Three Little Words

JOAN JONKER

headline

First published in 2004
by HEADLINE BOOK PUBLISHING

First published in paperback in 2004
by HEADLINE BOOK PUBLISHING

9

ISBN 978 0 7553 2121 6

Typeset in Times by Avon DataSet Ltd,
Bidford-on-Avon, Warwickshire

Printed and bound in Great Britain by
CPI Antony Rowe, Chippenham, Wiltshire

HEADLINE BOOK PUBLISHING
A division of Hodder Headline Limited
338 Euston Road
London NW1 3BH

www.headline.co.uk
www.hodderheadline.com

This book is dedicated to my family and friends, including my extended family – the readers of my books. Through their letters, which are warm and friendly, I feel I am blessed with a huge family of like-minded people who share my sentiments of kindness, love and a sense of humour. Long may our friendship last.

Hello readers

This Molly and Nellie story is bound to make you chuckle the whole way through. Its warmth and love shared will give you a feeling of contentment and well-being, honest! On behalf of myself and the Bennett and McDonough families and friends, I send you all my best wishes.

Take care.

Love

Joan

Chapter One

Molly Bennett stood on the top step and kissed her husband and daughter before they set off for work. They both started work at eight o'clock, but would part company when they reached the main road, for their jobs took them in different directions. The youngest of her four children, Ruthie, had only started work three months ago when she left school at fourteen, but to hear her talk you'd think she'd been working for years and knew the job inside out. She was much older in the head than Molly's other two daughters and son had been at that age, far more confident and sure of herself. There were times when Molly thought she was over-confident, but her husband Jack said children these days were all the same, and that it was because during the war their parents hadn't been strict with them.

A door on the opposite side of the street opened and a young girl stepped down on to the pavement, then turned to give her mother a kiss before hurrying across the cobbles to join Ruthie who had stopped to wait for her. They were best mates, Ruthie and Bella, friends from the time they could toddle, and it had been lucky that both had been taken on at Johnson's Dye Works. They were as different in nature as chalk and cheese, though, for Bella was an only child whose mother wouldn't let the wind blow on her, and hated to let her out of her sight. So while Ruthie was outgoing, Bella was very shy, blushing when anyone spoke to her. But she was a nice kid, and a good mate.

'Ta-ra, Mam!' Ruthie blew her mother a kiss, then linked her mate's arm and hurried to catch up with her father so she could give him a hug. And from the movement of her head, Molly could tell she was talking fifteen to the dozen. 'It's a wonder Bella doesn't suffer from a permanent earache,' Molly said aloud as she closed the front door. 'The poor kid can never get a word in edgeways.'

Standing in the doorway of the living room, Molly let her eyes go from the breakfast dishes still on the table to the grate that needed cleaning out, and the dust that had settled on the sideboard. Letting out a sigh, and holding her chin in her hand, she asked herself, 'Well, now, what shall it be? Shall I clear the table first and wash the dishes, or shall I take the ashes out and clean the grate down?' She didn't answer herself right away, as she considered her options. Then her face lit up in a smile and she chuckled. 'Or shall I do what my mate would do, and say sod them, I'll make meself a fresh pot of tea and relax for half an hour? I deserve a break, 'cos me body hasn't got over all the running round I did last week. And then there was the wedding on Saturday – that took it out of me.' She nodded, having made up her mind to pamper herself, but as she passed the table she found she couldn't break the habit of a lifetime. She'd clear up first, then relax with a cup of tea. Still talking to herself, she collected the dirty plates. 'It'll only take me half an hour to do the ruddy lot. I can have it done while I'm thinking about it. And the tea will taste better if I don't have to drink it while looking at the blinking ashes.'

When Molly finally settled herself on a chair by the table, a hot cup of tea in front of her and an arrowroot biscuit between her fingers, she smiled in contentment. That was better. The grate was clean and the paper and wood laid ready to light a fire when she came back from the shops. Everywhere had been dusted, and there were no fingermarks to be seen on the sideboard or the small table in front of the back window. At least, she couldn't see any from where she was sitting, and there were no visitors coming who would get down on their knees with a magnifying glass.

When the cup was empty, Molly put it back on the saucer and carried both out to the kitchen. It was only half past nine, so she had plenty of time to get herself washed and dressed before her mate called for her to go to the shops. Molly was not looking forward to going to the shops today, for she knew Nellie would talk non-stop about her daughter's wedding on Saturday. Not that you could blame her, because it was a wonderful wedding, and it had gone off without a hitch. The bride looked beautiful, the groom handsome, and the bridesmaids very pretty. And the reception was everything you could ask for. Hanley's, the confectioners, certainly knew how to lay on a good meal, well presented and plenty of it. And the party in the evening had been filled with fun and laughter until Tom Hanley had turfed them out at midnight.

It had been a smashing do, and Molly still hadn't got over it. She'd laughed so much she got a pain in her side. And she'd never forget the sight of George McDonough picking up his wife and putting her over his shoulder. He was a big man, was George, but to pick up eighteen-stone Nellie was no mean feat. The laughter from the guests was so loud it was a wonder the roof didn't cave in. It was some wedding party all right – fun and games all the way.

Molly sat up straight when there was a loud knock on the door. And it wasn't just one knock. Whoever it was intended to be heard, because they kept rapping hard on the knocker. 'Who the heck can this be?' Molly asked herself as she pushed her chair under the table. 'It's not the day for the rent collector, and he doesn't come this early anyway.' With a quick glance in the mirror to make sure she was presentable, she made her way to the door, calling, 'Whoever yer are, will yer stop making such a racket? Yer'll have the neighbours thinking ye're the bailiff, come to throw me and me few possessions out into the street.'

Molly opened the door intending to give whoever was standing there a piece of her mind, but the sight that met her eyes caused her jaw to drop. Looking up at her from the pavement, her face one big smile, was her mate Nellie McDonough. But not the Nellie who called for her every morning to go to the shops. 'In the name of God, Nellie, what are yer playing at? Have yer lost the run of yer senses?'

Nellie's smile never wavered. Dressed up to the nines in her wedding outfit with her purple dress, wide-brimmed lilac hat, beige gloves and shoes, and her bosom standing to attention, she looked as pleased as punch, and felt like Lady Muck. 'Well, girl, aren't yer going to ask me in for a cup of tea and a custard cream?' She didn't wait for a reply, but pushed Molly aside and swayed her way into the living room. 'I hope yer've dusted the chairs, girl, 'cos I don't want to dirty me frock.'

When Molly found her voice, she asked, 'What the hell are yer playing at, Nellie? What are yer dressed up like a dog's dinner for? I thought we were going to the shops?'

'Oh, we are, girl!' Nellie nodded her head, causing her chins to move upward and her wide-brimmed wedding hat to fall down over her eyes. Slowly, she took off one of her gloves, a finger at a time the way she'd seen Joan Crawford do it in one of her films. Then she pushed her hat back so she could see her friend, and explained, 'It's like this, girl. Seeing as we're going to the butcher's and the greengrocer's, I thought it would be nice to let Tony and Billy see me bride's mother's outfit. I mean, they didn't see the wedding, did they, girl, so I thought I'd give them a treat. Cheer them up for the day, like.'

'Over my dead body, Nellie McDonough! If yer think I'm walking to the shops with yer looking like that, well, yer've got another think coming.'

Nellie glared at her friend before turning her back and picking up the carver chair from its place beside the sideboard and putting it by the table. She then sat down, and took off her other glove, in slow motion, one finger at a time. Then, after laying them down on the table, very neatly and precisely, she glanced up at Molly, who had a look of disbelief on her face. 'If I'm not supposed to wear me wedding outfit, well, what am I supposed to do with the bleeding thing? Put it in the wardrobe and leave it there for the moths to get at? This hat cost me two guinea, so I intend getting some wear out of it.' Her eyes narrowed and her top lip curled. 'I know what it is, Molly Bennett, ye're jealous, that's what it is. I'm surprised at yer, acting like a flaming child.'

'I am not jealous, Nellie McDonough, and I am not childish.' Even as she was speaking, a voice in Molly's head was telling her that she wanted her bumps feeling, and it was childish to argue. 'Anyway, I don't intend to get meself all worked up about it, so I'll keep me cool and just tell yer I'm not going shopping with yer in that get-up. You go to the shops now and I'll go when I've put some washing on the line.'

'Yer mean I'm not even getting a cup of tea?' Nellie's voice rose. 'Well, you miserable bugger! I've a good mind to take yer at yer word and go to the shops on me own. That would teach yer to be sarky with me.'

'Yer know where the door is, Nellie, yer don't need me to show yer out. But as we're supposed to be mates, I'll go halfway with yer. Yer can have yer usual cup of tea, but I am definitely not walking down the street with yer looking like that.'

'I think ye're two-faced, Molly Bennett. Yer were full of praise for me dress and hat before the wedding. Now yer won't even walk down the street with me wearing it.'

Molly pulled a chair out and sat down. This was going to be a long session and there was no point in making her feet suffer. 'Nellie, sunshine, I love yer outfit, and I think yer look like a million dollars in it. But there's a time and place for everything, and this isn't the time to be walking down the street in a wedding outfit. Yer'd be the talk of the neighbourhood, a laughing stock, and that is something I don't want to see.'

Nellie spread out her chubby hands. 'Then when am I going to be able to wear it, girl? It's a sin to stick it in the wardrobe and never wear it again. It's not often we get clothes as posh as these, so why can't we enjoy them? Aren't yer going to wear yours?'

Molly nodded. 'Yes, sunshine, I'll be wearing mine, but at the right time.' She patted her mate's hand. 'Tell me, will your Lily be wearing her wedding dress often?'

Nellie lowered her head to think of a good answer to that, but one didn't spring to mind. 'Not to go to the shops in, girl. That would be daft.'

'Apart from going to the shops, when will she wear it again?'

Nellie was stuck. No matter how many faces she pulled, she couldn't think of an answer. Then suddenly her face lit up. 'I know, girl, she could wear it at the christening!'

'What christening?'

'When the baby gets christened!'

'Which baby is that, sunshine?'

'The baby what our Lily and Archie are going to have. Why don't yer use yer brains, girl?'

'Nellie, they've only been married forty-eight hours, and already yer've got them having a baby! And just so yer can wear yer ruddy hat! If Lily and Archie have got any sense they'll put off having a baby for a while. Let them enjoy each other a bit before starting a family. Once they have a baby they won't be able to get out to dances and the flicks like they do now. They'll be tied down. So don't be putting a spell on them just so yer can titivate yerself up and show off.'

'All that bleeding money spent on the wedding and we can't wear the clothes afterwards. What a waste when there's people in the world starving.'

Molly was dying to laugh. Never once had her mate ever mentioned the people in the world who were starving. In fact, Molly was surprised she even knew about them, 'cos although she loved the bones of Nellie, she had to admit she wouldn't go out of her way to help anyone. If she saw someone lying in the gutter she wouldn't offer to help them up, she'd say it was their own ruddy fault for being drunk. Then a little voice in Molly's head pulled her up, and reminded her that Nellie had been getting more generous and caring over the last few years. Why, it was only a few days before Christmas that she had let herself be talked into putting a penny in a Salvation Army collecting tin. The memory of that brought a smile to Molly's face as in her mind she saw a picture of Nellie holding the penny up to the collector's face so she could see it was a penny Nellie was putting in the box, and not a button like some folk she knew.

'What are yer smiling at, girl, 'cos I can't see anything to smile about. If I thought yer were laughing at me, I'd clock yer one.'

'I'm not laughing at you, sunshine, it was just something flashed through me mind. It was a long time ago, and I can't remember where or when. Anyway, how about you going to the shops? Otherwise they'll be closing for dinner.'

'What! Where's me cup of tea? Now that's breaking a promise, that is. Yer said I could have a cup of tea and a biscuit, and I ain't moving from here until I get it.' Nellie's sharp nod told Molly she meant what she said, and it told her chins to please themselves whether they did a quickstep or a slow foxtrot. 'So put that in yer pipe and smoke it, Molly clever clogs Bennett.'

Molly's head told her she was as daft as her friend, but it didn't stop her from saying, 'I never said yer could have a biscuit, sunshine, so don't be making me out to be a liar.'

Nellie was fast losing her patience. 'Bloody hell, girl, how long are yer going to keep this up? I don't know why ye're getting yer knickers in a twist, but if it improves yer temper, I'll leave me ruddy hat here while we go to the shops. Honest to God, girl, when I was wondering what to give yer as a Christmas present, I couldn't think what to get yer. It never entered me head to buy yer a dummy.'

'Yer didn't buy me a Christmas present!'

'I know I never, girl.' Nellie hands were spread out and her face looked the picture of innocence. 'As I said, I didn't know what to buy yer.'

'Okay, sunshine, I'll let yer off this time. But next Christmas, perhaps it would be a good idea to ask me what I'd like, save making excuses.'

Nellie's face was all sweetness and light. 'I'll remember to do that, girl. But can I have me cup of tea now, 'cos me throat is parched.' As Molly got to her feet, Nellie added, 'And if yer could see yer way clear to include a biscuit, it would be much appreciated.'

Molly tutted. 'I should have sent yer packing when I opened the front door, then I wouldn't have had to go all through this. I'm me own worst enemy.' She was putting a match to the gas ring when Nellie came into the kitchen with her lips pursed and her hands on her hips. 'What's up with your face, sunshine? Yer look as though ye're ready to kill someone.'

'I'll tell yer what's the matter with me, Molly Bennett, you little sneak. You never bought me no present at Christmas, that's what.'

The match had burned down to Molly's finger. She flung the spent match into the sink and turned the tap on to run cold water over the sore spot. Someone had once told her this would stop the skin from blistering. Pulling a face, she turned the tap off and rested the finger in the palm of her other hand. 'If you say I'm a sneak, Nellie, then I'm a sneak. And don't stand there doing nothing, put the tea in the pot and set the cups out.'

Nellie stepped back a couple of paces, horror on her face. 'Make the tea in me wedding dress! Not on yer life, Molly Bennett. If yer want a cup of tea yer'll have to make it yerself.'

Molly had an answer ready for that. 'I'm not fussy on a cup of tea, so put the gas out for us, if yer will. It's no good wasting money.' She held her sore finger to her chest and went back to the living room to sit down.

Nellie was in a quandary. She'd got herself into a mess and wasn't sure how to get out of it. All over her ruddy hat! Then she told herself it was her own fault because she'd talked herself into it, and the best solution was talk herself out of it. She followed her mate back to the living room. 'Ah, have yer burnt yer finger, girl?' She put her arm across Molly's shoulder. 'Yer poor thing. You just sit there and I'll make a nice pot of tea. That'll make yer feel better, girl.' She put her two hands on the brim of her hat and carefully set it down on the glass bowl on the sideboard. 'I know that'll be clean, girl, 'cos I can see yer've done yer dusting.' With that she swayed her way to the kitchen again. Then she cocked an ear, heard a chuckle, spun round and walked back. 'Did I hear you laughing at me, Molly Bennett?'

Still holding her finger, even though it wasn't as sore now, Molly looked the picture of innocence. 'Me finger is giving me gyp, sunshine, so what the hell have I got to laugh about? It just goes to show what a bad mind yer've got.'

Nellie was far from convinced, but nevertheless she went back to the kitchen and put a light to the ring under the kettle. But she kept her ear cocked all the time. Then she leaned against the sink and wondered how to get back in her mate's good books. And when the kettle boiled, her chubby face was creased in a smile as she silently complimented herself on coming up with a smashing idea.

In the living room, Molly was wondering what weird and wonderful scheme Nellie would come up with to get herself off the hook. And Molly had to admit to feeling a bit sorry for her mate, because she knew she only wanted to show off. But whatever, there was no way she was going to the shops with Nellie dressed up in her wedding regalia, stopping everyone they met, even people they'd never set eyes on before. They'd all be as sweet as honey to Nellie's face, for her reputation was well known, but they'd be laughing at her behind her back and Molly wasn't going to let that happen.

'Here yer are, girl, a nice cup of tea, just as yer like it.' Nellie set the saucer down in front of her mate, and with as much sympathy as she could muster, asked, 'How's yer finger now, girl? Is it any better?'

Molly asked God to forgive her before she answered, 'No, sunshine, it's still sore and throbbing like mad. I don't think it's going to come up in a blister, though, so I suppose I should be thankful for small mercies. I'll put a bandage on it when I've had me drink, and by the time I'm ready to go to the shops it should have calmed down a lot.'

Nellie put on her Florence Nightingale guise. 'No, I was thinking while I was in the kitchen, yer shouldn't go out if ye're feeling under the weather. You stay in and rest, and I'll get yer shopping in for yer.'

Molly lowered her head so she could bite on the inside of her lip. So that was what Nellie had come up with, eh? She was slipping, for it wasn't a patch on her usual excuses. 'No, thank yer all the same, sunshine, but I'd rather get me own shopping in. I haven't made up me mind yet what to get for our dinner, so I'll wait and see what meat Tony's got to entice me. But don't let me stop you, sunshine. You poppy off and get to the shops.'

Nellie narrowed her eyes. 'Yer know, girl, we could go on like this all day. I said before that yer were childish, but I'm as bad as you. So shall we both grow up and behave like responsible adults? I'll take me hat and go home, then I'll come back in me old clothes and we'll go shopping together like we always do. I mean, if I went in the butcher's or the greengrocer's on me own, they'd start a collection for a wreath for yer, thinking yer were dead.'

'Nellie McDonough, how d'yer think these things up? Why couldn't yer just tell Tony or Billy that I was busy, and that's why yer were getting me shopping in? Wouldn't that be less morbid than having me dead and neighbours collecting money for a wreath?'

The little woman puckered her lips and her eyes slid from side to side. 'Here we go again, girl, you with yer words what I sometimes think yer make up just to fool me. I can't wear me big hat, but it's all right for you to use big words that nobody but yerself understands.'

Molly looked puzzled. 'I didn't use any big words, sunshine, at least I can't remember using any. What was it I said?'

'If I knew that, I wouldn't have to ask yer, would I, soft girl? Whatever it was, it was as bad as having yer dead and buried.'

'Oh, I think I know the word yer mean, sunshine, but it isn't a long one. There's only six letters in it. Was the word morbid, by any chance?'

Nellie's face lit up. 'That's the one, girl, that's the one. It might not be a long word, but it's double Dutch to me. But 'cos I don't know what it means doesn't mean I'm thick, girl, it only means that you're a show-off.' She sniffed. 'Still, seeing as yer've used it, yer may as well tell me what it means, for future reference, like.'

Molly grinned to herself. This should be interesting. I bet me mate will be sorry she asked. 'It means someone who takes an interest in things that are unpleasant, such as disease or death. In other words, miserable buggers who don't know what it's like to enjoy themselves, or how to laugh.'

'Yer can't say I'm like that, girl, 'cos I'm not miserable, and I laugh more than I ruddy well cry. And being me best mate, yer should know that.'

'Of course ye're not, sunshine, or I wouldn't be yer best mate. And because you are me mate, I'll go to the shops with yer if yer go home and get changed.'

'Ah, ay, girl! I don't feel like getting changed, it's too much trouble! How about if I slip home and put me old coat on, and I leave me hat there? I can't say fairer than that, girl.'

Molly nodded. 'Okay, sunshine, and I'll be ready for when yer get back.'

Nellie hitched her bosom and narrowed her eyes. 'I see yer can use yer finger now. That's a miracle, that is, 'cos a minute ago yer were in agony.'

'Yes, I was, sunshine, and that's why I held me finger under the cold water. It does the trick if yer happen to burn yerself, sunshine, so there's a little tip for yer.'

Nellie picked her hat up and made for the front door, saying under her breath, 'Yes, Florence Nightingale, I'll do as yer say. You're the boss, Florrie, I'm only the ruddy lackey.'

Molly hurried after her. 'What did yer say, Nellie?'

'I said, girl, don't forget yer key.' With that the little woman stepped on to the pavement laughing her head off, feeling that everything hadn't gone her way so far this morning, but at least she'd got the last word in.

Molly closed the door and walked back into the living room shaking her head. 'She's a caution, is Nellie; yer don't get many like her in a pound. Which is just as well, I suppose. It's a wonder me ears aren't burning, 'cos I'd have a bet that right now she's standing in front of the mirror, with her hat on, telling herself what a miserable so-and-so I am. But I wouldn't have her any different. Just imagine what life would be like without her. I would know exactly what was going to happen each day, doing the housework, going to the shops, getting the dolly tub out every Monday and putting the washing in steep. All very predictable and dull. Whereas, with Nellie, yer never know what's going to happen from one minute to the next.' Molly smiled at her reflection in the mirror. 'I'd better be ready when she knocks, for it's going to take us longer to do the shopping today with my mate stopping to tell everyone about the wedding. She won't care whether they're friends or not, or if they don't want to hear it – they'll have little to say in the matter once Nellie gets her claws in them. Even Elsie Flanaghan would be received with open arms . . . that's if Nellie could catch her.'

Molly saw a shadow pass the window and hurried to take her coat off the hook in the hall. 'I'm ready, sunshine, so there's no need to bash the door in.'

Nellie was waiting with hands on hips for the door to open. 'What d'yer mean, don't bash the door in? Anyone listening to you would get the wrong impression of me. They'd think I was a loud-mouthed bully, instead of a respectable wife, mother and grandmother.'

'No, they wouldn't think that of yer, sunshine.' Molly closed the door behind her. 'Anyone with half an eye can see that ye're as cuddly and gentle as a little lamb.'

Nellie squinted up at her mate to make sure she wasn't being sarcastic before she smiled to show how pleased she was at the compliment. 'Ah, that's nice of yer, girl.' She linked arms. 'Where are we going to first, girl, butcher's or greengrocer's?'

'Greengrocer's last, sunshine. There's no point in lugging potatoes around with us. We'll see what meat we want first. I wouldn't mind a sheet of ribs, to have with cabbage and some mash.'

'Sounds good to me, girl, sounds good to me.'

They'd only gone a few yards when the door of a neighbour's house opened, and Nellie dropped Molly's arm as though it was a hot poker. Mabel Bristow was stepping down on to the pavement when she was confronted by Nellie. She put a hand to her chest and shook her head. 'In the name of God, Nellie, yer frightened the life out of me!'

But Nellie wasn't the least bit put out. 'Did yer see our Lily's wedding on Saturday, Mabel? There were so many people there I didn't get to see everyone. Oh, it went off a treat. Everyone said what a beautiful wedding it was.'

Mabel groaned inwardly. She liked Nellie, nearly everyone did, but once she got talking to you it was hard to get away. 'Yes, I was there, Nellie, and it was beautiful. Lily looked lovely, and so did the bridesmaids. The groom seemed a nice friendly lad, and I wish them the best of luck and hope everything goes all right for them.' Mabel made to walk away, but she should have known from past experience that it wouldn't be so easy.

Nellie put a restraining hand on her neighbour's arm in case she made a dash for it. 'Did yer like my outfit, Mabel?'

Mabel nodded. 'Yeah, I thought yer looked great, Nellie. Very ah, la, posh.'

To the poor woman's dismay, and Molly's, Nellie put her basket on the ground and began to undo the buttons on her coat. 'Yer wouldn't see me dress close up, like, Mabel, so I'll let yer see it now. Feel that material, girl. Don't yer think it's real classy?'

Mabel dutifully obliged. 'Oh, yeah, queen, it's real good quality.' She looked over to Molly, and her expression screamed out for help. 'But I'll have to go now, Nellie, 'cos I'm going to see me mam and dad.'

Molly obliged. 'You go on yer way, Mabel, 'cos me and Nellie are tied for time. When we've done our shopping I want to call at me daughters' and see if they need anything. So we'll love yer and leave yer, sunshine, and give our love to yer mam and dad.'

Mabel took off as though she was being chased by the devil himself, while Nellie watched her retreating back with surprise. 'Well, that wasn't very nice, was it? Another few minutes wouldn't have hurt her. I think that was bleeding rude, and I'll tell her next time I see her.'

Molly grabbed her arm and marched her forward. 'Yer'll do no such thing, Nellie McDonough. People have their own lives to live; they don't revolve around you. Mabel was going to see her parents, and we've got to see to our families. So no more moaning, and no more stopping to gab to everyone we see. If yer do, I'll leave yer to get on with it, because I'm going to see Doreen and Jill, whether you're with me or not. Understand?'

Nellie gritted her teeth. Fifteen minutes ago her mate had been Florence Nightingale, now she was talking like ruddy Hitler! But best to keep quiet: least said soonest mended. But Nellie couldn't help the way she was made, and when they were nearly at the corner of their street they came face to face with another neighbour coming back from the shops. Nellie had her mouth open ready to ask if Mrs Bamber had seen the wedding, and Molly had her hand ready to move her on. But they both got their eye wiped, for Ann Bamber beat them to it. 'I won't stay, 'cos I'm weighed down with shopping and me arms are dropping off, but I'd just like to say, Nellie, that the wedding went off a treat. I thought Lily looked lovely, and her new husband seems nice and friendly. You and your feller did them proud.' With a beaming smile, Ann went on her way, calling, 'Ta-ra. I'll be seeing yer.'

Molly squeezed her mate's arm. 'There yer are, sunshine, they all thought the wedding went off very well. And so they should because you and George did Lily and Archie proud.' Before Nellie had time to differ, Molly had cupped her elbow and steered her across the main road and along to the butcher's shop.

Tony happened to glance through the window of his shop and saw Molly and Nellie approaching. There were no customers in the shop, and he called through to Ellen in the stockroom. 'Yer mates are on their way, Ellen, d'yer think Nellie would take offence if I pulled her leg about the party? What yer told me was true, wasn't it? Her husband did pick her up, throw her over his shoulder, and Nellie did show everything she'd got, and something she hadn't got. Is that right? Yer weren't making it up?'

'I wouldn't make a joke about a woman's knickers, Tony, of course it was true. But whether Nellie will appreciate yer pulling her leg, well, yer'll have to see for yerself.'

Tony rubbed his hands in glee when the friends came into the shop. 'Here's yer neighbour, Ellen, Mrs No Knickers.'

Nellie glared at him first, with her eyes narrowed. But then laughter got the better of her and her whole body shook. And when Ellen, friend and neighbour, came through from the stock room, Nellie said, 'I suppose I'll never hear the end of it. And I bet when your feller goes to the pub tonight he'll tell all his mates. I'll get a name like a mad dog.'

Molly tapped her on the shoulder, 'If I were you, sunshine, I'd go careful with Ellen. She's got a chopper in her hand and blood all over her apron. So watch yerself, 'cos I'd hate to see yer in the mincemeat tray in the window.'

Ellen swung the chopper, Tony guffawed, Molly chuckled and Nellie was laughing so much she had to lean over the counter. When she got her breath back, she croaked, 'I hope yer put me with the best mince, Tony, not with that cheap stuff yer sometimes palm me and Molly off with.'

'I do not palm yer off with cheap mince, Nellie, not you and Molly, me two favourite customers.' He flicked his straw hat back off his forehead. 'Mind you, I can't be your favourite butcher, otherwise I'd get asked to these weddings of yours. I've missed three good dos in the space of a year.' He thought of the things Ellen had been telling him that morning in between customers. 'From what Ellen's told me, it was some party.'

'Fancy yer telling him about me knickers, Ellen. I'm surprised at yer, 'cos yer always seem so bleeding goody-goody. But I don't mind yer having a laugh. I've been laughing about it meself ever since. But I wouldn't like Corker to tell his mates in the pub tonight. I'd never be able to look them in the face again.'

'No, Corker won't tell them tonight, Nellie, I can promise yer that. Yer see, he told them last night, and I believe the pub was up. They were laughing so much, Tommy Baker couldn't see the dart board through his tears, and he lost the match.'

Molly and Nellie clung to each other laughing. 'Oh, dear,' Molly said, wiping her eyes with the back of her hand. 'We might not have much money, but we do see life. I enjoyed that laugh, it's cheered me up. But down to business, Tony, and I won't bother looking in the window, I'll have three-quarters of that mince we were talking about. And I might be back for more after I've seen what Jill and Doreen want.'

'I'll have the same as me mate, Tony, and I'll be back with her later, after we've been to see our grandchildren.' Nellie's bust stood to attention as she asked, 'Did Ellen tell yer that Jill and Steve are calling their baby Molly Helen McDonough? I hope she'll be a chip off the old block.'

Molly looked at Tony and groaned, 'Oh, no, not two Nellie Macs. I couldn't stand it.'

Chapter Two

'I'm going to throw this shopping in the hall, sunshine, then slip over to Doreen's to see if she's walking to the shops herself to give Bobby some fresh air, or if she wants me to get anything for her.' Bobby was Molly's eight-month-old grandson, and she was eager to see him for her daily hug and kiss. She turned the key in the lock and placed her basket inside before closing the door again. 'Go and put yours in the house, Nellie, or we won't make the shops before they close for dinner.'

Nellie rolled her eyes. 'It's only about half eleven, girl. We've got plenty of time.'

'I want to go up to see our Jill after I've knocked at Doreen's. So we haven't got all the time in the world.' When her mate made no move, Molly jerked her head. 'Put yer shopping in, sunshine, or I'll be going on without yer. I thought yer'd be eager to see the grandchildren.' A sly look came to Molly's eyes when she thought of a way to make Nellie put a move on. 'If ye're tired, sunshine, then why don't yer take yer shopping in and put yer feet up for a while? If either of the girls want anything, I can get it for them.'

'Oh, ye're not soft, are yer, girl? I know what ye're after, yer can't fool me. Yer think if our Steve's baby sees more of you, then he'll wonder who I am. Well, ye're not getting away with it, yer crafty so-and-so, 'cos I can see right through yer.'

'Hang about, Nellie! What d'yer mean, your Steve's baby?

Much as I love Steve like me own son, it was our Jill what gave birth.'

Nellie's eyes narrowed. 'Are yer saying my son had nothing to do with it? Your Jill, who I love the bones of, would have had a hard job to get in the family way without the help of my son, so there! Or are yer going to tell me it was a miracle?'

'Are yer going to put that shopping in yer hall, sunshine, or not? I'm not standing here any longer arguing the fat with yer. I'm crossing over to see Doreen, the baby and Victoria, but you can please yerself.' Molly had just put one foot down in the gutter when Nellie dragged her back on to the pavement.

'Wait for me, girl, 'cos I don't want yer saying anything behind me back. I don't trust yer to tell me what's said when I'm not there, 'cos I know yer leave bits out.'

A door on the opposite side of the street opened, and Molly's daughter Doreen stood on the step. 'Are you two coming over, or not?'

Molly waved. 'I'm coming, sunshine, but me mate hasn't made her mind up yet. I've got a feeling she'll still be standing here holding that basket when it gets dark. Which is sad, really, 'cos George and Paul won't get anything to eat. And after working all day, yer husband and son deserve to come home to a nice meal.'

'All right, girl, keep yer ruddy hair on.' Nellie leaned forward and stared hard into Molly's face. 'You stay right where yer are, girl, until I come back. I don't trust yer as far as I could throw yer.' With a sharp nod of her head, and chins, Nellie waddled to her front door, which was the fourth from Molly's. And after opening the door, she swung the basket back, then flung it with no concern for the contents, into the hall.

Tutting and shaking her head, Molly waited until Nellie was standing beside her again before saying, 'Nellie, I'm glad we didn't buy any eggs today, otherwise every one would have been broken.'

Nellie grinned. 'I could have done scrambled egg with them. My George is quite partial to scrambled egg on toast.'

'Would your George still be partial if he knew yer'd scraped it off the floor?'

'How would he know that, girl? I wouldn't have said nothing, and yer know the saying about what the eye don't see the heart won't know no difference.'

Doreen had been joined on the step by Victoria, and they both had smiles on their faces. Victoria Clegg was ninety years of age. A spinster, she'd lived a lonely life since her beloved parents had died forty years ago. But since the day she'd offered to share her home with newly-weds Doreen and Phil, her life had been transformed. She was part of a big family now, very much loved, and every day she counted her blessings. 'I don't know why me mam bothers, Aunt Vicky, 'cos half the time Auntie Nellie is winding her up on purpose.'

'Oh, Molly knows that right enough, Doreen, but wouldn't life be dull if they didn't have this little set-to every day? Just listen, now.'

'I've never heard that saying, sunshine. I think yer've just made it up yerself. The one I know, the right one, is what the eye doesn't see, the heart doesn't grieve for.'

'Oh, that's a new one on me, girl. I've never heard it said like that before.' Nellie linked her mate's arm and they began to cross the cobbles. 'Anyway, if it makes yer feel better, you being so good-living, I'll tell George I dropped the eggs but I dusted them off before putting them in the frying pan. He won't mind. He's easy-going, is my feller.'

'But yer don't need to tell him any lies, now, do yer, sunshine, 'cos yer never bought any eggs to ruddy well break!'

They had reached the opposite pavement by this time, and

Nellie winked at Victoria, causing her chubby cheek to move upwards. 'Good morning, Victoria, and you, Doreen. Mind you, if my mate had carried on acting daft much longer, I'd have been saying goodnight.'

'Don't be putting all the blame on my mam, Auntie Nellie,' Doreen said, holding the door open for them to pass. 'Ye're both as bad as one another.'

'We know that, girl, but it's better than going round with a long face and being miserable. And it helps to make the day go quicker.' Nellie brushed Doreen aside so she could get to the couch where Molly was bending over the baby, Bobby, whose arms and legs were punching the air with excitement. He could recognise his grandma's voice now, and knew he would be getting picked up and cuddled. 'Move along, girl, and let's get a look-in.' With a thrust of her hip, Nellie pushed Molly away so's she could bend down and chuck the baby under the chin. 'Ooh, he knows his Grandma Nellie, don't yer, sweetheart? Just look at the way his legs are going. He wants me to pick him up.'

'Oh no yer don't, sunshine, it's my turn first.' Molly looked down into the baby's laughing face and her heart went out to him. He was the image of Phil, his dad, and a better father he couldn't wish for. 'Oh, who's a lovely boy for his grandma? I'll swear yer've put weight on since yesterday, and grown another inch.' She lifted him from the couch and held him up in the air as he kicked and punched, gurgling with pleasure. She loved her mate, Nellie, and more often than not she gave in to her. But not where her grandson was concerned. When Bobby had first been born, Nellie was so jealous that her mate was a grandma, they had all agreed she could be an adopted grandma. And in her eyes, so she told all the neighbours and every customer in every shop they went in, she was Bobby's grandma. It was woe betide anyone who dared question how this could be. And even now, when she was a grandmother in her own right, she still insisted on sharing.

Nellie moved impatiently from one foot to the other. 'Ay, girl, give someone else a chance, or the day will be over before I get a look-in.'

Molly gave the baby a big hug and kiss before she passed him over. 'Here yer are, sunshine, before yer start crying. Ye're just like a big soft baby yerself.'

'D'yer think so, girl? Then how about putting me in the pram and going for a walk? Or yer could give me a piggy-back. I wouldn't mind as long as me corns weren't feeling the pinch.' Nellie was tickling the baby's tummy and the more he laughed, the more her own tummy and bosom rose up and down. 'Ay, listen, girl, I'll tell yer something for nothing. If Bobby is your grandson, as yer are always telling me, then how come he's got my sense of humour? I'm beginning to think there's more to this baby than meets the eye.' She nodded her head slowly. 'Yeah, I smell dirty works at the crossroads. And never mind laughing, Molly Bennett, 'cos yer might be laughing the other side of yer face before the day is out. We all know that Jill and Doreen are as alike as two peas in a pod, so what's to say that my Steve didn't mistake Doreen for Jill one night and indulge in a little hanky-panky? No, it's not far-fetched, Molly, 'cos that would account for the baby having a sense of humour. Our Steve takes after me, and this baby takes after him.'

Victoria chuckled behind her hand. 'Well, Nellie, I've heard yer come out with some amazing stories, but I think that one takes the cake. How do yer think these things up?'

'Easy, Victoria, just think about it. It's not as daft as it sounds, 'cos even I've often mistaken Jill for Doreen. It's easy done, especially in the dark.'

'Ah, well, sunshine, nothing you come up with surprises

me. But as Steve has black hair, and Phil is blond, don't yer think Doreen would have twigged something?'

'Listen, girl, when passion is at its height, who the hell is going to worry about the colour of someone's hair?' Nellie's tummy began to shake, bringing gurgles from the baby who thought he was bouncing on a cloud. 'On second thoughts, girl, I can well imagine you in bed, with a feller on top of yer, and yer suddenly pour water on his ardour by saying, "Ooh, but yer've got black hair!" '

Molly didn't know where to put her face. 'Yer'll be the death of me yet, Nellie McDonough. Yer don't care what yer say, or who yer say it in front of. Yer'll have to clear yer mind out if yer ever want to mind Bobby, or Molly. Left alone with you, they'll know the facts of life before their second birthday.'

Nellie's face was one big grin. She loved winding her mate up. 'Look at her blushing! A grown woman, what's had four children, and she's blushing. It's Jack I feel sorry for, the poor bugger. I bet she makes him turn the light out every night.'

Molly didn't know how she kept her face straight, for inside she was bubbling with laughter. She could hear Victoria's quiet titter, and Doreen's chuckle, but if she laughed it would only encourage her mate to come out with something more outrageous. 'That's it now, Nellie, that's yer lot. Put the baby down, we're leaving.' When she turned her head to ask her daughter if she wanted any shopping, little did Molly know that behind her back Nellie was pulling faces. With her tongue sticking out, she put a thumb in each ear and wagged her fingers, as she'd done as a child behind the teacher's back.

Doreen tried to focus on her mother's face so she wouldn't see her Auntie Nellie. 'I'm going to the shops meself, Mam, to give Bobby some fresh air and to stretch me legs. I'm trying to persuade Aunt Vicky to come with us, seeing as the weather seems to be milder.'

'Well, seeing as yer don't need me, I'll go to Jill's and see if she needs anything. She's probably not into a routine with the baby yet, only coming out of hospital four days ago. I can remember when Jill was born it took me ages to get used to washing her. I thought she was so fragile she might break. When you came along I was a bit better, then with Tommy and Ruthie I was a dab hand at it.'

She turned to her mate and asked, 'Are you ready, sunshine?'

Nellie's face was the picture of innocence. 'I'm ready, girl. I've been standing here as good as gold waiting for yer.'

But Molly knew her friend too well, and she was suspicious. 'What have yer been up to behind me back, Nellie? And don't say nothing, 'cos I can tell.'

Looking really put out, Nellie spread her hands, appealing to Victoria. 'Now, have I done anything behind Molly's back? I wouldn't do that, not to me best mate.'

Victoria chose to take a line between the truth and a lie. 'I know yer were standing there, Nellie, but I was busy watching the baby.'

'D'yer know what I think, girl?' Nellie asked. 'I think everyone knows their own tricks best, and that's what you do when my back is turned.'

'Oh, ay, what do I do when yer back's turned, sunshine?'

'Don't be acting the innocent, Molly Bennett, yer know quite well what yer do.'

'No I don't, so tell me.'

Nellie rolled her eyes. She knew her mate inside out, but wasn't quite sure whether today was a good day to test her humour. 'Okay, girl, I'll show yer. But only on one condition.' She cast her eyes at Doreen. 'You're nearest to yer mam, girl, so if she as much as lifts her arms, I want yer to promise yer'll grab her before she gets to me.'

Doreen was always glad to see her mam and Auntie Nellie, because they never failed to brighten the day. And it gave her and Aunt Vicky something to talk and laugh about afterwards. 'I promise I'll try, Auntie Nellie, but she might be too quick for me.'

Nellie shook her head slowly, allowing her chins to sway gently from side to side. 'Nah, girl, yer mam's too ruddy slow to catch cold. You just keep yer eye on her and I'll show her what she does behind me back, all sneaky, like.' But as a precaution, Nellie stepped back a few paces before sticking a thumb in each ear, wagging her fingers and putting her tongue out.

Molly pouted her lips and nodded. 'Not bad, sunshine, but yer haven't got it quite right, 'cos while I'm doing that, I also cross me eyes. But nevertheless, that's not a bad imitation.'

'Ooh, I couldn't cross me eyes, girl, 'cos they might stick like that. And while it might suit you being cock-eyed, I don't think it would do much for me. I mean, like, wherever I go I can see men gazing longingly at me voluptuous figure, and if I was cock-eyed I'd miss seeing that. Not that I'm big-headed, like, I wouldn't want yer to think that, but it really makes me feel good to know so many men desire me.'

'Now as though we'd think yer were big-headed, Auntie Nellie,' Doreen said, laughing. 'I think ye're very modest and shy.'

Nellie went into her drama pose. With her head lowered, and her two chubby hands spread on her tummy, she said, 'Oh, that is so kind of you. And you are so right, for I am shy and modest, but I try to hide it. And I have a good reason for hiding my true self, for if I were to act natural, as I really am deep inside, I'd show me mate up something rotten. People would look and listen to me, and then when she opened her mouth they'd think she was as common as muck. And I couldn't hurt her, not my bestest friend in the whole world.' She raised her head. 'Oh, dear, I've come over all soppy. Could someone pass the smelling salts.'

'Oh, I'm sorry, Auntie Nellie, but we ran out of smelling salts yesterday,' Doreen told her, straight-faced. 'But we do have Andrews Liver Salts. Would that help?'

Nellie's chubby face creased. 'I don't think so, girl, 'cos the last time I had a dose of salts I went through me housework in no time, and I couldn't be arsed doing that again. I had to sit twiddling me thumbs until it was time to call for me mate to go to the shops. Now I don't mind a bit of housework, girl, but the whole house in two hours, well, that's carrying things too far.'

'It's a good job we all know that these tales yer come up with are all fantasy, sunshine, and not deliberate lies. And it's to be hoped that Satan does, too, or he'd be stoking the fires of hell to welcome yer. But I'm going to put a halt to all this frivolity and you and me are going to hot-foot it to Jill's before the shops close for their dinner hour.' Molly crossed the room to drop a kiss on Victoria's cheek. 'See yer tomorrow, sunshine.' Then she gave her daughter a bear hug and a kiss. 'Yer know where I am if yer want me, sunshine, never forget that.'

'I know that, Mam, and thanks for the entertainment. It'll give Aunt Vicky and me something to laugh about all afternoon.'

Molly and Nellie strolled up to the top end of the street where Molly's daughter Jill, and Nellie's son Steve lived. For the year they'd been married they'd lived with Lizzie Corkhill, who had offered to share her house with them when her son, Corker, told her the Bennett sisters had been hoping to have a double wedding, but wouldn't be able to because Jill and Steve had nowhere to live. Steve was just out of serving his time and they hadn't been able to save enough to buy furniture for a house. And offering to share her home with them had been the best thing Lizzie Corkhill could have done, for she'd been lonely since Corker married Ellen and moved in with her and her children. But now, with Jill and Steve, she had a family, and there were no more lonely days. It was only supposed to be a temporary arrangement, but Lizzie wouldn't hear of their leaving, even when a very shy Jill told her she was expecting a baby, and that she and Steve had agreed they had enough money saved to furnish a house of their own now, for a baby in the house would be too much for Lizzie. But it was just the opposite: she was delighted and didn't want them to leave. And the newly weds had grown to love her deeply. It had been easy for Doreen, as Phil was already living with Victoria Clegg, and her house was fully furnished. So everything had turned out well for both sisters, and Molly thanked God every night for her blessings. For as well as her two daughters, her only son Tommy had a beautiful wife in Rosie, and they were living very happily with Molly's ma and da.

'Ye're very quiet, girl, are yer all right?' Nellie didn't like long silences. 'Yer haven't got a cob on with me for what I said in Victoria's, have yer?'

Molly squeezed her arm. 'Of course not, sunshine. I'll have a good laugh with Jack tonight over what yer said. No, I was miles away, actually, thinking how lucky I am with me family and me friends. Three of me children married and as happy as they could ever be. And they haven't moved miles away. I can see them every day. Two in the same street, and our Tommy just around the corner with me ma and da. What more could any mother ask for, Nellie, than knowing her children are well and happy?'

Nellie wasn't having any of that! 'I'm lucky, too, girl, with our Steve and Lily living in the street. I know yer've got three married, and have got two grandchildren, but I'll catch yer up when our Paul gets wed. And if Archie pulls his socks up, I could have another grandchild by the end of the year.'

Molly pulled them to a halt just two doors away from Lizzie's house. 'Nellie, they've only been married three days, for heaven's sake! Don't you dare repeat what yer've just said when we get inside the house. Lizzie probably wouldn't mind, but our Jill would die of embarrassment. And I can assure you that if Lily or Archie heard yer, they wouldn't think it was the least bit funny.'

Nellie cast her eyes up to the sky. Why did her mate have a mind as pure as the driven snow? 'Okay, girl, I'll keep me mouth shut the whole time I'm in there, then I can't get into trouble. But I must say I think it's bloody awful if I've got to watch every word what comes out of me mouth.' She took her arm from Molly's, a sign that she'd taken the huff. Then, with her bosom standing to attention, she rose to her full four feet ten inches. 'I just think it's a pity there's them what don't know what a sense of humour is. I don't half feel sorry for them, they must lead miserable bloody lives.'

'Nellie, most people do have a sense of humour, but not everyone appreciates the same things. I mean, you might not find their jokes funny, and they may not be amused by yours.' Molly smiled down into her friend's chubby face. 'After all, sunshine, it would be a dull world if we were all made the same.'

'You're telling me! I'd hate to be one of those miserable buggers what think it is funny when they see someone trip over and fall flat on their face.'

Molly clamped her lips together, and closing her eyes she could see Elsie Flanaghan flat out on the pavement. And she hadn't tripped, she'd been pushed. Oh dear, oh dear, she thought, my mate's got a terrible memory. But now wasn't the time to tell her, or they'd be here all day. 'Come on, sunshine, let's get in and see our grandchild. That should cheer yer up and put a smile back on yer face.'

Lizzie Corkhill beamed when she opened the door and saw who her visitors were. 'Come in, come in. It's good to see yer.'

Molly was the first to walk into an empty room. 'Where's our Jill and the baby?'

Nellie put on a fierce expression as she pressed her face close to Lizzie's. 'Yeah, what have yer done with her daughter and my grandchild?'

Lizzie grinned. 'Oh, it's quite a performance here when Jill washes the baby. She's terrified of hurting her, and takes ages just washing her down. I've offered to help, but no, she must learn, so she tells me. The most she'll let me do is bring the bowl of water in and take it out again when she's finished.' She waved them to the couch. 'Anyway, it all went smoothly, even though it took an hour, and the baby's dressed and smelling like a rose garden. Jill is in the bedroom feeding her now. She won't do it in front of me.' Lizzie smiled at Molly. 'Your daughter is the kindest, most gentle person I have ever met. She never raises her voice and never speaks ill of anyone. You brought her up well, Molly, she's a credit to yer.'

'She's always been the same, Lizzie, from the day she first learned to smile and crawl. I love all me kids, but they will agree with me that Jill is the most caring and gentle of the lot.'

Nellie's mind was working overtime, trying to find a way to get noticed. Then she grinned. 'Our Steve was the first one to know that. He's known from the age of two that Jill was the girl for him. It shows that good taste runs in our family, doesn't it, eh, girl?'

But Molly was ready for her. 'I would say it was good taste all round, sunshine, 'cos Jill chose Steve from a very early age as well.' She began to chuckle. 'Don't yer remember, Nellie? The kids were barely walking when you and me used to sit at the table having a cuppa and saying wouldn't it be nice if one of my kids fell for one of yours? We had Steve and Jill married off before they started school.'

'Yeah, I remember that, girl, and it's hard to believe it's nearly twenty years ago. The years go by real quick, don't they? If yer blinked, yer'd miss them.'

'I don't know, sunshine. Those far-off days weren't all milk and honey. The days when we hadn't a penny to our name, they didn't go quick, they used to drag. But they're gone now, and we've come through them with flying colours. No more times when our tummies rumble with hunger, thank God.'

Lizzie nodded in agreement. 'Some people these days don't know they're born. They don't have to scrimp and scrape, counting every farthing. But then, we can't begrudge them anything, because most of the fellers fought in the war, and without them God alone knows where we'd be.' She stopped her rocking chair and pushed herself to her feet. 'I'll put the kettle on. Jill shouldn't be much longer now.'

When Lizzie went into the kitchen, Molly stood at the bottom of the stairs. 'D'yer need any help, sunshine, or are yer managing?'

Jill's voice came back. 'I'm doing all right, Mam, after a fashion. It'll take me a few weeks to get into the routine, but I'll get there. Another five minutes and I'll be down.'

'I'm going to sit at the table, Lizzie,' Nellie called. 'I'm more comfortable sitting on a chair than the couch, 'cos it takes me ages to get meself up from here.' She shuffled her bottom to the edge of the couch and, making fists of her hands, tried to push herself up. But after three attempts at raising her bottom, only to fall back again, she was puffing like mad and still sitting on the couch. 'They're a bleeding death-trap, these couches.' She glared at Molly as though it was her fault. 'Why couldn't they put proper legs on them, so they'd be higher and I could get off easy?'

'Don't look at me, sunshine, I didn't make the ruddy things! Anyway, if they did put legs on, they wouldn't last long, not the way you plonk yerself down.' Molly stood in front of her and held her hands out. 'Take hold of these and I'll pull yer up.'

'It took yer long enough to think of that, girl, sitting there watching me puffing and blowing like an old carthorse.'

'You said that, sunshine, not me! Now take my hands and I'll pull.' After two attempts, when Molly thought her arms were being yanked out of their sockets, Nellie was still sitting on the couch. 'Unless yer help yerself, Nellie, yer'll still be sitting there when Steve comes in from work. Now, when I pull, you try and help by pushing yerself up, sunshine, 'cos I don't want to be here all ruddy day.'

When Lizzie came through from the kitchen carrying a tray, Nellie was standing, but her face said she wasn't in the best of moods. 'Don't ever ask me to sit on that contraption again, Lizzie. It's bloody torture.' Then her eyes lighted on a plate of biscuits on the tray, and this brought about a miraculous recovery. 'Ooh, fig biscuits. How did yer know they were me favourites, Lizzie?' Nellie pulled a chair out from the table and like Lady Muck she plonked her bottom down and pointed to the chair next to her. 'Come on, girl, park yer bottom on that and we'll have a nice cuppa and a fig biscuit.'

Molly sat down and her eyes met Lizzie's. 'D'yer know what my mate reminds me of sometimes, Lizzie? Have yer ever had a day when yer wash yer hair and yer can't do a thing with it? Well, that's how I feel sometimes.'

Nellie looked sideways. 'Ah, do yer, girl? Yer should have decent hair like me. I never have to worry about it. Run the comb through it every morning and it stays nice all day.'

Lizzie looked from one to the other. Molly had blond hair, which her daughters had all inherited, although while the girls were still shining blondes, Molly's hair was now well peppered with white. But with a fine healthy complexion, and a neat figure, she was a good-looking woman. Nellie had dark mousy-coloured hair, and she never spent any time on it. It only saw the comb in the morning and spent the rest of the day being untidy. And with her eighteen-stone body on her four-foot-ten frame, she was almost as round as she was tall. But Nellie's redeeming feature was her chubby face, with rosy cheeks that shone like polished apples, and a smile to melt the hardest heart. She wasn't a tidy person, and certainly wasn't fussy about how she looked, or what she said, but her friends saw beyond her looks to a heart that was as big as her body. But only her friends and family saw that side of her; strangers often just saw her as a loud-mouth.

'Here's Jill now,' Lizzie said. 'I'll wait until she's down before pouring, 'cos I know yer'll both be fussing over the baby and the tea would get cold.'

The two women scrambled from the table, each wanting to reach Jill and the baby first. But Jill anticipated this and turned her back on them. 'Take it easy, Mam, or yer'll frighten her. Wait until I sit down, then yer can both have a turn at nursing her. She's only tiny, and seeing and hearing a lot of people she'd be frightened.'

'Ye're right, sunshine, of course yer are,' Molly said, backing away and taking Nellie with her. 'We forgot the baby isn't two weeks old yet, and that's 'cos we're used to Bobby. But we'll sit down and have our tea, then have a little nurse of her.' She gave

Nellie a dig. 'And we'll keep our voices nice and quiet, won't we, sunshine, so we don't frighten her.'

Nellie looked from Jill, who was holding the baby close to her chest, to the plate of biscuits. 'Yeah, we'll have our tea and biscuits first, and give the baby time to settle down. And I've got to say, girl, it's going to be awkward having Molly the baby, and Molly the grandma. Yer must admit it is a bit confusing. Why don't yer call her by her second name?'

'Oh, you're not soft, are yer, sunshine?' Molly was up in arms. 'She was christened Molly Helen McDonough, that's two of your names, but ye're still not satisfied.'

Jill the peacemaker stopped what could have turned into a spat . . . friendly, but still a spat. 'Me and Steve have thought about that, and we're calling the baby Moll, so we'll know who we're talking about. She'll get Molly when she's a bit older and we won't get so confused.'

Molly turned to her mate. 'Now, does that satisfy yer?'

Nellie stuck her nose in the air and said, 'Will yer pass the biscuits, Lizzie, please?'

Molly winked behind her friend's back. 'Watch her hands, Lizzie, 'cos they're like lightning and she'll empty the plate.'

With a fig biscuit between her teeth, Nellie sighed with contentment, blissfully happy. And when Lizzie passed the plate for her to have a second one, she was filled with goodwill. 'Ay, Lizzie, d'yer know what Tony in the butcher's called me when me and Molly were in there before? He called me Mrs No Knickers.'

'Oh, I've heard from Steve and Jill about yer shenanigans at the wedding reception.' Lizzie chuckled. 'From the sound of things everyone had a marvellous time, and you had the place up, Nellie.' She leaned towards the little woman. 'Did yer really go to the wedding with no bloomers on?'

'Ah,' Nellie said, happy to be the centre of attention, 'that's for me and my feller to know, and for you to find out.'

'Nellie, don't make out things were worse than they were. It was bad enough seeing you hanging over George's back, without you saying yer had no knickers on.'

'Oh, did yer see them, girl? What colour were they?'

Molly was stumped, for she hadn't actually glimpsed any knickers, she'd been too busy laughing. But if Lily was wearing her mate's blue fleecy-lined drawers under her wedding dress, which was a joke that nearly brought the rafters down, then Nellie must have been wearing her pink ones. 'Yer had yer pink ones on, sunshine.'

When Nellie shook her head, her chins weren't very happy with her. For they had to shake as well, and they could easily miss her answer. And they'd been on pins since Saturday, waiting for someone to say whether she was knickerless or not. They could see most things that Nellie got up to, but there was so much of her it was impossible to know everything she did. 'Ye're wrong, girl! And that secret will go with me to me grave . . . or until the *News of the World* offers me a hundred pound for me story.'

Molly pushed her chair back. 'I think ye're telling fibs, Nellie, but if ye're not, then I'm ashamed of yer. I'm going to nurse the baby now, and while I am, I want yer to rid yer head of all these bad, stupid thoughts. Yer don't get yer hands on yer granddaughter until ye're as pure in heart as she is. Do you understand?'

'Not really, girl, yer lost me along the way. But while you're having a nurse of the baby, I'll get Lizzie to explain to me.'

Molly picked the baby up and felt a rush of love. She was so tiny, and so beautiful, just like her mother twenty-two years ago. Holding her gently, she whispered, 'I love the bones of yer, sunshine, and if yer grow up like yer mam, yer won't go far wrong in life.'

Nellie had been keeping her eyes on the clock, and how her mate was handling the baby so gently. She was more heavy-handed than Molly, she couldn't help it, she was born that way. But there was one thing she had that her mate didn't, and it was huge, soft-as-a-feather breasts. When her own children had been babies, she'd had no trouble getting them off to sleep by rocking them in the warmth and softness. And she wanted to do the same with her son's baby. 'Yer time's up now, girl,' Nellie said, leaving her chair. 'It's yer Grandma McDonough's shift now.'

Molly gave the baby a last kiss before handing her over. 'Here's yer other grandma, sunshine. Ye're a lucky girl having two grandmothers, aren't yer?'

Nellie looked down into the baby's face, and said, 'Why didn't yer answer her, girl? She'd have laid a duck egg with fright.'

Molly sat at the table with Lizzie and Jill. 'Did yer want anything from the shops, sunshine, 'cos me and Nellie will go for yer.'

Jill shook her head. 'I'm doing what you used to do on a Monday, Mam. I'm doing a fry-up of the leftovers from yesterday's dinner. But I'd be grateful if yer would do some shopping for me tomorrow. I don't want to take the baby to the shops yet. I couldn't bear to leave her outside in her pram in case someone ran off with her, or the noise frightened her.'

'You do everything at yer own speed, sunshine, there's no need to rush. Just take it easy until yer've got the hang of things, then washing and feeding the baby will be a doddle.' Molly had something on her mind and had to get it off. 'Look, I may as well be honest with yer. I don't like calling the baby Moll. It doesn't sound right, not for a tiny baby anyway. The only time I've heard it used is in films when they have a gangster's moll. Why not say Molly one and two? Or even little and big Molly?'

'I agree with yer, Molly,' Lizzie said. 'I don't like calling the baby Moll. I wouldn't have said anything if you hadn't, 'cos I didn't think it was my place, but I may as well put me oar in as well. I'd stick to baby Molly while she's so tiny, then sort something out when she's a bit bigger.'

Molly nodded. 'It's up to you and Steve, though, sunshine, she's your baby. Have a talk about it tonight, eh? Me and Nellie will come up in the morning before we go to the shops, and if yer have a list ready we'll get yer messages for yer.' She looked over to where Nellie was standing, her eyes fixed on the baby's face. 'She's like a little doll, isn't she, sunshine?'

'She is that. Our Steve's a clever lad.'

Molly winked at her daughter. 'Nellie's miles away so I won't disturb her, but we'll be here at half ten in the morning, sunshine, so have yer list ready for us.'

Chapter Three

'Mam.' Ruthie set her knife and fork down as she caught her mother's attention. 'Can I go to the first house pictures tomorrow, with Bella?' And before Molly had time to think of a reason why she couldn't, Ruthie went on, 'The nights aren't dark now, and we'd be home by half past eight.'

'You're only fourteen, sunshine, too young to be going to the pictures without an adult. And they wouldn't let you in, anyway.'

'Yes, they would, 'cos I don't look fourteen. I could easy pass for sixteen.'

'Don't be putting years on yerself,' Jack said. 'Time goes over too quick as it is, so don't try and be older than yer are.'

'Dad, me and Bella only want to go to the first house pictures, that's all. It's better than staying in every night playing snakes and ladders. We're too old for those games now.'

Molly's mind went back to when she was fourteen, and how she'd begged her mother to let her go to the pictures. Talking pictures were still a novelty then. She'd got her way in the end, by promising her mother that she'd come straight home from the cinema, with her friend Mary, and they wouldn't talk to a soul. 'Has Bella asked her mam yet? I can't see Mary agreeing – yer know what she's like with Bella. But if she says yes, then me and yer dad will probably agree. But only on condition that Mary says it's all right. I don't want her thinking ye're leading her daughter astray.'

'Mam, ye're old fashioned. Things have changed in the last fifty years, since you were my age.' Ruthie lifted her arm as though shielding herself from a blow. 'Only kidding, Mam. Don't hit me, please.'

Jack was smiling as he popped a piece of potato into his mouth. He could have told Molly that it was a foregone conclusion that their daughter would be sitting in the stalls at the picture house the following night. The last of their children left at home, she was going to be spoilt far more than any of the others had been. And, anyway, going to the first house pictures with her friend wasn't asking for too much. But he wouldn't interfere; it was up to Molly.

'I'll tell yer what I will do, sunshine. When we've finished our dinner and the dishes are washed and put away, with your help, then I'll go to Bella's with yer, and see what Mary thinks.'

'Yer will speak up for us, though, won't yer?' Ruthie knew only her mother could talk Bella's mother into agreeing. 'Auntie Mary won't even listen unless you're there. She thinks someone is going to run away with her daughter, or she'll get knocked down. Honest, I'm glad you're not like that, Mam, otherwise I'd still be wearing long black stockings.'

'Yer must remember that Bella is an only child, and it's natural that Mary will worry about her. I've had practice with yer sisters and brother, that's why I don't worry as much as Mary. Mind you, even if she says you and Bella can go to the pictures, what's to say she won't be sitting between yer with a bag of sweets on her knee?'

Ruthie was smiling as she swung her legs under the chair. 'If it was a box of Cadbury's chocolates, she'd be very welcome. That's as long as she let me have the Turkish delight one. That's me favourite.'

'Hang on a minute here, sunshine, let's backpedal a bit. Yer said fifty years ago, when I was fourteen, things were different. Just how old d'yer think I am, sunshine! Ye're putting years on me good style, 'cos according to you, I'd be sixty-four now. For your information, I am forty-three, and yer dad is forty-five.'

Jack put his knife and fork down and pushed the plate away. 'And, young lady, if you look as good at forty-three as yer mam does, then yer can thank her for it, for you and yer sisters inherited her good looks.'

Ruthie loved her mam and dad dearly, and she was proud of their looks. So she wasn't going to have one flattered and not the other. 'And our Tommy's got you to thank for being tall, dark and handsome.'

'I think yer've paid enough compliments to get permission from yer dad and me to go to the flicks, so if yer've got any more, save them for Mrs Watson.' Molly reached for the plates. 'I'll wash, sunshine, and you can dry.'

As soon as the dishes were put away, and the tablecloth shaken in the yard, Ruthie was all for going across the road to her friend's, but Molly put the block on it. 'Give them a chance to get their dinner down, sunshine, or they'll curse us. And it wouldn't put Mary in a very good mood, so let's bear that in mind. Give it half an hour and we'll nip over.'

As Molly had expected, Mary Watson shook her head before Ruthie had finished speaking. 'Not on your life, Ruthie. Ye're both too young to be going to the pictures on yer own.'

This was going to be hard work, Molly thought, before going to her daughter's help. 'The nights are light until nearly nine o'clock now, Mary, and they'd be home from first house before half eight. And I can't see what harm they'd come to. They can't play in the streets like they used to, and yer can't expect them to stay in every night, not after they've been working from eight in the morning.'

'But there's some funny people about these days, Molly, and I'd worry meself sick. What if a strange man started talking to them? Yer never know what would happen.'

Molly had an ally in Mary's husband, Harry, who was always telling his wife she shouldn't mollycoddle their only child so much, or she'd never learn to stick up for herself. 'Bella has got to be allowed to be independent like other girls, Mary, or she'll never have any confidence. Give her some credit for being able to look after herself.' He smiled at Ruthie, who was far more outgoing than his daughter. 'What would yer do, Ruthie, if a strange man came up to yer and started talking?'

'I'd tell him to get lost and walk away. And if he persisted I'd kick him in the shin and then run like the wind.'

Mary sensed she was fighting a losing battle, but she still wasn't happy about the prospect of her daughter's going out at night. She chewed on her bottom lip for a while, then said, 'I could meet them coming out of the pictures to make sure they get home safely.'

'Oh, no!' Harry decided it was time to put his foot down, or his daughter would be tied to her mother's apron strings for ever. 'No, Mary, you will not! Give the girl some freedom, for heaven's sake.'

Molly noticed that Bella had gone to stand beside Ruthie, and they were holding hands. It had always been like that. When they were little they had to play on the pavement outside the Watsons' house, because Mary wouldn't let Bella out of her sight. But Ruthie had never objected, and if any of the other kids made fun of Bella for being a 'mammy's girl', Ruthie soon chased them away. 'Mary, I worry about every one of my kids, always have done, no matter how old they were. I'm sure every mother in the land does. But yer have to start letting them spread their wings some time. None of my kids have come to any harm, have they? Never been in trouble for fighting or giving cheek, either. And that's because I've taught them how to behave, and given them some freedom at the same time.'

'What picture house are yer going to?' Mary knew she was outnumbered, but she still wasn't happy. 'Can yer get a tram there and back?'

'It's only two stops to the Astoria, Auntie Mary,' Ruth said. 'We can walk there and back and save the fare. The picture is a comedy, with William Powell and Myrna Loy, and one of the girls we work with said it was really funny. She laughed all the way home.'

'I'll give yer the fare, save yer walking.' Mary thought she was doing them a favour, but she could tell by their faces the offer wasn't very well received. 'Okay, if yer want to be independent, then you do what yer want. As long as ye're back here by half eight, Bella, otherwise yer won't be going out again for a long time, only with me and yer dad.'

'We'll be well home by then, Mam, I promise.' Bella squeezed Ruthie's hand. 'And I'll tell yer all about the picture.' She couldn't believe her luck. Never in her wildest dreams could she have imagined her mother agreeing. Mind you, she wouldn't have done if Auntie Molly hadn't been there. 'And if we buy any sweets, I'll save one each for you and me dad.'

'I'll give yer the money for sweets, pet,' Harry told her, pleased to see her so happy. 'I might even stretch to a tuppenny slab of Cadbury's each.'

Ruthie rolled her eyes and sighed. 'Oh, heavenly bliss, Uncle Harry. That's me favourite chocolate. Seeing as you're buying, I should promise to save yer a piece, but I know I wouldn't be able to keep me promise. Bull's eyes or blackjacks, yeah, I would have gladly saved yer one of them, but not Cadbury's.'

When Molly looked at her daughter, she wondered why some of her confidence hadn't rubbed off on to her friend over the years. For Bella could certainly do with being a little more outgoing. She was a very pretty girl, with her mother's dark colouring, and she was quite talkative when she was with people she knew well. In Molly's, for instance, she'd talk the hind leg off a donkey, but with strangers she was painfully shy.

'Come on, sunshine, let's go home to yer dad before he thinks I've run off with the coalman. Say goodnight to Auntie Mary and Uncle Harry, and we'll leave them in peace.'

Mary went to the door with them. 'I know yer think I'm over-possessive, Molly, and I know I'm holding Bella back, but it's the way I'm made. I'm going to have to change, though, 'cos it's not fair. I'll start tomorrow, when her and Ruthie go out. I won't sit biting me nails, I'll tear me hair out instead.'

Molly grinned. 'That beats cutting yer throat, sunshine, 'cos blood makes a hell of a mess. And it's the very devil to wash out of anything.'

'Look who's coming up the street, Mam,' Ruthie said, pulling on her mother's hand. 'Come on, let's say hello to him.'

Molly turned to see her next-door neighbour, Corker, walking on the opposite side of the street with another man. 'Molly, me darling,' he shouted, 'come and meet an old friend of mine.'

'I'll see yer tomorrow, Mary,' Molly said, taking Ruthie's hand. 'I mustn't keep me boyfriend waiting.'

Corker was Molly's hero. The man was six foot five in height, built like a battleship, with hands like shovels, and would stand out in any crowd. And it would take a very brave man to tackle Corker. But to Molly he was a gentle giant, who would go to the ends of the earth to help his friends. And she should know; he'd helped her out many a time. 'Are yer just getting home, Corker? Haven't yer had yer dinner yet?'

'Ah, well, yer see, me darlin', I was coming home from work when I bumped into me old shipmate here, and we went for a pint. We had such a lot to catch up on, the one pint led to another, and so on.' He put a hand on his friend's arm. 'This is the prettiest woman in the street, Molly Bennett, and her youngest daughter, Ruthie. And this, me darlin' Molly, is Derek Mattocks, who I sailed with during the war. We haven't seen each other since then, so we had a lot to tell each other.'

After Derek had shaken hands with Molly, he held out his hand to Ruthie, and she nearly burst with pride because she felt so grown-up. 'Corker insisted I come home to meet his wife, but I'm beginning to think he needs me as an excuse for being so late. But it was good to meet him after so many years, and we had a lot to catch up with. I'll stand in front of him if his wife takes the frying pan to him.'

Molly smiled. What a nice bloke he seemed, friendly and very handsome. He was about six foot tall, with thick jet black hair, deep hazel eyes, and a set of pure white teeth. Younger than Corker, she guessed, by about ten years. She reckoned he'd be about thirty-five or so. 'Ellen is far too gentle to take the frying pan to Corker, but if his dinner is ruined, well, no one would blame her if it ended up on his head.'

Corker's head dropped back and his hearty laugh filled the air. He was a fine figure of a man, with a mop of greying hair, a huge moustache and a bushy beard. 'Ellen couldn't reach me head, but, sure, I'm a big enough target for her to hit.'

Derek held his hands out and pretended they were shaking. 'I won't come with yer after all, Corker. I'll leave it for another day.'

Again Corker's laugh filled the air. 'Wait until yer see the size of me wife, Derek. Sure she only comes up to me waist. And she'd never hit me when I had a visitor with me.'

They began to walk up the street, with Ruthie clinging to her Uncle Corker's arm. He was a firm favourite with all the Bennett family, and the McDonoughs. 'Shall I come in with yer, Uncle Corker, and stop Auntie Ellen from hitting yer?'

Molly pulled on her arm. 'Not on yer life yer don't, sunshine. We'll let Uncle Corker face the music on his own. But if we hear the sound of crockery breaking, then I'll send yer dad in to sort them out before they wreck the joint.' They stopped outside her house, and she smiled at Derek. 'It was nice meeting yer, Derek. Perhaps we'll see yer again some time.'

'Oh, yer'll be seeing Derek again, me darlin', that's for sure. For I'll not be losing touch with him again.'

Molly was chuckling as she put the key in the door. 'When yer get inside, Derek, keep moving. Don't make yerself an easy target.'

He laughed back at her. 'I'll pretend I'm on board the ship in the middle of a storm, and I'll rock with the deck.'

Ellen must have heard them and popped her head out of the front door. 'I thought I could hear your voice, Jimmy Corkhill. What time d'yer call this to be coming in?' she asked, trying to look angry. 'Don't be expecting any dinner 'cos I threw it on the back of the fire half an hour ago. It wasn't fit to eat.'

'Come on, Ruthie, let's get in. I hate to see a grown man crying.' Molly pushed her daughter ahead of her, and as she was closing the door she heard Corker saying, 'Well, it was like this, me darling. I met this long lost shipmate, but I'll tell yer all about it inside. That's if yer've a mind to let us in.'

'Who were yer talking to?' Jack asked when Molly walked in. 'It sounded like Corker's voice. Is he on his way out to the pub?'

'Oh, I shouldn't think so, love.' Molly chuckled as she hung up her coat. 'He'll be in Ellen's bad books coming home at this time. He was on his way home at his usual time, when he bumped into an old shipmate. Of course, as yer would expect of Corker, they went in a pub to celebrate, didn't they, and as he said one pint led to another, and so on. He's probably getting down the banks off Ellen, 'cos she's just told him his dinner was ruined.'

'Is his friend with him?'

Molly nodded. 'His name's Derek Mattocks, and he seems a real nice bloke. He's younger than Corker. In his mid-thirties, I'd say.'

Jack rubbed his chin. 'D'yer think I should get shaved in case Corker knocks if they're going for a pint? I didn't shave last night 'cos I didn't feel like it, and I look scruffy.'

'It's up to you, sunshine, whether yer get shaved or not. But I don't think anyone will be knocking for yer to go for a drink tonight.'

'I'll leave it until later then,' Jack said, folding the *Echo* and pushing it down the side of his chair. 'How did yer get on with Bella's mam, Ruthie?'

She sat on the arm of his chair and grinned. 'Your youngest daughter is now old enough to go to the pictures on her own. Or at least with her best friend. This time tomorrow night, me and Bella will be sitting in the pictures with a tuppenny slab of Cadbury's each. And it's all thanks to me mam and Uncle Harry. It took some doing, but they talked Auntie Mary round. She was dead against it at first, and me heart sank. But we won in the end 'cos she was outnumbered.'

Jack put his arm round her. 'It'll be easier next time, pet, you'll see. Once she knows ye're capable of getting home safe, she'll not worry so much.'

Ruthie laughed. 'She wanted to come and meet us coming out of the pictures, but Uncle Harry put his foot down.'

'Good for him,' Jack said, 'but I hope yer don't think that because ye're being allowed to go to the pictures on yer own, yer can go on to do other things that grown-ups do, 'cos it doesn't work like that. You are still only fourteen, don't forget that.'

'Dad, I'm not only fourteen, I'm fourteen years and four months.'

'Oh, don't forget those four months, Jack.' Molly grinned. 'In another two months she'll be telling us she's nearer fifteen than fourteen, and that's plenty old enough to go to the dances in the church hall with a boy.'

Always ready with an answer, Ruthie said, 'How did yer know that, Mam? Are yer a mind-reader?'

'I would be if I could read everyone's mind as well as I can read yours, sunshine.' Molly kept her tone light, remembering the time she'd been fourteen and wished she was older. 'I know Gordon Corkhill goes to the church dances, and Jeff Mowbray.'

'Oh, them!' Ruthie shrugged her shoulder. 'I know them, but neither of them's me boyfriend.'

'Boyfriend! At your age, young lady, they better hadn't be!' Molly caught Jack's wink and was dying to smile. But if she did, it would send the wrong signal to her daughter, who would take it that it was all right to have a boyfriend. 'Yer've a long way to go yet before yer start bringing a boyfriend home. And if Bella truly is yer best friend, yer won't mention the word in front of her mam, 'cos if Mary so much as heard the word boyfriend, I wouldn't put it past her to have bars put on her bedroom window.'

'Oh, yer mean she might think someone would run off with Bella?' Ruthie's blue eyes were full of mischief. 'Like Romeo and Juliet? Ooh, I'll have to tell Bella to let her hair grow very long, so Romeo could use it as a rope to climb up to her window.'

'Yer've got part of it right, sunshine, but Juliet was on a balcony, she didn't have a window with heavy bars on.' Molly gave a soft sigh. 'Now, since we've discussed all there is to discuss about your life, sunshine, how about yer making me and yer dad a nice cup of tea. And there's some biscuits in the tin, only don't take too many out, or yer Auntie Nellie will curse yer in the morning when there isn't one to have with her morning cuppa.'

'Oh, we can't have that, can we?' Ruthie hummed as she made her way to the kitchen. She'd been lucky today, getting permission to go to the pictures, so she wouldn't push her luck by mentioning the dance in the church hall again. She'd leave that for another two months, when she was fourteen years and six months. That sounded much older, and would add more weight to her argument.

Nellie eyed the tray Molly carried through from the kitchen. She could see a plate on the tray, but because the teapot was in front of it she couldn't see what was on it. But she assured herself it must be biscuits, because her mate wouldn't bring an empty plate in. No, of course she wouldn't. There'd be no point.

'As I was saying, Nellie, Corker's shipmate seems a real nice bloke.' Molly pulled out a chair and sat down. 'I wonder if Corker got anything to eat in the end, or whether Ellen really had thrown his dinner on the fire.'

'Oh, Ellen would have something in to cook for him, girl. Working in the butcher's, she's bound to have chops or sausages in. Stands to sense, doesn't it?' Nellie was sitting in the carver chair with her legs swinging. 'I mean, like, if yer had a cow, yer wouldn't ever be short of milk, would yer?'

Molly grinned as she lifted the teapot. 'I suppose that's one way of looking at it, sunshine.'

It was then Nellie noticed the plate only had three custard creams on it. 'Yer've left yerself short, there, haven't yer, girl?'

Molly knew full well what her mate was thinking because she'd expected it, but she decided to act daft. 'What are yer talking about, sunshine? I don't understand. What d'yer mean by I've left meself short?'

Nellie nodded to the plate. 'Yer've only brought one custard cream for yerself.'

'What makes yer think I'm not having two?'

'Because that would be very bad manners, girl, that's why. I'm the visitor here, so it would make yer look very greedy if you had two biscuits and only left me with one. It would show yer hadn't been brought up proper.'

'Oh, so I'm lacking in etiquette, is that what ye're telling me?'

Nellie moved like lightning, and before Molly had time to breathe, two of the custard creams had disappeared off the plate. 'Ye're not only lacking in . . . er . . . in etic, ye're also lacking in two custard creams, girl, and that's what yer get for talking too much.'

'The word is etiquette, sunshine, and I'm not lacking in anything.' Molly put her hand in her apron pocket and brought out a custard cream. 'See, one whole custard cream.' She bit half of the biscuit off. 'Now, you see, one half custard cream.'

Nellie snatched the half biscuit out of Molly's hand and stuffed it in her mouth. And sending crumbs flying through the air, she spluttered, 'Now yer see it, now yer don't. Yer've got to be quick if yer want to get anywhere in this life. I keep telling yer that, girl, but yer don't take no notice.'

Molly didn't answer, but when she got in the kitchen she covered her mouth with a hand and laughed quietly. Then, when she'd composed herself, she reached for the long-handled stiff brush and marched back into the living room. 'This, sunshine, is a brush. And those bits on me clean floor are crumbs. So what you have to do is use one to get rid of the other. And will yer try and not knock me table or chair legs, 'cos they're in a bad enough state as it is, without you banging hell out of them.'

'Holy suffering ducks!' Nellie raised her eyes to the ceiling. 'Two ruddy biscuits, and yer expect me to brush yer floor!'

'You made the crumbs, sunshine, not me,' Molly told her. 'And it'll teach yer to be more careful in future.'

'Ay, you just listen to me, girl. I know me eticit as much as you do, and if yer were a proper lady what did the job proper, yer'd give yer visitors a plate for the crumbs to drop on.'

'But the crumbs didn't drop, yer spat them out 'cos yer were talking with yer mouth full. And anyone with etiquette would know that's not done in the best of circles.'

'Bloody hell! I get two flaming biscuits which were begrudged to me in the first place, and then I get a lecture in eticit. I'm sorry I had the ruddy things, 'cos I've got indigestion now.'

'That's because yer gobbled them down instead of eating them slowly.' Molly chuckled. 'Still, seeing as yer've got indigestion, I won't ask yer to brush the floor. We'll have another cup of tea, then we'll put our coats on and walk up to Jill's. I said we'd call this morning, remember, and she's having a list ready of the shopping she wants us to get for her.'

'So we've called a truce, have we, girl?'

'There has to be a war to do that, sunshine, but, yeah, yer could say we've called a truce. Like we've done every day for the last twenty-odd years. We've never once let a disagreement carry over until the next day. And that's how it should be with mates. Same as with a husband, yer should never go to sleep without making it up.'

Nellie nodded, but she had other things on her mind. 'When yer get down to pouring the tea out, girl, d'yer think yer could put a spoonful of sugar in, instead of counting each grain? Yer see, the last cup was too strong.' Then a smile spread across her face. 'Yer know I've got to have the last word, girl, or I wouldn't sleep a wink tonight.'

Chapter Four

As soon as Molly and Nellie walked into Lizzie Corkhill's house, Lizzie jumped from her rocking chair. 'Here yer are, Nellie, save yer sitting on the couch.'

Nellie's face glowed so bright, it was as though someone had switched the light on. 'Oh, that's very thoughtful of yer, Lizzie. I really appreciate yer kindness.' If she hadn't been eight inches shorter than Molly she would have looked down her nose at her. But as it was, she decided a haughty look would serve as well. 'Isn't that nice of Lizzie, girl, to think about me comfort? There's not many so thoughtful.'

'Any more sarcasm, sunshine, and I'll drag yer back to my house and make yer brush up the crumbs yer've covered me floor with.'

'What's Auntie Nellie been up to now, Mam?' Jill asked as she swayed from side to side with the baby in her arms. 'How did she come to put crumbs on yer floor?'

Lizzie sat on one of the dining chairs, a smile on her face before she even had anything to smile about. But these two friends had been to her house hundreds of times over the years, keeping an eye on her when Corker was sailing the seven seas, and never once had they failed to make her laugh. In fact sometimes she laughed so much she got a pain in her side. 'Come on, Molly, what's she been up to?'

'Seeing as she's sitting in the chair of honour, I'll let her tell yer herself. She won't tell the full truth, mind yer, but it'll be near enough.' Molly jerked her head, wondering what Nellie would come up with. It certainly wouldn't be a true account, but it was guaranteed to be funny. 'Come on, Nellie, tell them what yer did, and make it good, seeing as Lizzie gave up her chair for yer.'

'Why don't you tell them, girl, while I have a nurse of the baby.' Nellie rocked the chair with some speed, causing Lizzie to wonder whether she'd done the right thing. Her chair wasn't used to rocking an eighteen-stone woman. 'Ay, Jill,' Nellie said to her daughter-in-law, 'she'd soon go to sleep getting rocked on this. I could even rock meself to sleep.'

'The baby is fast asleep, Auntie Nellie, and I was just going to lay her down in her cot when yer knocked,' Jill said. 'So I'll take her up now before yer start telling us what tricks yer've been up to. Not a word until I come down.'

'Have yer written the shopping list out, sunshine?' Molly called after her. 'Or d'yer want me to do it?'

'She's done it, sweetheart,' Lizzie told her. 'It's on the sideboard, all nicely written out. She's a good writer, is Jill, very neat, and better at spelling than I am.'

'She takes after her mam,' Nellie said, her head nodding knowingly. 'In fact being good at spelling runs in the family. I think Molly used to feed them on a dictionary instead of a plate of sausage and chips.' She gave Molly a sly look. 'In fact, Lizzie, I've had a lesson in English this morning, and one in eticit.'

Lizzie looked puzzled. 'A lesson in English, yer said, and what was the other one, Nellie? Yer've stumped me there.'

Just then Jill came downstairs. 'I told yer not to say anything until I came down! Now, what have I missed?'

'Yer haven't missed much, sweetheart. Nellie was just telling me yer mam had given her a lesson in English this morning, and another lesson, but I didn't catch what it was.'

Nellie tutted. 'Eticit, Lizzie, eticit! Anyone would think yer'd never heard the word before.'

Jill shrugged her shoulders and pulled a face. 'I've never heard the word before, Auntie Nellie, so I must be as thick as two short planks. Tell us what it means.'

'It means not talking with yer mouth full, girl, and spitting crumbs on the floor. But it also means that the person what gave yer two custard creams without a plate to catch the crumbs on didn't know the meaning of it either. And then I wouldn't have had a brush stuck in me hand and been ordered to brush the crumbs up.' Then Nellie had what she thought was the best idea she'd ever come up with. 'I could act the scene for yer, Lizzie, word for word and action for action. Would yer like that?'

Lizzie's eyes sparkled as she leaned her elbows on the table and cupped her chin with her hands. 'Oh, that would be great, Nellie. I love it when yer do yer acting bit.'

'Well, to do it proper, Lizzie, yer'd have to put three custard creams on a plate for me. Then I could do me own part, and Molly's.'

Molly gasped. 'You hard-faced article! I don't know how yer've got the nerve, Nellie McDonough, asking for tea and biscuits when yer've had some not fifteen minutes ago.'

Nellie's face was the picture of innocence as she spread out her chubby hands. 'I was only trying to give Lizzie and Jill a laugh, girl, or is there a law against it?'

'I'd willingly give yer biscuits to have a laugh, Nellie,' Lizzie told her, 'but I haven't got any custard creams, only arrowroot.'

Nellie shook her head slowly, giving her chins the option of swaying or taking it easy. 'No good, Lizzie, I'm afraid. Yer see, yer don't get many crumbs from arrowroot biscuits, so I wouldn't be able to spit them all over yer floor.

I appreciate the offer, though, girl, and under any other circumstances I'd be glad of arrowroot biscuits. But my mate begrudged me the two custard creams so much, I ended up with indigestion.'

Molly was sitting on the couch, her legs crossed, and a half smile on her face. 'Go on, sunshine, yer might as well tell them the rest.'

'All right, girl, I'm coming to it, don't rush me.' Nellie wouldn't know what a look of disdain was, but that's the look she was trying for. 'It's your fault I've got indigestion, but yer don't feel a bit sorry for me.'

'If yer going to tell them the tale, tell them the truth. Yer pinched a custard cream out of me hand and gobbled it down, and that's how yer got indigestion.'

Nellie's nostrils flared. 'Ay, girl, who's telling this bleeding tale, you or me? Will yer kindly let me get on with it, please.' Then, as sweet as pie, she smiled at Lizzie and Jill, whose heads were going from one to the other as though they were watching a tennis match. 'Anyway, me and me mate called a truce. Because I had indigestion, Molly said I needn't brush the floor. And she gave me another cup of tea. And,' here Nellie paused for effect, 'yer'll never guess what she did. She put a spoonful of sugar in me tea without counting the grains. Now that's true friendship for yer.'

It wasn't so much what Nellie said, it was the way she said it. She could do so many contortions with her face you would think it was made of rubber. And the more she moved her head, the more her chins danced. She was a treat for Lizzie and Jill, for between her and Molly, they were left with plenty to talk and laugh about.

'Yer make a good team, you two,' Lizzie said. 'If yer ever fell out, not that I think there's even the remotest possibility of that, then yer'd both be lost.'

Jill nodded. 'Steve always says that Laurel would be no good without Hardy, and Nellie would be no good without Molly. And he's right.'

'There's a big difference between Laurel and Hardy, and me and Nellie,' Molly said. 'They get paid damn good money for acting daft, whereas we act daft because it comes natural.'

'Oh, you and Nellie get paid in appreciation, sweetheart,' Lizzie said. 'Yer've brightened my life all these years, for there's many a time I've gone to bed thinking about yer shenanigans and fallen asleep with a smile on me face.'

'I think ye're both wonderful.' Jill's pretty face was aglow. How lucky she was with her mother and her mother-in-law. 'I wouldn't change yer for the world. I love the bones of yer.'

'Ah, ay, girl, every time someone says that, yer mam comes off best 'cos she's got more bones than me. Why can't yer say yer love our bones and flesh, then I wouldn't feel left out.'

'If yer think of it that way, sunshine,' Molly said, 'I could moan and say that seeing as there is more of you than there is me, then you get more love.'

Nellie beamed. 'I never would have thought of it that way, girl. But then, I'm not as clever as you. More loved, but not as clever.'

'Well, seeing as yer've worked that out to your advantage and are feeling happy with yerself, sunshine, I think it's time we were on our way to the shops. So if yer hand me the list, Jill, we'll make a move.'

'I'll give yer five shillings, Mam,' Jill said, reaching for the list off the sideboard. 'That should cover it, but if not I'll give yer the difference when yer come back.'

Molly ran her eyes down the list then put it in her pocket. 'We may be an hour or more, sunshine, 'cos we've got our own shopping to do. And a lot depends upon how many people we meet that Nellie stops to talk to.'

Nellie got on her high horse. 'You speak to them as well, girl, so don't be putting all the blame on me.'

'Yes, I do speak to them, sunshine, because if I just stood there listening to you going on and on, they'd think I was gormless. But if I was on me own, I'd just wish them the time of day and keep walking. Unless it was one of me mates, when of course I'd stop and have a natter with them.'

Nellie leaned forward, her eyes like slits. 'What mates? I'm yer mate. Yer haven't got any other mates.'

'Don't be acting the goat, Nellie, of course I've got mates. What about Mary Watson, and Beryl Mowbray? They're not best mates, like you and me, but they are friends.' Molly leaned over the table and kissed Lizzie. 'I'll see yer later, sunshine. Jill can throw us out.'

'Before yer go, Molly, save me fretting about it all day, what does eticit mean?'

Molly chuckled. 'It's etiquette, Lizzie, but my mate can't get her tongue round that so she altered it to suit herself.'

'Come on, Mam, I'll go to the door with yer. I'm not chasing yer, but I'm hoping to get some ironing done before the baby wakes. I haven't got much, but I want it done and put away, then it's off me mind.'

Nellie let Molly and Jill go ahead of her, so she could whisper to Lizzie, 'Jill and Doreen both take after their mother. Too bleedin' fussy.'

Tony grinned when Molly and Nellie passed the shop window. 'Here's yer mates, Ellen. Come and serve them while I see to Mrs Whitworth.'

Ellen came through from the store room just as her neighbours walked through the shop door. 'Morning, ladies. Ye're a bit late today, aren't yer?'

'We went up to see what shopping Jill wanted, and yer know what it's like once yer sit down, yer start gabbing and the time flies over.' Molly jerked her head towards Nellie. 'Not that I do much talking. I leave it to me mate.'

'Only when it suits yer, girl, only when it suits yer. Most of the time yer can talk the hind legs off a donkey. Sometimes yer go on and on, forgetting to stop, and I can feel meself breathing for yer.'

Tony said goodbye to his customer and came down the counter. 'Shall I serve one of yer, and Ellen the other?'

'I want three-quarters of steak and kidney twice, Tony,' Molly said. 'Wrap them separate for us, 'cos one's for Jill. I don't know about me mate. What are you having for dinner, Nellie?'

'Same as you, girl, of course. Don't I always?'

'I'll see to them, Tony,' Ellen offered. 'You have a break.'

'What, and miss me usual laugh! Not on your life, Ellen. I'd be down in the dumps without me daily dose of Nellie and Molly. What treat have yer got in store for us today, ladies?'

'You can get to the back of the queue, Tony,' Molly told him. 'I want to know how Corker and his friend got on last night. Did yer tell him off, Ellen?'

Ellen pulled a face. 'I could hardly tell him off in front of a stranger. But I could cheerfully have strangled him for bringing a friend home without telling me. I looked a sight in the old dress I wear for work. But yer know what Corker is. He doesn't stand on ceremony, doesn't care how yer look. His dinner was in the oven, a bit dry by that time, but he ate it while I made his friend egg on toast. Then while they were busy eating and going over old times, I ran up and changed into a decent dress and combed me hair. Phoebe was out, but the other three were in and I've never known them so quiet as they listened to the men talking about the times they'd had during the war when they sailed in convoy. They talked about things I'd never heard before, about ships in their convoys being blown up, and how many near misses they'd had. It was very interesting, and Derek is a really nice bloke. But yer'll find that out for yerself, Molly, 'cos Corker's asked Derek down on Saturday to go for a pint, and they'll be calling for Jack, and George.'

Tony left them to serve a customer and Ellen felt guilty. 'I'll serve you now, and tell yer a bit more afterwards, if we don't have a rush of customers.'

But there was a steady stream of shoppers and they had no more time to talk. 'Here's yer three lots of steak and kidney, ladies, and that'll be two bob each.' Tony put the parcels on the counter and grinned at Nellie. 'Yer've ruined me day being so quiet, Nellie. I'll have nothing to tell the wife when I get home.'

'It's not my fault, lad, it's me mate. When she starts talking there's no stopping her. I just couldn't get a word in edgeways.'

'Well, that makes a change, sunshine. It's usually you doing all the talking.' Molly passed two silver coins over. 'That's four bob, for me and Jill.' She put the meat in her basket. 'Come on, Nellie, pay up and look happy.'

'You pay him, girl, and I'll pay yer when we get home. I've come out without me purse.'

'Oh, not that old trick again, Nellie. Yer can't expect me to fall for that. Get yer purse out and pay the man.'

'I've just told yer, girl, I forgot it! It's on me sideboard, I can see it in me mind. Anyone would think I was trying to diddle yer, the way yer talk. I'll pay yer as soon as we get home, and yer can charge me a penny interest on it.'

'What about the greengrocer's, Nellie? And we're going to Hanley's for bread. Do you expect me to pay in those shops, as well? Ye're a flaming smasher, yer are. How d'yer know I've got enough money on me to pay for everything?'

'Don't worry about it, Molly,' Tony said, even though he had a sneaking suspicion Nellie was pulling her mate's leg. 'She can pay me tomorrow.'

'Oh, no, lad, I wouldn't keep yer waiting for yer money, it wouldn't be fair. But I am beholden to yer for offering.' Nellie straightened up to look the pillar of respectability. 'My mate will help me out until we get home. She might say she won't, she always does, but she'll cough up in the end.'

Molly sighed as she opened her purse and rooted for another two shilling piece. 'I hope ye're not going back to pulling this trick every day, sunshine, like yer used to. I'll pay for yer today, but don't come back for more tomorrow.'

'Oh, I won't, girl.' Nellie made a cross as near to her heart as she could get. 'Look, I'll cross me heart and hope to die, if this day I tell a lie.'

Molly took a deep breath and let it out slowly. 'I feel sorry for you, Nellie McDonough, 'cos when the day of judgement arrives yer'll be asked to account for all these lies.' She put her basket in the crook of her arm and jerked her head. 'Come on, let's get the rest of the shopping in. That's if I've got enough money on me to pay for it.' She walked towards the door, 'See yer tomorrow, Tony. Ta-ra, Ellen. Come on, Nellie, get yer skates on.'

'Yes, miss, right away, miss.' Molly could hear the butcher and Ellen laughing, but her mind was busy on the shopping list and she didn't turn. If she had, she'd have seen Nellie with a thumb in each ear, her tongue sticking out and her eyes crossed.

Outside the shop, Nellie stood with an angelic look on her face. 'Where are we going to first, girl?'

'Jill needs a couple of nappies for the baby, so we'll go to the wool shop first for them, then the greengrocer's, and then Hanley's.'

Nellie linked her mate's arm. 'Why did yer say the nappies were for the baby, girl? I mean, who else could they be for? Not for you, 'cos yer grew out of them last year.'

'Oh, very funny, sunshine. D'yer know, ye're so sharp that one of these days yer'll be cutting yer tongue off.'

'Yer wouldn't wish that on me, would yer, girl? I mean, what would yer do if I wasn't able to torment yer? Yer'd have nothing to live for. Yer'd be lost.'

'Lost in a world of silence, doesn't that sound good, Nellie? What I mean is, I'd still have yer as me best mate, and we'd still go everywhere together, the only difference would be I would do all the talking and you could just nod or shake yer head. And I'd make sure yer were looked after. I wouldn't let Tony palm yer off with chops that were all fat, or Edna Hanley give yer a stale loaf. No, sunshine, I'd make sure yer got the best of everything.'

Nellie dropped her head sideways and squinted up at her mate. 'Has anyone ever told yer that yer talk too much, girl?'

Molly chuckled. 'Not yet, they haven't. But if you get any sharper and cut yer own tongue off, then they might have reason to say I talk too much, for I'd be talking for both of us.' They reached the door of the small wool shop. 'You stay here and hold the basket, sunshine. I'll be in and out in two minutes.'

Molly came out of the shop, and threw a bag in the basket. 'I told yer I'd only be two minutes. Now let's have a look at the list.' She whistled softly. 'Jill wants potatoes and a cabbage, and we both want potatoes and veg. It's going to be heavy carrying them to the cake shop, so shall we go to Hanley's first?'

'Good thinking, girl, good thinking.' Nellie passed Molly's basket back to her, then linked arms. 'Ye're not as daft as yer look, girl, and I'll crown anyone what says yer are. Some folk might say ye're cabbage-looking, but I'd soon tell them ye're not green.' She nodded her head for confirmation. 'No, sir, ye're definitely not green.'

Molly paused for a second, sensing her mate was up to something, but when she looked at Nellie's face, it was as innocent as a newborn babe's. So she carried on walking, little knowing that while the face was innocent, the mind was having a jolly good laugh.

Edna Hanley smiled when the two women walked into the shop. 'Good morning, Molly, and to you, Nellie. I hope you are both healthy and happy this fine day?'

'Yeah, it's not a bad morning, is it, Edna?' Molly rested the basket on the counter. 'Spring is definitely in the air, I'm happy to say.'

'Is it, girl?' Nellie frowned. 'What makes yer say that?'

'Well, two reasons, sunshine, which yer shouldn't need me to tell yer. We're into April, which is the start of spring, and in case yer haven't noticed, the weather is getting milder.'

'Oh, yeah, now yer come to mention it, girl, the weather is milder. I'll soon be able to leave me fleecy-lined bloomers off, and start wearing me cotton ones.'

'That is a very useful piece of information, Nellie,' Edna said. 'I'll pass the word on to anyone who comes in moaning and saying it's cold out. And now, ladies, what can I do yer for?'

'Three large tin loaves, Edna, please.' Molly had her purse ready in her hand. 'We're shopping for Jill as well, so we'll be weighed down.'

Edna turned to take the loaves off a rack behind her. 'How are Jill and the baby? When she is ready to come out, ask her to call in so I can see the baby.'

Molly chuckled. 'Edna, I think the baby will be ready for school before Jill ventures out with her. She's still coming to terms with bathing and feeding her.'

While Molly was talking to Edna, Nellie was eyeing the cakes in the glass display cabinet. The fresh cream oozing out of them was making the little woman's mouth water. She licked her lips, but that didn't help; the craving was getting worse. 'Molly, shall we take some cream slices home, to have with a cup of tea?'

'We certainly will not take any cream cakes home with us, Nellie McDonough. I might not even have enough to pay for the things from the greengrocer's. Take yer eyes off them and then yer mouth will stop watering.'

'I've tried that, girl, honest! I've crossed me fingers, and me legs, but it hasn't done no good. I want a cream slice.'

'I haven't the money for cream cakes, Nellie, so stop harping on it.'

'I'll pay for them, girl. I'll mug yer.'

'Oh, ay, get yer violin out, Edna, Nellie's going to sing us a sad song. She came out without her purse and I'm having to pay for her shopping, but I draw the line at cream cakes 'cos yer won't starve if yer don't get one. And don't be giving me that hard-done-by look, Nellie, because yer know damn well I'm counting the coppers.'

'But I've told yer, girl, I'll mug yer to one of those nice cream slices.'

'How can yer mug me when yer've got no money on yer?'

'I've just remembered I have got money on me, girl. I thought I'd left me purse on the sideboard at home, but I didn't. It's in the pocket of me apron.'

'Why you little sneak, Nellie McDonough. I don't know whether to clock yer one, or drag yer home by the scruff of the neck.' Molly turned to the woman behind the counter, who was having trouble keeping her face straight. 'What do yer think I should do with her, Edna? In my position, what would yer do?'

Edna scratched her head slowly, as though deep in thought. Then she said, 'If I were in your position, Molly, I'd punish her by making her buy four cream slices so Jill and Lizzie get one. But before I did anything, I'd ask to see the colour of her money.'

Nellie huffed and undid the buttons on her coat. Then she opened it to reveal the wraparound pinny with the big pocket in front. She put her hand in the pocket, but before she took anything out, her eyes went from Molly to Edna. 'D'yer know what, I think ye're a right pair of miserable sods, and I feel sorry for yer husbands. You can't take a bleeding joke, Molly Bennett, and what sort of mate are yer when yer don't trust me to give yer the money back what I borrowed? I hope yer feel ashamed of yerself.'

'Why should I feel ashamed of meself? It wasn't me what told lie after lie. And it wasn't a case of trusting yer to give me money back, 'cos I knew yer had yer purse with yer when we left the house. But if you enjoy playing silly buggers, who am I to spoil yer fun?'

'Yer didn't know I had me purse with me, yer big fibber.'

Molly chuckled. 'I knew yer either had yer purse with yer, or yer were pregnant.'

A slow smile spread across Nellie's face. She'd get her own back on her mate if it killed her. 'I could easy be pregnant, yer know, Edna, 'cos my feller is a very passionate man. If I didn't curb his passion, I'd be in the family way every month.'

'Ooh, every month, eh, Nellie? Your feller is not only very passionate, he's capable of performing miracles.'

Edna's daughter, Emily, was serving two customers at the far end of the counter, and they were all enjoying the banter. Nellie heard them tittering, and she turned, stuck her nose in the air, and informed them: 'Jealousy won't get yer nowhere.'

Molly gave Edna the eye. 'Before she starts world war three, will yer put four cream slices in a box, please? They'd get squashed to blazes in a bag 'cos I've got more shopping to do. Besides, if my mate wants to be generous, she can pay the extra penny for a box. And notice I said generous, Edna, where I could have said greedy.'

Nellie came out of the shop carrying the cake box in her two hands. She was so careful, anyone could be forgiven for thinking she was carrying the crown jewels. 'Shall I take these home, girl, and then come back and help yer with the spuds?'

'How crafty yer are, sunshine, but I've known yer too long to fall for that. If I was soft, and said oh, yes, what a good idea, the four cakes would be demolished by the time I got home. You stick with me, sunshine. I know where yer purse is now, so I can get the money out without you having to tip the box and make a mess of the cakes.' Molly grinned down into the chubby face. 'Cheer up, Nellie. Just keep yer mind on what it's going to feel like when yer sink yer teeth into the icing, and then the cream.'

'Ooh, yer make it sound like heaven, girl, so put a move on and let's get home quick.'

'I can't move any quicker, sunshine, and I don't know where the potatoes and veg are going to go. I'll not get them all in the basket.' Molly pulled up sharp. 'There's a woman on the other side of the road waving to us, Nellie, and I can't make out who it is.' Molly screwed up her eyes. 'Oh, yeah, I've got it, it's Tommo's mam.' She put the basket down and waved back, shouting, 'Are yer coming over to say hello?'

The woman nodded, and as she was waiting for a break in the traffic, Nellie muttered, 'Don't be asking her in for a cuppa, 'cos we've only got four cakes.'

Molly shook her head. 'D'yer ever think of anything but yer tummy, sunshine?'

'Yer know I do, but every time I mention George and the bedroom, yer do yer nut.'

When the woman joined them, Nellie said, 'Oh, I know yer now. It's Claire, isn't it?'

'That's it, Nellie. Yer've got a good memory. I was glad when I spotted yer, 'cos I often think of you and Molly.'

'D'yer live around here, then, Claire?' Molly asked. 'I never thought to ask where yer lived last time I saw yer.'

'Not far. Two tram stops or fifteen minutes' walk.' Claire Thompson was a woman of rare beauty. Tall and slim, with dark hair, high sculpted cheekbones, melting brown eyes and a fine set of white teeth. The two friends had met her at Christmas through her son, Ken. He'd left school that week and Billy, the greengrocer, had given him some work delivering to local customers. He was freezing when he got to Molly's, his clothes so threadbare they couldn't keep out the cold. Molly had made him a hot cup of tea and told him to come back when he'd finished work because she had some clothes that her children had grown out of and they might do him a turn. Molly had taken to the lad, who had told them his dad died before he was ten, and he was hoping to get a job soon so he could help his mam out with money. Of course Molly went round the whole family and had ended up with so many clothes, men's and girls', that she could have opened a second-hand shop. But she was well paid back when she saw the look on his face. She'd also collected some money for him, which had brought tears to his eyes, for he said he could buy his mam and his kid sister a present now. And to top it all, Doreen had told Phil, who remembered how he had no one to help him at that age, and he had offered to help the lad get a job. As he himself had that day been promoted to floor walker, he wanted to share his luck with someone less fortunate.

'I'm glad I spotted you,' Claire told them now. 'I've often thought of calling but I didn't want to be a nuisance. But I want yer to know that the day you helped our Ken was a turning point in our lives. The clothes gave us some pride back, and we were able to walk with our heads held high. Thanks to yer son-in-law, Ken now brings a wage home each week, and he's really proud when he hands the packet over. And I've got meself a part-time job in a laundry, working four mornings a week. We're not well off, far from it, but we are able to make ends meet now. And it's all down to you two, and Phil. You certainly changed our lives for the better, and our Ken calls yer our guardian angels.'

Nellie pulled herself to her full four foot ten inches, ordered her bosom to stand to attention, and beamed. 'Ooh, did yer hear that, girl? Guardian angels, young Tommo calls us.' Nellie was so proud she almost forgot the box of cakes as she put a hand up to pat her hair. 'We were glad to help yer, girl, weren't we, Molly?'

'If he hears yer calling him Tommo, sunshine, yer won't be his guardian angel for long. He likes to be called Ken, now he's working.' Molly straightened the cake box in Nellie's chubby hands before smiling at Claire. 'We didn't do much, sunshine, just gave yer some clothes the family had grown out of. I was made up that they were put to good use. And I'm really pleased that things are going well for yer. Phil said Ken is a good little grafter, works as hard as any of the men. It would be nice to keep in touch, so why don't yer come round one afternoon for a cuppa and a natter? We'd like that, wouldn't we, Nellie?'

Nellie and her chins agreed. 'Yeah. We've got loads to tell yer. My daughter got married last week and yer should have seen me all dolled up. Everyone said it was the best wedding they'd ever seen.' She suddenly felt Molly's eyes on her, and added, 'Mind you, it would have to have been good to beat

Molly's weddings. They were great.' Thinking she'd got herself out of that nicely, Nellie thought of something else to brag about. 'Oh, I'm a grandma now. Me son had a baby two weeks ago.'

Molly winked at Claire. 'I think yer mean my daughter had the baby, sunshine. It is usually the woman that gives birth. Steve made it possible, I'll agree with yer on that before yer raise any objections, so let's say we both became grandmas two weeks ago. And any other news yer've got, would yer keep it until Claire comes to visit, 'cos I think we better get cracking, or Jill will think we've forgotten her. But how about coming round on Friday afternoon, Claire, when yer finish work? We'll have a butty and a cup of tea ready for yer. And if my mate is feeling generous, we might even run to a cream slice.'

Claire grinned. 'I'll look forward to that. It'll be about half one, give or take ten minutes. So, ta-ra till then.'

Chapter Five

'I really enjoyed that, love,' Jack said, patting his tummy. 'Yer can't beat steak and kidney. It was very tasty and very filling.'

'Yeah, it was nice, Mam.' Ruthie nodded. 'But I could have done with a potato less, 'cos I'm bloated and I'll be getting fat.'

Molly clicked her tongue as she gazed across at her youngest daughter. 'Listen, sunshine, yer have to eat to be healthy. Look at yer grandma and granddad. They've had a good meal every day, and it hasn't done them any harm. Both of them are slim and look younger than their age.'

'Never mind yer grandma and granddad,' Jack said, 'look at yer mam! She eats everything in front of her, and she's still got a good figure.'

Molly grinned. 'Thank you for the compliment, sunshine. It's bucked me up no end to know me husband still notices what I look like.' She remembered Nellie's antics over the cream slices and thought she'd give her husband and daughter a laugh. 'I won't give yer chapter and verse 'cos it would take too long, and I want to go over to Doreen's tonight, and to me ma's. But my mate Nellie is so funny at times, yer'd need a face made of concrete not to laugh. First, in the butcher's she said she'd forgotten to bring her purse out with her, and would I pay for her shopping until we got back home. Now, if yer think on, she used to try this trick nearly every day until I got wise to her. And I knew she was lying today because her purse is one of those big ones that me ma used years ago, and I could see the bulge of it through her coat. Anyway, I didn't let on, I just played the fool like I always do with her, until we got to Hanley's, and Nellie saw the fresh cream cakes. I was busy talking to Edna, but I could see Nellie looking longingly at the slices, and she kept licking her lips. In the end she got so desperate, she had to tell me she'd just remembered she did have her purse with her after all. And I had to pretend to be mad with her, so she offered to mug me. And it ended up with her buying four cream slices 'cos I was shopping for Jill, and we could hardly walk in with a cake box and not offer one to her and Lizzie. But Nellie would have paid for ten if she'd had to, 'cos she can't resist a fresh cream cake. Anything sweet come to that. She's really got a sweet tooth.'

'She's very funny, Auntie Nellie is,' Ruthie said. 'Half the time I think she makes things up just to make people laugh.'

'She fills my days with laughter,' Molly said, collecting the dirty plates. 'My life would be very dull without her. For instance, I don't know anyone else who could make a half-hour drama out of one custard cream.' She put the plates down and went through the shenanigans of the crumbs on the floor: the speed with which Nellie had swiped the biscuit from her hand and the speed in which it disappeared into an eager mouth. She was very good at taking her mate off, with the facial contortions and the hoisting of the bosom. The latter had to be left to the imagination of those watching, because when it came to comparing bosoms, Molly wasn't in the meg specks. 'And if she ever says yer have no eticit, take that as meaning yer haven't a clue when it comes to etiquette. Nellie has changed quite a few words in the English dictionary because she can't get her tongue round them.'

Jack and Ruthie were in stitches, and Molly herself was chuckling as she picked up the plates. 'Honestly, yer have no idea what she's like. And she can keep it up for hour after hour. Whether it's in the butcher's, the baker's, or the greengrocer's, she never stops talking, and she never repeats herself. I've never met anyone like her, and I bless the day she moved in next door.'

'Why did she say she'd forgotten her purse, Mam, when she'd have to pay yer the money back when yer got home anyway?' Ruthie asked. 'I mean, she would pay yer back, wouldn't she? She'd have to, or yer wouldn't speak to her again.'

'Well, she started that trick years ago, and I believed her for ages. Sometimes I'd ask her for it when we got home, but as she always comes in with me for a cuppa, she'd make the excuse she'd give it to me first thing in the morning. It was ages before it dawned on me that she was pulling me leg. And even then I let her get away with it because some of the expressions on her face when yer know she's telling her whopping big lies, well, it's better than going to the pictures.' Molly pushed her chair back and stood up. 'I meant to have the dishes washed and put away by now, 'cos I want to slip over to Doreen's before she puts Bobby to bed. I haven't been over there today, what with doing Jill's shopping as well as me own, and I don't like to let a day go by without seeing them.' She got to the kitchen door before adding, 'I'm going round to see me ma and da, too.'

'I'll come with yer, love, if Ruthie is going over to the Watsons',' Jack said. 'I don't see much of either of me grandchildren, and I don't want to be a stranger to them.'

Ruthie's eyes widened. 'Dad, have yer forgotten this is a big day in my life? Don't yer remember me and Bella are going to the pictures? She'll be standing by the window waiting for me, 'cos we should be on our way now. It's a good job I got washed and changed as soon as I came in from work, or we'd be too late.' She scraped her chair back. 'That's what I get for listening to me mam.' Her coat was ready on the couch, and she slipped her arms into it. 'I won't be late, Mam, but if ye're out, I'll go in with Bella until I see the light go on.' With that she was out of the door and halfway across the street by the time Molly got to the step.

'Enjoy yerself, sunshine, but take care!'

'I will, Mam. Ta-ra.'

Jack put his arm across his wife's shoulder. 'I can tell by yer face that ye're going to be as worried about her as Mary is about Bella, but yer've no need to be, for our Ruthie has got her head screwed on the right way. She's much more advanced than the others were at her age. I'd feel sorry for any man who tried to take advantage of her, 'cos they'd get more than they bargained for.'

Molly let out a sigh. 'Yeah, I know, sunshine, but she's the last one left in the nest, and I don't want her to grow up too quickly. In fact, selfish though it may sound, I would like her to stay fourteen years and four months for ever.'

'Not much hope of that, love, so make the most of her while she's here. And now, I'll help yer with the dishes and then we'll go and see our grandson.'

'Look at yer dad, Doreen, he's like a child with a new toy.' There was love in Molly's eyes as she watched her husband with the baby. Bobby was eight months old now, and beginning to recognise different faces and voices. And when Jack tickled his tummy, his laugh was really hearty as his arms and legs kicked out.

Jack felt very proud as he gazed down into eyes that were as blue as the sky on a summer day. Doreen and Phil had blue eyes and blond hair, but it was too soon to say who the baby would favour in looks, his mam or his dad. 'With legs like you've got, Bobby, yer could well make the Liverpool team when yer grow up.'

'Watch it, Mr B.,' Phil said. 'Don't forget his dad's a red hot Evertonian. It'll be blue for him, not red.'

'My son will make his own mind up when he's old enough,' Doreen said. 'Yer never know, he could end up a film star, like Alan Ladd. He's got blond hair. Mind you, I have heard he's very small and has to have his shoes built up to make him look taller.'

'Ah, yer shouldn't be making plans for the lad,' Victoria said. 'Then yer wouldn't be disappointed if he wanted to be a ballet dancer.'

'Ooh, I think I'd be very disappointed if he wanted to be a ballet dancer, Aunt Vicky,' Phil said, a smile on his handsome face. 'Can yer imagine me introducing him to the men I work with, and saying, "This is my son, he's a ballet dancer"?'

'You talking about yer work, sunshine, has just reminded me that I saw Ken Thompson's mother this afternoon. Me and Nellie were talking to her for a while, and I invited her to come for a cuppa and a chinwag on Friday afternoon. She works four mornings a week now, in a laundry, and she seems quite happy. Have yer ever seen her, Phil?'

Phil shook his head. 'No, but I've heard a lot about her from Ken. I travel home with him some nights, and he talks non-stop about her. Her name's Claire, isn't it?'

'Yes, and I'm not surprised at Ken talking about her so much, 'cos she's got to be the most beautiful woman I've ever seen. All our girls are lovely, but Claire is something else. She would knock any film star into a cocked hat.'

'Ooh, would yer bring her over on Friday when she comes to yours?' Doreen asked. 'I'd like to see her. Phil often talks about what a nice lad Ken is.'

'He's a good worker, I'll say that for him,' Phil said. 'I'm really glad I put a word in for him with the boss, because he certainly hasn't let me down. In fact, the boss has asked me a few times if I know any more lads as good as him.'

'Tell him if he waits fourteen years he'll have one as good as his dad,' Jack said, talking to the baby. 'It's an idea, if yer can't make it to the Liverpool team, lad.'

'Shall I make yer a drink, Mam?' Doreen asked. 'I never thought because we'd not long finished our dinner when yer came.'

'No, thanks, sunshine. We've not long finished our dinner, either. And me and yer dad are going round to me ma's for half an hour, just to see how they are. I don't want Tommy and Rosie to feel left out 'cos I see much more of you and Jill than I do of them. Mind you, they'll understand it's only natural with you and Jill having babies.' Molly chuckled. 'Talking of babies, my youngest baby has gone to the pictures tonight with Bella. Which she thinks makes her grown-up now. Only first house, mind; I wouldn't let her go to the last house. We had a job talking Mary into it, and I bet she stands at the window all night waiting for her daughter to come home safe and sound.'

'Mary can't help the way she's made, Molly,' Victoria said. 'She's always been of a nervous disposition, and Bella is her only child.'

'She's a good neighbour, Mam.' Doreen went to their neighbour's defence. 'Never a day goes by that she doesn't ask how Aunt Vicky is. If she hears me in the yard she'll shout over the wall, but if not, she'll knock on the door to see if we want anything.'

'Yer don't have to tell me that, sunshine, for Mary was keeping an eye on Victoria long before you and Phil moved in. Yer couldn't ask for a better neighbour, or friend.'

Doreen looked at the clock. 'I'm sorry to interrupt yer conversation with me son, Dad, but it's time to get him ready for bed.' She held out her arms. 'Pass him over, and don't look so scared, he won't break.' She held the baby close and kissed his forehead. 'I'm trying to get him into a routine by putting him to bed at seven o'clock every night. He slept right through last night until six this morning, which was great.'

Phil's blue eyes twinkled. 'The only thing was, he didn't tell us he was going to sleep through, and we both slept with an eye and an ear open.'

'It was really inconsiderate of him not to tell yer, sunshine, but if he sleeps through again tonight, that's his way of telling yer that the routine is working.' Molly was proud of the way her once wayward daughter had turned out to be a fantastic housewife and a loving mother, and at the same time was taking such good care of the woman who had offered her and Phil a home. Victoria's hair was always neat and tidy, her clothes were immaculate, she was well fed, and her face told of her happiness and contentment.

'Shall I sit down and make meself comfortable?' Jack asked with a grin. 'Or are we on our way round to yer ma's?'

'Don't park yer bottom, love, 'cos we'll have to move. I want to try and be back for when Ruthie comes home from the pictures. It's a big step for her, paying at the kiosk for her ticket and then following the usher to her seat. She'll be so excited she'll want to talk about it, and I think you and me should be the ones she tells. Sometimes she reminds me a bit of Nellie. She can be just as funny when she puts her mind to it, and she says exactly what she thinks and to hell with the consequences.'

'I think Lily is like Auntie Nellie,' Doreen said. 'She's a real hoot when she takes her mother off, and she's just as quick on the uptake.'

Victoria had a habit of putting a hand to her mouth when she laughed, and she did that now. 'Have you ever shown your mother how you can impersonate Nellie?'

When Doreen blushed, Molly said, 'No, she hasn't! Oh, when she was little, she used to try and walk like Nellie, and pull faces, but I think Nellie's bad language got in the way of her doing a good job. For I wouldn't have found it funny if a daughter of mine came out with some of the words my mate uses.'

'Oh, Doreen is very good at it,' Victoria said. 'When we see yer standing outside your house having one of yer make-believe arguments, we stand by the window and Doreen has Nellie's body and face movements off to a T.'

'That's an exaggeration, Aunt Vicky, 'cos me mam does it better than anyone could. I only do it for a laugh.'

'Isn't that why we all do it?' Molly chuckled. 'It just goes to show, though, that yer never know when ye're being watched. But next time, I'll tell Nellie to have an argument with herself, and I'll nip over here and watch. And that's not as daft as it sounds, 'cos she'd be prepared to do it if she knew we were watching. There's nothing my mate likes better than playing to an audience. I think if it came to a choice between a cream slice or applause, Nellie would opt for the applause.' Molly's head dropped back and she roared with laughter. 'And when the applause had died down, yer wouldn't see her heels for the dust as she ran like hell to Hanley's for a cream slice.'

Phil sat listening, a warm glow inside him as he thought how lucky he was to have such a wonderful family and friends. The big family that was the Bennetts, the McDonoughs and the Corkhills had taken him in and made him one of them. 'When yer go to the shops tomorrow, Mrs B., will yer get seven cream slices? That's if yer can carry them with the rest of yer shopping.'

'Seven!' Molly's voice came out in a squeak. 'What in heaven's name d'yer want seven cream slices for?'

'Four for yer to take to Mrs Corkhill's for her, Jill, Auntie Nellie and yerself. And we three are partial to cream slices, so as I said, if yer can manage to carry them, I'll pay for them.' Phil suddenly realised he'd left Jack and Ruthie out. 'I'm out with me counting. It'll be nine cakes, not seven.'

'There's no question of being able to carry them, son, for Nellie would carry them on her head if she had to. But you don't have to pay for them all. We'll pay for our own.'

'I want to, Mrs B., so don't put up an argument.'

'No, Mam,' Doreen said. 'Remember the saying that yer should never look a gift horse in the mouth. And you've done plenty for us, so a cream slice is a very small repayment.'

'Okay, yer twisted me arm.' Molly stood up and wagged her finger at Jack. 'Come on, sunshine. I want to spend an hour at me ma's, not run in and out.' She gave a throaty chuckle. 'I let yer twist me arm over the cakes, but I wonder if Nellie will be willing to let yer mug her to a cream slice. She's very independent, yer know.'

It was Victoria's turn to chuckle. 'You could play a joke on her for a change, sweetheart, and tell her the cake was for George.'

Molly put her bag down, stood in the middle of the floor with her hands on her hips and became Nellie. With her eyes like slits, and her face screwed up, she snarled, 'It'll be over my dead body, girl, that George gets his bleeding hands on that cake. What does Phil think he's playing at, the miserable bugger, leaving me out. I'll be over there tonight, as soon as he gets in from work, and he'll get a piece of me mind.' The pretend bosom was hitched up. 'I'm having one of those cakes when we get to Lizzie's, girl, or no one gets one. So put that in yer bleeding pipe and smoke it.'

'Very good, love,' Jack said. 'If I closed me eyes I'd think it was Nellie.'

'Yer know, I'm daft,' Molly told them. 'I'm with her every day; yer'd think I'd have had enough of her. But I get a kick out of taking her off! I don't know about daft, I'm crazy!'

'We should be going, Molly, if yer want to spend some time with yer mam,' Jack said. 'I think we'd better be home for Ruthie. It wouldn't seem right her having to wait in Bella's for us to get home.'

'I'm ready, sunshine.' Molly kissed Victoria, Doreen and Phil, then had a special one for her grandson. 'You sleep all night for yer mam and dad, d'yer hear, Bobby? There's a good boy.'

'I'll see them out while you take the baby up,' Phil said. 'He goes down easier for you than he does for me.'

When Molly stepped down on to the pavement, she linked Jack's arm, then smiled up at Phil. 'Doreen's with the baby all day, son, so he's bound to be more used to her ways than he is to yours. But just wait till he's a bit older. He'll be taking yer hand and asking yer to take him to the park and on the swings.'

Jack wasn't going to let that pass. 'And a few years after that, Phil, he'll be asking yer to take him to the match at Anfield.'

'Yer mean Goodison, don't yer, Mr B.?'

Molly pulled on her husband's arm. 'Come on before you two start talking football. Honest, women have so many chores on their minds, and all you men think about is ruddy football.'

'I'm coming.' Jack chortled as he tried to keep his feet on the ground. 'This is what marriage is when the novelty has worn off, Phil, so don't say I didn't warn yer.'

* * *

Tommy raised his brows in surprise when he opened the front door. 'Hi, Mam, Dad. I wasn't expecting to see you tonight. Yer never mentioned yer were coming when I called in from work.'

Molly swept past him. 'Yer dad didn't know, sunshine. I don't tell him everything, yer see.' She smiled when she saw her mother and father sitting beside each other on the couch, holding hands. Ooh, she felt like eating them, she loved them so much, but she had to make do with a kiss. 'Did Tommy tell yer our Ruthie's gone to the first house pictures with Bella?'

'He did, me darlin'.' Bridie nodded. 'And he said she was as pleased as Punch.' Still a fine-looking woman in her seventies, Bridie Jackson, like her husband Bob, thought they were the luckiest couple in the world, with the most wonderful family in the world. They'd only had the one child, Molly, but she had given them four grandchildren, and recently a great-grandson, and now a great-granddaughter. Their cup of happiness was overflowing. Born in Ireland, Bridie still had that lovely Irish lilt to her voice, and she and her husband were adored by their family and all their friends. 'I imagine she'll be coming round tomorrow night to tell us all about her great adventure, so she will. And, sure, me and Bob are happy for her, right enough, but we'll not be wanting her to grow up too quickly, and that's the truth of it.'

'Don't worry, Ma, I'll be keeping her on a tight leash. This is her first step into being independent, and it'll be a while before she takes her second.'

Tommy's wife, Rosie, came through from the kitchen, a broad smile of welcome on her bonny face. 'Auntie Molly, sure it's good to see yer, so it is.' After giving her mother-in-law a bear hug and a kiss, she turned to Jack. 'And it's yerself come to see us, Uncle Jack. Sure, it's not often we have the pleasure.'

'Then don't I get a kiss?' Jack, like the rest of the family and friends, had taken this beautiful Irish colleen to his heart. 'It's not that I don't want to come and see yer more often, love, but usually I have to stay in with Ruthie when Molly comes around.' He chuckled. 'But me baby-sitting days are over now, with our youngest daughter grown up enough to go to the pictures with her friend.'

Tommy's eyes never left the face of the wife he adored. 'Doesn't yer dearly beloved husband get a kiss?'

Rosie turned away from Jack, her face stern and her hands on her hips. 'Wasn't it yerself that stole a dozen kisses while we were washing the dishes?'

Tommy shook his head. 'No, it was thirteen kisses, my dearly beloved, and yer know thirteen is an unlucky number.'

'Did not yer think of that when yer were stealing the kisses, Tommy Bennett?'

'When I'm kissing you, Rosie, I'm not capable of thinking of anything else.'

'How can I refuse when yer say things like that?' Rosie put her arms round his neck and kissed him soundly on the lips. 'That's for being the finest figure of a man on this earth, and having the sense to choose me for yer ever-loving wife.'

Molly slipped her coat off and sat in a chair by the table. She had a half smile on her face as she watched her son and his beautiful wife. Years ago she could never have imagined her shy son kissing anyone in front of her. And he probably would still be as shy if he didn't witness, every day, the love his grandma and granddad had for each other. They held hands and kissed no matter who was there. And Rosie was the same. She would never dream of telling a lie, or doing things on the sly. She had plenty of love to give, and she gave it freely. With Rosie, what you saw was what you got.

'D'yer feel like a game of cards?' Bridie asked. 'Or would yer prefer to relax, have a cup of tea, and tell us how our great-grandchildren are?'

'We won't play cards, Ma, 'cos it takes well over an hour to have one game, and I really do want to be home for Ruthie.'

'I'll put the kettle on,' Rosie said, 'and yer can have a piece of the sandwich cake Auntie Bridget made with her own fair hands.' She turned to go to the kitchen when she said, 'Sure a little birdie must have told yer it was a good night to come visiting. For isn't the dear woman one of the best sponge cake makers ever, so she is.'

Molly licked her lips. 'Me mouth is watering already. I can remember me ma's baking. When I was at school I could always smell it as soon as I came through the door.' She smiled at Bridie. 'Remember, Ma, yer always saved me a bit of pastry so I could make a little cake for meself. But somehow, it always came out of the oven as hard as a rock, while yours were as light as a feather.'

'Oh, yer can't learn how to make pastry in a few minutes, me darling. It's something that comes with practice. Yer have to have a feel for it, that yer have the right mix of flour and margarine. And yer have to have the time and patience. Sure, when my mammy first taught me, there was many a time when the cake hadn't risen and was as flat as a pancake.'

Molly pulled a face. 'I stick to fairy cakes, Ma, or the occasional Victoria sponge. I haven't the patience for these fancy concoctions. But our Doreen's not bad. She makes nice sponges, and she'll have a go at making bread. Victoria taught her, and she's a dab hand at it now.'

When Rosie carried the tray in, followed by Tommy with the teapot, they all sat at the table. Molly was the first to reach for a piece of cake, and she closed her eyes. 'This is bliss, Ma. Yer haven't lost yer touch.'

'Yer never do, me darlin',' Bridie told her. 'Once yer've learned, yer never forget. And now, tell us how the babies are.'

'Both doing well, Ma. Bobby is getting to be quite heavy now, and he's all there. He knows who's who, and he points to things in the room now. Doreen's trying to get him into a routine at bedtime. She's putting him to bed at seven o'clock every night, to get him used to it. And last night he slept through, until six this morning.'

'She's wise to do that, so she is,' Bridie said, nodding in agreement. 'A baby soon learns when his life is run on an even keel, and he'll be more happy and contented.' She pointed to the plate. 'Have another piece, me darlin'. Sure I can easily make another tomorrow.'

'I won't say no, 'cos it's delicious. It's a good job Nellie's not with me. She'd scoff the lot and think nothing of it.' Molly swallowed the piece of cake in her mouth before going on. 'But we'll leave me mate for another time. Yer want to know about Jill and the baby. Because Molly is so small, Jill is afraid of hurting her and takes ages to bathe and feed her, so she hasn't really had time to get into a routine. But the baby is beautiful, just like a little doll. And with the first one, it does take a long time to get yerself organised, feeding and washing the baby, and trying to make dinners and keep the place tidy. I wasn't a bit organised when Jill was born. I always felt I needed another pair of hands. But she'll sort herself out in time, and I'm happy because she's with Lizzie, and not on her own all day.'

With the three women talking about babies, the men looked at each other and shrugged their shoulders. 'Are yer going to see Liverpool play on Saturday, Dad?' Tommy asked. 'They're playing at home, and it should be a good match. Any chance of you coming, Granda?'

'No. I couldn't stand for so long, but there's nothing to stop you and yer dad going.'

'Yes, I'll go, son. I haven't been for a couple of weeks. That's if the wives have no objection.'

But the women were so rapt in baby talk they didn't hear. So Jack winked at his son. 'We could say we asked them but they mustn't have heard us. We'll both stick to the same story.'

Chapter Six

'Don't forget Claire's coming this afternoon, sunshine, so we've no time to mess around.' Molly looked down into Nellie's face. 'D'yer think it would be better if we take this shopping home, then come out again?'

'What would we need to come out again for, girl? We've got all the shopping we want.' Nellie moved the basket to her other arm. 'These potatoes are not half heavy, so don't hang about, let's go home.'

'Claire's coming straight from work, sunshine, so she'll be starving. I'll have to have a sandwich ready for her. I thought ham sandwiches and a cream cake. D'yer think that's enough?'

'Ooh, I think so, girl, she's not going to expect more than that. Are yer thinking of making a sandwich for us as well?' Nellie forgot her aching arm when food was mentioned. 'I mean, like, girl, she would feel dead embarrassed if we sat there watching her eating. We'd have to have something ourselves, or she'd feel like a monkey in the zoo with everyone gawping at her.'

Molly nodded. 'I wouldn't say no to a sandwich and a cream cake meself, anyway. And I could put a fancy doily on each plate to make them look a bit more posh. D'yer think that would be all right?'

'I'd say putting a doily on the plates is a good idea of yours, girl. It shows we know what eticit is.'

Molly sighed. How many times was she going to have to tell her? 'Nellie, the word is etiquette, not eticit. Try and remember, eh?'

'I don't know why yer keep telling me that, girl, 'cos I'll never get me tongue round saying it the way you do. Anyway, nine out of ten people won't know what I'm talking about no matter how I say it. They're not all clever bleeding clogs, like what you are.'

'Okay, sunshine, we'll discuss that when we've got more time. Let's take this shopping home and come straight out again. Then we'll split up, one go for the boiled ham and the other for the cakes. Do those arrangements meet with your approval?'

Nellie's eyes narrowed. 'Are yer being sarky, girl?'

'Of course I'm not being sarky,' Molly said. 'I've got more to do than play silly beggars. So when we come out again, do you want to go for the ham or the cakes?'

Nellie didn't need to give that much thought, but being crafty she didn't want to appear too eager. 'I'm not going for the ham, girl, 'cos the last time I got some for yer, yer had a face like thunder, and yer said there was more fat than ham. So, if it's all the same to you, I'll let you get the ham and I'll get the cakes.'

Molly looked doubtful. 'I don't think I could trust yer to get the cakes, 'cos I can still remember when yer went for some when I was having visitors, one time, and yer'd run yer finger all along the side of the cream slices and licked all the cream out.'

'Yer've got a ruddy good memory, girl, I'll say that for yer. Ye're talking about something what happened a couple of years ago! Don't tell me ye're going to harp on that again?'

'I'm not harping, I just don't want to open the bag and bring out cakes what yer've squashed on purpose so the cream would ooze out and yer could lick it. I'd die of humiliation, sunshine, so if yer go for the cakes yer've got to swear on yer heart that yer won't finger them before yer get home.'

'Molly, if yer don't trust me, go for the bleeding cakes yerself!'

'No, your promise is good enough for me, sunshine. Besides, the cake shop is nearer than Irwins, so it isn't so far for yer to walk. And now that has been sorted out to both our satisfaction, let's get home with this lot.'

It wasn't a quick walk home, for Nellie insisted on linking Molly, and as she swayed from side to side Molly was pushed against the brickwork and sills of the houses they passed. She thought about asking Nellie to swap sides, but knew it would be a waste of time, because she'd only end up walking in the gutter. She was glad when they stopped outside her door, and pleased all the heavy shopping had been done. 'Just put yer shopping in the house and come straight back, Nellie, so I'll have a bit of time to make the place presentable for Claire coming.'

Nellie nodded and walked away, and as Molly put the key in the lock she could hear her mate muttering, 'She's a fussy cow. Anyone would think she was expecting a visit from the Queen.'

'What did yer say, Nellie? I didn't quite catch it.'

'I said the meat we got off Tony was the leanest I've ever seen.'

Molly chuckled as she walked through to the kitchen. You could lay money down that Nellie would have an answer for anything you came up with. Still grinning, Molly placed the basket on the draining board and began to put the groceries away. She didn't bother taking her coat off because Nellie would be coming any minute. And if she saw her mate with her coat off, she'd plonk herself down and play the drama queen, pretending she couldn't walk another step because she was dying of thirst. And there was no time to waste: this house was going to look like a new pin when Claire came. Molly wasn't a snob, she told herself, putting the potatoes and vegetables in the pantry, but she did have her pride.

'I'm here, girl. Are yer coming?'

'Okay, sunshine, I'm on me way. Just give me a minute to make sure I've got enough money on me.'

Ten minutes after walking up the street, the two friends were walking down, but this time they were minus the baskets. 'If yer insist on linking arms with me, sunshine, will yer try and stop yer hips from banging into me,' Molly said, fighting against the odds to make Nellie walk in a straight line. 'Then I won't be having to explain to Jack why I've got ruddy big bruises on me thighs.'

Nellie tilted her head. 'Ay, girl, we've only been out of the bleeding house one minute, and already ye're moaning.' She pulled Molly to a halt. 'How would Jack see any bruises on yer thighs? Yer don't wear yer skirts up to yer backside, so how could he see them?' A sly look in her eyes, she said, 'Yer must lift yer clothes up and show him, yer brazen hussy.'

Molly had to do some quick thinking. 'He doesn't see them, sunshine, I never said he did. What he does see is the way I grimace when I get into bed.' That should give me mate something to think about, she thought. 'And I don't grimace on purpose. I can't help it, 'cos it can be very painful lying on a big bruise.'

'Oh, I'm sure it is, girl, although I can't speak from experience. Yer see, being so fat comes in handy sometimes, 'cos no knocks can get through to the bone.' They walked on in silence for a while, then, as Molly expected, Nellie pulled her to a halt. 'What did yer say Jack sees when he gets into bed?'

'I said he sees a look of pain on me face.'

'Yer never said no such thing, girl, yer said he grinned. And I don't think that's a very nice thing for a husband to do. I'd clock my George if he did that.'

'I did not say he grinned, Nellie. Fancy you saying that!' Molly knew they weren't going to be home early, the rate they were going. And she knew she'd brought it on herself, but she couldn't help winding her friend up now and again. 'My husband is very solicitous when he thinks I'm not well.'

'Bloody hell, girl! When your Jack's reading the *Echo* every night, do yer sit at the table with the ruddy dictionary in front of yer? Yer must do, 'cos ye're the only one I know what comes out with foreign words. And for spite, and to teach yer a lesson, I'm not moving from here until yer tell me what Jack sees on yer face, and what he does when he thinks ye're not well. So go on, clever clogs, or yer'll have me thinking yer make words up just to confuse me and make me look daft.'

'Oh, I don't think ye're daft, sunshine, not by a long chalk. Yer can knock spots off me at most things.' Molly pinched a chubby, rosy cheek. 'Let's move, and I'll tell yer while we're walking. I don't want to be out very long. Now, first, what Jack sees on me face is a grimace. And that means I pull a face 'cos the bruise hurts. And when I said Jack is solicitous, it means he worries about me, and is concerned. Fusses over me, yer know, like, runs round after me, putting cushions or pillows behind me back.'

'D'yer know what, girl, if yer'd said it like that to begin with, we'd be on our way back from the shops, not on our way to them. And all this on account of bruises what we both know bleeding well yer don't have. I've got too much padding on me hips to cause yer any bruises, so don't come that with me.'

They turned into the main road, and Molly said, 'Yer basket hasn't got any padding, and neither has the walls yer push me into. But I'll put the white flag up for now, sunshine, and give in to yer.'

Nellie had a smug smile on her face. 'I knew yer'd give in, girl 'cos yer always do. I know yer wind me up; I'm not soft, yer know. I've known all along that yer've made up those big words yer come out with in yer head, and yer only do it to get me going. I mean, as though there'd be such a word as solicitous.'

Molly pulled them to a halt and faced her friend. 'How come yer can say that one perfectly, when yer asked me what it means a few minutes ago, and have just said there's no such word?'

In the butcher's shop opposite, Tony said to Ellen, 'There's yer mates over the road, and it looks as though they're having an argument over something.'

'They won't really be having an argument, they never do. They'll go on like that for a few minutes, then they'll carry on walking arm in arm.' Ellen handed some change over to the customer she'd served. 'Thanks, Mrs Brocklehurst. We'll see you tomorrow, I suppose. And I'm going to have a dekko at me friends, see what they're up to.'

'I'm in no hurry,' the elderly lady said, 'so I may as well watch the antics of Molly and Nellie. It's one way of passing the time away, save going back to an empty house.'

And Tony's two customers, after they'd paid him, decided that Mrs Brocklehurst's idea was a good one. She might be a complete stranger to them, but there's nothing wrong with a stranger having a good idea. So they stood looking out of the window with her, while Tony and Ellen hoped they wouldn't have any more customers for a few minutes so they too could watch the couple on the opposite side of the road.

Meanwhile, oblivious of the fact they had an audience, the friends faced each other. 'What word was that, girl?'

'Don't start that, Nellie, yer know we're pushed for time.' Molly was wagging a finger. 'Now yer know damn well what word I mean, and we're not moving until yer say it again.'

From his vantage point opposite, Tony was giving a running commentary. 'Ooh, it looks as though Molly's got her dander up, wagging her finger as though she's telling Nellie off about something or other.'

Ellen chuckled. 'There's something up, 'cos Nellie's got her hands on her hips.'

On the pavement opposite, Nellie was doing contortions with her face, but howling with laughter inside. 'I am trying to think, girl, but how can I when ye're shouting and wagging yer finger? If yer keep quiet for a minute I'll soon remember the word was sisitus.' Her face beamed. 'See, girl, I knew I'd get it when yer shut up.'

'Listen to me, sunshine, I know ye're having me on for a joke. Yer know exactly how to say the word and what it means.'

'Cross my heart and hope to die, if this day I tell a lie.' Nellie was never sure which side she should cross, whether her heart was on the left or the right. So she settled for making a quick cross in the middle. 'I couldn't say it proper again if yer paid me, girl; I surprised meself when it came out. But I do know it means yer husband putting pillows or cushions behind yer back to make yer comfortable. And yer can bet yer sweet life that I'll be telling my feller that as soon as he comes in from work.'

'Nellie's crossed her heart, so that means she's made a promise,' Ellen said, leaning into the window as far as she could. 'But she'll have forgotten she's made it by the time she gets to wherever they're going, and Molly will pretend to get mad with her and they'll go through the whole rigmarole again. Just watch, they'll link arms in a minute, the best of friends until the next time they feel like livening things up a bit.'

True enough, Molly held her arm out and Nellie linked it. 'I'll walk with yer to the next street, sunshine, then we'll split up. I'll go to Irwins for a quarter of boiled ham, and you go to Hanley's for three cream cakes. It doesn't matter if they don't have any cream slices left, any cream cakes will do. But I'd like them all in one piece, Nellie, don't forget.'

Nellie pulled her arm free. 'Hang on a minute, girl, let's wave to Tony and Ellen.'

'Why? Have they seen us?' Molly did as her friend did, and waved. 'They must have just noticed us.'

Nellie looked up at her and rolled her eyes. 'Tony and Ellen, and all their customers, have been watching us from the time we stopped here. Honest, girl, yer might be able to say grimace, and solicitous, but yer can be as thick as two short planks sometimes.'

'I don't mind yer saying that, sunshine, because at some time in their lives everyone can be as thick as two short planks. I bet Tony and Ellen do daft things now and again. Even Mrs Brocklehurst isn't perfect.'

Nellie's eyes flew open. 'Mrs Brocklehurst! What made yer bring her name into it? We hardly know the woman!'

'We know her well enough to wave to her.' Molly kept her face straight. 'She waved back to us, as well. Didn't yer see her?'

'We haven't seen Mrs Brocklehurst all week!'

'Yes, we have, she's in the butcher's now! She was the one in front of the other ladies who were waving to us.'

'Molly Bennett, if we weren't on the main road, I'd clock yer one.'

'Now, don't be getting yer paddy up, sunshine. I'm going to part company from yer here. I'll see yer back home, and don't forget I want three cream cakes which are the same shape as they were when Mr Hanley put them on the tray. No squashed ones, none with finger marks on, and most definitely none that have had a certain person's tongue licking the cream from the sides.'

Molly watched her mate walk away, and smiled when she heard a muttering. 'She's a miserable cow. Wouldn't give yer daylight.'

'Did yer say something, Nellie?'

'No, girl, I was just telling meself how nice the day is. You know, nice and bright.'

Molly was in the kitchen humming to herself as she placed a doily on two of the plates on the wooden tray. 'Yer look proper posh today,' she told the plates. 'In fact I've only ever seen yer looking this posh on Christmas Day.' She started when she heard the window frame rattle. 'Oh, my God, I'll swing for her if she ever puts one of me windows out. I don't know why she can't use the knocker, like everybody else.' She was still cursing her friend when she opened the door. 'Haven't yer ever wondered what that brass thing on me door is for, Nellie McDonough, the one . . .' Molly's words petered out as she bent down to look at her mate's face, to make sure she wasn't imagining the blob of white cream on the tip of Nellie's nose, and traces of it in the corners of her mouth. And in her mind's eye she could see her nice posh plates, with their white-as-snow doilies, being covered by three squashed cakes with most of the cream missing. 'Why you miserable article, Nellie McDonough, after crossing yer heart and hoping to die.' She could see Nellie's mouth moving but she was too angry to listen. 'It's very seldom I have a visitor, and yer knew I wanted everything to be just right. Now yer've gone and spoilt it for me.' She reached down and carefully took the cake bag from her neighbour's hand. 'I'll talk to yer tomorrow, ye're not getting in here now.'

'But I haven't done nothing wrong, girl. What are yer getting all het up about?'

'What have yer done! Go home and have a look in the mirror, Nellie, and yer'll see the evidence on yer nose, and in the corners of yer mouth. Yer've let me down, so go home.'

'I ain't going nowhere, girl. I'll stand here and wait for yer to apologise.'

'Yer'll wait a long time.' Molly wasn't sure of her ground now, for her mate didn't look a bit guilty. 'I'm going to shut the door.'

'Please yerself, girl, but I'm staying here. And if the neighbours ask me why I'm standing like a lemon in front of a closed door, I'll tell them yer called me a liar and I'm not budging until yer say ye're sorry.'

'Please yerself,' Molly said, turning to go back into the living room. But she only half closed the front door because she was only half certain of whether she was doing the right thing. She walked straight through to the kitchen and placed the cake bag next to the plates. Her hands curled into fists on the draining boards. She was frightened to open the bag for two reasons. The first was she would see three squashed cakes, the second because she didn't like falling out with her mate. She was so lost in thought she didn't hear a sound, and she jumped when she heard a voice behind her.

'Go on, open the bleeding bag, girl, it's not going to bite yer.'

Molly was now so unsure of herself a voice in her head was telling her she should be certain of her facts before opening her mouth. 'If yer weren't so fond of playing tricks on people, sunshine, then they wouldn't always look sideways at yer.'

'Don't be such a wet bloody week,' Nellie said, pushing Molly aside. 'Yer might know I wouldn't let yer down today, not when yer've got Claire coming.' She tore the bag from top to bottom, revealing three cream slices that were as perfect as they were when the baker put them on the rack. 'That'll teach yer to cry before ye're hurt.'

'Oh, I'm sorry, sunshine, I should have trusted yer not to let me down. But what was I supposed to think, when yer've got a blob of cream on the end of yer nose, and in the corners of yer mouth?'

Nellie's face dropped. 'I haven't, have I, girl?'

'Go and look in the mirror if yer don't believe me.' Molly followed her through to the living room and stood behind her as the little woman stood on tiptoe to try to see her face.

'What have yer got the mirror so high up for, girl? I can only see the top of me forehead. Haven't yer got another one?'

'There's the broken one in the kitchen, but it's got marks all over it and it makes yer look as though yer've got chickenpox.'

Nellie pushed her aside and waddled to the kitchen. She picked up the piece of mirror that was leaning against the window, which Jack used when he was shaving. The silver was off it in places, and if you wanted to see your full face you had to keep moving until you found a clear space. 'Oh, my God.' Nellie ground the words out. 'I'll marmalise Edna Hanley for letting me walk through the streets like this.'

'What's Edna got to do with it?' Molly asked. 'And I don't know how yer couldn't see the blob on yer nose for yerself.'

Nellie could pull some faces, but as Molly was to tell Jack later, she'd never seen anything like the one she was pulling now. Nellie could see the blob of cream in the mirror, but she was blowed if she could see it without. She tried looking down her nose, putting her head back and looking up her nose, crossing her eyes, but all to no avail. 'I've crossed everything but me legs, girl, and I still can't see no cream. I probably could if I stood on me head, like I used to do when I was at school, but I don't think I'll be trying that.'

'Not in my house yer won't,' Molly said, 'I couldn't lift yer up if yer fell. Anyway, just out of curiosity, how have yer come to have cream on yer face?'

Nellie had the grace to blush. 'I couldn't resist, girl. Yer know I've got no willpower. And there was this cream bun in the glass cabinet, and it was looking at me as if to say, go on, girl, yer know yer fancy me.'

'And what did yer say back to it?'

'I didn't say nothing to it, girl, honest! But I did say to Edna, "Give us that cream bun, will yer, Edna, and I'll eat it while I'm waiting for yer to serve me." And d'yer know what, girl, that bun tasted better than any cake I've ever had. But it's been spoilt for me now, knowing everyone I passed must have had a good laugh behind me back. And I bet Edna Hanley's still having one.'

'Don't be saying that, sunshine, 'cos the chances are, Edna never noticed yer.'

'Of course she did! You did, didn't yer?'

'Ah, yeah, but I was on the front step looking down at yer, not serving in a shop with customers to worry about. I'd say Edna had more on her mind than you standing there filling yer face. And I'll bet a pound to a pinch of snuff that yer devoured that cake in two bites.'

Nellie grinned just thinking about it. 'It was three bites, girl, I'm not greedy.'

'Not much, ye're not,' Molly told her, shaking her head. 'Anyway, I apologise for thinking ill of yer, sunshine. I won't be so hasty in future.'

'And I owe you an apology, girl.' Nellie couldn't stop her tummy from shaking, and Molly wondered what she was in for. 'I only had the sixpence you gave me for the three cakes, as yer very well know, so I asked Edna to take the money for two of the cream slices and the cream bun, and you'd pay her for the other cream slice tomorrow.'

'You cheeky hound, Nellie McDonough! Have yer heard that saying when anyone does something they shouldn't, that they take the biscuit? Well, you take the ruddy cake!'

Nellie's chubby face creased. 'Ay, that's good that is, girl. It's not very often that ye're so quick off the mark.'

Molly looked at the round, happy face, and couldn't resist. She put her arms round Nellie's shoulders and gave her a hug. 'Ye're the bane of me life, sunshine, but I love the bones of yer.' Then she remembered and quickly added, 'And all your fat as well.'

Chapter Seven

'Hello, sunshine. Me and Nellie were just about giving up on yer.' Molly welcomed her visitor with a smile while thinking she had never seen a face so perfect. 'We expected yer to be here earlier.'

Claire lifted the canvas bag she was carrying by its string handles. 'I had to do a bit of shopping for tonight's meal. I just managed to get everything I need before the shops closed for their dinner hour.'

A loud voice called out, 'What are yer keeping her at the door for, girl? Why the hell don't yer just tell her to wipe her feet and come in.'

Molly rolled her eyes as she held the door wide. 'I think yer will recognise the dulcet tones of my mate, who, I might add, has been waiting for yer to come so she could have a cuppa. And, I might also add, she hasn't been waiting patiently, either. It's a wonder yer ears haven't been burning.'

Claire smiled when she saw Nellie sitting at the table in the elegant carver chair. 'My goodness, Nellie, yer look very important sitting in that chair. Like a managing director in charge of a meeting with his staff. I've got to say it really is an impressive chair.'

Nellie looked like the Cheshire cat who had just licked the cream off the top of the milk. And she quickly decided a posh chair required a posh voice to go with it. 'My friend Molly bought this chair hespecially for me, hand no one helse his hallowed to sit hin hit.'

'Shall I translate that for yer, sunshine?' Molly asked, as she took the bag off Claire and stood it at the side of the couch. 'It's Nellie's way of telling yer to keep yer eyes off it.' She chuckled. 'Her backside, and hers alone, is allowed the great privilege of sitting in it. I bought the ruddy thing because she talked me into it. Not that I didn't take a liking to it, for I did, but Nellie's encouragement was the deciding factor. But I never thought for one second that I wouldn't be allowed to sit in it in me own house. I'm allowed to polish it, and keep it looking good, but with regards to my sitting on it, well, that's out of bounds.'

Nellie nodded her head knowingly. 'Don't be trying to fool me, girl, 'cos I know ruddy well that as soon as I'm out of the door, your backside is on this chair.'

'I know what yer could do, Nellie,' Claire said jokingly, 'yer could put a reserved notice on it. That would stop anyone else using it.'

'Ooh, ay, girl, that's a bleeding good idea. Why didn't I think of that?'

Molly tutted. 'Because yer can't spell reserved, sunshine, that's why.'

Nellie's eyes narrowed. 'No, clever clogs, but I can spell crafty, and that's what you are. I'm not going to ask you to write the word down for me, 'cos I know yer'd cheat, so I'll ask Claire instead.'

'And when yer know how to spell it, sunshine, what are yer going to do then? Yer don't think I'd let yer paint the word on the chair, do yer?'

'I'm not going to tell you, girl, 'cos I don't trust yer. Yer'll find out soon enough, though, and it'll put yer off plonking yer backside on it for a little rest when ye're on the way to the kitchen. And talking about the kitchen, girl, which yer weren't, like, but I think it's my place to remind yer that the kettle must have burnt its backside out by now. So hadn't yer better see to it, and while ye're out there, will yer remember yer manners and make yer visitors a cup of tea and some refreshment?'

'I've only got one visitor, sunshine, and that's Claire. You're here so often ye're part of the ruddy fixtures. And it wouldn't do you any harm to get off that chair and give me a hand.'

'I'll give yer a hand, Molly, if yer don't think I'm being pushy,' Claire said. 'I'd hate to part Nellie from that chair. She looks really content there.'

Nellie grinned, thinking what a nice person Claire was. 'That's real kind of yer, Claire, very thoughtful. Not everyone is as thoughtful as that, are they, Molly? And I don't want to upset yer, girl, but don't let the cakes see that look on yer face, 'cos it'll turn the cream sour.'

Molly dipped a knee in a curtsy. 'Yes, Miss Nellie, three bags full, Miss Nellie. I've a good mind to drop your cake on the floor for spite.'

'Wouldn't worry me, girl, 'cos ye're always telling me how fussy yer are about cleaning yer house. So unless ye're telling lies, yer floor should be clean enough to eat off.'

Claire was grinning when she followed Molly into the kitchen. Keeping her voice low, she said, 'She is hilarious. Is she always pulling yer leg like that?'

Molly didn't bother keeping her voice low. 'If yer whispered in me ear, Claire, she'd still hear yer 'cos she's got the ears of a hawk. And she does often pull me leg, but this is one time she's in earnest. If I dropped her cream slice, she'd be out here like a shot to lick the cream off the floor.'

'I heard that, girl! Don't yer be pulling me to pieces and telling lies about me.' Nellie's voice came loud and clear. 'Don't you take no notice of her, Claire, I'm not a bit like she's making me out to be. I was brought up proper, I was, not dragged up like what some people are. To hear them talk yer'd think they were born in a castle, with servants to wait on them.'

Molly gave Claire a light dig and winked. 'So, are yer saying, sunshine, that if I did drop one of the cakes, the one that happens to be yours, then yer wouldn't eat it?'

There was silence for a while as Molly poured the boiling water into the pot. Then she put a finger to her lips and mouthed the words, 'Just wait for it.'

Nellie was in a quandary. Well, she wasn't really in a quandary, she knew exactly what she would do, but how could she tell them and make it sound acceptable? 'Well, girl, it's like this. D'yer remember during the war when we went short on food? I remember sitting at me table one day, me tummy rumbling, and I made a vow that day that I would never ever waste food again, 'cos it would be a sin. And I've kept to that, girl, I've never wasted a crumb since that day. So me conscience wouldn't let me throw a good cream slice in the bin, especially when the floor it was on was spotlessly clean. And on top of that, I wouldn't sleep tonight thinking of those poor souls in the world what are starving.'

'What part of the world is that, sunshine?'

They couldn't see her face, but she looked fierce as she stuck out her tongue towards the kitchen. 'How the hell do I know the names of those far-off places, yer silly sod. But I do know there's loads of them. And before yer decide to give me a lesson in geography, girl, will yer bring that flaming tea in before I die of thirst.'

Molly burst out laughing. 'I'll carry the tray through, Claire, if you fetch the plates. I'd hate me mate to die in my house; it wouldn't feel right, somehow. I couldn't live in it if she did, 'cos she'd haunt me.'

When they were sitting round the table, with Nellie presiding over events from her special chair, Molly began to pour the tea out. Then she noticed Nellie's eyes going to the plate on which the cakes stood. She was stretching her neck to see which cake had the most cream in it, and it would be true to say her mouth was actually watering.

'It's a pity yer can't remember the place where the people are starving, sunshine, 'cos if yer did yer could give them your cake.'

'Sod that for a joke,' Nellie said, leaning forward and taking a cake from the plate. 'Fancy having to go through torture for a tuppenny cake.' She gazed lovingly at the cream oozing out of the sides, then her tongue shot out and she licked down one side, practically purring as she did so. Then she looked at her mate. 'Ay, girl, d'yer think they'll have cream slices in heaven? If I knew for certain that they did, I'd be as good as gold. I'd never tell no more lies, nor would I speak ill of anyone. But I'd need a guarantee before I got serious over it. I wouldn't just take your word for it, girl, so I'll ask Claire and see what she thinks.'

'Well, Nellie, rather than getting religious, if I were you I'd hedge me bets. Because, even if they don't have cream cakes in heaven, it would be a far better place to go to than down below. For yer certainly wouldn't get cream cakes or ice cream down there, 'cos I believe the fires are red hot and the cream would go off in no time.'

Nellie nodded. 'Good thinking, girl, good thinking. But yer see, I don't know meself when I'm telling lies. They just come out of me mouth without asking me first. So I hope God knows this, and takes it into consideration.'

'Nellie, will yer stop talking so me and Claire can have a sandwich? Claire's been working all morning. She must be hungry.' Molly passed the plate of ham sandwiches over to

Claire. 'Put a couple on yer plate, sunshine, while the going's good. And drink yer tea before it gets cold. There's nothing worse than lukewarm tea.'

Claire bit into the sandwich and nodded. 'Mmm, the ham tastes nice, Molly. Where did yer get it from?'

'From Irwins. Yer can always rely on it being lean and tasty. I sometimes get it from the butcher's for convenience, but it's usually got a lot of fat on.'

Nellie was munching on a sandwich, her head going from Molly to Claire. In the end she got fed up being left out. 'Have yer forgotten I'm here, girl? I heard yer saying yer'd got the ham from Irwins, but yer never said I went to Hanley's for the cakes. Anyone would think yer'd done everything yerself.'

It was Claire who answered. 'Oh, I know you and Molly share everything, Nellie, because she's told me. And I can tell yer I feel jealous because I haven't got a close friend I can share a laugh with, or tell me troubles to.'

Nellie showed her soft side now. 'Oh, yer can always come to me and me mate, girl. We'll always help yer, won't we, Molly?'

'Yes, of course we will! And if yer don't live far away, there's no reason why yer can't call in and see us whenever yer feel like a natter, or yer want to get something off yer chest.' Molly tilted her head. 'If yer don't mind me asking, Claire, how long have yer been a widow?'

'It's five years now, although it seems like it was only yesterday that Bill died. I still miss him, and many's the night I cry meself to sleep. I try not to let the kids know, for it would serve no purpose to make them sad, as well. But never a day goes by I don't think of the lovely man who was my husband.'

'Yer said Ken takes after him for looks, didn't yer?' Molly

asked. 'If he does then yer husband was a fine-looking man, for Ken is a good-looking boy.'

Claire nodded. 'Yes, he's very like him in looks. And he takes after him in other ways, too. He walks like him, talks like him, and has a lot of his mannerisms. Yer know, the way he smiles and holds his head. While Ken is alive, my husband will never be dead.'

'Can I ask how old yer are, Claire?' Molly didn't want to seem nosy, but she was interested. 'I'd say not more than thirty-five.'

'I am thirty-five, so that was a good guess. But sometimes I feel like an old woman. That's 'cos I don't go out much because of the shortage of money, and I've no neighbours like you and Nellie. Although I have to say I feel better since I started work. I meet people every day, 'cos I work in the shop part of the laundry. People bring their sheets, pillowcases, men's shirts, things like that, and I'm getting to know a few of them for they're in every week.'

'Blimey, they must be loaded with money,' Nellie said, her face screwed up. 'It costs a bleeding fortune taking clothing or bedding to be laundered. I took a couple of sheets once, and they charged me a shilling. That was me first and last time. Highway robbery it was, and I told them so.'

Molly had her eyes on Claire's face. 'Would yer every marry again, sunshine, if a nice bloke came along?'

'I've never thought about it, Molly. I don't think I would, though, 'cos no one could ever take Bill's place.'

Nellie didn't agree with that. 'Ye're only young, girl, yer've got a long life ahead of yer. And without a man yer life will be lonely.'

'She's right, Claire,' Molly said. 'I'm not suggesting yer go out and find a man to marry just to stop yer from being lonely, sunshine, for life with a man yer didn't love would be no life at all. But ye're only young, Claire, and ye're blessed with the looks of a film star. Surely if yer met someone who fell for yer, and he was a good man, yer'd consider getting married again, wouldn't yer? After all, the children won't be with yer for ever.'

'Chance is a fine thing, Molly, and it may never come my way. And yer can't say yer'd get married, or yer wouldn't get married, until yer have the opportunity to choose.' Claire put a finger to her chin. 'I won't say I've never had the opportunity, for that would be telling lies, but not from anyone I could take to.' She grinned at Nellie. 'Here's a nice bit of gossip for yer to keep under yer hat. There's a man comes in the shop twice a week. He brings his shirts and collars to be laundered, and last week he brought in a suit to be dry cleaned. He has taken to holding a conversation with me, just for a few minutes, but I think he's got his eye on me. So look out for further instalments in the near future.'

Nellie leaned forward so quickly she banged her bosom on the table and grimaced. But it didn't stop her from saying, 'Go 'way, girl. What's he like?'

'He's presentable, quite good-looking, in fact, but we haven't got as far as exchanging names or anything like that. He could be married with half a dozen kids for all I know.'

'I doubt if he's married, sunshine, for if he was he wouldn't need to bring things to the laundry. His wife would be doing the washing.' Molly was now showing interest. 'How old would yer say he was, sunshine, just out of curiosity?'

'I'm not very good at guessing ages, Molly, but I'd say he was probably a little bit older than I am. And he always seems to be well dressed.'

This was like manna from heaven to Nellie who loved a bit of tasty news. 'He must have money, then, girl? Ooh, yer could have hopped in lucky.'

Molly tutted. 'Don't be marrying the girl off, sunshine. She doesn't even know the bloke's name. She's only telling us all this to satisfy your curiosity.'

Nellie managed a look of disgust as she eyed her mate. 'It's better than talking about the bleeding weather, isn't it? I don't care if Claire is making the whole thing up. At least it's got more life in it than saying the price of fish has gone up.'

Molly feigned surprise. 'It hasn't, has it, sunshine? Blimey, it was dear enough as it was. We bought some last week, but I don't remember the bloke behind the counter saying it had gone up. I'd have told him to keep his ruddy fish if he had. And I don't trust him, anyway. His eyes are too close together for my liking.'

Claire was enjoying this, and feeling really at home. None of her neighbours were like these two, worse luck. 'I wouldn't know, 'cos it's very seldom I buy fresh fish. Ken and Amy prefer it in batter from the chippy.'

'Bloody hell, what's the matter with you two! We've gone from a nice man what comes in the laundry to have his shirts washed to the price of bleeding fish! Can we get back to the feller what's got his eye on Claire, if yer don't mind. Otherwise I'll put a curse on both of yer, and the next time yer buy fish the feller will give yer a piece what's been in the window for a week and pongs to high heaven.'

'Ooh, my mate's getting a cob on, Claire. We'd better go from the fish shop to the laundry,' Molly said. 'What colour eyes has this man got? And I hope they're not close together, 'cos, like I said, I don't trust people with eyes close together. And what about his hair, what colour is that?'

'To tell yer the truth Molly, I've never taken much notice. I don't like looking at him too closely in case he thinks I'm forward. But I'd say from the colour of his skin that he'll have mousy hair and hazel eyes.'

'Listen to me, girl, never mind what me mate says.' Nellie lifted her bust when she leaned forward; she'd had one knock today and didn't fancy another. 'To hell with what colour his hair is, or if his eyes are close together. What yer want to be finding out is has he got a wallet full of pound notes? If yer find out he has, well, then, yer should start to work yer charms on him. You know, a nice smile to show yer've still got yer own teeth, and perhaps yer could come out from behind the counter to give him his cleaning, and he'll see what a smashing figure yer've got. Then next week yer could perhaps have a little chat with him. Yer'll have to encourage him, yer know, girl, 'cos faint heart never won rich man with fat wallet.'

'And the third week, sunshine, d'yer want Claire to flaunt herself at him? Perhaps lift her skirt and show a bit of ankle?'

'Yeah, let him see what he'd be getting for his money. I mean, no man will fork out for something that's wrapped up. They want to see what they're spending it on.'

Claire laughed. 'The poor man probably wouldn't recognise me if he fell over me in the street, and here's Nellie asking me to do a striptease for him.'

'I never said no such thing, girl, and don't yer be putting words in me mouth.'

'Nellie, you don't need anyone to put words into yer mouth, sunshine, yer've got enough of yer own. Yer might not be able to spell them, might not even know what they mean, but yer've got them all the same. In twenty-odd years, I've never known yer be lost for words.'

Nellie's chin jutted out to put emphasis on what she had to say. 'Yeah, and if it was me working in that laundry shop, instead of Claire, I'd be using every word I know. And with a few tricks thrown in.' Nellie's chins were wishing she would keep her head still, for they were getting dizzy being thrown sideways and then up and down. 'It's a pity yer haven't got a big bust like me, girl. That would make him take notice of yer. Yer see, men like something to get hold of.'

Molly took exception to that remark. 'Ay, sunshine, not all men like well-padded women. Your Steve didn't, did he? He's crazy about our Jill, and she's very slim. And Phil, Tommy and Archie, they've all married girls with slender figures.'

'Take no notice of me mate, girl,' Nellie said. 'She's always been green with envy over my voluptuous body, and the way men turn their heads when they see me. I don't blame her, mind; I'm not the type to take offence. I feel sorry for her, if the truth be known, 'cos it must make her feel jealous when men pass her by to look at me. But, as they say, girl, if yer ain't got it, then yer ain't got it! We can't all have everything, but I can't help feeling sorry for them what were behind the door when figures were being given out.'

The table began to jump up and down as Nellie took a fit of laughing. 'Ay, me saying if yer ain't got it, then yer ain't got it, well, it's reminded me of something the three of us ain't got. And that's a ruddy cup of tea. And don't try and palm me off by telling me to pour meself a cup out, girl, 'cos what's in the pot will be stiff by now.' She rubbed her hands together. 'Go on, don't sit there like a stuffed dummy, show Claire what a good hostess yer are. And while ye're out there, see if there's enough ham left for another sarnie.'

If looks could kill, Nellie would have been a dead duck. For she knew Molly had only bought a quarter of boiled ham, and she also knew it had been used up on the sandwiches. It couldn't have been stretched any further or they wouldn't have been able to taste it, and Nellie must have been aware of that.

'I don't want another sandwich, Molly,' Claire said. 'They were very nice, and I enjoyed them, but if I had another it would put me off me dinner. I'd love another cup of tea, though, and then I'll be on me way. I like to be home when Amy comes in from school.'

'I'll put the kettle on,' Molly said, jumping to her feet. 'I could do with another drink meself.' She was in the kitchen lighting the gas under the kettle when she heard Nellie talking.

'It's been nice having a visitor in the afternoon, girl, yer'll have to come again.'

'Yes, I've enjoyed it,' Claire told her. 'It's not very often I go anywhere on a social visit, what with working four mornings and having to be home in time for Amy. Friday is the only day I have any time to spare.'

'Come again next Friday, then, girl, it'll be a break for yer. Me and Molly would love to see yer and have a natter. Yer could tell us how ye're getting on with the man what comes in the shop.' Nellie raised her voice so Molly could hear her. 'We'd be made up to see Claire next Friday, wouldn't we, girl?'

Molly's eyes were rolling. How kind it was of her mate to be giving invitations out for afternoon tea in Molly's house! Nellie wasn't soft, and neither was she backward in coming forward. Well, it was time to give her a taste of her own medicine. 'I'm not too sure about next Friday.' She poked her head round the kitchen door. 'Phil wants us to pick his mam up one day next week, and bring her to his house by taxi, but he didn't say what day.' She moved further into the room. If the kettle came to the boil she'd hear the whistle. 'Did yer know Phil's mam is very ill, Claire? She can't make it here on her own, so me and Nellie pick her up at least once a week, and Phil fetches her on a Saturday. So I wouldn't like to make arrangements for Friday until I've had a word with him. What I could do is give Phil a message to pass on to your Ken. That would be the best plan. If Friday's okay, then yer could come at the same time, and Nellie can play hostess. She'd go mad if she thought yer were coming to my house every week, 'cos she likes nothing better than to entertain.' She smiled sweetly at her mate, who was sitting with her mouth open. 'Yer'd like that, wouldn't yer, sunshine? And what are yer sitting with yer mouth open for? Anyone would think yer were catching flies.'

Molly jumped when she heard the kettle whistling. 'Entertain our guest while I see to the tea, sunshine.' She couldn't get into the kitchen fast enough to double up with quiet laughter. The look Nellie had given her was enough to turn the milk sour. Never once in the twenty-odd years they'd been friends had Nellie had visitors. If anyone knocked at her door she didn't make them welcome, didn't even let them over the doorstep, but brought them straight along to Molly's.

'Have you gone to China for that bleeding tea, Molly Bennett? Me and Claire are sitting here with our tongues hanging out.'

'I'm coming, I'm coming, I'm coming! Keep yer ruddy hair on, sunshine, I've only got one pair of hands.' Molly carried two cups of steaming tea through and put them on the table. 'Who was yer servant before I came along, Nellie McDonough?'

Nellie gave her daggers, but she knew better than to argue in front of Claire. 'My feller was, girl, and when he was at work I had to do it meself. I wasn't half glad when I got pally with you and found yer were daft enough to put up with me.'

'Aye, and I have lived to rue the day, sunshine. I hardly knew yer when one day yer asked me if I was going to the shops would I get yer a small loaf and four ounces of margarine. Yer said yer'd pay me when I got back, and like a fool I believed yer.' Molly turned and winked at Claire. 'To this day I've never been paid that money back.'

Nellie waved her hand, nearly knocking her cup over. 'Go on, tell her how many cups of tea I've had off yer.'

'No, sunshine, I don't want to embarrass yer.'

'Yer won't embarrass me, girl, it's yerself what will be embarrassed. Anyway, I'll tell her meself. At the last count, my mate reckons I've had one thousand, four hundred and fifty-six cups of tea off her over the years.'

'Ye're well out, Nellie, it's over two thousand by now. And it must be well over a million grains of sugar.'

Claire was being well entertained; she thought they were hilarious. 'Well, two can play at that game, Nellie, so why don't yer tell her how many cups of tea she's had in your house? And yer could guess how many grains of sugar.'

Molly was delighted. 'Yes, that's a good idea, sunshine, to get yer own back on me. Go on, tell Claire how many cups of tea I've had in your house.'

Nellie ground her teeth together. Just wait until Claire had gone, she wouldn't half give Molly a piece of her mind. 'I don't know, I'm not very good at figures. Anyway, I wouldn't keep count like you do, I'm not that tight.'

'Just tell the truth, sunshine, that's all yer've got to do. But don't forget what Claire said about not having cream slices in hell.'

Nellie was beginning to see the funny side. She propped her elbows on the table and cupped her face in her chubby hands. 'Let's see if I can get this straight, girl, 'cos I don't want to make a liar of meself. I'm sure I gave yer a cup of tea one pancake Tuesday. The reason I remember, I asked yer to lend me some sugar to put on the pancakes. And I said to meself that I couldn't let yer go without offering yer a cuppa after yer being so good.'

Molly nodded. 'I remember that, too, sunshine, 'cos it was the first and last time I got a drink off yer. It was before the war, I remember that, too! But what the heck, what's a couple of thousand cups of tea among friends? We're still best mates, and that's the main thing.'

When it was time for Claire to leave, she didn't feel like moving. She felt as though she'd known Molly and Nellie for years. 'Yer won't forget to send a message through Ken, will yer? I've really enjoyed meself and I don't want to lose touch with yer.'

Molly followed her to the door. 'I'll send a message, don't fret. Next Friday will probably be fine, but I'll have to check with Phil.' She stood on the step until Claire turned, then they waved to each other and Molly went back inside and closed the front door behind her.

Nellie was waiting for her, nostrils flared and eyes narrowed. 'What d'yer think ye're doing, inviting her to my house? Yer had a bleeding cheek, Molly Bennett. Yer know I don't like having visitors.'

'I know yer don't, sunshine, that's why I was so surprised when I heard yer inviting Claire to come next Friday. I couldn't believe me ears.'

'I didn't invite her to mine, I invited her here! Don't yer be telling fibs, Molly Bennett.'

'Nellie, yer've either got a very short memory, or a very convenient one. Who was it said, "Come again next Friday, girl, it'll be a break for yer"?'

Nellie grunted and lowered her head. 'When I said come again, I meant come again here, and yer know ruddy well I meant here.'

'I have no objection to her coming here, sunshine, 'cos I like her and I think she's lonely.'

'Then what are yer making a song and dance about it for?'

'There's a condition attached to it. If it's going to be a regular visit, then we share the cost. Next week you pay for the ham and cakes, I'll pay the week after. Isn't that fair?'

'I suppose so, but ye're not half getting tight in yer old age.'

'Oh, I'm going to be really tight with yer right now, Nellie, and I don't care what names yer call me. I want the money off yer for the cake yer got off Edna Hanley. Yer said I'd pay her tomorrow, and I will, but it'll be with your money, not me own.'

Nellie looked up at the ceiling. 'All I can put it down to, Lord, is that this morning she got out of bed on the wrong side.'

Chapter Eight

'What day do yer want me and Nellie to pick yer mam up, Phil?' Molly asked, tickling Bobby's tummy as he lay on the couch kicking his legs. 'It doesn't make any difference what day, it's just that when Claire called this afternoon for a cuppa and a chat, my mate was very generous, very hail fellow well met, and asked her to call again next week 'cos it was nice having a visitor in the afternoon. The invitation wasn't for Claire to visit her house, mind, Nellie's not that soft. No, she invited her to mine.'

Doreen laughed, thinking that was hilarious. 'Trust Auntie Nellie. I bet she sat in that posh chair, waving her hand about like a lady of the manor. But why won't she ever have visitors at her house? I know it's not often that Uncle George's brother and his wife come to see them, but when they do she brings them straight to yours.'

'I know. It's all me own fault. And it's not as if I don't tell her what I think, 'cos I do, but she looks at me as though it's me that's in the wrong. She's got a skin as thick as a rhinoceros – insults just bounce off her. Anyway, in this instance I don't mind, because Claire is a lovely woman, and I feel a bit sorry for her being left a widow at her age.'

'Yer'll have to bring her over next time she comes,' Victoria said. 'Phil is always saying how well brought up young Ken is, and I'd like to meet his mother.'

Doreen nodded. 'Yeah, bring her over next time she comes, Mam.'

'Yer don't know what ye're letting yerself in for, sunshine, 'cos yer wouldn't only get Claire, yer'd have to take the whole package. That means me and Nellie come with her.'

'Well, we didn't expect her to come on her own, Mam, 'cos we knew Auntie Nellie wouldn't be left out. And we wouldn't want her to be, would we, Aunt Vicky?'

'Certainly not!' Victoria was quite definite. 'We wouldn't leave her out for the world.'

'Yer wouldn't get the chance, Victoria,' Molly told her. 'If yer didn't open the door to her she'd have the street out by banging like hell on yer window until yer let her in.'

'Oh, I know Auntie Nellie's tricks, Mam. I'd open the door before she had time to lift her hand.' Doreen smiled at a memory. 'Ay, Mam, do yer remember the night she sneaked up the back yard, and was peering through the curtains to see what you and me dad were up to?'

Molly chuckled. 'She got her eye wiped, though, 'cos Jack was reading the *Echo* and I was darning a sock. But we both jumped when she banged on the window because we thought some kid had kicked a ball over, and we expected the pane to break.' She could see the scene in her mind. 'I was blazing when I opened the kitchen door. I felt like strangling her. But she just pushed me aside and walked into the living room. And before Jack, or me, could say anything, she put her hands on her hips and said, "What a miserable pair of buggers you are. I thought yer'd be enjoying yerself with all the kids out and the house to yerselves. Here's me thinking I'd catch yer in a passionate embrace, and what do I find? One's reading a ruddy paper and the other's darning a flaming sock!" I won't give yer chapter and verse of what else she said, but I can say I blushed to the roots of me hair, and Jack didn't know where to put his face. He's not easily embarrassed, he enjoys a laugh as well as the next man, but Nellie doesn't leave anything to the imagination.'

'Did yer tell her off, Mam?'

Once again Molly chuckled. 'What good would it do to tell Nellie off? It's like water off a duck's back with her. No, she just plonked her backside down, as large as life, and said, "Well, seeing as yer've nothing better to do, girl, yer can make me a cup of tea." I opened me mouth to tell her what I thought of her, and when I looked into her face she gave me that innocent, butter wouldn't melt in me mouth look, and I just threw me hands in the air and went to put the kettle on. I'm a sucker where me mate's concerned, I know that. I can be calling her for everything under the sun, telling meself I'm going to play hell with her when I see her, but talking to meself is one thing; looking into her face and telling her she's a bloody nuisance, well that's another. She's always been me mate, and she always will be. Even though she can be outrageous at times, especially in the butcher's or the greengrocer's, I wouldn't change her for the world, and I'd be lost without her.'

'There's not many people that can say they've been the best of friends for over twenty years, and never fallen out, Mrs B.,' Phil said, while Victoria nodded her head in agreement. 'You are both very lucky. And we all gain from your friendship.'

'Yeah, I know that, lad. But before Jack thinks I've left home and gone off with the coalman, can we sort out what day yer want us to pick yer mam up?'

'How about Wednesday? I can tell her tomorrow when I go for her.' Phil looked down at his clasped hands. 'How d'yer think me mam looks, Mrs B.? I don't think she looks any worse than she did a month ago, but I wonder to meself whether it's wishful thinking on my part.'

'To tell yer the truth, Phil, me and Nellie were talking about that only yesterday. And we both said we didn't think there'd been any change in her for months. We didn't think she'd make the wedding, but she did. I know she didn't stay for the reception, but she made it to the church. I'm no doctor, but I think it's having you back in her life, and Bobby, that's doing it. She's got more to live for now, and who knows what will happen? But she certainly is no worse now than she was at Christmas, and that must mean something. What does the doctor have to say about her?'

'She doesn't see him now, hasn't done since Christmas. He said then that when she needs him she should get someone to ring his surgery and he'd come right away, night or day. And me mam won't send for him 'cos she's frightened of what he might say. I'd like to have a word with him meself, but I don't want to upset her.'

'What about Tom Bradley? Surely he should ask the doctor to come out to see if she's any worse, or if there's an improvement?'

'I don't talk to him, Mrs B., and I don't discuss him with me mam. She says he's good to her, and so are the children, and I'm not going to upset her by going into it too deeply.' Phil was talking about his stepfather and the children his mother had by him. He had been a terrible stepfather to Phil, and although the lad was happy to have his mother back in his life, he could never forget the way Tom Bradley had treated him. 'I don't like to keep asking her about her health, and whether she feels worse than she's letting on, but I wondered if you could find out for me, without it seeming too obvious.'

'I do ask her, Phil, but she always says she feels the same. She never complains of pains or anything, but I'm as puzzled as you are. It's nine months nearly since me and Nellie found out she was very ill, and she did say the doctor said it was only a matter of time. But although she's still very weak, and all skin and bones, she keeps going. I really don't know what to make of her, lad, I really don't. I will try and find out how she feels, and then perhaps coax her to agree to see the doctor again for a check-up. That would be the best thing all round. Anyway, me and Nellie will pick her up in a taxi at the usual time on Wednesday, and take her home again.'

'Thanks, Mrs B. I'll tell her tomorrow.'

'I'll see her meself tomorrow, son, I always come over for half an hour, as yer well know. And as I'm a creature of habit, I'll be here for a chinwag tomorrow afternoon.'

'Why not make it tomorrow night, Mam?' Doreen asked. 'Uncle Corker's taking all the men to the pub for a drink to meet his old shipmate, so we'll all be husbandless for a couple of hours. But I've warned Phil if he comes home drunk I won't let them in.'

'Considering he never goes over the door without you, sweetheart,' Victoria said, 'I don't think yer've anything to complain about.'

'Nellie and Ellen are coming to sit with me,' Molly told them. 'Corker is bringing a few bottles of milk stout down for us.'

'Ah, come over here, Mam, and we'll have a hen party.' Doreen raised her brows and looked at Victoria. 'Yer wouldn't mind, would yer, Aunt Vicky?'

'Oh, I'd be delighted! It would be nice to have some company, and we're bound to have a laugh if you and Nellie are coming, Molly.'

'Yeah, I'd like that!' Molly was pleased with the idea. 'I'll mention to Corker that we want an extra couple of bottles of milk stout. I don't see why the men should have all the fun while the women sit at home twiddling their thumbs.'

Victoria was nodding her head in rhythm with her rocking chair. 'I'll make some fairy cakes.'

'And I'll make sandwiches,' Doreen said. 'They'll be my contribution.'

Molly giggled. 'My contribution will be bringing the entertainment, in the shape of the one and only Helen Theresa McDonough.'

'Ay, d'yer think Uncle Corker would be upset if I didn't go to the pub?' Phil asked. 'It seems like it's going to be a good night here.'

'Corker wants all the men to meet his old shipmate, and he'd be upset if yer refused. Besides, tomorrow night is a ladies only night. Apart from little Bobby, no men are allowed.'

When Molly opened the door on Saturday night at half seven, it was to see Corker standing with his friend, Derek. 'Molly, me darlin', I'm just walking up to the pub with Derek to get the bottles of milk stout for the ladies. Will twelve bottles be enough?'

Molly smiled at his companion. 'Hello, Derek. It's nice to see yer again. If yer take my advice, sunshine, only have one drink to Corker's two, otherwise yer'll never find yer way home. See how he's leading me and me friends astray with twelve bottles of milk stout?'

'Molly, me darlin', are yer not forgetting this is an old mate, who not only sailed with me, but drank with me as well? He can hold his drink, can Derek, but if it so happens he has one over the eight, he's welcome to flake out on our couch.'

Derek grinned. 'I'm out of practice, Corker, so I'll not be able to keep up with yer. Three pints will be me limit.'

'I should think so!' Molly pulled a face at the very thought of anyone being able to down three pints. 'My husband doesn't drink often, so one pint makes him happy. And I don't mind him getting a little tipsy now and again, but I draw the line at him being blotto.'

'What about the drinks for the ladies, Molly?' Corker asked, eager to get things organised so he could start some se[illegible] drinking. He could drink any man under the table, but never appeared to be drunk. 'Would they like a bottle of sherry, as well as the stout?'

'No, thanks, Corker, we'll be quite happy with the stout. Phil's mother is down, so there will be six of us.'

'What about my princess, will she be down?'

Molly shook her head. 'The baby's only a few weeks old, Corker. Jill wouldn't leave her. Besides, she's feeding the baby herself, so it wouldn't do for her to drink. Another couple of months, perhaps, and she'll be able to get out more.'

'Right, well we'll love yer and leave yer now, me darlin', and we'll drop the bottles off over the road. And tell Jack we'll see him at the pub.' His weather-beaten face creased in a smile. 'I'm looking forward to seeing the gang all together. Tommy, Steve, Paul, Phil, Archie, George and Jack. Sure, it should be a good night.'

'Well I hope the gang don't get so drunk they come down the street singing and waking the neighbours. Yer'll have us getting a name like a mad dog.'

Corker guffawed. 'If there's any complaints, me darlin', pass them over to me and I'll deal with them.'

'Enjoy yerself, Corker, and you Derek, and I'll see Jack hurries himself up.' Molly smiled as she closed the door. Corker was in his element when surrounded by friends, and he would really enjoy tonight. And he would be the one who forked out the most money, for there was more going into his house than any of the others. Apart from his own earnings, Ellen had a weekly wage, and Phoebe, Dorothy and Gordon all brought home a weekly pay packet.

'Yer'd better put a move on, Jack,' Molly said when she returned to the living room and found her husband standing in front of the mirror over the mantelpiece combing his hair. 'If ve got yer tie handy, I'll tie it for yer. I make a neater knot than you, 'cos I'm more fussy.'

Jack pointed to where a tie was draped over the back of a dining chair. 'I couldn't find the maroon one yer bought me for Christmas, but that one will do.'

'Over my dead body will yer wear that tie, Jack Bennett. It's got a couple of stains on it. Honest, have yer no pride in yerself?'

'Molly, it's dark in the pub. No one will notice.'

'I don't care whether it's dark in the pub or not, ye're not wearing that tie! They'll wonder what sort of woman ye're married to, who lets yer go out looking like a tramp. So don't bother putting it on. I'll slip upstairs and find the maroon one. I know yer won't have looked properly, and I'll probably put me hand right on it.'

Jack's reflection in the mirror pulled a face back at him. 'Women! What would yer do with them?' Then he grinned. 'Ah, but what would we do without them, that's the question.'

'Are you talking to yerself, Jack Bennett?' Molly came back in waving a deep maroon tie. 'It's a bad sign when yer start talking to yerself.'

'Yer found the tie, then, love?'

'It's a wonder it didn't bite yer hand off, soft lad. Yer didn't look very hard. All I did was open the wardrobe door, and there it was, lying on the bottom where yer'd thrown it.' She turned her husband round to face her. 'Move yer hands out of the way while I put this tie on. When yer walk out of this door, Jack Bennett, yer'll hold yer own with any of the other men.'

Jack looked into her eyes and asked, 'D'yer think any one of them will notice what I've got on? Men aren't like women, yer know, love. We don't scrutinise each other from the top of our heads to our shoes.'

'No, I know that, sunshine, yer don't need to tell me.' Molly looked pleased with the neat knot she'd tied. 'Yer'll have a pint put in yer hand as soon as yer walk in the pub, and that will go down very quickly 'cos yer've all got a thirst. So the second round arrives, and after that no one will notice whether yer tie is maroon or sky blue pink with a finny haddy border. But at least I'll know I sent yer out looking respectable.' She gave him a peck on the cheek. 'And yer'll be the most handsome man there.'

Jack grabbed her round the waist. 'Seeing as our daughter is over at her mate's, and you and me are alone with five minutes to spare, why don't we put them to good use?' He nuzzled her ear. 'Molly Bennett, after all these years, yer can still send me pulses racing.'

She slapped his hand. 'Behave yerself. I'm expecting Nellie here any minute, and I can just imagine what she'd make of that.' Molly grinned. 'I can see her now, telling everyone from here to the Pier Head, and that includes the butcher, the baker and the candlestick maker, that when she called for me she caught you with yer pulses racing, and so filled with passion were yer that yer couldn't help yerself, and yer threw me on to the couch and had yer wicked way with me. And knowing Nellie, she'd milk it for all it was worth. Like, she was so shocked she couldn't move, her feet were stuck to the floor. And although she didn't want to, being a sober religious woman what goes to church every Sunday, she was forced to stay and witness our mad, uncontrollable passion, until it reached its peak. And when yer desire was satisfied, yer just got up, fixed yer trousers, and went off to the pub without a word of apology to her. Oh, she'd have a ball, sunshine, and I'd never hear the end of it.'

Molly spun round when she heard a tap on the living-room door. And standing there, with her face beaming and a look of devilment in her eyes, was Nellie. 'If yer don't want people to hear what ye're saying, girl, then yer should make sure yer shut the front door properly.'

'How long have yer been standing there?' Molly asked, her face crimson. 'And why didn't yer knock on the front door instead of just walking in?'

'If I'd done that, girl, I'd have missed the best part, wouldn't I? I mean, I was wondering what I could do to entertain the ladies tonight, something different, like, and I walk in here and it's handed to me on a plate.'

Jack was longing to laugh, for Nellie's face was a picture, but he knew he might land himself in trouble with Molly if he did, so he made his escape. 'I'll have to leave you two ladies, 'cos I'm late as it is.'

Nellie winked at him as he passed. 'If yer ears are burning, lad, yer'll know it's me what's talking about yer.'

Molly shook her fist. 'Nellie McDonough, Jack never opened his mouth.'

'No, I know that, girl, but he didn't have to, 'cos you said enough for both of yer. And when I add my little bit, well, it should pass half an hour away and give the ladies a good laugh.'

Molly knew from experience that the ladies would get a laugh, but she didn't fancy being the butt of Nellie's sense of humour. So she thought it was time to reverse the situation. 'What are yer looking so smug about, sunshine? I was only repeating to Jack what you had told me. I don't mind who yer tell; it's got nothing to do with me.'

Nellie came further into the room and stood in front of Molly. 'Don't be coming that with me, Molly Bennett. I know ye're mad inside because I caught yer out, but it's yer own fault for leaving yer front door open.'

'I'm not worried about that, sunshine, although yer did give me a fright. I mean, not many people would walk in someone's house without knocking. But with regards to yer wanting to tell the ladies what yer heard, then you do that and we'll all have a good laugh. I remember what yer told me word for word, so if yer get stuck I can help yer out.'

'Are you going soft in the head, girl? It was you what told Jack about pulses racing, and how he threw yer on the couch and had his way with yer. So just tell me where I come into this? And don't be trying to change things round 'cos yer can't fool me.'

'Not for one second would I try and fool yer, sunshine, but I have to admit I did change one thing round. I said he threw me on the couch, but when you told me the tale, yer said on the bed, not the couch. Apart from that one word, though, the rest was just as yer told me. But when yer tell our mates tonight, I don't care whether yer say bed or couch. Makes not a scrap of difference.'

'Have yer lost yer marbles, girl?' Nellie's face was being pulled in every way imaginable. 'I've never told you a tale like what I've just heard you telling Jack, so don't be making me out to be doolally.'

'Oh dear, oh dear, oh dear! Yer've got a short memory when it suits yer, sunshine. I can see yer as plain as day, sitting facing me, with yer elbows on the table and holding yer chin in yer hands. And yer were relishing every word as yer told me what you and George had been up to the night before. And I also remember I had to shut yer up because yer were going too far. I told yer I didn't want to know what went on in yer bedroom.'

There was no sign of a smile on Molly's face, and she sounded so sincere Nellie was beginning to believe her. After all, Molly never mentioned what went on in her bedroom, and she was always saying she didn't want to know about the shenanigans that went on in one a few doors away. 'Yer've got me flummoxed, girl, and no mistake. I mean, I know I do go on about me and George being passionate, but I only do it to see yer get worked up. But I can't say I remember telling it like you told Jack, and I don't remember any night when my feller threw me on the bed 'cos he'd got himself all worked up. The other way round, yeah, 'cos if I didn't throw my feller on the bed, I'd never get me share of nuptials.'

Molly scratched her head, looking thoughtful. 'I don't understand that, sunshine. What d'yer mean by saying yer'd never get yer nuptials?'

'Well, yer know what I mean, girl. It's when a man and woman are getting married and they're standing in front of the altar, and the priest tells them they must love, honour and obey. And he also says something about honouring with yer body, which means whether yer husband feels like it or not, he's bound to keep his wife happy in that department of their marriage. I think it's something like conjukerler rights. Me and George often have words about it, 'cos he swears the priest never said no such thing. And, to add insult to injury, he says that even if the priest did say it, he can't do anything about it 'cos he's tired out. I should remember he's been working all day while I spend the day sitting on me backside.'

Molly turned her head slightly so her friend wouldn't see her biting her lip to keep the laughter at bay. Wait until she told Jack that Nellie insisted upon getting her conjukerler rights. He'd split his sides. How Nellie came up with these words she'd never know, but it wouldn't be the same if her friend spoke perfect English. 'What does George say when yer tell him yer don't just sit on yer backside all day?'

'Oh, he doesn't say nothing, girl, 'cos he knows I wouldn't think twice about clocking him one if he said the wrong thing.'

'Quite right too, sunshine. But we should be over at our Doreen's by now. She'll wonder what's keeping us. I'll get me coat and we'll be on our way.' Molly slipped her arms into the coat sleeves, and shrugged her shoulders until the coat was hanging properly. Then she faced Nellie. 'I've been thinking, sunshine. It might not be a good idea repeating what we've been talking about. Our Doreen's too young for that sort of talk, and I don't think Victoria would appreciate it. So skip that, and I'm sure yer'll think of plenty of ways to amuse us. Ye're very good at that. I've never known yer to be short of ideas.'

That was praise indeed, and Nellie was flattered. She linked her friend's arm as they walked across the cobbles to Doreen's. 'Ye're right, girl. I'll put me thinking cap on. It's a long time since I took off Tessie O'Shea, so I'll start with her.'

Molly squeezed her arm. 'Yeah, that's a good idea. Anybody but Betty Boop, sunshine, 'cos I don't want yer using all Phil's black boot polish to make yer kiss curls.'

Chapter Nine

Corker's loud guffaws rang out in the smoke-filled bar room of the pub on the corner of the street. The manager, Alf, had pulled three of the small round tables together to cater for the nine men, who were in very high spirits. The big man was always a welcome sight at the pub, for on the nights he was there the takings were sky high as he was very generous. Corker liked his pints of bitter and could hold his drink. No one had ever seen him drunk: merry, perhaps, but never drunk. In fact on a Saturday night, when all the local men had a few bob in their pockets, there would always be the odd one who would cause trouble. But even though they might be the worse for wear and full of fighting spirit, with their fists punching the air and thinking they could conquer the world, they could always be talked round by Corker. And they would stagger home, lurching from side to side, believing they had conquered the world.

Derek Mattocks, Corker's old shipmate, had soon made himself at home with the men from the street, and he and Corker had a captive audience as they related some of their experiences in the many countries of the world they had visited, and some of the sights they had seen. 'Mind you, yer can't get a pint of beer anywhere in the world as good as this here. I don't know what they put in it, but it's deadly.' He punched his old mate on the shoulder. 'Ay, Corker, d'yer remember that night in a port in India, when you and me went into this dive for a drink? And the next morning we both woke up with big heads and didn't even remember how we got back to the ship?'

Corker, his weather-beaten face wreathed in a smile, wiped the froth from his huge moustache before saying, 'Ah, well, yer see, I'm like a homing pigeon. I always find me way back to where I came from.'

Derek laughed. 'That's why I was glad I was yer mate. I can only drink half the amount you can, and there's been many a time I'd have missed the ship if it hadn't been for you.'

'What would have happened if yer had missed the ship?' Jack asked. 'Or did they send out a search party looking for yer?'

'Did they heck! There was a war going on – they couldn't afford to miss a tide. If yer didn't make it back in time, they sailed without yer.'

Corker put his glass down and wiped a hand across his mouth. 'There's lots of low-life dives in some ports. Places of ill-repute, which our captain would warn us about. Where the women were two a penny, and would drape themselves round yer as soon as yer walked in the door. That's how they made their living. The more they could get yer to drink, the more wages they got. And if any of the men were daft enough to accompany them to a seedy room upstairs, then they made a bit more money. But while yer could understand men being attracted to these places after being away from home for weeks on end, many of them found themselves picking up more than they bargained for.'

Jack and George were used to Corker's tales of life at sea, but the young men – Steve, Phil, Tommy, Archie and Paul – were hanging on to every word. Archie thought Derek was in his mid-thirties, and took it for granted he would be married. 'How many children have yer got, Derek?'

Corker's head fell back and his guffaws brought a smile to every face in the room. 'That is something he hasn't got an answer to, Archie, me boy.'

The room was filled with smoke but it didn't hide the blush that covered Derek's face. 'That's one of Corker's jokes. I admit I strayed a few times while I was at sea, but because I'm not married I wasn't hurting anyone.'

'Not married?' George sounded surprised. 'I would have thought a fine-looking feller like yerself would have had a wife in every port.'

'No, I'm footloose and fancy free. I wouldn't take up with anyone in the foreign countries we visited because we weren't there long enough to get to know anyone well. And the same when we were home on leave: no time to make friends. My dad died when I was fifteen, yer see, and as I'm the only child, I didn't want to leave me mam on her own.'

'He tells me he's packing up the sea and getting a shore job,' Corker said. 'He'll find it takes a while to settle to being a landlubber, 'cos I still miss the sea. Once it's in yer blood, it's hard to get it out.'

'You wouldn't want to go back to sea, would yer, Uncle Corker?' Steve asked. 'I thought you were settled in yer job.'

'Yeah, so did I,' Phil said. 'Yer've never mentioned it before.'

Tommy chuckled. 'Is it the drink talking, Uncle Corker? And have yer told Auntie Ellen how yer feel?'

'Oh, she knows right enough, lad. I have told her. And, God bless her, she said if I really wanted to stretch me sea legs, she wouldn't try and stop me.'

'Are yer serious, Corker?' Jack asked. 'I thought yer'd settled down now, and liked being home with Ellen and the children.'

'Ay, Uncle Corker, have yer forgotten I'm courting your Phoebe?' Paul's dimples showed as he grinned. 'And we should have a say in whether yer can go back to being a seaman.'

Corker raised his bushy eyebrows. 'I think I could sail to a few countries in the world before you and me daughter tie the knot. If I had to be on it, son, I'd say it would be next year before you and Phoebe wed.'

'We're both happy to leave it for another year,' Paul said. 'We haven't got enough money saved. But we do put so much a week away, Phoebe sees to that. When it comes to money, she's got a better head on her than me.'

George stubbed his cigarette out in the ashtray before looking across at his son. 'It strikes me, son, that Phoebe's got a lot more sense than you. If the saving up was left to you, there'd never be a wedding.'

'There better had be,' Steve said, his dimples deeper than his brother's. 'You're the only one left, and we expect a big do with all the trimmings.'

Tommy was sitting next to Archie, and he gave him a dig in the ribs. 'Has the word blackmail entered yer head at all?' He spoke quietly. 'If we play our cards right we'll be set for free beer every Saturday.'

It didn't take long for the light to dawn, and Archie's deep brown eyes lit up. 'Nice thinking, mate, nice thinking. Do you want to start the ball rolling, or shall I?'

'You do it. Ye're a better boxer than me.'

Corker was busy chatting to Jack and George, stopping only to down half a pint of bitter every so often. 'Aye, those were the days all right. Good skipper and fine mates. There was never any trouble on board, was there, Derek?'

'Not when you were around, no! They knew better than to start anything, 'cos they knew they'd get their heads banged together. They'd rather risk the German U-boats than you. I've seen yer lifting two blokes, one in each hand, about four foot off the ground as though they were rag dolls. That's why I was always yer best mate. I was terrified not to be.'

Archie pressed his hands on his knees and leaned forward. 'Corker, yer know these low dives yer were talking about, the dens of iniquity, well, did Ellen know about them? Yer see, me and Tommy were wondering what it would be worth to yer for me and him to keep our mouths shut?'

Corker chuckled. 'There's not much mileage in that, lad, 'cos I wasn't married to Ellen at that time.' His gaze covered all their faces. 'Most of yer here know the tale about me and Ellen, but I'll tell it anyway to put everyone in the picture.' He picked up his glass and took a long drink before he started. 'When I was a young lad, like most of yer here now, I went courting Ellen. When the ship was in port I would see her every night, and we'd go dancing or to the flicks. I was crazy about her, and had every intention of asking her to marry me. But like a soft lad, I didn't tell her me intentions were honourable because I believed she would take it for granted. Anyway, when the ship docked after a three-month trip, it was to find she'd married Nobby Clarke. He was a tall, dark, handsome bloke, who could charm the birds off a tree. But I knew a different Nobby to the face he showed to the girls, and I knew he was a rotter. Still, there wasn't anything I could do about it. But the bottom had dropped out of my world, for I really loved her, and I've never looked at another girl since.' Corker picked up his glass and drained it. 'Another round, everyone?'

Archie shook his head. 'Yer can't leave it like that, Corker, not without telling us how you came to marry her in the end.'

Steve, Tommy and Paul all had reason to remember Nobby Clarke, for each of them had suffered from his violent temper. If they were playing in the street, not hurting anyone, he never passed without clipping one of the kids round the ear, or booting them up the backside. He had his hands round Tommy's throat one night, because a ball had broken one of the Clarkes' windows, and Tommy was the one who got the blame because he didn't run away. He hadn't done it; it was his mate, Ginger, who had picked up the ball and run hell for leather up the street, leaving his friend to face the music. Molly had tried to prise Nobby's hands from Tommy's throat, but the more she tried the tighter his grip became. In the end, Nellie came out to see what the commotion was, and when she saw what was happening she managed to free Tommy and sent Nobby sprawling on the pavement. Oh, yes, they all remembered Nobby Clarke, and the way he treated his wife and four children.

However, Corker had no intention of speaking ill of the dead. 'He died just after the war, and after waiting a suitable interval Ellen agreed to marry me. I wouldn't wish a man to die so I could marry his widow, but I am a very happy man now. A wife I adore, and four kids that I'd lay me life down for.'

While the other men were thinking it was just like Corker not to say anything nasty about Nobby Clarke, or anything that would bring back bad memories to Ellen if it was repeated in her presence, Archie was really moved by the tale. 'That was just like sitting in the picture house watching a romantic film, Corker. It's a one in a million love story, that is, and I'm really happy it ended the way it did.'

'So am I, son, so am I! And I hope you and Lily find the same happiness in yer married life. Yer've got some very good examples here, except for Derek, but he'll soon find himself a good woman when he gets a shore job. The rest of the men, young and not so young, have all been lucky in love.' He chortled. 'D'yer know, Archie, yer've had me yapping away and losing valuable drinking time. I'll not get me quota in, and that will never do.' He raised his arm as a sign to the landlord, who was waiting patiently for a signal. He couldn't afford to miss a nine-pint round, that would never do. 'Same again, Alf, and one for yerself.'

'Coming up, Corker.' With his hand on the pump, Alf felt well satisfied. The takings would be good tonight, but heaven help them if Corker ever became teetotal. The pub would have to shut down.

'Yer'll have to move the table back,' Nellie said, feeling very important as the entertainer. 'How d'yer expect a professional artist like meself to perform if I can't move around? Yer wouldn't find Tessie O'Shea working in a small place like this. She'd turn her nose up at it.'

'Ooh, is that who ye're going to be tonight?' Doreen asked, picking up a dining chair to take out to the kitchen. 'What song are yer going to sing?'

Nellie shook her head, her chins and her bosom. 'Blimey, yer'll be asking for programmes next. Ye're getting me talent for nothing, so be satisfied. Get those ruddy chairs out and we can push the table back.'

Molly patted the couch. 'Come and sit next to me, Frances, before me mate says ye're putting her off her stroke.' When Phil's mother sat down next to her, Molly grinned. 'Yer know what these professionals are like. Very temperamental.'

'Ay, watch it, girl. Don't be calling me for everything.'

'I haven't called yer for everything,' Molly answered. 'I never mentioned yer name!'

'I heard yer, girl. I haven't got cloth ears. Yer told Frances I had a temper and was soft in the head.'

Frances shook her head. 'Molly didn't say that, Nellie.'

'I heard her with me own ears, Frances, so don't be sticking up for her.'

Victoria was rocking in her chair, loving every minute. It was nice to have visitors and have a laugh with them. Yer couldn't beat good friends, especially when they were Molly and Nellie. So the old lady sat back and rocked, knowing it would all end up in laughter, but wondering what it would go through to reach that stage.

'Listen, sunshine, don't be making up things,' Molly said. 'Frances told yer I never mentioned yer name, and I didn't. If yer heard me, then ye're hearing things and yer should go and see yer doctor.'

Oh, that did it! Nellie's hands went on her hips, her jaw jutted out and her eyes narrowed. 'Ye're a bleeding fibber, Molly Bennett, 'cos I definitely heard yer tell Frances I was bad-tempered and I was daft in the head.' Nellie put a finger to her temple. 'The word yer used was mental, and I know ruddy well what people mean when they say a person is mental.'

Ellen was sitting on the couch now next to Frances, after being turfed off her dining chair. And both women were waiting to see how this would end up. Molly knew how it would turn out, but not until she'd pulled her mate's leg. 'What was the exact word yer heard, sunshine?'

'Words, girl, not word. Temper and mental are two words, and even a clever clogs like yerself can't say they're not.'

'Try putting the two words together, sunshine, and see what yer get. If yer say it quickly, yer might just see the light.'

'Don't start being sarky as well, girl, 'cos I'm confused as it is. And why should I say those words quickly, just to please you? It's not that I can't say them, so don't be thinking I'm making excuses, but I'd like to know why I should.'

'Well, if yer do, it'll become clear to yer, and yer won't have a cob on with me. Go on, sunshine, it's nearly time for Tessie O'Shea to come on stage.'

Nellie held her hands out, palms upward, and appealed to Frances, who looked the most sympathetic. 'If she wasn't me best mate, Frances, I'd have clocked her one by now. So doesn't that prove I haven't got no bad temper?'

'Oh, I'm saying nothing, Nellie.' Phil's mother looked very frail, as though a puff of wind would blow her away. She'd been told six months ago that there was nothing more the doctors could do for her, and it was only a matter of time. But although it was an effort, for she had little energy or strength, she looked forward to the twice-weekly visits to her son's house. They were the highlights of her week. 'I'm not coming between friends.'

Molly patted her hand. 'Yer don't have to, Frances, 'cos even if Nellie strangled me to death, I'd still be her best mate. Wouldn't I, sunshine?'

'Oh, all right,' Nellie said, rolling her eyes. 'Tempermental.'

There was a burst of applause, and Molly said, 'There yer are, Nellie, that's what I told Frances yer were. Yer missed a letter out in the middle, but yer know what temperamental means, don't yer? So are yer satisfied now that I didn't tell Frances yer had a temper and were mental?'

'Yer must think I was born yesterday, Molly Bennett, to think I'd fall for that load of bleeding rubbish. There's no such word as tempermental, and yer ruddy well know there isn't.'

'Yes there is, Auntie Nellie, honest!' Doreen said. 'And it's got nothing to do with having a temper and being mental.'

'What does it mean, then, girl? Go on, tell me, seeing as ye're so bleeding clever.'

But Molly didn't want that. She wanted to be the one to make Nellie swell with pride. 'Let me tell her, Doreen, 'cos she is me best mate and I don't want her falling out with me.' She gave Nellie a sweet smile. 'D'yer know all the well-known artists, like Tessie O'Shea, Gracie Fields, George Formby, and all the big film stars in Hollywood, such as Greta Garbo and Katharine Hepburn? Well, they are said to be temperamental 'cos they think because they are big stars they can do and say what they like. It's because of their profession, their talent, that they are different to other folk. And because they are famous, they get away with being temperamental.'

Nellie was torn between wanting to believe her mate, and not wanting to appear foolish. But it was Victoria's nodding head that did the trick. With a smile on her face, she hoisted her bosom and stretched to her full height. 'I had yer going there, didn't I, girl? Yer see, I knew all along what tempmental meant, but I thought I'd string yer along. Us gifted artists are different to you what have no talent. I've been tempmental since I was a young girl: that's how I knew I would be a great singer.'

'And yer've been keeping that secret to yerself for over twenty years, have yer, sunshine? I thought we were never going to have any secrets from each other, but seeing as you are different to the rest of us, you being a great singer, I'll forgive yer.' Molly felt like leaving her seat to plant a kiss on her mate's chubby cheek, but decided to ask one more question. 'Are yer going to tell George about this talent of yours? This gift that makes yer . . . er . . . what's the word now? It's gone right out of me mind.'

'Tempmental, girl,' Nellie said, looking proud of herself. 'Ye're getting forgetful in yer old age.'

'And will George know what tempmental means, d'yer think?'

'Of course he will. He's not daft, my feller. Any fool knows what tempmental means. And now, if yer've got it all off yer chest, girl, I'll go in the kitchen and run through a short rehearsal, make sure me singing voice is in order. So if yer hear me going up and down the scales, don't think yer've got a skylark in the yard, it'll only be me.' As Nellie turned to go to the kitchen, she stopped by Victoria's chair and, in a loud whisper, said, 'There's one born every minute, girl.'

'Oh, one what, Nellie?'

'A temperamental fool, girl, that's what. And I should know, I've been mates with one for God knows how long.' Nellie kept her voice above a whisper. 'Don't let her see yer looking or she'll know we're talking about her. But the blonde one sitting on the couch, to look at her yer'd think butter wouldn't melt in her mouth, but take it from me, Victoria, yer can't go by looks. If you were to knock on her door at twenty-nine past ten in the morning, she'd leave yer standing on the pavement until the big finger on the clock was dead on ten thirty. She wouldn't care if yer were standing in two feet of snow, she still wouldn't let yer in. So if that's not being temperamental, then I'll eat me bleeding hat.'

Nellie swayed her way to the kitchen with laughter ringing in her ears. And the loudest laugh came from Molly, who was telling herself she'd never get the better of her mate. 'Nice one, sunshine,' she called. 'I got me eye wiped there, and I deserved it.'

Nellie leaned back against the kitchen sink, her arms folded beneath her mountainous bosom. She was racking her brains to remember which song Two Ton Tessie was most famous for. There were three she could think of, but which one was the best? Still, it wasn't a matter of life or death, 'cos she could sing all three if it came to that. But she'd need a bottle of milk stout after the first, just to oil her throat. If Molly hadn't started that rigmarole, they could have had at least two bottles each by now, and they'd all be in a happy frame of mind. Still, she'd soon have them singing their heads off.

As she pushed herself away from the sink, the washing on the clothes rack hanging from the ceiling caught her eye. It was mostly baby clothes, nappies and bibs, but Nellie noticed a towel and a tablecloth hanging on the back rail. And a grain of an idea worked its way into her head and started to take root. With her imagination working overtime, Nellie's eyes glinted with mischief. It was only an idea, but she'd bear it in mind for consideration after she'd seen how her Tessie O'Shea act went down. She coughed to clear her throat, then holding up the front of her dress she made her entrance, belting out at the top of her voice a well-known song which was a favourite in many a local pub on a Saturday night just before closing time.

> 'Oh, my old man said follow the van, and don't dilly-dally on the way,
> Off went the van with me old man in it, I followed on with me old cock linnet,
> I dillied and dallied, dallied and dillied, lost me way and don't know where to roam
> And yer can't trust a Special like the old time copper,
> When yer can't find your way home.'

The skirt of Nellie's dress was lifted as she copied the actions of the singer, showing her elastic garters, an expanse of bare leg and a glimpse of blue bloomers. And as her audience clapped and sang along, she put her heart into the song. She was so good, if you closed your eyes you could picture Two Ton Tessie entertaining the audience at the Liverpool Empire.

'That was very good, sunshine,' Molly said, when her mate finished and was bent over trying to get her breath back. 'Well worth the sixpence we paid for these seats in the front row of the stalls. But I do have one little, teeny-weeny complaint.'

Nellie straightened up and glared at her. 'And what's that, then, girl?'

'Well, yer looked like Tessie O'Shea, and yer sang like her, but to my knowledge that is not one of her songs. At least I've never heard her sing it.'

Nellie shook her head, and her chins agreed that she had a right to be upset. 'Trust you to find something wrong, yer long string of misery. Honest to God, if yer were walking down the street and saw a sixpence lying on the ground, yer'd moan because yer had to bend to pick it up. And then yer'd moan again because it wasn't a shilling.'

'Oh, I wasn't being critical of yer, sunshine. I only thought yer should know, so yer could leave it out of yer repertoire.'

Victoria was quick to put a hand across her mouth to keep the laughter at bay. For Nellie's face was going through the most unbelievable contortions as she tried to decide whether to clock her mate, or act daft and pretend she knew what that long word meant. In the end she opted for the safest way out. 'I won't sing it no more then, girl, if you say it isn't one of Tessie's songs. Just to be on the safe side, like.'

'There's nothing to stop yer singing it, sunshine, 'cos it's a free country. Just don't say that it's one of Tessie's.'

'I won't do any more of her, not tonight, anyway. I'll do something new for a change.' To get to the kitchen, Nellie had to pass Doreen, and she winked at her. 'Yer can't please some people, can yer, girl? Honest, it makes yer feel like going to the nearest funeral parlour and giving yerself up.'

Before closing the kitchen door, Nellie said, 'Nobody is to come out here. I want to prepare meself for the second part of the show.'

Once in the kitchen, Nellie gazed up at the clothes rack. If she was a bit taller, she might have been able to reach the things she wanted, but even on tiptoe she was nowhere near. But she wasn't one to give in without a fight, and she looked round the kitchen for something that would be of use to her. Her eyes lit up when she saw the long-handled brush leaning against the wall in the corner. Ah, she thought, that is just the job. Now I'll give Molly Bennett something to cry about. Then she slapped a hand across her cheek, muttering, 'Silly bugger, I haven't got a pin.' Hand on chin, and eyes narrowed, she wondered how to get round her problem. 'Me bloomers,' she told herself softly. 'I've got a pin in me ruddy bloomers!'

'What's Nellie doing out there?' Ellen asked. 'She's been ages.'

'She'll be thinking of some way to get her own back on me,' Molly said. 'So batten down the hatches – yer never can tell with my mate.'

Just then a knock came on the kitchen door. 'Are yer all sitting comfortably, 'cos here I come.' The door burst open and it was hard to say who was the first to gasp in surprise, and who was the first to bend double with laughter. For Nellie had taken the tablecloth from the rack, folded it into a nappy and was wearing it over her clothes, held together with the safety pin from her bloomers. And she had one of the baby's bibs tied around her neck. She skipped into the room like a young girl, singing one of Shirley Temple's songs, 'On the Good Ship Lollipop'. What a sight she was, with her clothes sticking out from the sides of the nappy, her chubby, dimpled legs on show, and her stockings crumpled round her ankles. And to top it, her round face was beaming as she skipped around the room with her arms waving, imitating the child film star.

The three women on the couch were in convulsions as they clung to each other, their laughter loud. Doreen had her head in her hands, her elbows resting on the table as her shoulders shook, and Victoria was pressing at the stitch in her side. Before they had time to recover, Nellie stopped in front of Molly and said, 'Now don't try telling me Shirley Temple never sang this song, girl, 'cos I'll marmalise yer.'

It was about this time that the men came out of the pub, all happy and hail fellow well met. Tommy was the first to leave the group as he lived at the top of the next street, then Archie and Steve said their farewells. Corker took a deep breath of the cool night air, then led the men down the street. 'I enjoyed meself,' he said, stroking his large moustache. 'A night out with good mates does yer the power of good.'

Derek said, 'I'm glad yer offered to let me sleep on yer couch, Corker, 'cos I don't think I could make it home.'

'Me and George are lucky, we only live a few doors down.' Jack chuckled. 'And at least I can see the number on the door tonight. Many's the time I've been out with Corker and would have ended up getting into a strange bed if he hadn't been with me.'

'Oh, I don't think yer'd have got as far as getting into a strange bed, Mr B.,' Phil laughed. 'The man of the house would have sent yer packing.'

'Shush!' Corker cocked an ear. 'Just listen to the noise coming from your house, Phil. The ladies seem to be enjoying themselves.'

There came a loud burst of laughter from the house opposite, bringing a smile to the faces of the men. 'I bet that's Nellie, up to her tricks.'

They could hear the sound of merriment, but if they could have seen the cause of it, they would probably have felt a pang of regret. It was nice to have a drink with your mates at the pub, but nothing could come up to Nellie when she was in good form. And from the sound of it, she was in excellent form. 'Next time yer come down, Derek,' Corker said, 'we'll stay in and have a party with the two best hostesses in Liverpool.'

Chapter Ten

Frances Bradley was watching from her front window when the taxi drew up outside. She slipped on the coat she had ready, hanging over the back of a chair, then picked up her handbag. Her tummy was turning over with excitement as it always did at the prospect of seeing her son and her grandson. And she had the door open before Molly had time to knock.

'That was quick, Frances,' Molly said, smiling at her. 'Yer must have been watching out for us.'

'Oh, I haven't been waiting long, queen, just a few minutes.' Frances pulled the door behind her, then pushed to make sure it was firmly closed. Then as she walked down the path, she waved to Nellie, who was spread out on the back seat of the taxi. 'Hello, Nellie. I see yer haven't got yer nappy on today.'

'No, I'm back to me fleecy-lined bloomers, girl, 'cos I find them more comfortable. It's what yer get used to, isn't it?' Nellie moved along the seat to make plenty of room for Frances, while Molly sat on one of the pull-down seats opposite. 'Ye're looking well, Frances. Yer've got a bit of colour in yer cheeks today.'

'Yeah, I was just thinking the same thing,' Molly said, as the taxi pulled away from the kerb. 'It's probably the nice weather, making yer feel better.'

Frances shook her head. 'No, the weather's got nothing to do with it, 'cos I never go over the door only to our Phil's. I've had colour in me cheeks since Saturday, and I'll tell yer why. I keep seeing Nellie in me mind, with that tablecloth on like a nappy, and the bib round her neck. I've never seen anything so funny in me life. Ye're a hero, queen. I wouldn't have the guts to do anything like that.'

'Thank you, girl, it's nice of yer to say so. Not everyone appreciated my artistic talent, though, but I suppose that's the price I have to pay for being famous.'

'What are yer talking about, sunshine?' Molly asked. 'Everyone thought yer were a scream. They all enjoyed it. In fact we were laughing so loud the men could hear us as they came down the street from the pub.'

Nellie's eyes narrowed as she leaned forward in her seat to get her face as close as possible to her mate's. 'Oh, aye, clever clogs. Well, in that case, why did your Doreen stick the tablecloth under me arm when I was leaving, and tell me to take it home and wash it? She had the nerve to say it wasn't going on her table after it had been on my backside, not until it had been washed.' With a plaintive expression on her chubby face, she turned to Frances. 'I'd understand if I was a dirty beggar, but I wash me backside religiously once a month. If I could reach it meself I'd wash it every fortnight, but because me figure is so voluptuous, I can't get to it and have to wait until George feels like helping me out.'

Molly gasped, and gave her mate daggers before turning her head to see if the driver had heard. When she saw him grinning, she shook her fist. 'Nellie McDonough, yer'll be the death of me. Have yer no pride at all?'

Nellie wasn't the least bit concerned. 'Everything you've got, girl, I've got. The only difference is, I've got more of it.'

'I don't mind yer having more of it, sunshine, but do yer really have to share it with everyone, even strangers?'

'You and Frances are not strangers, girl, so don't be coming all prim and proper with me.'

'We're not strangers, no, but the taxi driver is. And right now he'll be wondering what sort of women he's got in the back of his cab.'

Without lowering her voice, Nellie said, 'Oh, I know he's watching, girl, 'cos I could see his eyes all over me when he came to pick us up. But I'm used to men ogling me, and I don't mind 'cos they can't help it. It's not often they see a figure like mine, and I bet they don't half envy my George.'

Molly could hear the driver chuckling and she knocked on the pane of glass separating them. 'Take no notice of me mate. She's usually as quiet as a lamb, and butter wouldn't melt in her mouth. But when there's a man around, she has to show off. So take my advice, keep yer eyes on the road and whistle a happy tune.'

'Oh, I'll whistle a happy tune, missus, 'cos I'm going home to someone twice the size of yer mate. And believe me, I wouldn't swap her for anyone . . . except perhaps Mae West. Yer see, I like a woman with plenty of flesh on her.'

Molly could see the gloating expression on Nellie's face and wished she'd kept her mouth shut. As sure as eggs, she'd never hear the end of it. And how right she was. For while she was paying the taxi fare, Doreen had opened the door and been pushed aside by Nellie.

'She's in a hurry, isn't she, Mam?'

Molly had a hand cupping Frances's elbow. 'I'll tell yer when we get in, sunshine, if I get the chance. But I've got a horrible feeling that Victoria is being told something she would rather not hear. There's nothing on God's earth that will stop my mate from saying something she wants to say. That taxi driver has lots to tell his wife when he gets home.' She waited until Phil's mam was in the hall before laughing. 'He didn't hear all the story, so he'll only be able to tell her that he had an eighteen-stone woman in his cab who wears a nappy.'

Doreen put a hand to her mouth. 'She didn't tell the driver that, did she?'

'Not in those words, sunshine, but she was telling Frances about you giving her the tablecloth to wash because yer weren't going to put it on your table after it had been on her backside.' Molly couldn't keep the laughter back as she followed Frances into the living room. 'She also let it be known that she isn't as dirty as you seem to think, for she washes her backside every month. She'd do it every fortnight if she could reach it, but with her voluptuous body she can't manage and has to rely on George helping her out.'

Nellie was looking her mate up and down, her lips clamped together and her chins swaying rhythmically. 'D'yer have to tell them me business? Yer always want to get there first, even though it's my tale, not yours.'

'Oh, I'm sorry, sunshine. I keep forgetting yer like to be centre stage. So me and Frances will sit on the couch and our lips will be sealed while yer bring Victoria and Doreen up to date with yer latest antics.' Molly plumped a cushion and put it behind Frances. 'We've both heard it, but we'll be quiet and see what interpretation you put on it. Go on, I'm sure it'll be very interesting.'

Nellie glared. 'Yer've told them everything now; there's nothing left for me to say. Why don't yer tell them about yer own carryings on, and leave me to do me own thing?'

'I didn't mean to steal yer thunder, sunshine. I wouldn't want to do that. Not to me very best mate. Anyway, I've hardly said anything! There's bags they haven't heard yet. What about a woman who's twice the size of you?'

Nellie's face beamed. 'Oh, yeah, I forgot about that, girl. Thanks for reminding me. And I wasn't really mad at yer, I was only pretending.'

'Before yer start, though, can yer hang on until Doreen

makes us all a cuppa?' Molly smiled at her daughter. 'Be an angel, me throat is as dry as a bone.'

Doreen jumped to her feet. 'It won't take two ticks – the water's been on the boil for about ten minutes. Not a word out of yer, Auntie Nellie, until I'm back in the room. I don't want to miss out on anything.'

Nellie pulled out a chair from the table. 'I don't mind waiting, girl, not when I'm going to get two custard creams with me tea.'

Molly gasped. 'Nellie, don't be so flaming hard-faced! If Doreen hasn't got any biscuits, she's going to be really embarrassed.'

'She's no need to be, girl, 'cos if she gives me the money I'll nip to the corner shop to get some for her. I don't mind doing her a favour.'

Victoria grinned behind her hand, Frances and Doreen laughed, but Molly kept her face straight. 'Don't yer mean doing yerself a favour? Yer've got some cheek, Nellie McDonough. I don't know how yer've got the nerve.'

'It's all right, Mam, I've got biscuits in,' Doreen said. 'I don't know about custard creams, but there's ginger snaps and arrowroot.'

The chair groaned when Nellie sat down without giving any warning. As one leg said to the other, if she'd let them know, they could brace themselves. 'Yer see, girl, all that fuss over nothing.' There was a smug smile on the chubby face. 'Yer'd cause trouble in an empty house, you would.'

Molly was ready with a quick retort. 'I never have the luxury of being in an empty house, sunshine, you're always with me. Most people have a shadow, but I've never seen mine 'cos yer stick to me like glue.'

'Oh, that's a good one, girl. I would never have thought of that. But then I'm not as clever as you.'

'Nellie, ye're a damn sight more clever than I'll ever be.' Molly looked thoughtful for a few seconds as she gazed up at the ceiling. 'No, I take that back 'cos I've changed me mind. I am more clever than you, 'cos what you are is crafty.'

The little woman jerked her head at Frances. 'Would yer say that was a compliment, girl, or an insult? Should I kiss her or thump her?'

'Don't bring me in, queen, 'cos I haven't got the strength to be referee. Why don't yer just shake hands, kiss, and make up?'

Molly doubled up at the thought that was running through her head. 'I'll shake hands, sunshine, but I don't fancy kissing someone what only washes their backside once a month.'

'Ay, don't be so bleeding funny, Molly Bennett. I'll have yer know I'm very fussy who kisses my backside. So now yer know.' The chair began to groan and creak as Nellie's body shook. 'It's due for a wash in a week's time, and I'll let yer know, just in case yer change yer mind.'

'Don't bother, sunshine. I'll leave that part of yer anatomy to George.'

Nellie's eyebrows nearly reached her hairline. 'That part of me what?'

Doreen left her chair. This could go on all morning, she thought, and the baby will be awake soon. 'I'll see to the tea, and whatever biscuits we've got.'

'That's the first sensible thing I've heard since I walked through that door.' Nellie's chins were in complete agreement with her, but the chair wasn't. All four legs were wishing she'd keep still and not be moving her bottom around so much. Did she have no consideration for what she was putting them through? And why couldn't she sit on the couch, which was sturdy, and could take her weight better than a dining chair?

When Doreen came through carrying a tray laden with five

cups of tea, Nellie was delighted to find two custard creams on her saucer. 'I'll say this for yer, Doreen, ye're a better hostess than yer mam. When I have me morning cuppa in her house, she puts a plate on the table with three custard creams on. And I have to grovel to get the spare one.'

Molly slowly shook her head and tutted. 'For once in yer life, Nellie, why don't yer tell them the truth? That before I've taken me first bite, the other two biscuits have disappeared like magic. Your hands are so fast they're like a blur. They're faster than my eyes. And you eat the ruddy biscuits so fast I can't prove I even brought them in.'

'I can't help it if ye're too slow to catch cold, girl, can I? Yer've got to be quick on the draw if yer want anything in this life. That's my motto. And I still say yer daughter is a better hostess than you are.'

Molly gave Frances a light dig in her side. 'Well, yer can show your prowess as a hostess on Friday, sunshine, and see if yer make an impression.'

Nellie could see Molly had her legs crossed, as did Frances, and she tried to cross hers. It was a wrong move, though. She got her right leg halfway over her left, but it slipped off. So she tried again, more determined this time. If her mate could do it, and look so comfortable, then she saw no reason why she couldn't. So, once again, huffing and puffing with the exertion, she tried to cock her leg over and look nonchalant at the same time. For a few seconds she thought she'd made it, but, worse luck, the leg refused to stay put and slid off. 'Oh, sod yer, then,' Nellie said. 'Stay on the bleeding floor, see if I care.'

'That wasn't your fault, sunshine,' Molly told her. 'It was yer tummy. I saw it pushing yer leg off.'

'To hell with it,' Nellie said, thinking it was too much trouble to be nonchalant. 'Anyway, what's this yer were saying about Friday?'

Molly's willpower was stretched, for she was dying to laugh. 'I hope yer haven't forgotten that you're playing hostess on Friday?'

'Yer've lost me now, girl, 'cos I don't know what ye're on about.'

'Don't tell me yer've forgotten that yer've invited Claire?'

'I hadn't forgot she was coming, girl, so why the fuss?'

'Because she's your guest, Nellie, and yer need to make an effort. I hope yer have the house tidy for her coming, and yer've got something in for her to eat.'

'There's no point in me tidying me house, girl, 'cos she won't see it. It's your house she's coming to, not mine.'

'Oh, no, Nellie, I didn't invite Claire, you did. "Why don't yer come again next Friday, girl, and have a natter?" Those were yer very words, so don't be trying to get out of it.'

'Uh, uh! Got yer there, girl, 'cos you told Claire we might not be able to see her on Friday 'cos we might be picking Frances up.'

'Yes, but I asked Phil to tell young Ken that it was all right for his mam to come on Friday. So she'll be here the same time as last week.'

Nellie rubbed her nose, pushing it out of shape. 'I don't see what it's got to do with you, Molly Bennett. Seeing as she's coming to your house, she won't see the dust on me sideboard and the ashes in me grate.'

'Oh, no, yer can't do that, Nellie! She'll be expecting to go to yours, seeing as you were the one what invited her.'

Nellie nodded her head. 'Yes, I agree with yer on that, girl, but I was sitting in your house at the time, so that's where I invited her. And no matter how yer look at it, there's no getting away from that.'

'No, no!' Molly shook her head vigorously. 'Ye're not getting out of it, Nellie, so ye're wasting yer time trying. Claire would think it funny if she was plonked in my house again when the invitation came from you.'

Nellie was getting all flustered by now. She didn't fancy cleaning her living room to have it looking spick and span for a visitor; that was too much like hard work. She'd fight this battle to the bitter end, and she'd win. Pressing her hands flat on the table, she pushed herself up, allowing the chair to sigh with relief. But its relief was to be short-lived, for Nellie turned the chair to face her mate, then plonked herself down again. 'Now listen, girl, and we'll go over what was said last Friday. Yer were listening hard enough, so yer'll know every word I'm about to say is the truth. Listen and watch carefully, now. "I'm glad yer've enjoyed yerself, girl, so why don't yer come again next Friday?" ' Nellie curled the four fingers on her right hand, then pointed her thumb downwards to the floor. She did this several times, to make sure they all saw it. 'That's what I did, girl, and if I'm pointing to your floor, then it's only natural she'll know the invitation is to your house.'

All eyes were on Molly's face with its look of incredulity. It was several seconds before she found her voice. 'Nellie, d'yer remember when the war was on, and I said it was a pity Mr Churchill don't know about yer, 'cos yer could be his secret weapon? It was one day when yer were trying to pull a stunt like yer're doing now. I can clearly remember saying that if they put yer in a room with Hitler for half an hour, then the war would be over in no time 'cos yer'd baffle him with ruddy science and he'd give up.'

Nellie's jaw dropped. 'In the name of God, girl, what's that got to do with the price of fish?'

Molly gave in, and her laughter was the loudest. What could you do with someone like Nellie, who had an answer to everything?

Wiping away the tears of laughter, Doreen stood at the bottom of the stairs with her ear cocked. 'Bobby's awake. I'd better go and get him – he's due for a feed.'

'Me and Nellie will just say hello to him, sunshine, then we'll leave yer in peace. Frances will be happy to hold her grandson while yer put the dinner on.'

'We share him,' Frances said, smiling across at the older woman who had taken her son in when he had nowhere to go. 'Don't we, Victoria?'

'We certainly do. But he's getting to be quite a weight, you know, Molly, and pretty soon he'll be too heavy for me and Frances to hold him for long.'

Molly, the proud grandmother, smiled. 'When I was over the other day, Doreen had put a blanket on the floor for him to lie on, and blow me if he didn't roll over and try to crawl. Another few weeks and he'll be all over the place.'

Nellie's eyes narrowed as she glared at her mate. 'When was that? I don't remember him being on the floor and trying to crawl.'

'No, yer wouldn't, sunshine, 'cos yer weren't with me. I slipped over one night for half an hour.'

'Why didn't yer give me a knock? I'd have come with yer.'

'Nellie, I only came over to see how things were. Doreen is me daughter, yer know. I'm entitled to come and see her without asking your permission.'

'Don't be sarky, girl, 'cos it doesn't suit yer. It might suit me, 'cos I've got the face for it, but it doesn't suit you. And next time yer just come over to see how things are, well just knock at my door and I'll come with yer. If it's not too much trouble, like, and yer haven't anything to say what yer don't want me to hear.'

'What could I have to say that I didn't want you to hear? I can't breathe without yer knowing about it.'

The look of devilment in Nellie's eyes should have warned her mate she was about to say something outrageous. 'One of these days yer might be glad of me listening to yer breathing. What if yer ever stop and I'm not with yer? Yer'd be in a right pickle then, with no one to get a doctor for yer, or pull yer clothes down so anyone passing can't see yer knickers.' Nellie's face was serious as she nodded her head knowingly. 'Do yer know that if yer stop breathing yer die? And that's why I follow yer like a shadow, and never leave yer on yer own. Ye're me best mate, girl, and I can't afford to lose yer. After all, where am I going to find another friend what will make me a cup of tea every morning, and lend me money when I forget to take me purse to the shops? No, girl, I'm not soft. I know a good thing when I see it. I'm going to keep you alive even if I die in the process.'

'I can't see the sense in you dying to keep me alive, sunshine, but I somehow think you can. Anyway, you do what makes yer happy.'

Doreen came down the stairs at that moment with the baby, and Molly pressed her curled fists into the seat of the couch to push herself up, a smile of pride on her face at the sight of her grandson. But she was no sooner on her feet than she was pushed down again by Nellie, who had a look of determination on her face. 'Seeing as yer sneaked down the other night to see the baby without telling me, I'm making sure I get in first today, so that makes us even.'

By the time Molly struggled to her feet again, Nellie was patting Bobby's cheek. 'Hello, there, lad! This is yer grandma Nellie come to see yer. And d'yer know, lad, ye're getting to look more like me every day.'

'You're his adopted grandma, courtesy of his real grandma,' Molly said, pushing her mate aside and holding her arms out to take the baby. 'I did it 'cos ye're me best mate, but give you an inch and yer take a ruddy yard.' The baby's arms and legs were thrashing out as he tried to free himself from Doreen's hold on him. 'Look, he knows his grandma now, don't yer, sunshine? And you're not half getting heavy. Ye're a ton weight, my darling.'

Behind her, Nellie's head was lowered and her eyes narrowed, a sure sign she was up to something. Then she nodded at the floor, as though satisfied with her decision. 'In that case, Molly Bennett, I've decided that you can only be an adopted grandma to Steve's baby. Ye're not the only one who is mean enough to pull a stunt like that. So there, see how yer like getting your eye wiped.'

'We've been through this dozens of times, Nellie. I'm surprised it hasn't sunk in yet.' Molly was chuckling as Bobby pulled on a handful of her hair. 'Yer'll have me looking a sight to go to the shops, sunshine, so leave grandma's hair alone.'

'What have we been over a dozen times, girl, I'd like to know?' Once Nellie got the bit between her teeth she wouldn't leave well alone. 'Go on, tell me?'

Molly sighed. 'Listen, do yer want to hold Bobby for a while? We've got shopping to do, and we'll have to look sharp if we want to catch the shops before they close for dinner.'

Nellie was immediately all sweetness and light. She held the baby close and covered his face with kisses. 'Who's a lovely boy for his grandma then, eh?'

Molly smiled at Frances. 'We go through this grandma lark every day, Frances. Doreen and Victoria are used to it. But it's only a bit of fun. We all know you are, like meself, Bobby's grandma.'

'Can I put him on the floor and see if he crawls?' Nellie asked hopefully. 'I'd like to see him crawl for the first time.'

'Nellie, we haven't got much time,' Molly reminded her. 'Remember we want to catch the shops.'

Doreen saw her Auntie Nellie's face drop, and although she knew it was probably an act to get her own way, she felt sorry for her. 'I'll put the blanket on the floor, Mam. It won't take long and yer'll have time to get to the shops.'

Oh, the look of pleasure on Bobby's face when he had the freedom of the whole floor. He gurgled and punched the air with his arms and legs. And as all women are emotional when it comes to babies, the four women had smiles on their faces. Then when he rolled over on to his tummy, and worked his feet to push himself forward, there was much excitement as the women declared him to be very forward for his age. 'Just look at his face,' Molly said. 'He's looking at us as if to say aren't I a clever boy?'

She happened to glance at Frances and saw a look of sadness on her face. She knew Phil's mother was wondering how much longer she had to see her grandson growing up. 'He's the spitting image of Phil, isn't he, Frances? He won't go far wrong if he takes after his dad.'

'I was just thinking how well Frances looks.' Victoria had also seen the sadness and her heart went out to her. 'I may be mistaken, sweetheart, but have yer put a bit of weight on?'

'That's what I said, girl, when I saw her this morning,' Nellie said. 'She's got some colour in her cheeks, too!'

Doreen was praying one of the women would ask the question she didn't like to raise. And her prayers were answered when Molly said, 'Have yer been back to the doctor's for a check-up Frances? Like Victoria and Nellie, I think yer look a lot better.'

Frances dropped her head. 'I'm too much of a coward to see a doctor, 'cos I'm afraid of what he'll tell me.'

'Don't be daft, sunshine. Better to know than worry yerself sick when it's not necessary,' Molly told her. 'Me and Nellie will come to the doctor's with yer one morning, won't we, Nellie?'

'Of course we will, girl. And as Molly said, the doctor might have good news for yer, and yer'd have been worrying yerself sick for nothing.'

Frances seemed to brighten up. 'Would yer really come with me? Oh, that's very kind of yer. Tom is always at me to go, but men don't understand like women. I'd be fine if you and Nellie came, Molly, and I'd be ever so grateful.'

'What times does he have his surgery?'

'He starts at nine o'clock every morning, and then again from two in the afternoon. He sometimes gets called out on an urgent call, and that means waiting till he gets back. But it's only happened to me once.'

'Nine o'clock is too early for me and Nellie to get to your house, but we could take yer to the afternoon surgery. Is it all right with you, Nellie, if we get to Frances's tomorrow about half one?'

'Suits me fine, girl, suits me fine.'

'That's settled then. We'll be there tomorrow, Frances, so don't even think of changing yer mind. Have yer coat on ready.' Molly lifted the baby from the floor and hugged him tight. 'Ye're my little ray of sunshine, and I love the bones of yer.' She put him down gently on Frances's lap. 'We'll be on our way now, so come on, Nellie, get a move on.'

'Okay, girl, keep yer flipping hair on! I'm right behind yer.'

Doreen went to the door with them, and when she was giving her mother a kiss, she said, 'Thanks for helping Phil's mam. He'll be really pleased when I tell him.'

'We'll call tomorrow, sunshine,' Molly said, 'and let yer know what the doctor said.'

Doreen didn't close the door right away, but watched her mam and Auntie Nellie walk away, arm in arm. And she heard the little woman ask, 'Ay, girl, what was it yer said we've been through a dozen times?'

'Well, let this be the last time, Nellie, because it's getting monotonous. You can't decide to make me an adopted grandma to Jill's baby, because I am her grandmother. Jill is my flesh and blood, and so is little Molly. And Steve is your son, your flesh and blood, and so is Molly. So get that into yer head and let's hear no more about it.'

'But why can't I be a real grandma to Bobby? Just tell me that.'

'Subject closed, Nellie, once and for all. Now, what are we getting for the family's dinner?'

'I'll get what you get, girl.'

Doreen closed the door with a smile on her face.

Molly and Nellie took an arm each as they led Frances out of the doctor's surgery. 'How did yer get on, sunshine? What did the doctor say?'

'He said my condition hasn't deteriorated, queen, and I could see he was surprised. I'm still a sick woman, he told me that, but I'm no worse than the last time I saw him. That's good news, isn't it, queen? I'm to see him again in four weeks' time.'

'That's wonderful news, and Phil will be very happy when we tell him. God works in mysterious ways, yer know, so we'll all keep on praying for yer.'

Nellie wasn't to be left out. 'You just keep telling yerself ye're going to get better girl, and yer never know, it could happen.'

'Yer will tell Phil and Doreen, won't yer, Molly? I know they worry about me.'

'We'll see you safely in yer house, sunshine, then hop on the first tram to take us home. Doreen will be watching out of the window for us, and the news will bring a smile to her face. And me and Nellie will see yer on Saturday, as usual.'

Chapter Eleven

Nellie was very quiet as she sipped her tea in Molly's on Friday morning. Usually she never stopped talking, even when her mouth was full. But there were no custard cream biscuits to fill her mouth today, for Molly had run out of them. Normally, the lack of a biscuit would have brought forth complaints, but even they were missing today. There was good reason for Nellie to be quiet and thoughtful, for she had a lot on her mind. Claire was due to visit this afternoon, but Molly hadn't said a dickie-bird about it since Wednesday, when she said Claire was invited by Nellie, and would therefore expect to go to Nellie's house. And looking round Molly's sitting room now, all nice and tidy with furniture highly polished, Nellie was filled with despair. For her living room wasn't a patch on it.

Molly could read her friend like a book, and she had sensed right away that she had something on her mind. She guessed what it was too, but was waiting for her mate to speak up. When she thought the silence had gone on long enough, and not liking the idea of her friend's being really upset, she asked, 'Has the cat got yer tongue, sunshine? Yer've hardly said a word since yer've been here.'

'It's this bleeding visit, that's what's wrong with me.' Nellie blurted it out. 'I can't have Claire coming to my house and that's the top and bottom of it. Looking round your room now, I feel sick in me tummy. I've tried to make me living room respectable, honest I have. I put a clean duster over me brush head and went round all the picture rails and skirting boards with it. But I can't get down on me knees and polish the table and chair legs, 'cos if I got down I'd never get up again. I miss our Lily, 'cos she used to do those jobs for me.'

'I'm sure Claire wouldn't get down on her hands and knees to check yer chair legs, sunshine. She won't be going over yer room with a fine-tooth comb. And never be ashamed of yer house, Nellie, for though yer might not be as tidy as yer should be, yer house is far from being dirty.'

Nellie wasn't to be pacified. 'Look round your room, girl, and then go and look at mine. The difference would hit yer in the face.'

'Look, if worrying about it is going to make yer ill, then yer needn't take Claire to your house. She can come here.'

Nellie's body slumped as she let out a huge sigh of relief. 'Thank God for that! Why didn't yer say so yesterday, girl? Then I could have got some sleep last night. It's been worrying the life out of me, and George got a right cob on with me for tossing and turning in bed and keeping him awake.'

'Have I ever let yer down, Nellie?' Molly asked. 'I know I've refused yer hundreds of times, but never once have I gone through with it. Yer always get yer own way in the end, even though I tell meself I'm a ruddy fool for giving in to yer. So Claire is welcome to come here this afternoon, but don't be handing invitations out right left and centre in future, not without asking me first.'

'No, I won't, girl,' Nellie told her, full of good intentions. 'And ye're a real smasher, the best mate anyone could have.'

'Oh, ye're not getting off that easy, sunshine, so don't be thinking ye're out of the woods yet. Claire can come here by all means. I'll be glad to see her, I'll make her very welcome and very comfortable, but I will not be feeding her. And I don't care what excuse or stunt yer pull, the boiled ham and the cakes are being paid for out of your purse.'

Nellie scratched her head and pulled faces as she wondered how far she should go, and how much she'd get away with. 'D'yer think that's fair, girl?'

'Fair! It's more than fair, yer cheeky article! Yer don't really expect me to pay for the ham and cakes, do yer?'

'Well, Claire will think yer have, won't she?' Nellie saw this as a great injustice. 'It's you what will get all the praise, while I sit here like a stuffed duck listening to her saying how kind it is of yer.'

'Ooh, yer forget I know yer too well for that, Nellie McDonough. There's not a snowball's chance in hell of you letting Claire think I paid for the food. I'll bet that every time she takes a bite, there'll be a running commentary on how much it cost. I can see it in me mind now! You leaning towards her, saying, "The cream slices are nice, aren't they, Claire? Tuppence each I paid for them." She'll hear that with every bite she takes, and be so embarrassed she'll never want to come again.'

Nellie, being crafty, soon found a way round this. 'I won't say nothing, girl, I promise. But you could say, off hand, like, that the sandwiches and cakes were my treat. If yer like, yer could even say yer had offered to buy them but I wouldn't hear of it. Then Claire wouldn't get it into her head that you were too tight to pay.'

Molly shook her head slowly. 'Nellie, yer never cease to amaze me. Not satisfied with getting yer own way, yer want me to lie for yer! And with all yer cunning and lies, yer still expect Saint Peter to let yer through the pearly gates to heaven.' A smile hovered around her mouth. 'Mind you, with your gift of the gab, I'll bet he not only lets yer in, but makes sure yer get a seat on the front row.'

'Well, he'd have to, wouldn't he? I wouldn't be able to manage if I didn't have plenty of room in front of me.'

'Nellie, I know I'm daft for asking, but why would yer want plenty of room?'

'For me harp, of course, girl. What did yer think?'

'Silly me. Fancy me not knowing that.'

'You wouldn't need to be in the front row, girl, 'cos yer haven't got an ear for music. Not like what I have, anyway. I imagine you'll probably get a flute, or a tin whistle.'

'Just out of curiosity, sunshine, does a halo come with your harp?'

'Of course it does, soft girl. How daft I'd look, playing me harp when I hadn't been issued with a halo.' Her chubby face screwed up, Nellie stroked her chin. 'I think I'll have to wait a while for me wings, though, 'cos they'll have to make them special. That's with me being a different size and shape to all the other angels, yer see.'

'So I'll be stuck at the back, will I, and not be able to talk to yer?' While she was speaking, Molly was telling herself she didn't know who was the daftest, her or Nellie. Still, it was better than having her mate sitting there not speaking and looking really down in the dumps. 'Yer'll miss me, yer know. Who are yer going to borrow off if yer forget to take yer purse with yer when yer go to the shops?'

'There's no shops in heaven, girl, everything is free. And yer won't be stuck at the back, I'll see to that. Wherever I go, you'll be coming with me. We'll sit on a nice, white, fluffy cloud, and wave to the aeroplanes as they go past. And yer won't have to count how many cups of tea I'm drinking 'cos, as I said, everything is free in heaven.'

'Well, I'll say this for yer, sunshine. Fifteen minutes ago yer had a face on yer that would turn milk sour. And between then and now, yer've made friends with Saint Peter, talked him into giving yer a front seat in heaven, and learned to play the harp. Not bad going in a quarter of an hour, when yer consider yer did all this without the halo slipping off yer head. And yer've done it without uttering one swear word.'

Nellie's face creased, hiding her eyes. 'Yeah, it's not bad going, is it, girl? But I meant what I said. Me and Saint Peter will make sure yer get a good seat, and a halo what fits yer.'

Molly's chuckle was hearty. 'I'll look forward to all this, sunshine. It'll give me something to fill in the time when I'm in bed before I drop off to sleep with a smile on me face. But first I'd like to ask a favour of yer.'

Nellie lifted her bosom on to the table. 'What is it, girl? I'll do anything yer want, for being such a good mate and helping me out over Claire. You just name it, and I'll do it.'

'Well, I'd like yer to ask Saint Peter if he'd leave it for thirty or forty years. Yer see, sunshine, I'm quite happy down here now. I don't feel like moving house, even if the new one did come with a halo.'

'I'll have a word with him tonight, girl, and tell him we're not quite ready yet. But I will say we're looking forward to making his acquaintance.' Nellie thought that was a nice little touch, posh, like. 'Best to keep on the right side of him, yer see, girl.'

Molly reached for the cups. 'Now our future lives are sorted out, hadn't we better make tracks to sort today's dinner out? I'll leave these few dishes in the sink until we get back.'

Nellie rushed to open the door when the knock came. Her face beaming, she stood aside to let Claire pass. 'Hello, girl. It's nice to see yer again.'

'It's nice to see you again. I've been looking forward to today.' Claire waved a cake bag. 'I've brought us a cake each. Cream slices, 'cos I know they're yer favourite.'

Nellie's heart nearly burst. Oh, joy of joys, an extra cream slice. 'Molly's in the kitchen making the tea.'

Claire went straight through to the kitchen and put the bag on the draining board. 'It's nice to see yer, Molly. I stopped at the cake shop, so I hope I'm not too late for yer.'

'No, ye're dead on time, sunshine, the kettle was boiling as yer knocked on the door.' Molly nodded at the bag. 'Yer shouldn't have bothered, Claire, we've got the sandwiches and cakes ready.'

'I can't keep sponging off you and Nellie, and anyway, it's only a couple of cakes.'

Nellie was standing behind Claire, but she was too small to see over her shoulder so she popped her head round the side. She was making signs, pointing first to the laden tray, and then at Claire's back. When there was no reaction, she took the bull by the horns. 'Claire brought cakes with her, girl. Isn't that kind of her?'

Molly turned to the sink so Claire couldn't see her grin. 'Yes, it is very kind of her, sunshine. I'm doing really well for meself today, what with you treating us to ham sandwiches and cakes, and now Claire! It's my lucky day.'

Satisfied that their new friend knew of her generosity, Nellie pushed Molly aside and picked up the tray. She couldn't stand there gabbing when her mouth was watering at the picture in her mind of lashings of cream oozing out of the cakes. 'I'll take this through, girl, while you carry the teapot.'

Molly winked at Claire. 'Yer better hurry up, sunshine, or Nellie will pinch the cake with the most cream in.'

'Got a sweet tooth, have yer, Nellie?' Claire pulled out a chair and sat down. 'I'm rather partial meself, I must say. When I was a kid, my father used to bring me sweets in every night. On his way home from work, he'd call in to the sweet shop for his baccy and a ha'p'orth of sweets for me. My mam used to tell him off for spoiling me.'

'I enjoy a cake,' Molly said as she poured the tea out. 'But I don't drool over them like Nellie does. We've only got to pass Hanley's and her mouth waters. I'm glad I'm not that bad 'cos I couldn't afford them every day.'

Nellie got on her high horse. 'I don't have a cake every day, girl, only when we go in Hanley's and I see them in the case. Then I can't resist them.'

'And how often do yer get fresh bread, Nellie?'

'Every day, yer know that. My feller won't eat stale bread. He said he'd rather starve.'

'And where do yer always buy yer bread from?'

'That's a daft question to ask when ye're with me every day when we go to Hanley's.'

'Which means, that, apart from Sunday, yer have a cream cake every day. Am I right, Nellie, or am I wrong? And before yer answer, remember Saint Peter and your speck on the front row.'

'Oh, aye,' Claire said, her face even more beautiful when she smiled. 'What's all this about Saint Peter?'

Nellie glared at her mate before answering. 'Take no notice of her, Claire, she's being sarky. I keep telling her it doesn't suit her, she hasn't got the face for it, but she doesn't take no notice of me. She'll never get to heaven when she dies, will Molly Bennett. She forgets Saint Peter can hear everything she says, and he keeps a note of it. That's why I keep me nose clean and watch what I say. I'm pretty sure of a place in heaven, but I have grave doubts about me mate.'

'Don't speak with yer mouth full of bread, sunshine, it's not very ladylike. And why don't yer give Claire a laugh and tell her about the front row, the harp and halo? Oh, and don't forget my flute.'

In between the laughter, the sandwiches and cakes Nellie had bought were eaten. And not once did she brag about having paid for them. That was because she liked to hear people laughing, and Claire and Molly were in stitches. 'D'yer think you'll get into heaven, Claire?'

'I would like to think so, Nellie, but who knows what's going to happen to them when they die? I have always believed, from being very young, that when yer die yer go to heaven and meet all yer family again. That's still what I like to believe, for I want to see my husband again, and me mam and dad. Not everyone believes the same, but it suits me because that's what I'm hoping for.'

'You and I think alike, sunshine,' Molly said, 'and I'll keep on thinking that because, like you, it's what I want to happen.'

'Yer've never told me that, girl.' Nellie was peeved. 'In all these years we've been mates, yer've never once told me about that.'

'I could say the same to you, sunshine! All the years we've known each other, yer've never once mentioned Saint Peter was a friend of yours.' Molly took a bout of laughing which brought tears to her eyes. She gulped, and took a deep breath before saying, 'Talk about having friends in high places, well, they don't come any higher than heaven.'

Nellie's tummy lifted the table, then her bosom pushed it down again. 'Oh, that's a good one, that, girl. Yer deserve a treat for that little gem. So shall I bring in the cakes what Claire brought?'

'I wondered how long yer could last out, sunshine. It must have been agony for yer, knowing they were so near.'

Nellie nodded. 'Worse than agony, girl, it's been torture. And if I had to wait for you to offer, I'd have been waiting all day.'

'Go and get them, Nellie,' Claire said. 'I can't bear to see a woman suffering.' She fell back in her chair, her eyes wide with surprise when she suddenly realised she was talking to an empty chair. Nellie had moved like lightning, there one second, gone the next. 'My God, she can certainly move, Molly. I didn't even see her leave her chair.'

'Yer should thank yer lucky stars she didn't push the table over! My mate would walk a million miles for one cream slice. She'd slay dragons and choke crocodiles on the way, if need be. Nothing, or no one, would keep her from that cake.'

Nellie walked in carrying the cake bag in one hand, and a half-eaten cake in the other. There was cream round her mouth and on the tip of her nose. And on her face there was a look of indescribable bliss. 'I'll have to have a word with Saint Peter, girl, and tell him to have a stock of these cakes in for when we get there. Otherwise I might be forced to consider what other options are open to me.' She placed the bag on the table. 'Help yerselves, girls, before I scoff the lot.'

Molly quickly reached for the bag. 'Not on your sweet life, sunshine. Don't even think about it.' She tore the bag open and offered it to Claire. 'Take one while the going is good, 'cos yer've seen how quick my mate can move. She wouldn't think twice about snatching it out of yer hand, and I should know.'

Nellie's tongue was out, licking the cream from round her mouth. 'Take no notice of what Molly says, girl, 'cos I'm not that bad. The only time I would pinch a cake off yer is if yer took a long time to eat it, taunting me, like.'

'Oh, I wouldn't taunt yer, Nellie. I'm not cruel. But as I told yer, I have a very sweet tooth as well, so don't expect me to share with yer.'

Molly didn't even look at her mate while she was eating, for she knew there'd be a look of longing on the chubby face, and that would take the pleasure out of the fresh cream and soft sticky icing. So she kept her eyes averted until the only thing left in her hand was the white crinkly paper. 'I enjoyed that, Claire, and I think another cup of tea is called for. I'll boil some water for a fresh pot.'

As she leaned against the sink waiting for the kettle to boil, Molly heard Nellie asking, 'Ay, Claire, how are yer getting on with that feller yer told us about? The one what comes in every week?'

'Hang on a minute, Claire, wait for me.' Molly lowered the light under the kettle and hurried through to the living room. 'You can either do without another cup of tea, or keep quiet until I come back with a fresh pot. It's up to you, but I'm not missing out on any news.'

'Make the tea, Molly,' Claire said. 'We'll wait for yer.'

'But don't take too long, slow coach,' Nellie called as her mate headed for the kitchen again. 'We haven't got all day.'

'Yer can get off yer backside, sunshine, and rinse the cups for me.' As Molly spoke, she would have bet any money that Nellie would be pulling faces. Her mate wasn't exactly keen on work of any description, and even rinsing cups was work. 'Come on, or the afternoon will be gone.'

'I'll help,' Claire said. 'Save Nellie moving.'

'Ah, that's nice of yer, girl, but if I let yer do that, I'd never hear the end of it off my best mate. I'd get a lesson in how to be a good hostess, and I'd rather clean the house from top to bottom than get one of Molly's lectures.'

'You cheeky article!' Molly carried the tray through. 'Yer deliberately kept on talking so I'd have the tea made. It's to be hoped they have servants in heaven, 'cos they'll never get you off yer backside.'

'It doesn't get dirty in heaven, girl, surely yer must know that? How can it get dirty when it's up in the sky where there's no smoking chimneys and no soot?'

'D'yer think yer could find the strength to pour the tea out,

Nellie? I don't think that would tire yer out. Yer know I take one sugar, and so does Claire.'

'Ye're getting sarky again, girl, and what have I said? It just doesn't become yer. Me now, I can get away with it, but not you.'

'Pour the tea, Nellie, and try not to spill it in the saucers, like yer usually do.'

Nellie's chubby fingers wouldn't fit through the handle of the teapot, so she had to use both hands to take the weight. 'Ah, ay, girl, this is bleeding hot! I can't hold on to it. I'll have to let it fall.'

Molly was round the table like a shot. 'You break that teapot, Nellie McDonough, and I'll do more than have yer guts for garters. I'll pulverise yer.'

Nellie placed the teapot carefully on the tray, gave Claire a huge wink, then wiped her hands together as she sat down. 'Why the hell didn't yer buy a decent teapot while yer were at it, girl? Our Lily was about six when I bought her a doll's tea set for Christmas, and it was a damn sight easier to manage than that one.'

'Shut up, Nellie, and be thankful ye're getting a cup of tea,' Molly said. 'I was rooting in the sideboard drawer this morning for something, and I happened to come across the little book I keep notes in. And with the second cup of tea ye're getting now, it brings the grand total of cups yer've had off me over the years to two thousand, five hundred and twenty-six. And that's not counting high days and holidays.' She passed the cups over. 'Don't look so surprised, Claire. We'll tell yer about that another day. Right now we'd be more interested to hear if there's been any progress in the romance department.'

'Ay, don't be getting ideas about the man I told yer about. It was only said in fun, 'cos I hardly know the bloke. For all I know he might just be a friendly person who makes conversation with everyone out of politeness. He came in on Monday morning, at eleven o'clock, on the dot as usual, with three collars and three shirts. Then on Tuesday, again as usual, he came at eleven o'clock to collect them. He's quite a toff: well spoken and always immaculately turned out.'

Nellie was getting impatient, wanting to go straight to the nitty-gritty. 'Is he getting more friendly with yer, chatting yer up, like?'

'Don't read anything into it, Nellie, 'cos as I say he's probably just being polite. I would imagine he's a boss of some description. He certainly has the air of someone in authority, very sure of himself. And he's become more friendly, stays a little longer after he's been served, and seems interested in my life. He knows I'm a widow with two children, although I didn't volunteer the information. It came out in the questions he was asking. Only out of interest, of course, 'cos he's not forward or anything like that. He's nice to talk to, and doesn't look down on me, even though I'm only serving behind the counter.'

Nellie was so agog with interest, she didn't even feel the pain when she pressed her bosom too hard against the table. 'Is he married, d'yer think? If not, perhaps he's got his eye on yer.'

Claire shook her head. 'He's out of my league, Nellie, and I certainly wouldn't have the nerve to ask the man if he was married.'

'Ay, girl, yer could ask, casual like if he's married.' This was Nellie's advice. 'And if not, yer want to start giving him the glad eye. If he's got money, then don't let him get away because ye're too shy. Get in there, girl, while yer can. If you don't snap him up yer want yer bumps feeling.'

'I wouldn't put it so bluntly, Claire, but for all yer know he might be a lonely bachelor,' Molly said. 'He could turn out to be your knight in shining armour.'

'Yeah, that's what I mean.' Nellie's legs were swinging under the chair. 'He could give yer a life what the rich people have. And yer could invite me and Molly to visit yer, so we can see how the other half live.'

Claire shook her head. 'He's a real gentleman, very pleasant and quite attractive. But I'm only the woman who takes his laundry in, and that's as far as it will ever go.'

'I suppose ye're right,' Molly said, 'but just out of curiosity, if he did ask yer to go out with him one night, would yer go?'

'Well, I'd want to know a bit more about him. There's a big difference between standing behind a counter serving a customer, and sitting on the back row of a cinema or theatre with a man. I would never go out with anyone just because they were paying to take me to somewhere I couldn't afford to go to meself, 'cos that would give him the impression I was out for what I could get.' Claire started to giggle. 'Yer know, if the poor man heard this conversation, he'd find another laundry to take his cleaning to. All I do is serve him, and here's you two talking about marrying me off to him.'

'In all seriousness, Claire, yer must look in the mirror to comb yer hair now and again, so yer know ye're not an ugly duckling. Many a man would jump at the chance of marrying yer. And there's no shame in serving behind a counter, either, so don't put yerself down. Young and beautiful, yer should be enjoying life. If yer get the chance, then don't turn it down, but grab it with both hands, for your sake and the kids'. But only if ye're quite sure the man is one you would be happy to spend yer life with, and who yer think will make a good father for Ken and Amy.'

Claire nodded. 'I would consider meself very lucky if the right man came along. As long as he was good to the kids. They come first in my life.'

'Come again next week, sunshine, and yer can tell us if

there's been any further advance with this man and his three shirts and three collars. I'm not pushing yer 'cos I'm nosy, I'm just interested. And apart from that it'll be nice to see yer. Unless yer've got other things to do, of course. We can't expect yer to be free every Friday afternoon.'

'I've got nothing else on, Molly, and I look forward to seeing you and Nellie. So I'll be here next week, same time.'

Nellie was gazing at Molly with admiration. 'I'm not half lucky to have a mate as clever as you, girl. You always know what to say, and the right words to use.'

Molly smiled. 'I might know more words than you, sunshine, but I don't know about clever. When it comes to getting yer own way, yer beat me by a mile.'

Nellie stopped swinging her legs while she folded her arms and hoisted her bosom. She was feeling well pleased with herself.

Chapter Twelve

'I'm doing me rounds of visiting tonight, love,' Molly said, her hands on the arms each side of her husband's chair. 'Yer don't mind, do yer?'

Jack lowered his paper and smiled up into her face. 'I know, love. I heard yer telling Tommy yer would be going round to see them. Yer know I don't mind, and I'd go with yer if I wasn't feeling so tired. Now the weather's getting warmer it's like an oven in the workshop, and sweating all day tires yer out. Give my love to Jill, and yer ma and da. Tell them I'll see them at the weekend.'

'Nellie's coming with me, so we're calling to see Lily and Archie as well. I'll try not to be too late, but yer know what me mate's like – when she starts talking she forgets to stop.' Molly bent down and kissed his forehead. 'Not that I'd want her to stop, because the family love her coming. She always has something to say to make them laugh. Heaven knows what little gem she'll make up tonight.' She slipped her arms into a beige knitted cardigan. 'I won't bother with me coat, it's not cold out.'

Jack watched her picking the door keys out of the glass dish on the sideboard. 'Don't be too late. I get lonely once I've read the *Echo*.'

'I've told Ruthie she's to be home by ten at the latest, and if I can manage to shut me mate up, I'll get home for the same time.' She waved from the door. 'See yer later. Ta-ra.'

When Molly opened the front door, there was Nellie standing waiting for her. 'What are yer standing there for? I would have knocked for yer.'

'I don't trust yer, girl, 'cos many's the time yer've bent down when yer were passing our window so I wouldn't see yer. Once bitten, twice shy, that's my motto, girl.'

Molly tutted as she bent her arm. 'Stick yer leg in, sunshine, and put a smile on yer face. Anyone looking at yer would think we were on our way to a wake.'

Nellie's body shook. 'Ay, that's a good one, girl! Yer know, yer can be funny sometimes. Not very often, but sometimes.' She tilted her head to gaze up into her mate's face. 'I've never been to a wake, have you, girl?'

'I haven't, sunshine, and I don't fancy going to one. Why, do you?'

Nellie shook her head, and her chins quivered at the thought. 'No, girl, I don't. I don't know what they do there, or why they have them. I mean, like, what's the point of a wake if the person is dead? They can't suddenly wake up and join in the fun, can they?' Her warped sense of humour got the better of her. And even though she knew Molly would disapprove she couldn't keep her thoughts to herself. They were too funny. 'If I went in a house where someone had died, and took some flowers with me to put on the coffin, I'd jump out of me skin if the corpse sat up and thanked me for them.'

Molly stopped in her tracks. 'Nellie, may God forgive yer, for that's a terrible thing to say. Yer should never make fun of someone dying.'

As she was expecting this reaction, Nellie was ready for it. 'Well, I thought it was funny, anyhow. And it's their own fault for calling it a wake.'

Molly looked down at her. 'I shouldn't say it, 'cos it makes me as bad as you, but the way yer said it, well, it was funny.'

They carried on walking, but hadn't gone very far when Molly stopped again. 'Yer won't mention it in front of me ma and da, will yer? I don't think they'd appreciate yer humour, and it might upset them. Yer might not know it, but they always hold a wake in Ireland when anyone dies.'

'I'll be as good as gold, girl, so don't be worrying.' They had reached the top end of the street by this time, and Nellie asked, 'Who are we going to first, our Lily or your Jill?'

'I'd like to go to Jill first, so I can see the baby before she's put down for the night. Not that she sleeps all night – she'll need feeding three times before morning. But Jill wants to get her used to going to bed at a certain time. I agree with her, too, 'cos even when they're only weeks old, they get used to a pattern.'

'Right, that suits me, girl. I've got all the time in the world, so I'll fit in with anything yer want to do.'

Steve opened the door and his face lit up when he saw their visitors. 'Hello, Mam, and you, Mrs B. This is a nice surprise, come on in.'

'I hope the baby's not in bed yet,' Molly said, as she passed him on her way in. 'I like to see her every day so she gets to know me voice.'

Nellie pulled on the back of her cardigan. 'Ay, don't forget this is one house where we are both equal. I'm a grandma and ye're a grandma. Yer rub it in when we're in Doreen's about me being an adopted grandma, but yer can't do it here. This is neutral territory.'

'What's neutral territory?' Jill asked. 'Are you and me mam having an argument over my baby?'

'Now just as if!' Nellie put on a pained expression. 'When have yer ever heard me and me best mate argue?'

Jill had always been a beautiful girl, with her blond hair, bright blue eyes, lovely complexion and a slim figure. But motherhood had added to her beauty. She looked so happy and contented with her own little family. Her and her beloved Steve, the baby, and Lizzie Corkhill, their adopted grannie. 'Auntie Nellie, I have heard you and my mam arguing at least once every day of my life. I've never seen yer come to blows, but argue, yes, very often.'

'What yer've heard isn't real arguments, sunshine,' Molly said. 'We're only messing. If we ever did have a real argument, the whole street would know about it.' She bent to kiss Lizzie Corkhill on the cheek. 'While me and Nellie are having a fight to see who gets to the baby first, her third grandma is sitting here as proud as Punch, nursing her.'

Lizzie grinned. 'I was going to say I'd hand her over to yer, Molly, but with Nellie giving me daggers, I think Jill can take the baby and sort the pair of yer out.'

Molly shook her head. 'No, let me mate have her, or she'll have a cob on all night and I couldn't stand that. We're calling to see Lily and Archie when we leave here, then we're off to me ma's, and I'd have to put up with her having a face like a wet week. Let her have little Molly for ten minutes, and then I'll take over.'

Nellie pushed her out of the way and bent to take the baby. 'Come to yer grandma, sweetheart, and let me have a little cuddle.' With her chubby hands she pressed the baby to the softness of her bosom, and the tiny face smiled up at her. 'Ay, she knows me, Molly. She's smiling at me.'

'Let's see,' Molly said, her head over Nellie's shoulder. 'Oh, yeah, she really does know yer, sunshine. She must recognise yer voice.'

Steve was leaning on the sideboard, pride written all over his face. He loved everyone in this room in a different kind of way. He loved his mother dearly, for she had always been there for him and the other kids. And she had made their home happy with her warmth and humour. And Mrs B., now his mother-in-law, had always been like a second mother to him and he loved her very much because through her he was married to the girl he'd adored since he could toddle. And Corker's mam had been so good to him and Jill, giving them a home when they first got married. He loved her like a grandma. Then there was the baby who had come along to make his life complete. He couldn't find enough words to say how proud he was of that small bundle of humanity, or the right words to say how much he loved her.

'Steve, will yer put the kettle on and make a pot of tea, please?' Jill saw him shake his head and laughed. 'Yer were miles away then. What were yer thinking of?'

His dimples appeared. 'Yer'd say I was soppy if I told yer. I'll put the kettle on.'

Jill grabbed him round the waist. 'Oh, no, yer don't, my love. Tell us what yer were thinking and we won't think ye're soppy.'

'All right, if yer must know. I was thinking how lucky I am. A beautiful wife, a lovely mother and mother-in-law, a new granny, and a wonderful daughter. I love everyone in this room, and I don't care if yer do think I'm a sissy. If I am, then I'm a very happy and contented sissy.' He cupped his wife's face and kissed her. 'And now I'll put the kettle on.'

Molly whispered in Nellie's ear. 'Yer did a good job bringing up a son like Steve. Not many men would say what he's just said. They might think it, but wouldn't be able to put it into words. He's a credit to yer, sunshine, and I take my hat off to yer.'

Lizzie couldn't help but hear, and she nodded her head as she brought her rocking chair to a halt. 'Yer'll never speak any truer words than that, Molly. He's a wonderful husband; they don't come any better. It's a pleasure having him and Jill here.

They've brought a lot of joy into my life. And I'll tell yer something else: that baby will never go short on love.'

With tears stinging the back of her eyes, Nellie sniffed. 'I did my best with all the children. It was probably the one thing I was ever good at.'

Molly put an arm across her shoulders. 'I think yer were a marvellous mother, sunshine. All your children love the bones of yer.'

'Will yer stop being so nice to me, Molly Bennett? I'm not used to it, and yer'll have me bawling me eyes out.'

Jill peered down into her face. 'Can yer take just one more compliment from yer daughter-in-law? I have always wanted to tell yer, but was too shy. I've plucked up the courage now because the compliments are flying, and I'd like to thank yer for making my husband into the man he is. Kind, thoughtful, and loving. I reckon I'm the luckiest girl in the world.'

Steve called from the kitchen. 'The kettle's boiled and I've filled the teapot. But yer better come and do the rest, love, 'cos yer know I usually spill tea into the saucer. And I've looked in the biscuit tin and it seems to be pretty bare. So you'd better be the one to tell me mam there's no custard creams, 'cos she won't hit you.'

'What, no custard creams?' Nellie narrowed her eyes and tried to look fierce. 'What sort of daughter-in-law are yer what doesn't have custard creams in the house?'

Lizzie chuckled. 'He's only pulling yer leg. There's always a packet of them in the larder for when yer come. If we're getting low, I run to the corner shop for more, just to make sure. It's a standing joke in the house.'

Nellie, who was swaying with the baby held close to her bosom, smiled down into the face that already showed signs of blond hair and blue eyes. 'Did yer hear that, sweetheart? Well,

I don't think it's a joke having no custard creams in the house.' She gave the baby one last kiss, then handed her over to Molly. 'I think my time is up, girl, so you can have her until it's time to go. Otherwise yer'll moan all the way round to yer ma's, and I couldn't stand that, not after all the praise I've been getting. Not that I've let it go to me head, like, but I'd like to savour it for a bit longer. And if you've got a face on yer like a wet week, well, it'll take all the pleasure away.'

'I'll go and give Steve a hand,' Jill said, knowing her mother wouldn't let a remark like that pass without a quick reply. 'The tea won't be long.' In the kitchen, she walked into Steve's waiting arms. 'Not a word, love, just listen.'

'Nellie McDonough, yer were crafty enough to pass the baby over before pulling me to pieces. Yer knew I couldn't raise me voice 'cos it would frighten her. Well, I can be just as crafty as you, and I'll smile at little Molly while I'm talking to yer so she'll think I'm telling her a joke.' She tickled the baby's tummy and when she gurfled Molly said sweetly, 'Anyone listening to my mate would think I was a long string of misery, sweetheart, but I'm not. At least I don't talk about taking flowers to a wake, and the corpse sitting up in the coffin and thanking me for them.'

Lizzie's chair stopped rocking and she spluttered, 'Yer didn't say that, did yer, Nellie?'

Nellie's face was contorted into every shape imaginable. 'Ye're not half two-faced, girl, have I ever told yer that before? Yer tell me to keep me mouth shut about the wake, and then yer go and bring it up yerself! And if that's not being two-faced, well I don't know what is.'

Jill came in with the teapot, followed by Steve carrying a tray. 'What's all this about a wake?' She put the pot down before shivering and rubbing her arms. 'It's not a subject I'd like to talk about.'

Keeping her voice low so as not to frighten the baby, Molly said, 'It was just me and Nellie talking, and the word happened to come up. We didn't have a conversation about it, just a few words.'

Nellie huffed. 'It was you what used the word first, girl, telling me I looked so miserable anyone would think I was going to a wake. And in the end yer said yer thought what I said was very funny. That's before yer told me not to mention it in front of yer ma in case she didn't see the funny side.'

There was affection in Steve's eyes when he looked at his mother. 'Go on, Mam, tell us right from the beginning.' He put his arm round Jill's waist. 'It's only a joke. Yer won't be frightened of going to bed tonight.'

Nellie was in her element. She started off with where she was standing outside Molly's house. And she added more to the story than there really was, doing all the actions and changing the tone of her voice. Her actions and the expressions on her face were funnier than the tale, for she really put her heart into it. And when she came to the part where she was putting the flowers on the coffin when the corpse sat up and thanked her, she jumped back so quickly for effect, Jill closed her eyes and gripped Steve's hand. But Steve, Lizzie, and even Molly, thought it was hilarious and roared their heads off.

There was so much noise in the room they didn't hear the knocking at the door, and the rap that came on the window was so unexpected, Jill nearly had a heart attack. 'Ooh, that gave me the fright of me life. You go and see who it is, Steve. Yer'll not get me to the door for love nor money.'

Steve was chuckling when he opened the door to his sister, Lily, and her husband Archie. Only married at Easter, they showed all the signs of newly weds, never more than a few inches separating them, except when they were at work. Lily had kept her job on in spite of Archie's wanting her to pack in. She loved her work, and her workmates, and also the independence, even though Archie had a very good job and was more than generous. Right now they were holding hands as they looked up at Steve.

'Well, this is our night for visitors, but come in and join the crowd.' Steve held the door wide. 'Have yer been knocking long?'

Lily nodded. 'We nearly banged the door down, but with the racket going on inside we knew we wouldn't be heard. Hence the rap on the window.' She grinned. 'I resorted to one of me mam's tricks.'

There was bedlam in the room for a short while, as greetings, hugs and kisses were exchanged, and everyone seemed to be talking at once. Lizzie was as happy as a child in a sand pit, for the more visitors there were the more she liked it. She'd spent years living alone when Corker was away at sea for long periods, so it was a treat for her to hear so many voices and so much laughter. But the noise was too much for baby Molly, and she began to whimper.

'Ay, keep yer voices down,' Molly warned, holding the baby close. 'The poor mite is terrified.'

Jill held out her arms. 'I'll take her upstairs and bed her down, Mam. It's past her bedtime, anyway.'

'We're not staying,' Lily told them. 'We only called to tell yer me and Archie are going to the pictures, in case yer intended paying us a visit. We knew me mam and Auntie Molly were here, 'cos I saw them through the window.'

'We were going to call on yer,' Nellie said, her chubby face screwed up in a smile. 'Me and Molly are doing the rounds, and yer were next on our visiting list. But we can call another night, girl, so you and Archie poppy off or yer'll miss the beginning of the big picture.'

'What was all the laughing about, Mrs Mac?' Archie got on well with his mother-in-law. He thought she was the funniest person he'd ever met, and the warmest-hearted. 'We were knocking the door down and yer couldn't hear us for the racket yer were making.'

Molly gripped his arm. 'Are yer going to see a horror picture where there's people dying by the minutes, or are yer going to see a comedy?'

'It's a tough gangster film, Mrs B., with James Cagney as the bad guy. One of the blokes I work with said it was very good.'

'Then I suggest yer ask yer mother-in-law some other time what the laughing was about. Otherwise it might spoil the picture for yer, 'cos yer can only stand so much death in one day.'

It was Lily's turn to pull on Archie's arm. 'It's not a gangster picture, is it? Yer know I don't like them. I sit with me eyes closed through most of them.'

Archie grinned. 'It's only a picture, love, and I'll be there to hold yer hand.'

Lily wasn't convinced. 'Why can't we go to the Astoria instead? Cary Grant and Jean Arthur are on there, in a comedy.'

Archie lifted his hands in surrender. 'I'll give in quietly, 'cos I know if I don't there'll be sulking all night.' He was well over six foot, was Archie, and he had to bend to look into Nellie's face. 'Is it you that Lily takes after for being stubborn, Mrs Mac? Once she gets something in her head there's no moving her.' He put a finger under Nellie's chin and lifted her face. 'But I'll tame her eventually, you'll see. I'm giving her an easy ride 'cos we've not long been married, but she'll not have it so easy when I start putting me foot down.'

'Ooh, I wouldn't recommend that, lad, it would be a bad move on your part.' Nellie winked up at him. 'My George tried putting his foot down with me, but he only tried it once. I stamped on it so hard he couldn't walk for a week. He said I'd broken every one of his toes.' She chuckled. 'I hadn't, though. I'd only broken three of them.'

'Oh, I get the message.' Archie turned round to face his wife. 'What picture house did yer want to go to, my love?'

Molly, thinking it was going to be very late when she and Nellie finally got to her ma's, tried to hurry them along. 'If yer don't make a move, the big picture will be halfway through.'

'Yes, me Auntie Molly's right.' Lily tugged on his arm. 'They say women talk a lot, but yer don't do so bad, Archie Higgins. Come on, let's be having yer.'

Lily and Archie had just left when Jill came down the stairs. 'I think the noise upset the baby. I couldn't get her off so easy tonight. She's asleep now, though, so we can have a cup of tea in peace.'

'Me and Nellie will have to be on our way after we've had a drink, sunshine, 'cos I don't want to be too late getting to me ma's. Her and me da go to bed early some nights.'

'But a cup of tea will go down well, girl. Make us refreshed for the long walk, like.' Nellie turned her head from Molly before adding, 'And a couple of custard creams will give us the strength.'

'Oh, aye she'll need her health and strength for that walk.' Molly laughed. 'It takes all of five minutes.' Then she added, 'Unless we're unlucky enough to meet Elsie Flanaghan.'

Nellie even had an answer for that. 'If we met Elsie Flanaghan, girl, it wouldn't be us what was unlucky, it would be her.'

The two friends got the same warm reception when they got to the Jacksons'. Bridie and Bob were always happy to see the daughter who was ever there for them.

Tommy had known his mam and Auntie Nellie were coming, and the noise of the knock had barely died down before the door was open. 'Where the heck have you two been? We expected yer ages ago.'

Molly lifted her cheek for a kiss, even though she'd had one off him when he'd called in from work, as he did every night. 'Oh, well, yer know things never run to course, sunshine. We stayed longer at Jill's than we intended to. Lily and Archie came over to say they were going to the pictures, and their five minutes turned into twenty.' She could feel the strings of her heart pull when she saw her ma and da sitting close together on the couch. What a fine example they were of happy married bliss. They'd married young and spent a lifetime loving and caring for each other. And their only daughter had followed their example, then three of their four grandchildren.

Molly bent to kiss her parents, asking, 'How are the two lovebirds tonight? I must say ye're both looking very healthy, and also very smart. Ye're better turned out than I am!'

'Oh, Rosie makes sure of that, right enough, me darlin',' Bridie said. 'Sure, she'll not let the wind blow on us.'

Tommy was standing with his arms round his wife's waist, happy and content as ever. And the lovely Rosie was always happy in his arms, for wasn't he her dearly beloved husband? 'I'll not be taking all the credit, Auntie Molly, for isn't Auntie Bridget one for being independent? I've only to turn me back, so I have, and she's got a duster in her hand.'

'Ay, don't I get a look-in here?' Nellie asked, not liking to be left out of anything. 'I'm not a statue, yer know. I can move and speak.'

Rosie escaped from Tommy's arms and within seconds Nellie was held tight and being smothered with kisses. 'We'd not be leaving yer out, Auntie Nellie, for sure, it's yer dear self we love the bones of. And that's the truth of it.'

Tommy was next in line. And as always, he had the right words to use. 'I never think of yer as just a visitor, Auntie Nellie, for to me ye're one of the family. Like Jill, Doreen and Ruthie, I've always looked on yer as our second mam.'

As Bob was to say to Bridie in bed later, he would swear that Nellie grew six inches in front of his very eyes. She loved to be the centre of attraction, and when the praises came her way her cup of happiness was overflowing. 'It's nice of yer to say that, lad, really nice. Of course I've always looked on Molly's kids as me own, same as she has with mine. Just one big happy family, which is getting bigger and bigger. The way we're going on, every house in the street will be occupied by a McDonough, Bennett or Higgins.'

Molly winked at her ma before saying, 'What d'yer mean by saying the way *we're* going on? You and me are not likely to be adding any more children to the population, sunshine. Yer mean the way our children are going on.'

Nellie's face creased into layers of fat. 'Trust you to stick a spoke in the wheel, Molly Bennett. Honest to God, ye're enough to drive anyone to drink. Does it matter whether I say we, or they? The world's not going to come to an end because my bloody English isn't what it should be. Everybody else understands what I'm talking about, so yer can just sod off and leave me in me ignorance. Yer see, I'm as happy as a pig in . . . well, you know what.'

'Yes, we all know what yer mean, Nellie, so there's no need to spell it out for us.'

Nellie looked downhearted. 'Ah, that's a pity, that is, 'cos it's the one word I do know how to spell.'

Bridie laughed, Bob roared until the tears ran down his cheeks, and Tommy and Rosie held on to each other. Over his wife's shoulder, Tommy asked, 'Mam, have yer ever known a time when Auntie Nellie hasn't had an answer to anything yer said?'

Molly shook her head. 'No, sunshine, I can't remember a time when me mate hasn't been quick to wipe me eye. But I don't give in easy. I'll bide me time, 'cos the day will surely come when I get one over on her.'

Nellie huffed. 'Yer'd have to be up with the larks to get one over on me, girl. If yer take my advice, yer won't bother getting out of bed.'

'Oh, ye're not better at everything than I am, sunshine, so don't let yer head get any bigger. I can beat yer at a game of cards any day.'

'Will yer be having a cup of tea, me darlin'?' Bridie asked. 'And I made a tray of fairy cakes, and, sure, ain't they as light as a feather?'

Molly could sense Nellie was going to rub her tummy in expectation, so she got in before her. 'Ma, we've not long had a cup of tea in Jill's. I couldn't drink another one right now. How about a game of cards? Then I'll feel more like a drink.'

'And a fairy cake, girl. Don't forget we'll feel like a fairy cake, as well.' There was a message in Nellie's eyes, daring her friend to disagree. 'It'll give us the strength for that long walk home.'

They had two games of cards, one won by Molly, the other by her mother. Then they had a cup of tea and a fairy cake. At least in Molly's case the word cake was singular, whereas in Nellie's it was plural. For she just couldn't resist the offer of a second, and then a third.

It was a quarter to ten when Molly looked at the clock. 'Come on, Nellie, I promised Jack I'd be home by ten.'

'I'll walk you and Auntie Nellie home, Mam,' Tommy said. 'It's dark now, and it won't take me fifteen minutes there and back.'

'There's no need for that, sunshine, but thanks for the offer. Yer see, I'm never afraid when I'm out with me mate, 'cos there's not a man breathing she couldn't get the better of if it came to a fight. They'd be on the ground before they knew what had hit them.'

Nellie pushed back her chair and jumped up. With her fists curled, she took up a fighting stance. Then punching the air, while doing a bit of nifty footwork, she did her version of shadow boxing. Much to the amusement of her audience, every time she threw a punch, she said, 'Take that, yer bugger.' And for someone carrying so much weight, she bounced like a rubber ball, as light on her feet as one of Bridie's fairy cakes.

The two mates were linking arms on their way home, saying goodnight as they passed neighbours who were standing talking. Then Molly felt Nellie squeezing her arm. 'What is it, sunshine?'

'Yer know what day it is tomorrow, girl?'

'Well, I know it's Monday today, and I know that Tuesday usually follows. Why?'

'I was thinking about Claire and that man what comes in her shop to have his shirts and collars laundered. Monday he brings them in, so she said, and he picks them up on Tuesday, eleven o'clock on the dot.'

'Yes, I know, sunshine. I was there when Claire said it, or had yer forgotten?'

'I'm not going to say anything about yer being sarky, girl, 'cos yer don't take no notice of me. So I'll forget yer said it, and go back to what I had in mind.'

'Oh, what had yer got in mind, sunshine? Go on, I'm all ears.'

'Well, we could walk down to the shop tomorrow and see him for ourselves. It's not far to walk, just down the side of the greengrocer's to the main road.'

'What would we want to do that for?'

'Just so we could see for ourselves what he's like. It won't do us no harm, just a few minutes' walk.'

'I'm not really interested in what he looks like, sunshine. And anyway, what would Claire think of us? She'd think we were a pair of nosy beggars, that's what. She wouldn't be very happy to see us spying on her. I know if it was me I'd go mad, and I wouldn't want to be friends with someone who was that nosy.'

'Don't be getting yer knickers in a twist, girl. Yer take things too much to heart. Claire wouldn't know what we were up to. She wouldn't have to see us.'

'Of course she'd see us. We're not exactly invisible.'

'We wouldn't have to stand facing the shop! I know where it is, and we could stand on the next block and just see him coming and going. Claire won't even know we're there.'

'But I don't see any point! What good would it do if we did see him? We couldn't tell Claire what we thought of him, so why bother?'

'I don't know, girl, yer can be really bloody miserable when yer want to be. We ask her enough questions about him, and isn't that being nosy? I'd just like to see him for meself, that's all. I don't care if yer do think I'm nosy, I'd still like to see what kind of man he is. Is he a toff, is he well dressed and handsome? I'm curious, girl, that's all. I don't want the ruddy man for meself.' They came to a halt outside Nellie's house, and she said. 'All right, girl, if yer don't want to go, we won't go. I just thought it would put a bit of excitement back in our lives, like when we open the McDonough and Bennett Private Detective Agency. Wouldn't cost nothing and wouldn't hurt no one.'

Molly was being talked round. 'Nellie, how many times do I have to remind yer that it's the Bennett and McDonough Private Detective Agency, not the other way round? So when we go tomorrow just remember who's boss.'

Nellie beamed. 'I'll come to yours a bit earlier for me morning cuppa, so we can get down to the laundry about ten to eleven.' She stood on the top step to slide the key in the lock. 'Goodnight and God bless, girl.'

'Goodnight and God bless, sunshine.'

Chapter Thirteen

As they passed the greengrocer's the next morning, the two friends waved to Billy who was serving behind the counter inside the shop. Then they turned the corner into the street that ran down to Westminster Road. Molly wasn't feeling good about this; in fact she was very apprehensive.

'Nellie, I'm not sure we're doing the right thing. I feel like a sneak, and I'd die of humiliation if Claire happened to see us.'

'She won't see us, girl, unless she can see through thick brick walls. We won't go near the shop, we'll stand a block away from it.' The little woman glanced up at her mate. 'I hope yer didn't lose any ruddy sleep over this? What about when we were playing detectives and trailing people? Yer never worried about that so much.'

'That's because we were doing the right thing, helping someone we knew. What we're doing now is just out of curiosity, and it won't help anyone.' Molly sighed. 'It certainly won't help my nerves, 'cos they're shot to pieces.'

'Well, I think ye're being ridiculous.' Nellie's chins were in complete agreement with her. 'It's a public road and we have as much right to be there as anyone. And anyway, if Claire did see us, we could say we were going to a shop in Westminster Road 'cos Beryl Mowbray told us they had cheap shoes.'

Molly's jaw dropped. 'Nellie, telling lies comes too easily to you. Yer don't seem to see any harm in telling whopping big fibs. They roll off yer tongue, one after the other.'

'Ah, now ye're exaggerating, girl, 'cos they don't roll off me tongue one after the other. It isn't easy making up lies, yer know. There's a bit of headwork attached. Besides, I never tell one after the other. I always leave a few words in between.'

Molly gave another sigh before giving up. She could talk till she was blue in the face, but it wouldn't have any effect on Nellie. Her mate didn't see any harm in bending the truth a little, and even Father Kelly couldn't convince her otherwise, even though he'd been trying for the last twenty-odd years. Giving her six Hail Marys as a penance was no deterrent. He had to admit she had one redeeming feature, though: she never pretended to be holier than thou, and was quite open in confessing to her sins.

The main road was busy, with women going about their shopping, delivery vans in front of some of the shops, and a man sweeping the pavements. 'It's a good road for shopping, this is,' Nellie said. 'We should come down here more often.'

'Don't push yer luck, sunshine, 'cos this is not going to be a regular outing. If yer think I'm coming here again with yer next week, then yer've got another think coming. I'll be glad when we're back in Scotland Road, where we belong. The shops there and in Walton have suited me for over twenty years, and with the grace of God they'll suit me for the next twenty.'

Nellie stopped in the middle of a parade of shops. 'Better not go any further, girl, 'cos the laundry's in the middle of the next block.' She didn't believe they were doing anything wrong; lots of people snooped on their neighbours. 'I don't see why we can't walk in the shop, as bold as brass, and tell Claire we were just passing.'

Molly huffed. 'And yer don't think she'd put two and two together, and remember she'd told us what time the man came each morning?'

A two-year-old child could not have looked more innocent than Nellie when she said, 'Did she, girl? I don't remember. But then I've got a head like a sieve.' She looked into Molly's eyes. 'See, girl, it would be as easy as that.'

'It would be to someone who was used to telling fibs, sunshine, but as it happens I am not used to it. And yer may not know it, but every time a lie passes your lips, I say a prayer for yer to be forgiven.'

'That's real nice of yer, girl, and I appreciate it. But it's too late for yer to change yer mind and go home now, 'cos there's a man going into the shop. And he's very well dressed from what I could see of him. Nice trilby, posh suit, and if I'd have been a bit nearer I could have told yer what colour his shoes were.'

'Are you pulling my leg, sunshine? 'Cos if yer are I wouldn't think it was funny. Did yer really see a man like that going into the shop?'

'Cross my heart, girl, cross me heart. Yer'll see for yerself when he comes out. I bet he's the man Claire talks about. He's very tall, and I'd guess he's around forty, maybe a few years older.' Nellie tutted. 'Yer call me nosy, say ye're not interested, then ask me what the man's wearing. I'm sorry I can't tell yer whether he's wearing long johns, girl, but perhaps when I get better acquainted with him I'll find out.'

Molly moved from one foot to the other. 'He's a long time, Nellie. It shouldn't take him this long to pay his money over the counter and collect his laundry.'

'Oh dear, oh dear, oh dear! We don't want him to come out too soon, girl, we want him to stand chatting to Claire for a while. The longer he's there, the more interested he must be. And the more Claire will have to tell us on Friday.'

'Nellie, if you put yer imagination to good use, yer could write a book. Yer come out with things I would never dream up in a month of Sundays.'

Her friend chuckled. 'I'd need a dictionary to find the big words, girl, and I'd need you to tell me what they mean. And if I couldn't use any swear words, then it wouldn't be me, would it? So it would be a very short book.'

Molly, who had been keeping an eye on the shop in the next block, gave Nellie a dig. 'Ay, sunshine, is that him?'

'Yeah, that's him.' Nellie was bursting with excitement. 'Ay, look, he's turned back to look in the shop, and he's raised his hat! Ooh, that's a proper gent for yer.'

'Oh, dear God,' Molly groaned, 'he's coming this way. What shall we do, Nellie, walk past him?'

'Just stay where yer are, girl, and pretend we're talking. Then we can get a good look at him.' Nellie huffed. 'For heaven's sake pull yerself together, girl, and start talking. Tell me what we're having tonight for our dinner.'

The man passed them without a second glance, and they were able to get a good look at him. When he was out of earshot, Nellie said, 'Ay, he's not half good looking.' Her eyes followed him as he walked briskly on his way. 'I bet that suit didn't come from Burton's. It will have set him back a pretty penny. He's definitely not short of a bob or two.'

'Can we make our way back now, sunshine?' Molly was a nervous wreck in case Claire spotted them. 'The sooner we're away from here, the happier I'll be.'

Nellie linked her arm and they turned to face the way back. 'I don't know why yer worry so much, girl, 'cos it's not good for yer. Yer'll not live a long and happy life if yer worry over every little thing what's not worth worrying about.'

'I felt guilty, 'cos Claire is a friend of ours and I don't think we should have been spying on her. It's got nothing to do with us whether a man who comes in the shop talks to her or not. And I'm damn sure that Claire would tell us that if she knew what we've been up to.'

'Ye're looking at everything the wrong way round, girl, that's your trouble. Why don't yer see it from my point of view? Claire is our friend, and because she is, we are taking an interest in her love life. We want to make sure that any man what fancies her is good enough for her.'

'That's not why we came down here today, Nellie McDonough, and you know it. We came because ye're a nosy beggar who likes to know everyone's business. And I came because I'm daft enough to give in to yer.'

They walked in silence for a short while, and then Molly could feel her friend's body shaking. 'What are yer finding so funny, Nellie? 'Cos I don't think it's a bit funny. We're a pair of nosy beggars what should know better, and I'll tell yer straight I am not feeling very proud of meself.'

'I don't feel the least bit guilty, girl, so don't be harping on it. At least when Claire comes on Friday and talks about the man, we'll know what he looks like. But that wasn't why I was having a little laugh with meself.'

'I know I'm daft for asking, but why were yer laughing then?'

'I was wondering whether the toff liked women what have a voluptuous body. I know Claire's beautiful, with the face of an angel, but if I put a pillowcase over me head when we were in bed, he wouldn't know the difference. And by the time I'd finished with him, he wouldn't ever be interested in any other woman. And just imagine, girl, if I had a man what was rich, and money was no object, I could lie on the couch all day stuffing meself with custard creams and cream slices.' She pretended to let out a long sigh. 'Now, that would be my idea of heaven, and I'm afraid Saint Peter couldn't match that. I mean, there's no comparison between a halo and a cream slice from Hanley's.'

Molly didn't want to laugh, but she couldn't help it.

She might have been able to suppress it if she could rid her mind of the picture of Nellie lying in bed with a pillowcase over her head. But she wasn't going to let her mate get away with thinking she was the only one who could raise a laugh, while Molly was a stick-in-the-mud. 'Nellie McDonough, what am I going to do with yer? Ye're past the post. Incorrigible.'

Nellie's eyes slid sideways, to see if her friend looked as though she was serious, or was taking the mickey out of her. Then she thought, oh, sod it, why worry. 'Oh, I agree with yer, girl. I'm definitely that.'

Molly knew when she was beaten. She should do – it happened every day. 'I'm glad we agree on something, sunshine. It doesn't happen very often. So, all we have to think about now is what to have for dinner tonight.'

'Don't bother me with it right now, girl, I've got too much on me mind.' With every step Nellie took, her hips swayed, pushing her mate sideways. And Molly had to hold herself stiff so she wouldn't be pushed into the gutter and into the path of a car or a bus. But it was no use telling Nellie. As she said, if Mae West could walk like that, why couldn't she?

'What have yer got on yer mind, sunshine, apart from what to get in for dinner?'

'Yer'd be surprised what I've got on me mind, girl. I'm not always empty-headed. For instance, right now I'm wondering how Claire can attract a toff with loads of money, when all she's got going for her is that she's beautiful. And yer know what they say about beauty being in the eye of the beholder. So, if she can land herself with someone what's got more money than sense, why couldn't I?'

'Is that what ye're asking yerself, sunshine? Well, if I can stick me oar in, I'd remind yer that Claire is a nice woman, as well as being beautiful.'

'So, are yer telling me I'm not a nice woman, and I'm as ugly as sin?'

'Ye're a lovely woman, sunshine, me very best mate. And ye're certainly not as ugly as sin. I mean, your George isn't blind, is he? Yer were beautiful in his eyes – that's why he married yer.'

Nellie stopped in her tracks. 'Are you being funny, Molly Bennett?'

'Of course I'm not being funny. What are yer on about?'

'Because yer know my feller's short-sighted. He can't see a thing without his bleeding glasses.' Nellie was in her element now she could rile her mate. 'So what ye're saying is, the first night I met George, when I was in the Grafton with me mates, and he asked me to dance, he thought I was a blond-haired, blue-eyed beauty? And by the time he'd saved enough money to buy himself a pair of glasses, we were married and he couldn't get out of it?'

Molly roared. 'Oh, Nellie, I have never known anyone with such a vivid imagination as you've got. What a pity it is that yer don't know enough big words to write a book.'

'You know all the big words, girl, so I could tell yer the story and you could write it down. I'd always mug yer if I made any money out of it.'

Molly shook her head so vigorously it nearly fell off. 'Oh, I don't think so, sunshine, 'cos I've got a sneaking feeling most of the story would take place in your bedroom. I'd be far too embarrassed.'

'There'd be no need for yer to be embarrassed, girl, 'cos my feller wouldn't even know yer were there. I told yer, he's short-sighted.' Nellie's tummy was shaking at her thoughts. 'Mind you, having said that, I couldn't guarantee he wouldn't grab hold of yer by mistake, and he'd have yer flat on yer back in the bed before he realised the woman he was wrestling with didn't have a figure like mine.'

'I think yer can forget about the book, sunshine, 'cos me conscience wouldn't let me write down the words yer were saying. I'm not a prude, but I do draw the line at some things. So forget it. Put it right out of yer mind and concentrate on what we can get for dinner for a change.'

'I had yer going there for a while, didn't I, girl? And just for the record, my feller's got perfect eyesight. He said he's glad he has, 'cos he can see every inch of me, and wallow in the beauty of me voluptuous body.'

'Nellie, the dinner, if yer don't mind.'

'What have yer been up to today, love?' Jack asked. 'Have you and Nellie done anything exciting?'

'Not really.' Molly knew her husband would think she was crazy if she told him what she'd been up to with Nellie. 'The most exciting thing we did was go to the butcher's and the baker's. And it doesn't come more exciting than that.'

'Why don't you and Auntie Nellie go to the pictures one afternoon?' Ruthie asked, 'It's only sixpence in the stalls at a matinee.' There was a reason behind the offer she was about to make. 'Me and me dad would pay for yer between us, wouldn't we, Dad?'

'I think yer mam could pay for herself if she really wanted to go to the pictures,' Jack answered. 'I know she doesn't get enough money to throw around, but I'm sure she would have the odd sixpence to spare.'

Molly could tell by her daughter's face that there was something in the wind. 'What brought on this bout of generosity, sunshine? It's usually you trying to cadge off me, so what are yer after?'

'I'm not after anything, Mam.' But the girl's blush told a different story. And after a few seconds, Ruthie decided it was now or never. 'Yes, I am, Mam, but promise yer won't bite me head off?'

'Oh, I can promise I won't bite yer head off, sunshine, 'cos after eating this big dinner I won't be hungry. Anyway, whatever it is ye're after, get it off yer chest and I'll give it very careful consideration.'

'Then promise yer won't shout at me.'

'Okay, I'll keep me voice down. So come on, out with it.'

'Me and Bella were talking to Gordon Corkhill in the street last night, and I told him we were going to the first house pictures one night this week, if yer said we could. And he offered to take us, and pay for us.'

Jack lowered his head and concentrated on spearing a potato with his fork. This was something he'd leave to his wife to sort out.

'Just Gordon with you and Bella? No other lad?'

'No, only Gordon. We don't know any other lads, only the Corkhills and Jeff Mowbray.'

'Oh, so yer Auntie Nellie must have got it wrong, then?'

Ruthie's heart sank. 'Why, what did Auntie Nellie say?'

'That a boy in the next street, by the name of Johnny Stewart, was sweet on yer, and follows yer everywhere.'

'How does Auntie Nellie know that?' Ruthie was indignant. 'I'm in Bella's nearly every night, and when I'm not there, we're only in the street.' Then she remembered. 'Oh, we sometimes go window shopping, and there's nothing wrong with that. There's not much else for us to do.'

'So, yer don't know this Johnny Stewart, then?'

'Yes, I know him,' Ruthie said. 'Me and Bella are sometimes on the same tram as him coming home from work.' There was no need for all this, the girl was thinking. Why did her Auntie Nellie have to go telling tales? 'You know Johnny Stewart, Mam. He's lived in the next street all his life. He's nearly fifteen, the same age as Gordon, and they're mates.'

Jack came to the conclusion his daughter needed a bit of help. 'I know the Stewarts. The father drinks in the corner pub. He's a nice respectable bloke, doesn't use bad language and is always polite. Like meself, he's not a heavy drinker, just the odd pint at the weekend. Johnny works with him.'

Molly grinned across the table at her daughter. 'That's a good reference yer dad's given, sunshine. So in six or seven years' time, if this Johnny comes asking for yer hand in marriage, then he's in with a good chance. That is, he stands as much chance as Gordon or Jeff who, so I'm told, are also in the running.'

'Oh, Mam, don't be daft. And yer can tell Auntie Nellie she talks too much.'

'I'll tell her that tomorrow, sunshine. But right now, I'll remind you that you are still only fourteen years of age and too young to be going out with boys.'

There was mischief in Ruthie's eyes. 'Mam, I have just turned fourteen years and seven months. Which means I'm nearer fifteen than fourteen.'

'That is still too young, sunshine, so give yerself another year or two before yer start thinking about boyfriends.'

Ruthie thought she might get more sympathy from her father. 'Dad, how old was me mam when yer first met her?'

Jack was stumped. Should he tell the truth or embroider it a little to suit his wife? But it would be a stupid thing to lie over, and if Molly didn't like it, he'd soon get round her. 'Yer mam was only fourteen when I first laid eyes on her. She'd just left school and came to work in the store room of the factory where I worked. Where I still work, come to that. Anyway, that's when I first saw her. But I was sixteen and thought meself a man, while she was just a kid as far as I was concerned.' He gazed across at Molly and knew his wife was looking back to those years, as he was. 'Then after about eight or nine months, I began to notice how pretty she was. Long blond hair, bright blue eyes, and a figure that promised to be a smasher. And although I was too shy to talk to her, I started to give her a smile. And honest to God I felt like Rudolph Valentino when she smiled back at me. That was the start, pet, and although it was months before I dared ask her out, I knew she was the one for me.'

Ruthie could see it all happening in her mind, and thought it was dead romantic. Then it dawned on her that at that time, her mother would be the same age as she herself was now. 'Why have yer never told me before how yer came to meet me dad, and how old yer were at the time?'

'Yer sisters know, but you came along years after them, and I never thought yer'd be interested.'

'But Mam, ye're telling me I'm too young, yet yer were only the same age as me when yer started going out with me dad.'

'Don't be so quick off the mark, sunshine, until yer've heard the whole story.' Molly nodded to her husband. 'Go on, love, tell her what yer had to go through before yer were allowed to date me.'

Jack laughed. 'I had to go through hell, fire and water, pet, and suffer wobbling knees, nerves and attacks of stammering. For yer grandma wasn't easily won over. She said I could come to the house one night a week for a game of cards, and also on a Sunday to have tea with them. But under no circumstances was I allowed to take her daughter out on her own. Not until yer grandma and granda were satisfied I was fit to court for her.'

Ruthie was round-eyed. 'Ooh er, I can't imagine me grandma being so strict.'

'That's because I let yer get away with murder, being the baby of the family,' Molly told her. 'I was fifteen years and nine months old before I was allowed to walk out with yer dad unaccompanied. And I had to be home at a certain time, whether I liked it or not. If I was ten minutes late I used to shake in me shoes. And don't forget, yer dad was seventeen then, going on for eighteen.'

'Me grandma would never hit yer, would she?'

'Of course not, soft girl! Yer grandma was like all mothers, worried that their daughters would get in with the wrong type of man. She was strict with me, but I probably asked for it as I was like you, wanting all me own way. And wanting to be old before me time. It's only when ye're older that yer look back and think how stupid it was to be wishing yer life away.' Molly leaned across and patted her daughter's hand. 'It's nice to be young, sunshine, and I want yer to enjoy life. But don't grow old too soon. Enjoy the teenage years and yer'll have them to look back on in later life.'

Ruthie tilted her head. 'Mam, d'yer want me to tell Gordon that me and Bella can go to the pictures with him, but it'll have to be in a year's time?'

'I doubt if that's quite what he wants to hear, sunshine. But there's nothing to stop yer asking the lads to come for a game of cards one night. It's better than hanging around the streets. Then perhaps I can get to meet this Johnny Stewart and form me own opinion of him.'

Ruthie shuffled her bottom to the edge of her chair. 'That would be great, Mam, but how many can I ask?'

'We've only got four chairs, sunshine, but as a treat I'll let yer use Auntie Nellie's. And there's one in the bedroom, so that makes six.'

'Ooh, thanks, Mam, that would be great. And Auntie Mary can't object to Bella coming over here, can she?' The legs were swinging and hitting the bottom of the chair, as Ruthie thought of the fun they would have with the lads playing cards. Bella's mam was very good with them and they had a laugh. But it would be better with her mates. 'Mam, would I be able to give them a drink of tea? Or even lemonade, that would be better.'

'Ruthie, if yer give me advance warning when ye're inviting yer friends, me and yer dad will be making ourselves scarce. We wouldn't be going far away, only to Doreen's or Jill's for an hour. But you would have to act as hostess and see to yer mates. I think that's only fair, don't you?'

Her daughter thought it was more than fair. 'Oh, yeah, that's fine. Me and Bella will make the tea, and we'll make sure nothing gets broken, and no one makes too much noise.'

'They better hadn't, sunshine, because if there's any complaints from the neighbours, then that will be your lot. Your days as a hostess would be short and sweet.'

While she was on a winning streak, Ruthie thought she might as well go the whole hog. 'And me and Bella can go to the flicks with Gordon?'

Molly nodded. 'As long as it is only with Gordon. And I think it would be nice on his part if he came and asked me and yer dad if it's all right.' She saw a look of rebellion on Ruthie's face and hurried to put a halt to it. 'Yer dad had to do it, and Tommy had to ask yer grandma before Rosie would go out with him, so I don't think it's asking too much of Gordon. God knows, he's known me and yer dad since he was born, he knows we won't bite his head off. I just think it would be a nice touch. A little touch of class, eh? I'm sure Corker would expect that of any son of his.'

'Ah, ay, Mam, we're not going to mention it to Uncle Corker, are yer? And if yer tell Auntie Nellie the whole street will know inside half an hour. They'll know before I've had a chance to speak to Gordon.'

'Yer can see Gordon tonight, sunshine, and I won't be seeing Nellie until tomorrow. So help me with the dishes, and then get yer skates on.'

Molly told Jack later that she'd never known the dishes be dried and put away so quickly. 'I hope I haven't been too lenient with her, love. I should have told her how many kids she can invite.'

'Oh, I think I can tell yer that, love.' Jack nodded. 'There'll be Bella, Gordon Corkhill, Jeff Mowbray and Johnny Stewart. So five chairs will be enough.'

Molly gasped. 'How d'yer know that?'

'Nellie is your mate,' Jack said, chortling, 'but she keeps me up to date with what's going on in the street as well. Sometimes I get more news from Nellie than I do from the *Echo*.'

Chapter Fourteen

'Hurry up, Ruthie, or yer'll be late clocking in.' Molly pulled out a chair from the table and faced her daughter. 'Yer usually go out the same time as yer dad, and he went out ten minutes ago.'

Ruthie swallowed a piece of toast before saying, 'It's only five minutes since me dad went out, Mam. Yer don't half exaggerate. I'll just drink me tea and then be off.'

'It's a wonder Bella hasn't been over for yer. She must wonder what's keeping yer.'

Her daughter gulped her tea down, then scraped her chair back. 'Me and Bella can make the time up by running. But I'd have given anything to have stayed in bed, Mam. I felt like turning over and pulling the sheet over me head.'

'That's because I was daft enough to let yer stay up late,' Molly told her. 'I should have put me foot down and made yer go earlier. The trouble was, I couldn't stop yer talking. Yer went on and on without stopping to take a breath. The only way I could have got yer upstairs was by carrying yer.'

'That's because I was excited.' Ruthie slipped her coat on and picked her handbag up from the couch. 'I'll run now, Mam, 'cos I can see Bella standing outside.' She gave Molly a quick kiss. 'See yer tonight. Ta-ra.'

But Molly had never missed a morning seeing any of her children off to school or work, and as she didn't intend to change the habits of a lifetime, she followed her daughter to the front door.

Bella was waiting. 'Why are yer so late, Ruthie? We'll never be in time for our usual tram.'

Ruthie linked her arm through her mate's. 'We'll get that tram, so don't be worrying. I bet me dad will still be at the tram stop when we get there. We're younger than him, we can run faster.'

'A few seconds won't make any difference, sunshine,' Molly said. 'So tell me if I've got things right. Ye're not going to the pictures with Gordon until next week, and yer've invited yer mates here on Friday night for a game of cards. Right?'

Bella was pulling on her friend's arm, and soon the pair were hurrying down the street, with Ruthie's voice calling, 'That's right, Mam! Oh, and will yer tell Auntie Mary for us, 'cos I bet Bella hasn't mentioned it to her.'

Molly shook her head as she watched them take flight as though they had wings on their heels. Then aloud she said, 'That daughter of mine isn't soft, leaving me to get round Mary.' She closed the door and walked inside, still talking aloud. 'I'll nip over after, when me and Nellie are on our way to the shops. I'm sure Mary won't mind. Bella can't come to any harm having a game of cards here.' Blowing out her breath, Molly gazed at the breakfast dishes cluttering the table. Then she asked herself a question. 'Shall I get stuck in now and clear the table and wash the dishes? Or shall I sit meself down for a quiet ten minutes with a nice cup of tea?' The tea in the pot was still hot, so as she told the tea cosy when she took it off, 'No contest, really. The tea wins hands down.'

Nellie brushed past Molly and swayed her way into the living room. 'What was the commotion this morning, girl, when Ruthie was going to work?'

Molly's face was blank. 'What are yer talking about, sunshine? There was no commotion. Yer must have been hearing things.'

Nellie pushed one of the dining chairs along the table, then slowly walked to where her special chair stood by the sideboard. Without a word, or a by your leave, she picked it up and placed it in her special spot by the table. When she was seated, like a queen on her throne, she said, 'I heard Ruthie shouting to yer, girl, so don't be trying to fob me off.'

'If yer heard, sunshine, then why are yer bothering to ask me? I'm sure yer've got ears like a ruddy hawk, 'cos yer don't miss a trick.' Molly walked through to the kitchen to put a light under the kettle. 'If yer must know, and I know that yer won't rest until yer know every word that was spoken, our Ruthie was asking me to do a favour for her.'

'Oh, aye, girl, and what's the favour?'

A smile played around Molly's mouth as she said, 'I'm afraid that's my daughter's secret, sunshine, and she's not very happy with you right now.'

Nellie gawped. It had never been known for any of Molly's children to find fault with her. 'Ye're making that up, girl, and I don't think it's the least bit funny. There's no reason for Ruthie to fall out with me. I haven't done nothing to upset her.'

'She hasn't fallen out with yer, Nellie, and I suppose it was my fault for snitching on yer. But I happened to let it slip that yer said Johnny Stewart had taken a fancy to her and followed her around. She wasn't best pleased about that.'

'I don't know about her being not best pleased with me, girl, but I do know if she said it wasn't true, then she's telling fibs. Why, I saw her talking to him just last night, and with Gordon Corkhill and Jeff Mowbray. And I still say she takes after you for liking the men. I bet yer were just the same at her age.'

The kettle began to whistle, and Molly jerked her head. 'If yer want to hear any more, yer can come out to the kitchen and get the cups ready. I don't see why I should do it every morning while you sit there like Lady Muck.'

Nellie sighed, as though she had all the worries of the world on her shoulders. 'I don't know, it's coming to something when yer can't even make yer mate a cup of tea. I could understand if I was asking yer to make me a dinner with roast beef and Yorkshire pudding, or even if I was asking yer to give me a bath. But blimey, all this bleeding palaver over a lousy cup of tea. I've a good mind to tell yer where to stick it.'

'All right, don't bother getting up,' Molly said, chuckling inwardly. 'Yer look nice and comfortable there, and as I'm not that fussy on a drink, and you're not, then I won't bother. I'll switch the kettle off and we can sit and have a nice quiet natter.'

'Sod that for a laugh, Molly Bennett.' The chair was pushed back and Nellie was on her feet in seconds. 'You see to the tea, while I get the cups ready and look in the larder to see what the biscuit situation is today.'

'My God, yer've soon perked up, Nellie Mac. Yer came in here with a face on yer like thunder, and now ye're happy to go mooching in me larder for biscuits! I don't know whether that's a good sign or not, sunshine, 'cos they do say there's always a change before death.'

'Yer should have learned by now that yer can't insult me, girl. It's like water off a duck's back. So get cracking with the tea, I'll see to the cups and biscuits, and then we'll sit and have that nice quiet chat. All about Ruthie, and what favour she's asked yer to do for her.'

Five minutes later the friends were sitting at the table with cups of tea in front of them, and two custard creams in each saucer. Before Molly had touched the biscuits, Nellie's had disappeared. She rubbed the back of a hand across her mouth, and sighed with pleasure. 'I enjoyed them, girl, so now yer can tell me what the favour is.'

Molly stroked her chin as though in contemplation. 'I find it a bit confusing, sunshine, so see if yer can put me straight. Yer heard Ruthie shouting to me, yer said. What did yer hear her say?'

Nellie's head swung slowly from side to side, like a pendulum on a clock. Her chins found it so pleasing they went to sleep. 'I'm beginning to worry about you, girl, ye're not half getting forgetful. Fancy not remembering what yer daughter said to yer, when I can remember every single word.'

'Go on, then, sunshine, remind me what she said.'

Nellie sat up straight and squared her shoulders. This movement was enough to wake her chins and set them in motion with her bosom. If Molly had had a baton to hand, she could have conducted an orchestra. 'I might just get a word wrong, girl, but I'll do me best. Ruthie shouted to yer, "That's right, Mam! Oh, and will yer tell Auntie Mary for us, 'cos I bet Bella hasn't mentioned it to her." '

'If me memory serves me right, sunshine, that's exactly what she said. Word for word. But what's puzzling me is what more d'yer want to know. Ruthie asked me to do her a favour, I heard her, and so did you! What else is there?'

'The favour, girl, the favour! It's no good me knowing half the tale, 'cos I won't sleep proper tonight. What is the favour?'

Molly pretended to let out a weary sigh. 'If I don't tell yer, yer'll only watch for Ruthie coming home from work, and yer'd have the nerve to ask her. So what I'll do, I'll let yer come with me to Mary's. That way yer'll find out what the favour is, and the answer at the same time.'

'I don't see why yer can't tell me now what the favour is, then I can wait for the answer until we get to Mary's.' When she saw by her friend's expression that she wasn't going to give way, Nellie quickly drained her cup, and said, 'Drink up and let's be on our way. Yer can be a right pain in the backside when the mood takes yer, Molly Bennett. I don't know how yer can keep things from me, yer very best mate. I don't keep anything from you.'

'Nellie, sunshine, that's yer trouble. Yer don't keep anything from anybody! After we've been to Mary's, and yer have all the information ye're so keen to have, I bet yer'll be dying to pass it all on to every person we meet. It won't matter if they're strangers yer don't know from Adam, nor will it matter if they're cursing yer up hill and down dale 'cos they've got more to do than listen to a perfect stranger who they think must be barmy. Even if it's Elsie Flanaghan, yer worst enemy, yer'll still want to stop and gossip. But this is one time I'll make sure yer don't repeat one word of what yer hear. For this is my daughter's business, not yours or mine.'

Molly's words made no impression on Nellie. 'Listen, girl, are yer going to drink that tea or not?'

'Yer eyes are not as keen as yer ears, sunshine, or yer'd have noticed me cup's been empty for a while. If yer'll just be patient for a few minutes I'll rinse the cups and then we'll be on our merry way.'

'Leave the bleeding cups.' Nellie was huffing and puffing. 'I'll wash them when we get back, save having to listen to yer moaning.'

Molly looked horrified. 'I'm not going out and leaving me place looking like a tip! What if burglars broke in! They'd think I was a lazy beggar who couldn't keep me house clean.'

Nellie rolled her eyes to the ceiling. 'With a bit of luck, girl, they might be houseproud burglars, and they'd tidy up for yer.' She blew out in exasperation. 'Oh, go on, you wash and I'll dry. But don't mess around. Make it snappy.'

* * *

Mary Watson was closing her front door when she heard her name called. 'Good morning, Molly, and you, Nellie. Off to the shops, are yer?'

'Yeah, but I was calling to see you first.' Molly smiled at the mother of her daughter's best friend. 'Lucky I caught yer. Are yer going to the shops? We can walk down with yer.'

Mary shook her head. 'No, I'm going to see me mam and dad, and I'll be walking up the street while you're walking down. Did yer want to see me over anything in particular?'

'Nothing more exciting than a game of cards, I'm afraid, Mary.' Molly could see her mate's ears being cocked, and was amused to think Nellie would be expecting to hear something that would add a little spice to her life. How disappointed she was going to be. 'I've told Ruthie she can have some of her friends in on Friday night for a game of cards. I thought it would be better than them hanging around the streets: at least we'd know where they were. Just Bella, Gordon Corkhill and Jeff Mowbray.' Molly wasn't going to give Mary a chance to object. 'My mam always encouraged me to bring me friends home so she'd know who I was mixing with. And I did the same with my eldest three. At least I know Ruthie's in good company and won't come to any harm. And I can't see you objecting to Bella coming, but knowing what ye're like, I thought I'd better ask. Me and Jack will make ourselves scarce, but we'll only be across the street in Doreen's.'

Nellie spoke before Mary had a chance. 'But Friday's the day Claire comes to visit us. Couldn't Ruthie pick another day?'

'What difference does that make? Claire comes in the afternoon, sunshine; she's on her way home at four o'clock. Anyway, that's got nothing to do with the kids having a game of cards. It's all right for Bella to come, isn't it, Mary? I want to know how many, so I can get some lemonade in for them.'

'That's fine, Molly, as long as she's home for ten o'clock. It's a good idea, and nice of yer to think of it. I'm never happy when Bella's hanging around the street. Perhaps she can ask them over here sometime, so I can get to know them. I know the Corkhills, of course, and they're a good family.'

'Salt of the earth, Mary,' Nellie said. 'Salt of the earth.'

Molly smiled. 'That's settled, then, Mary, so we'll let yer get on yer way.'

'Shall I get a bottle of lemonade for Bella to bring with her?'

It was on the tip of Molly's tongue to say it didn't matter, but her brain told her Mary would feel more a part of it if she got involved. 'Yeah, I bet she'd like that, Mary. And yer can always slip over and see for yerself that they're all right.'

Mary went on her way a happy woman. She knew she worried about her daughter too much, and was in danger of spoiling the years that should be happy ones for Bella. She often wished she was more like Molly, who loved her children dearly, but was wise enough to give them enough freedom not only to enjoy themselves, but to build up their confidence and prepare them for what the future held.

Nellie was disgusted. 'D'yer mean yer've kept me waiting for hours, girl, for that? After all I've gone through, it was a load of nothing.'

Molly bent her elbow. 'Stick yer leg in, sunshine, and stop yer moaning. If yer hadn't been so nosy, it wouldn't have been such a let-down, would it? But yer have to know every little thing what goes on, so yer deserve to get yer eye wiped occasionally.'

Her mate wasn't going to let the incident pass without gaining something from it, though. 'I'll come to Doreen's with yer on Friday night, girl. It'll be an excuse to get out of the house for an hour and hear some human voices. My feller's in a world of his own once he gets the *Echo* in his hands, and I can't drag a word out of him. And I get bored stiff being on me own and no one to talk to. Our Paul is out every night as soon as the dinner's over. Well, after he's spent an hour dolling himself up. He takes longer combing his hair and cleaning his teeth than I do all week cleaning the house down.'

Molly squeezed her arm. 'He's only young, Nellie. He's bound to want to look nice when he calls for Phoebe. I remember I used to stand for hours titivating meself up when I first started courting Jack. Me ma used to tell me off for being vain.' She began to chuckle. 'And our Tommy used to fight with the two girls to get to the mirror in the kitchen first. He never had a hair out of place when he knocked on me ma's door for Rosie.'

Nellie pulled her to a halt. 'D'yer know why I never bothered with meself when I was their age? Because I never knew what I looked like. The bleeding mirror on the wall over the fireplace was far too high up. I couldn't even see what me hair looked like. And I still have to guess, 'cos I can't see in our mirror properly, either! I don't mind so much now, though, 'cos I know you'd tell me if I looked a sight, or me knicker legs were showing.'

'Nellie, if yer knicker legs were showing I'd be too embarrassed to tell yer. And d'yer know why I'd be embarrassed? Because I know yer wouldn't turn a hair. I wouldn't put it past yer to stand in the road, lift yer dress and pull yer knickers up. In full view of anyone who was unfortunate enough to be passing at that particular moment.'

'Ye're a fussy bugger, you are,' Nellie said with feeling. 'If the worst thing anyone ever sees in their life is the leg of someone's knickers, then they're bleeding lucky. And that's all I've got to say.'

'And yer said it well,' Molly said, also with feeling. 'And

don't ever worry if it happens, 'cos I won't run away and leave yer. I'll open me coat wide and stand in front of yer so yer can hold on to yer modesty.'

'It's not me modesty I'd have to hold on to, girl, it's the leg of me ruddy knickers! Yer see, I couldn't just pull them up, 'cos I always have a pin in them for safety reasons.'

Molly shook her head in disbelief. 'That cotton dress yer've got on, the one yer bought for two bob down at Paddy's market? Well, it must be hiding a multitude of sins. Ye're a walking disaster, Nellie, d'yer know that?'

'I've been called worse things than that by George. But as ye're so pure at heart, I can't tell yer 'cos some of his language is very strong.'

'You do surprise me!' Molly said. 'I've never heard George use strong language in all the years I've known him.'

Nellie grinned back at her. 'He said it's me what makes him swear. In fact, he said I'm enough to make a saint swear.'

'Does George know that ye're well in with Saint Peter? If he doesn't, I think it would be wise of yer to tell him. Yer see, his bad language might tell against him and he might not be admitted to heaven. And I'm sure he'd want to meet up with yer again in the after-life.'

Nellie laughed so much her whole body shook. 'If I told George what yer said, every other word would be a swear word. After a lifetime with me down here on earth, I don't think he could stand the thought of meeting up with me when he's dead.'

'Nellie, this is not a pleasant conversation. Think of something nice to talk about.'

'Yeah, okay, girl. Let's talk about who's paying for the sandwiches and cakes on Friday for when Claire comes?'

'We'll go half each, sunshine. I think that's the best way. Then we won't be squabbling every week about who pays.'

'I'm looking forward to seeing her, girl, to find out how she's getting on with the man we saw coming out of the shop.'

'Yer wouldn't say that to her in those words, would yer, sunshine? If yer let on that we spied on her, I swear you and I will have our first row and I'll never speak to yer again.'

Nellie thought it would be in her best interest to change the subject. 'Ay, wouldn't it be smashing if Claire brought cream slices with her, like what she did last week?'

'I take me hat off to yer for invention, Nellie. In one big swoop yer've taken us from life after death to Claire and her cream slices. And there's not many people could do that and keep their face straight.'

'I might be able to keep me face straight at a funeral, girl, 'cos I'd be frightened that Saint Peter would be looking down at me. But it's more than me heart could stand to keep me face straight in Hanley's with all those cream cakes in the glass case.'

'Ye're short on willpower, sunshine, that's your problem. Yer don't have a problem with telling lies, or making up stories to make people laugh, but I'm afraid the sight of cream is your downfall.' Molly happened to glance across the road, and she saw two faces pressed against the inside of the butcher's window. 'There's Ellen and Tony waving to us, Nellie, so we may as well cross over and get our meat.'

Nellie pulled on her coat. 'Can I tell her about their Gordon coming to yours on Friday night for a game of cards? There's no harm in that, surely?'

'Okay, sunshine, if it makes yer feel better. But only what yer've just said. Ye're not to add one more word to it.' Molly took her friend's arm, looked both ways to make sure the road was clear, then hurried her across. She wasn't taking any chances of an accident, not now she knew Nellie had a pin keeping her knickers up.

* * *

It was Friday afternoon and Claire was due any time. Molly stood back and her eyes went over the table. It looked really nice, set off by a pure white linen tablecloth, which had been embroidered by her mother many years ago. Tiny colourful flowers were in each corner, and a circle of flowers in the centre. It was very seldom used as Molly treasured it, but she thought she would give it an outing today. And there were three place settings with her best cups and saucers, and two plates of sandwiches and cakes were set in the centre. 'That looks nice, doesn't it, sunshine?'

'I'll say it does, girl, it looks proper posh. There's not many houses yer'd go in where they have those fancy bits of paper under the sandwiches and cakes. Only the likes of Buckingham Palace would have them.'

'Those fancy bits of paper, as yer call them, are doilies, Nellie. And please don't show yer ignorance when Claire is here, or she'll think we're not used to anything.'

'I'll be on me best behaviour, girl, but don't expect me to be all lah-de-dah. I am what I am, and if anyone doesn't like it, then sod 'em. That's what I say.'

Just as Molly chuckled, there came a knock on the door. 'This will be Claire, sunshine, and I'm sure she likes yer just the way yer are, so there'll be no need to tell her to sod off.'

Much to Nellie's delight, Claire came in carrying a cake bag. 'I haven't forgotten yer have a sweet tooth, Nellie, so I brought an extra cake each.'

Nellie's cheeks moved upwards and nearly covered her eyes. 'That's what I call a friend. I definitely won't be telling yer to sod off, girl, no matter what Molly says.'

Molly lifted her hands. 'Don't ask what she's talking about, Claire, 'cos I couldn't tell yer. My mate has a mind that only she can understand. Anyway, the kettle's on the boil, so sit yerself down while I make the tea.'

Nellie rested her elbows on the arms of the carver chair, and folded her arms under her bosom. 'Me and Molly went half each with the ham and cakes, girl, so there'd be no argument over whose turn it was to pay.'

Molly came through carrying the teapot in one hand and the chrome stand in the other. When they were safely on the table, she glared at her mate. 'Have yer told Claire how many blankets I've got on me beds, Nellie?'

'Why would I do that, girl? Even if I knew how many blankets yer've got on yer beds, I'm sure Claire wouldn't be interested. I mean, it's hardly exciting enough to send her into raptures, is it?'

'Well, the fact that we went halfy-halfy with the ham and cakes is hardly newsworthy enough to make the front page of the *News of the World*, is it?'

Claire was thinking what a pleasure it was to be in the company of these two women, who were gifted with such a fabulous sense of humour. 'Why don't yer sit down, Molly, and I'll pour the tea?'

Nellie nodded. She would never have offered to pour the tea herself, but it was nice that Claire did. 'You muck in, girl, and make yerself at home. And when ye're settled, me and Molly are dying to know how ye're getting on with yer mystery man. Have yer got any further with him, d'yer think? I mean, has he asked yer for a date yet?'

'Nellie McDonough, I'm ashamed for yer!' Molly was red in the face. 'Give the girl time to sit down before yer bombard her with questions. I've never known anyone so cheeky in all me life. Claire will tell us as much as she wants, when she wants.'

'Ooh, ye're a sly article, Molly Bennett. Ye're sitting there like little Miss Prim and Proper, while all the time ye're as nosy as me.'

'I am not as nosy as you, sunshine, and you know it. I'll admit to being inquisitive, but I am not as nosy as you.'

Nellie's tongue clicked on the roof of her mouth. 'Did yer hear that, Claire? She can't be nosy in a common way like me, she's got to be nosy in a posh way.'

Claire handed the cups out. 'Be quiet, both of yer. I have got some news, and I will tell yer, but only after I've had a sandwich and a drink of tea. I'm hungry and thirsty.'

'Go ahead, sunshine, and we'll join yer.' Molly smiled sweetly at Nellie. 'Pass the sandwich plate over, Nellie, after yer've taken what yer want.'

Nellie smiled back just as sweetly. 'Ye're not half polished, girl. If my sideboard was as highly polished as what you are, I'd only ever have to dust it.'

Much to Claire's delight, the insults kept flying across the table, one mate trying to outdo the other. Neither of them ran out of answers, and they were hilarious. 'Do you two ever fall out? I mean, really fall out?'

The two friends looked at her as though she'd gone soft. 'What would we want to fall out for, girl?' Nellie asked. 'When ye're lucky enough to have a good mate, yer don't want to be falling out. Life's too short.' She picked up the plate with the cakes on and held it out to Molly. 'Here yer are, girl, you have first pick. But I wouldn't advise yer to take the one near me thumb, 'cos by accident, me thumb ran right down the side of it and got itself covered in cream. It's still on me finger, so I could put it back. But I know yer wouldn't enjoy the cake if I did that, so I'll lick me finger when yer've made up yer mind which one to have. I don't know why ye're taking so long – they're all the same. Oh, and don't forget the three Claire brought, so that's another one each still to come.'

'We'll have them with a fresh pot of tea before Claire goes.

I couldn't eat two cream cakes one after the other, but I'll enjoy one later.'

Claire could feel Nellie's eyes on her as she bit into her cake and then ran her tongue over her lips to lick the cream. 'Two more bites, Nellie, then it'll be news time. Nothing to write home about, like, but still a bit of news.'

'I don't care if yer make it up as yer go along, girl, as long as yer put a bit of spice into it.'

Molly felt so awful when Claire began to describe what the man looked like and how he dressed, she couldn't look the other woman in the face. But Nellie sat there drinking it all in, even asking what colour hair he had, when she'd been as close to him on Tuesday as she was to Claire now. Never again, Molly was telling herself. I'll never again do anything so underhanded. But as Claire started to tell them her news, Molly relaxed a little and sat forward to listen with interest.

'It was just friendly conversation at first, after I'd served him. You know, how the weather was getting warmer now, and wasn't it nice to walk in the park and see the trees and flowers in bud. Then he asked how long I'd been a widow. He told me he'd never married because he didn't want to leave his mother after his father died suddenly. He said she was heartbroken, and he felt he should stay with her. Time passed, and he's still living with her.'

'Ooh er, he must be interested to have told yer all that,' Nellie said, 'Did he tell yer where he worked, or where he lived?'

Claire shook her head. 'Not on Tuesday he didn't.' She looked from one intent face to the other. 'But he came back on Wednesday. I nearly fainted with shock when he walked in. He's only ever come the two days. Anyway, a customer came in straight after him, and I had to serve her. Then another came in, and I just shrugged my shoulders and told him the shop got busy just before we closed for the dinner hour. And I was really surprised when he said he'd come back later in the afternoon.'

'Ay, he's keen, isn't he, girl? He's a man what means business.' Nellie was over the moon. This news would keep her mind active until bedtime. 'He's not short of a bob or two, either, is he?' The kick Molly aimed at her shin was hard enough to warn Nellie to watch her words. 'That's according to what you told us, girl.'

'Oh, he's not short of money, yer can see that by his clothes. He is always immaculately dressed. And he's polite and well spoken.'

Molly asked, 'And did he come back in the afternoon?'

'Yes.' Claire nodded. 'He asked if I would like to go to the theatre with him one night. I got all flustered, and he must have thought me really childish. Me mind was split in two, 'cos he seems quite genuine, and he's very easy to talk to, but I hardly know the man. It all seemed to be happening too quickly. I would prefer to wait a while until I know him better and feel more easy in his company.'

Nellie waved her hand as though brushing these objections aside. 'Yer'll never get to know him if yer don't go out with him. Yer can't build up a romance over a ruddy shop counter. I think yer'd be daft if yer didn't jump at the chance.'

But Molly thought otherwise. 'If ye're not sure, Claire, then put him off for a while. At least until yer feel more confident. No matter how much money he's got, or how nicely he dresses and speaks, that still doesn't automatically make him a nice person. Don't rush into something unless yer feel right about it.'

Nellie huffed. 'What bleeding harm can she come to in a theatre? He's hardly likely to ravage her, or strangle her in front of hundreds of people. Where's yer sense of romance, Molly

Bennett? If she finds she doesn't like him there's no harm done, and at least she'll have been to the theatre and lived it up for one night. And I bet he'd have bought her one of those big boxes of chocolates what are tied with a ribbon and have a big bow on the front.'

Molly winked at Claire. 'My mate would sell her soul for a box of chocolates. She doesn't just have a sweet tooth, she has a craving.'

Nellie was quick to turn the tables. 'Ye're right, girl, as usual. But it's not me biggest craving, as yer would know if yer lived next door to me. The noises coming from me bedroom most nights would tell yer what me biggest craving is.'

Claire's laugh ricocheted off the walls, while Molly looked horrified. 'I thought this was one time I'd be spared yer bedroom antics, Nellie, but yer don't seem to have any shame in yer. Now, if yer can clear yer mind of cravings, could we ask Claire what the eventual outcome was? Is she going out with the man or not?'

'Nothing was arranged, Molly, so he's coming in again on Monday. Yer see, it was all so quick, I didn't have time to think it out properly. The children were on me mind, and I wondered what they'd think about me going out with a man. Amy doesn't remember her dad, but Ken idolised him. And me going out with a man might upset him. So I explained this to Graham, and to give him his due, he said he understood.'

'Is that his name?' Molly asked. 'Graham?'

'Yeah, Graham Collins. He said if I explained to the children, he was sure they would understand. Especially Ken, who might be pleased his mother was getting some pleasure out of life. Anyway, I said I'd let him know when he comes in on Monday. So I've got the weekend to think it over. In me head, part of me is saying I should throw caution to the wind and go out with him. I'm not old yet, and I should be glad of the opportunity to get some social life. Then the other part is telling me it would be wrong.'

'Have yer said anything to the children yet?' Molly asked. 'It might help yer decide if yer know what their views are.'

'I intend to do that tonight, and get it over with. A lot will depend on their reaction. I'll call again next Friday and let yer know.' Claire turned in her chair and reached for the cake bag she'd put on the sideboard. 'Now, anyone for another cake? Nellie, can I tempt yer?'

Molly chuckled. 'What a silly question to ask.'

'I think I could manage another one, girl, seeing as yer asked.' Nellie took a cake from the bag, and by the time Claire and Molly each had one in their hand, Nellie's had disappeared. All that remained to prove she had been given a cream slice was the line of cream round her mouth. And her tongue soon took care of that.

Chapter Fifteen

Claire left about half past four, after saying she'd see them the following Friday to let them know if she'd decided to go out with Graham Collins. It all rested on the reaction of her two children. If they showed signs of being upset, then she would turn him down, no matter what her own feelings were.

After saying goodbye to her at the door, Molly walked back to the living room, but she didn't sit down. 'You can go home now, Nellie, so I can clear the table and then start on the dinner. Yer've got yer own dinner to see to, anyway.'

'Ah, ay, girl, just give us another few minutes. It doesn't take long to cook sausage and mash. I'll easy have it done before George and Paul get in from work.'

Molly shook her head, a look of determination on her face. 'No, I'm not sitting down, Nellie. I want to get cracking. Ruthie's having friends in tonight, and I want everything to be ready for her.' There was a message Molly wanted to go on after she'd got the dinner on the way, but she wasn't going to tell her mate because she'd insist on coming with her. 'So up yer get, sunshine, there's a good girl.'

It was not with good grace that Nellie pushed back her chair. 'I don't know. Five bleeding minutes won't make any difference to yer.'

'I've been with yer since half ten this morning, sunshine, and now I want to see to me house and family. Anyway, I've said yer can come over to Doreen's with me tonight, so what more d'yer want, for heaven's sake?'

Nellie had forgotten about the visit tonight, and that cheered her up somewhat. It was only over the road, but it was better than sitting at home talking to herself. 'Oh, okay, girl, you win. What time shall I call for yer?'

'I'll call for you, sunshine, after I've made sure everything is ready for Ruthie and her friends. So don't knock for me, or I'll brain yer. Just be patient, and wait for me.'

'Okay, girl, keep yer ruddy hair on! I'll wait for yer, but don't make it so late I'll have me nightdress on.'

Molly watched as Nellie lowered herself down to the pavement. 'Oh, so yer wear a nightdress in bed, do yer, sunshine? The way yer talk, I was under the impression yer slept in the nuddy.'

Now this was the sort of conversation Nellie most enjoyed. And her friend had walked right into it. 'Of course I go to bed in a nightdress, girl, what did yer expect? Mind you, I may as well not bother, 'cos as soon as I'm under the sheets, George has me nightie off.'

'I asked for that, didn't I, sunshine? But I'm not sure I believe yer, so I'll ask George tonight. I know I'll get the truth off him.'

'You do that, girl, you do that.' Nellie grinned up at Molly, then waddled away with her whole body shaking with laughter. There was more chance of her mate flying to the moon than there was of her asking George about anything so personal. It would be a toss-up who would have the redder face, her husband or her mate.

Molly closed the door, and as she walked through to the kitchen she was humming a song which she thought was very appropriate right now. It was called 'The Very Thought of You'. And as she peeled the potatoes, she began to sing. But she'd only sung a couple of lines before she took a bout of laughing. For in her mind's eye, she could see Nellie in her tent-like nightie and George ripping it from her. And the very thought was enough to bring on tears of laughter. Even when she told herself she shouldn't be laughing at her best friend, she couldn't stop. To salve her conscience, though, she vowed to be truthful and tell her mate tonight how she'd laughed at her expense.

When the potatoes were washed and put in lightly salted water, Molly placed the pan on a very low light. She'd run over to Mary's now, and by the time she got back the potatoes would have reached the boil, and she'd have time to fry the sausages slowly.

'Hello, Molly.' Mary held the door open. 'Are yer coming in?'

'Just for a few minutes, sunshine, 'cos I've left me spuds on the stove.' Molly shook her head when waved to a chair. 'No, I can't stop. I've only come to see if yer'd like Bella to come over a bit early tonight, so she can help Ruthie with the sandwiches? With it being the first time they've invited friends, I thought it would be better to leave them to get on with it. Give them a bit of confidence for next time.' Molly looked round the living room, where nothing was allowed to be out of place. 'I was going to do the sandwiches, then I thought Ruthie would feel more grown-up if I let her do them herself. A bit of responsibility, like.'

'That's a good idea, Molly, and I'm sure Bella will be thrilled to bits. I bought four large sausage rolls when I was out, for her to take over with her. They can be cut in half, and they'll fill a plate up. Not much, but every little helps.'

Molly was inwardly pleased that Mary was taking part. It showed that at least she was going to give Bella some freedom. 'They'll go down a treat, Mary, and it was a nice thought. I bought some ham, a jar of salmon paste, and a large home-made loaf. With two bottles of lemonade, that should be plenty for them.' Molly was edging towards the door. 'I'll have to love yer and leave yer, sunshine, or me pan of spuds will be boiling over.'

Mary followed her. 'What time shall I tell Bella to be at your house for?'

'Seven o'clock will be fine. It will give them half an hour at least to get things organised. I can always give them a hand if they get stuck.' Molly began to cross the cobbles, then slowed down to look over her shoulder. 'I've told yer, Mary, that ye're welcome to nip over to see they're all right. Me and Jack won't be there, but there's nothing to stop you going if it'll make yer feel better.'

'We'll see,' Mary called. 'Ta-ra for now.'

Molly waved a hand in the air and hurried into the house, to find the water had just come to the boil and no harm had been done.

Ruthie was so excited she couldn't keep still on her chair. With butterflies in her tummy, she didn't feel hungry. 'Dad, will yer have one of me sausages? I couldn't eat two, and yer know me mam doesn't like wasting good food.'

Jack looked at his wife. 'What d'yer think, love? I suppose it's no good making her eat it if she doesn't feel like it. And I'm sure I can fit it in me tummy.'

'Oh, go on, then.' Molly could practically feel her daughter's excitement. 'There'll be sandwiches later if she feels hungry.' She rested her knife and fork. 'Are yer getting changed, sunshine? If yer are, put that pretty floral dress on. It really suits yer.'

'Yes, I had a good think about what to wear, and that came out tops. Bella is wearing her green cotton dress, so we could look posh.'

Jack's eyes went from his wife to his daughter. 'D'yer know, love, when yer said yer'd marry me, I told meself I was getting the most beautiful girl in Liverpool. Little did I know yer would give me three beautiful daughters. I'm sitting here now looking at Ruthie, and I could be looking at Jill or Doreen at her age. The likeness is uncanny.'

Ruthie's cup of happiness was flowing over. She knew her sisters were beautiful, the prettiest in the street. And to be told she looked like them was a real compliment.

'Aren't yer forgetting something, love?' Molly asked, her blue eyes holding the deep brown ones of her husband. 'I didn't only give yer three beautiful girls, I also gave yer a son who is every bit as handsome as the man I married.'

With the last of the mashed potato on the end of her fork, Ruthie made a vow. She would marry someone who would love her like her dad loved her mam, and would tell her so every time he looked at her. She might only be fourteen years and seven and a half months, but she knew a look of love when she saw it. And she saw it every day of her life, each time her parents looked at each other.

'You get washed in the sink, sunshine, before I start on the dishes. There's a drop of hot water left in the kettle, so yer can use that. Then yer can get changed while I'm doing the washing up.'

'Am I coming to Doreen's with yer?' Jack asked, passing his empty plate over.

Molly chuckled. 'Unless yer want to stay in and play cards with the young ones.'

'Then yer won't mind if I bring the *Echo* over with me, will yer? I'll sit quiet and read me paper while you women do what yer do best. Talk about everything under the sun.'

'Yer know Nellie's coming with us, I told yer last night! So I doubt very much if yer'll be able to concentrate on the paper.'

Ruthie was running the water in the sink, so she didn't hear her dad say, 'There's not much to choose from, really. Unless I knock to see if Corker wants to come for a pint. And we could give George a knock.'

Molly nodded. 'Yer might be better off doing that, love, 'cos yer know what Nellie's like once she starts. It's all right for us women, but one man on his own I would feel heartily sorry for. So Corker and George are yer best bet.'

'Doreen won't be upset over me not going, will she?'

'Of course she won't, sunshine, she'll understand. And I'll lay odds that Phil will be following yer.' Molly was standing with the dirty plates in her hand. 'I'll get these done when Ruthie's finished at the sink. Then yer can give yerself a shave. Yer can't go to the pub with a stubble on yer chin.' She grinned across at him. 'And yer skin will be nice and smooth when yer get amorous in bed tonight.'

He grinned back. 'Ye're beginning to sound like Nellie.'

Molly's eyes went to the ceiling. 'Heaven forbid! Yer should have heard what she said to Tony in the butcher's, this morning. Ellen didn't hear, thank goodness, 'cos she was in the back room. But Tony's face was the colour of the blood on his apron. Twenty years we've been going in that shop, and yer'd think that nothing Nellie said could affect him any more. But he found out today that she can still bring a blush to his face.'

'Make who blush, Mam?' Ruthie came through drying her face on a piece of towelling. 'I bet it was Auntie Nellie?'

Molly walked past her into the kitchen. 'Yer Auntie Nellie doesn't blush, sunshine. She leaves that to other people.'

When Molly stepped down on to the pavement, she almost collided with a young couple who came out of the house next door. 'Oh, Phoebe, did I stand on yer foot, sunshine?'

'No, Auntie Molly, yer missed me by an inch.' Phoebe

Corkhill was linking Nellie's son Paul, and they made a handsome couple. 'Are you and Uncle Jack off somewhere?'

Jack banged the door behind him and joined his wife on the pavement. 'No, love, me wife is deserting me tonight, so I'm going to knock for yer dad to see if he feels like a pint.'

'Uncle Corker is going for a drink, so ye're in luck,' Paul said, his dimples showing. 'His mate came down, and I heard them saying they were going to the pub.' He winked at Molly. 'I believe you and me mam are going over to Doreen's, to let Ruthie have a few of her friends in for a game of cards? Me mam's been thinking of ways to entertain yer.'

'Then I'm definitely going to join Corker in the pub,' Jack said, pulling a face. 'Can yer imagine me sitting there when all the girlie talk and laughter is going on? And I'm going to do Phil a favour and rescue him.'

'We'll have to leave yer,' Paul said, his arm moving to Phoebe's waist. 'We're off jazzing, to the Grafton, and I'd hate to miss the first slow foxtrot.'

Molly smiled at the young couple. 'Oh, what it is to be young, eh? You get what yer can out of life, and when ye're old, like me and Jack, yer'll have good memories to look back on.'

'Ay, don't be putting years on me, love. I've still got plenty of life in me,' Jack told her. 'I've got twenty working years to go yet, so don't be making me old before me time.'

'Ye're as old as yer feel, love, and that's what counts. Anyway, you two lovebirds be on yer way. I'd hate yer to miss the slow foxtrot.'

Paul pulled on Phoebe's arm. 'Yer heard what Auntie Molly said. Come on.'

The young couple had just walked away when Corker came out of the house, followed by his friend Derek. 'Molly, me darlin'!' Molly was lifted in the air and spun round. 'Still the prettiest woman in the street.'

'Put me down, yer silly nit,' Molly said, laughing as she struggled to free herself. 'Half the street can see everything I've got.'

'Never mind half the street,' Jack said, 'what about me? That's my wife up there, and I demand yer put her down right now.'

Derek was leaning back against the wall, his guffaws as loud as Corker's. 'He has a very delicate approach to women, Corker has. He always gives his seat up on a tram, for he thinks it's ungentlemanly to leave a woman standing. So don't take it to heart 'cos he's holding yer wife up in the air, Jack, for as I said, he doesn't like to see a woman standing.'

Ellen had been watching the goings-on from behind the curtains, and now decided she might as well have a laugh herself. So she stepped from the house, and with her hands on her hips said, 'Take yer hands off that woman this instant, James Corkhill, or I'll get the rolling pin out to yer. And then the whole street will have something else to watch.'

Her feet firmly on the ground, Molly ran a hand down the back of her skirt to make sure it was straight. 'Ay, Ellen, over the years, if we'd charged the neighbours every time there's been a peep show, we'd be on Easy Street today.'

Ellen nodded. 'Either that, Molly, or in one of the cells at the local police station.'

'At least it would be a change of scenery, Ellen, like a short holiday.'

The loud banging of a front door had all heads turning. And they saw Nellie walking towards them with a look of determination on her face that told them she was ready to do battle. 'Is this a mothers' meeting for fathers only, or can anyone join in?'

'Oh, I was just coming to call for yer, sunshine, but I got held up.'

'Yeah, I saw yer being held up by a strange man.' Nellie glared, head forward in a fighting stance. 'I've been standing waiting for yer, with me coat on, for half an hour. What the hell have yer been doing with yerself, apart from messing with a man what isn't yer husband?'

'Nellie, me darlin',' Corker roared, 'it's always good to see yer. Me favourite woman, after Ellen and Molly.'

'I notice I don't get the same treatment as me mate, though, do I? I mean, yer don't lift me up in the air and twist me round, showing all me knickers, do yer?'

Her mind on Derek, who wasn't used to Nellie and her lack of social manners, Molly tried to change the subject. 'We'll go over to Doreen's now, sunshine, and Jack can ask Corker if he wouldn't mind him joining them for a pint. And he mentioned knocking for George to see if he fancied a drink.'

'Don't be changing the subject, Molly Bennett. We'll go over to Doreen's after Corker has greeted me the same as he did you. What's good enough for you is good enough for me.'

While Nellie was facing Molly, Corker winked at Derek and jerked his head. The two men approached the little woman from behind. Without a word, they each put a hand under one of Nellie's arms, and cupped her elbow with the other. Then they lifted her off the pavement and swung her round. Nellie's face was a joy to behold. It was creased in a smile and her laughter filled the air. 'Oh, this is the bloody gear, girl. Yer want to ask them to give you a turn.'

'I don't think so, sunshine, 'cos I can see Doreen and Victoria watching through the window. Besides, I don't want everyone to see me knickers. It's all right for you, 'cos yer don't mind who sees yer pink bloomers, do yer?'

'Yer've no need to tell everyone what colour me bloomers are, girl. I'm sure Corker and his friend aren't interested. Nor is your feller, who seems to think everything is a huge joke. But I don't care, I'm enjoying this. It's like being in one of them eariothings.'

'I didn't tell them what colour yer bloomers are, sunshine.' Molly thought she had never seen anything so funny in her life. And how the men were holding Nellie's weight for so long, and spinning her round, well, it was a mystery. 'They can see them for themselves, 'cos the pin in them must have come undone.'

Nellie's mouth opened in horror and she began to kick her legs. 'Put me down, yer silly buggers. Have yer nothing better to do? And as for you, Jack Bennett, yer better shut those eyes or I'll shut them for yer.'

When her feet were firmly on the ground, Nellie grinned like a Cheshire cat. 'Thanks, lads, I enjoyed that. It made a nice change to be able to look down on people instead of always looking up and getting a crick in me neck. And I also enjoyed seeing yer all laughing when me mate told yer about me knickers falling down. Well, she's had her eye wiped, good and proper. Yer see, I put an extra pin in me knickers before I came out. Just in case I got run over crossing the road, like.' Nellie shrugged her shoulders once, then squared them. 'Yer won't believe what I'm going to tell yer, but I swear to God it's the truth. This morning, my mate told me that if I ever got run over while I was out with her, she'd pretend she wasn't with me. Now what sort of a friend would yer say that was?'

Even the customers sitting in the corner pub must have heard Corker's guffaws. 'I'd say she was a wise friend, who believed in taking precautions.'

Jack kept his face straight. 'I'd say that Molly is such a good friend, she would lie down in the road beside yer.' He put a curled fist in front of his mouth and coughed. 'That's after she'd checked to make sure yer were respectable. Yer see, I remember her once saying that although they're called safety pins, yer still shouldn't put all yer trust in them. Not where knickers are concerned, anyway.'

Ellen tapped Molly's arm. 'Doreen's waving to yer, Molly.'

Molly looked to the house opposite to see her daughter standing on the step. 'We're coming now, sunshine.'

'I should hope so,' Doreen called back. 'The kettle's been on the boil for nearly half an hour.'

'Before yer go, me darlin',' Corker shouted, 'will yer ask Phil if he'd like to come for a pint with us? We're giving George a call, as well.'

Phil's head appeared over his wife's shoulder. 'I'll follow yer up, Uncle Corker. Ye're like a knight of old, come to rescue a prisoner from torture.' He laughed. 'Not that sitting all night with four women is torture exactly, but it's near enough.'

'You cheeky beggar!' Molly was grinning when she shook her fist. 'For your information, it's five women now, 'cos I'm inviting Ellen. And if you're not gone by the time we get over there, we'll tie yer to a chair and force yer to listen to five of us nattering all night.'

That really took Nellie's fancy. 'Yeah, we'll tie yer to a chair in the middle of the room and do a war dance round yer. You know, like what the Red Indians do. We've haven't got no tomahawks, but Doreen will lend us some knives.' She began to dance in a circle, bending and then straightening up, with a hand patting her open mouth to make a war cry.

Phil was pulling on his jacket as he crossed the cobbles. 'Very realistic, Mrs Mac. It's a pity there's no Indian tribes living round here, 'cos ten to one the chief would make you his number one squaw.'

Nellie rose to her full four feet ten inches. 'Now that's nice of yer, lad. And although I haven't seen no Indians round here, I have seen a tent in Walton Park. So if yer come across an Indian chief on yer travels, let me know and I'll ask him if he feels like making me his number one squaw in a wigwam in Walton Park. Mind you, yer'd have to tell him the truth. There's no buffalo round these parts, but we do have a good butcher what sells beef.'

It was Corker who told her, 'Yer best bet, Nellie, is to ask Derek. He travels the world and is more likely to come across what you're looking for.'

Derek waved an open palm. 'I don't travel the world any more, Mrs Mac. I've signed on for one more trip, and that's only Rotterdam. And I know for a fact that Red Indians are few and far between in Holland.'

By this time Doreen had lost her patience. 'Mam, are yer coming or not? It'll be nearly time for us to go to bed.'

Molly nodded. 'Yeah, ye're right, sunshine. Come on, Nellie, let's be having yer. And you, Ellen. There's nothing to stop yer coming for an hour. It'll get yer out of the house.'

'I'll nip in and put the fireguard in front of the fire, Molly, just to make sure. Tell Doreen to leave the door open for me.' Ellen wagged a finger at Corker. 'Don't you dare come home the worse for wear, or yer'll get the length of me tongue. And that goes for you, Derek. Yer mam will wonder what sort of friends yer've got if yer go home tiddly again.'

'Me mam's known Corker a long time, Ellen, and she won't hear a wrong word said against him.' Derek smiled at what he was going to say. 'In fact, if me mam saw me and Corker staggering along the road, it's me she'd clout, for getting him drunk. She'd say I was leading him astray.'

Phil saw his wife was agitated and he touched Molly's arm. 'Doreen's waiting to put the baby to bed, Mrs B. She kept him up so yer could see him. I think yer'd better get over there.'

'Right! Nellie, come over with me. Ellen, you follow when ye're ready. Jack, don't drink so much I'll have trouble getting yer up for work. And from me and Nellie, it's goodnight to Corker and Derek.'

* * *

'That's the second game I've won,' Ruthie said, bragging as any fourteen-year-old girl would in front of boys. 'We should have been playing for money.'

'If we'd been playing for money, yer wouldn't have got away with cheating,' Gordon Corkhill said. He wasn't very happy because Johnny Stewart had beaten him to the chair next to Ruthie, and Jeff Mowbray had bagged the chair next to Bella. Which meant Gordon and his kid brother, Peter, had been left with the chairs each end of the table.

'I didn't cheat,' Ruthie said with indignation. 'I won fair and square.'

Gordon was equally indignant. 'Yer did too, Ruthie Bennett! I saw with me own eyes that on two occasions Johnny passed yer a card. Yer did it sly, under the cover of the cloth, thinking yer wouldn't be seen. But I saw yer.'

'It's only a game of cards, for heaven's sake,' Johnny said. 'It's not as though yer've lost money. And I didn't pass Ruthie a card twice, it was only once.'

Ruthie blushed. 'What did yer have to go and tell him for? It was only in fun.'

'He's me mate, that's why,' Johnny said, also rather red-faced. 'And yer never tell a lie to a mate.'

Bella's jaw dropped. 'That's not fair! I could have won if I'd cheated. In fact we could all win if it came to that.'

'Yer'll win the next game, Bella, I'll see to that,' Jeff Mowbray said. 'If I've got a card yer can use, I'll throw it on the pack and yer can pick it up.'

'We won't have another game yet.' Ruthie pushed back her chair. 'Me and Bella are going to make us all a drink.' She didn't mention the food, she wanted it to be a surprise. 'Will yer put the cards back in the packs while me and me mate play hostess?'

Out in the kitchen, Bella said softly, 'Hadn't yer better put a white tablecloth on, in case something gets spilled on the chenille? Yer mam would go mad.'

Ruthie nodded. 'Yeah, I better had. I don't want to give me mam anything to complain about, or she won't let me invite them again.'

'Oh, ay,' Gordon said, 'what's the cloth for?'

'To stop tea stains on me mam's best cloth.' Ruthie felt very grown up shaking out the white cloth and throwing it on the table. She was helped the other end by Gordon, who would have done anything to get in her good books. 'If any spills on the chenille, it's hard to get out. But any stain will come out of this if it's steeped in bleach.'

When the two girls came in carrying a plate in each hand, the boys' faces lit up and they cheered.

'It's not much, but me mam and Bella's mum thought yer might be glad of a snack. And yer can either have tea or lemonade.'

The boys opted for lemonade, and once they were all seated again, the atmosphere was happy and noisy. The sandwiches and sausage rolls were much appreciated, and in what seemed no time at all the plates were empty and the girls were carrying them out again.

'Shall we wash them?' Bella asked. 'Or leave them until later?'

'Leave them for now,' Ruthie replied. 'Me mam said she thought our guests should leave by ten o'clock, so we'll wash them when they've gone. They'll only take five minutes.'

'Did yer mam really say that?' Bella couldn't believe this was happening. Any minute she was expecting her mother to come knocking on the door. 'We'll have to make sure everywhere is clean and tidy for when she comes home.'

'Don't let's play cards again,' Johnny suggested when they were all seated. 'Let's play a parlour game and have a laugh.'

* * *

The youngsters were having the time of their lives playing 'pass the parcel'. They took turns in standing with their back to the table and shouting 'Stop'. And the one who did that was allowed to choose the unfortunate loser's forfeit. The one left holding the parcel wasn't allowed to choose what they did for a forfeit, they had to do as they were told. It might be to tell a joke, to sing or even dance. And the whole house seemed to be alive with the laughter of young friends enjoying themselves.

It was nine o'clock when Mary Watson thought she would call, as Molly had said she could, to see her daughter and friends were all right. And she had her hand on the knocker when she heard an outburst of young laughter. She listened for a while, and there was a smile on her face as she dropped her hand. She didn't have the heart to spoil the night for her daughter, so she turned and crossed the cobbles, content and happy that Bella was enjoying herself.

When she set foot on the pavement opposite, Mary heard another burst of laughter. This time it came from her neighbour's house. And once again Mary smiled, as in her mind's eye she could see Nellie McDonough standing in the middle of Miss Clegg's living room, and either impersonating someone, or making up the most outrageous stories as she went along. She was never short of stories, was Nellie, and she never failed to cheer people up and make them laugh.

Mary wasn't to know this, but had she been in the street about half past ten, she would have heard still more laughter. This time it came from five men who strolled down the street after enjoying more than a few pints in each other's company. They'd exchanged jokes, discussed their jobs, and finally decided the world wasn't such a bad old place after all.

Chapter Sixteen

In the butcher's on the Tuesday morning, Tony was in fine fettle. There were no other customers in the shop and he had the two friends in stitches with tales of his next-door neighbour. And for once, Nellie didn't object to not being the centre of attention.

'She's got up to some queer tricks, has Mrs Middleton.' Tony was leaning back against the thick wooden cutting table, his straw hat pushed to the back of his head. 'The funniest thing was when her washing line snapped one day, and she hung her husband's long johns out of the front bedroom window to dry.'

'Go 'way! She didn't, did she?' Nellie was tickled pink. 'I bet the whole street had a good laugh at that. And eh, I bet her husband had to put up with a lot of stick from the neighbours.'

Molly wasn't so sure that Tony was telling the truth. She had a feeling he was making it all up for a laugh. It was something he often did, and a lot of his regular customers knew him well enough to take everything he said with a pinch of salt. But Nellie was enjoying herself so much Molly didn't want to spoil her fun. So she joined in. 'Your wife wouldn't be too happy, would she, Tony, having a pair of long johns dangling from the window next door?'

'The wife was blazing, Molly, and knocked to give the woman a piece of her mind. It didn't do no good though, 'cos Mrs Middleton told her to sod off. Her husband needed those underpants to wear the next day. And as the sun was shining on the front of the house, then that's where they were staying, to dry off. And if the neighbours didn't like it, well it was just too bleeding bad.'

Nellie was bent double as her imagination took over. In her mind she could actually see the long underpants hanging from the window, blowing when there was a gust of wind. A rare sight to be seen. 'Ooh, she must be a right one, your neighbour, as daft as a brush.' She wiped away tears of laughter with the back of her hand. 'Mind you, I wouldn't mind her coming to live in our street. It would cheer us all up.' She quickly added, 'But a few doors away, not right next door.'

Tony was really enjoying himself. It wasn't often he could hold forth when Nellie was in the shop, for she usually took over. 'Oh, yer wouldn't want her for a neighbour, Nellie, she can be quite dangerous. I remember one day, she set fire to her living room. Her curtains were alight, and her carpet. If the fire engine hadn't come as quick as it did, our house could have gone up in flames along with hers.'

Nellie's face was a picture as she drank in every word. 'Go 'way! Ay, Tony, yer want to move away from there. She sounds doolally.'

Two more customers came into the shop then, followed quickly by another two. 'I'll tell yer the rest of the tale next time yer come in.'

As Tony attended to the first two customers, Ellen came from the store room to help serve. She winked at Molly. 'He's almost as good as Nellie when he gets going. They make a good pair.'

Outside the shop, Molly put her basket in the crook of her arm. 'Come on, sunshine. It's Hanley's now for the bread, and we'll get our spuds on the way back. They're heavy to cart around when there's no need for it.'

Nellie linked her arm, but her mind was back at the butcher's. 'Ay, girl, I wouldn't like to live next door to Tony's neighbour, would you? I wouldn't feel safe in me bed with a maniac like her living next door.'

Molly looked sideways. Should she tell her mate that everything Tony told them had been made up, just for a laugh? No, better leave her with something to think about. It would keep her out of trouble. Or halfway, or somewhere in between, perhaps. 'I wouldn't take what Tony told us as gospel, sunshine. I think he exaggerated a bit, to give us a laugh.'

'Oh, I don't think . . .' Nellie's mouth gaped in surprise as she was unceremoniously pushed across the pavement towards the wool shop. 'What the hell . . .'

'Keep quiet and pretend to look in the window,' Molly said, in hushed tones. 'There's someone coming towards us that I think we know. Yer can take a sly look, but don't make it obvious.'

Nellie was almost cross-eyed as she tried to look without appearing to. 'What is it, girl? I can't see nothing.'

'Look to your right, sunshine, and see if yer recognise the man walking towards us. He's got a blonde hanging on to his arm.'

Nellie took another peep. 'Oh, yeah. That's the bloke . . .' A hand across her mouth prevented Nellie from saying any more. But as soon as she could breathe, she said, 'Ay, that's the bloke what's asked Claire to go out with him.'

Molly nodded as the couple passed. The woman was looking up into the man's eyes, all lovey-dovey, and neither noticed the two friends. 'By no stretch of the imagination is she his mother,' Molly said. 'More like a girlfriend.'

'I wonder what he's doing round here, girl? We've never seen him before, have we?' Nellie's eyes narrowed, a sure sign her brain was working. 'And what's he doing with that woman, when he's asked Claire to go out with him? There's something fishy going on.'

Molly nodded. 'It certainly looks that way, sunshine. The woman he's with is certainly not his sister, that's for sure.'

'Ay, let's follow him,' Nellie said, 'and see where they go.'

'I don't think so, Nellie. We may get caught.'

'It won't be us what gets caught, girl, 'cos we wouldn't be doing nothing wrong. It's a public street: we've as much right to be on it as he has. And even if he sees us, so what? He doesn't know us from Adam, and my curiosity is roused now. Come on, girl, before he gets too far away and we lose sight of him.'

Molly wasn't so sure. 'What good will it do us if we do find out where he's going?'

Nellie was prepared to follow the couple on her own if it came to the push. 'So I'm nosy, Molly, is that a crime? And why am I nosy? Because he's asked a friend of ours to go out with him, and for all we know he could be a rotter.'

That was enough to sway Molly. 'Okay, but we stay well behind. I don't want him to see us. So promise to behave yerself.'

'If I behaved meself every time yer told me to, I'd have a miserable bleeding life. And as this involves a friend of ours, I think we should open the McDonough and Bennett Private Detective Agency. So come on, girl, we're in business.'

Molly allowed herself to be propelled forward, but she wasn't going to let her mate have it all her own way. 'Yer've got a terrible memory, sunshine. Yer keep forgetting it's the Bennett and McDonough Private Detective Agency. Unless we get caught and hauled off to the police station. Then you can be senior partner.'

'Right now I don't care what we call it, we can argue about that later. Just put a move on, girl, before they get too far ahead of us and we lose them.'

The friends kept up a steady pace until they were about thirty yards away from the couple, who were arm in arm and laughing into each other's face. 'They're like a young courting couple,' Molly said. 'Yer were right about there being something fishy going on, sunshine. And it would be interesting to see what they are up to, and if they live together. I know he told Claire he wasn't married and lived with his aged mother, but it could have been a pack of lies. So we'll carry on following them to see if they split up, or go into a house together.'

Nellie was in her element. She loved playing detective, and she often said to anyone who would listen that her and Molly made good sleuths. They'd never lost a case yet. 'Yeah, we'll find out what he's up to. We don't have to rush home, so we've got plenty of time.'

'I think we should split up, though,' Molly said. 'Two of us together are more noticeable than one on their own. So what d'yer think about one on the opposite side of the street, and one walking behind them?'

'I think that's a good idea, girl,' Nellie agreed, feeling very important. 'You go on the other side, and I'll stay behind them. I'll move a bit closer, see if I can hear what they're saying. But from the looks of them, it's all lovey-dovey.'

'Perhaps we shouldn't jump to conclusions, sunshine, because there might be a very good reason for their behaviour. She could be a long-lost cousin, or something.'

Nellie huffed. 'Aye, and pigs might fly! No, they're no more cousins than the man in the moon. I keep expecting him to kiss her any minute. You mark my words, there's something phoney about that man. He's a wolf in sheep's clothing.'

'Let's not hang the man until we know he's guilty, sunshine. For Claire's sake I hope there's a good explanation for what we're seeing.'

'That's your trouble, Molly Bennett, yer can never see bad

in anyone. But I'll have yer a bet on this. I bet he's not what he makes out he is. Still, time will tell, so let's wait and see.'

'I'll cross over now, sunshine, and we'll meet up at the bottom of the street. I've got a feeling they'll go into one of these houses. Or at least one will, and the other will carry on walking. We'll see whether I'm right or not.'

Molly crossed the street, and when she glanced back over to the other side she was horrified to see Nellie had quickened her pace, and was shortening the gap between herself and the couple. Trust her mate to pull a stunt like that. She was probably trying to get close enough to hear what was being said. 'Let's hope she doesn't get so close they notice her,' Molly said under her breath. Not that Nellie would be in the least bit put out, even if they accused her of following them. She'd have a good excuse: she always had an excuse for everything.

Molly had to walk faster to keep abreast of her mate, but when she saw the couple stop outside one of the houses she automatically slowed down. But Nellie didn't slow down until she was only a couple of yards from the couple, and she was able to hear clearly when the man she thought of as Graham said, 'What about half past two this afternoon? The kids won't be in from school then.'

'Aren't yer coming in now?' the woman asked. 'We'd have a couple of hours on our own.'

The man shook his head. 'I'd love to, darling, but I have a job to do. I'm going home to pick up a case, then I have two calls to make. But I'll be here at half two.'

Nellie was walking very slowly, but to have listened in any longer she would have had to stand still. So she had to walk past the couple, and missed seeing the kiss they exchanged. But Molly had a good view, and when the mates met up on the corner of the street the words poured from her lips. 'Yer should have seen the kiss he gave her! In broad daylight, too!'

'That's nothing, girl. Listen to this.' Nellie repeated what she'd heard, and did it in a very dramatic style. 'What d'yer make of that?'

Molly shook her head. 'I don't know what to make of it, sunshine. I only wish I did.'

Nellie made up her mind quickly, and with determination. 'Let's follow him. He told the woman he was going home to pick something up, so if we follow him we'd at least know where he lives. It won't have been a waste of time then.'

'Ooh ay, Nellie, he might live miles away! He might even get on a bus, or a tram. We've got a bit of time to spare, but not enough to follow him if he's going a long way.'

'He doesn't live far away, girl, 'cos he's coming back to the woman's house at half two.' Nellie jerked her head back. 'And he certainly ain't coming for a cup of tea, that's a cert. Unless he likes a cup of tea in bed.'

Molly watched the man putting distance between them, and she quickly made up her mind. 'Fifteen minutes, sunshine, and no longer. Okay?'

Nellie was on the move before Molly had finished speaking. 'We'll have to leg it, girl, if we want to catch up with him.'

They didn't have to follow him far, for he turned into the next street. 'You go first, Nellie, and I'll follow. We look too conspicuous together.'

The little woman took to her heels and covered the ground fast. For someone carrying so much weight, it didn't seem to be an effort, and she bounced along. Molly was forced to pull herself together and walk quickly to keep up. And she turned the corner of the street just in time to see the man she knew as Graham turn in to the path in front of one of the houses. These were six-roomed houses, and all had a tiny garden in front. And the first thing Molly noticed was how well kept they were.

Nellie had slowed down when she saw the man turn in to the

path, and as she sauntered along her eyes slid sideways to see him putting a key in the lock. She hesitated long enough to see the number on the door, then carried on until she was halfway up the street, where she stopped and waited for her mate to catch her up.

Molly grinned when she reached Nellie. 'Ye're enjoying this, aren't yer, sunshine?'

'Ye're not kidding, girl. I'm having the time of me life. He lives in number thirty-two, so at least we've found something out about him. Just wait until we tell Claire. She won't half get a shock.'

'She won't get a shock, Nellie, 'cos we're not going to tell her.'

Nellie's voice came out in a squeak. 'Not going to tell her! Why aren't we? She has every right to know what the man's like. He'll be having it off with a bit of stuff at half past two this afternoon, and yer don't think we should tell her?'

'It's not up to us to tell her,' Molly said. 'She'll soon find out for herself what sort of man he is, she's not soft. And anyway, just tell me how yer would put into words what we've seen and heard today? Yer can't prove he's having it off, as yer call it, because we haven't seen it with our own eyes.'

Bedroom talk was always interesting to Nellie. 'Ay, I wouldn't mind being in the bedroom watching what they get up to. I bet some private detectives do get those sort of jobs. But we'd never be that lucky.'

'They do say that small things amuse small minds, sunshine, and you certainly have a small mind when it comes to things that happen in bedrooms. Me now, I'm not narrow-minded, and I am very satisfied with Jack in all those matters. But I'd rather read a good book than have nothing better on me mind but sex.'

Nellie chuckled. 'There yer are, girl, yer said it! Yer actually said "sex", and that's the first time since I've known yer.'

Molly was facing down the street, and she gave a start. 'Ay, here comes the man himself, and he's swinging what looks like a large attaché case. Let's move. We're too obvious standing here, and I don't want him to get a good look at us. Walk round the corner, sunshine, and we'll pretend to be looking in a shop window.'

Nellie had a quick glimpse before turning the corner. 'He looks dead respectable with that case, doesn't he? A real businessman.'

'I'll go to the far end of the window, sunshine, so he doesn't see us together. One woman he won't even notice, but two might just register.'

Nellie tutted. 'He's got more on his mind than remembering two working-class women in their forties. All he'll be thinking about is what he's got waiting for him at half past two.'

The man came round the corner, and without a glance at the two women he kept on walking. They waited until he was out of earshot, then Nellie said, 'Come on, girl, let's follow and see where he's off to.'

Molly had no choice but to follow, for Nellie was already in her stride. But her intention of following the man was thwarted when he stopped by a bus stop just as a bus came to a shuddering halt. And he had hopped on board and was away before Nellie could talk her friend into following him. 'Damn and blast!' She was so disappointed, Molly thought she was going to stamp her feet. 'Missed him by ten seconds.'

'You might have missed him, sunshine, but I didn't. I had no intention of following him if he took a bus or a tram, and I told yer that. I've got more to do with me time than chase after a man we don't know.'

'But that's the whole point, girl, we don't know him! And our job, as private detectives, is to find out who, and what, he is. We've missed our chance today though, through you dithering. Wasted a whole day.'

'Yer don't half exaggerate, sunshine, for if we've wasted any time, it's only been half an hour. And for your information, I wasn't dithering, I was being realistic. He could be on his way to Aintree for all we know, or even Fazakerley. And that would be an hour's travelling, plus the bus fares. And we haven't got all day to waste following some strange man. Plus, I have better things to spend me money on than forking out fares. The pennies would be better spent on food.' Molly took a deep breath. 'Take that scowl off yer face, Nellie, and don't you dare sulk all the way home because yer didn't get yer own way. Why can't yer be satisfied that we now know where he lives? At least we haven't completely wasted our time.'

Nellie forced a smile. 'Yeah, and we know he's going to bed with a woman at half past two. I must remember that, and keep me eye on the clock.'

Molly's brow creased. 'What d'yer want to keep yer eye on the clock for?' Then it suddenly dawned on her. 'Don't get the idea into yer head that yer can sit in my house at half two, 'cos yer can't. And all I'll say is, it's a pity yer've got nothing better to do. Bed, and what goes on in it, has become an obsession with yer, Nellie, and at your age yer should have a bit more sense.'

Nellie was feeling mischievous and goaded her friend. 'It's the only thing in life that's free, girl, so yer may as well get yer fill of it.' She pretended she'd just thought of something. 'Ay, isn't there a song called "The best Things in Life are Free"?'

Molly didn't rise to the bait. 'Yes, I think so, sunshine. I bet the man what wrote it had you in mind. Did yer know him by any chance?'

Nellie rolled her eyes. 'Yeah, he used to live next door to me mam, when I was a young slip of a girl. I remember him 'cos he had bandy legs. Me ma, God rest her soul, used to say he was so bandy, he couldn't stop a pig in an entry.'

'Oh, yer ma used to say that, did she?' Molly suddenly burst out laughing. 'Nellie, that was a useful piece of information, but don't yer think we should start making our way back to where we come from? The shops will be closing for dinner soon, and I don't want to have to come out again this afternoon.'

'Okay, girl, let's go.' Nellie linked arms. 'Have yer still got the notebook that yer had for writing down the details of the jobs Bennett and McDonough did?' She waited for Molly's nod. 'Well, when we get home, yer'll have to start a new page for our latest assignment. I'll tell yer everything what we did, and you can be writing it down. It's no good me trying to write, I can't even spell me own name.'

'That's not quite true, sunshine, and you know it. Oh, it's true ye're hopeless with big words, but ye're far from being as thick as yer make out yer are. What yer've done very cleverly, Nellie, is turn acting daft into a profession. I've seen yer standing looking as innocent as Shirley Temple, while the wheels of yer brain are working overtime to find a way of turning the situation to your advantage. Yer've got as much nous as our Prime Minister. Yer may not be able to spell his name, but I'd put yer up against him any day, and I bet yer'd come out the winner.'

'Ah, that's nice of yer, girl, and I'm really grateful to yer.' When Nellie nodded decisively, her chins were happy to go along with her. 'By the way, girl, what is the name of our Prime Minister?'

'Ooh, I couldn't tell yer that, sunshine, 'cos I don't take much interest in politics. But whatever his name is, you're just as clever as him. In a different way perhaps, but every bit as clever.'

'I'll ask George when he comes in from work. He'll know

who the Prime Minister is. He should do, he reads every word printed in the newspaper. He'll be surprised that I'm as clever as him, though, 'cos George is always saying I've got nothing between me ears only fresh air.'

'That's only George's little joke, Nellie. He doesn't mean it.'

'I don't give a bugger whether he means it or not, girl, 'cos him thinking I'm tuppence short of a shilling comes in handy sometimes.'

'How d'yer mean, Nellie? What times are they?'

'When he gives me half a crown to get him twenty cigarettes, and I forget on purpose to give him sixpence change. When he asks me for it, I swear it was only a two-bob piece he gave me. If he argues, I tell him he should get himself a pair of glasses 'cos his eyesight must be going if he can't see the difference between a two-bob piece and a half-crown.'

Molly gasped. 'Yer don't get away with it, do yer?'

'Of course I do! I've told yer, girl, it doesn't pay to be honest. That's a big fault of yours, and I'm fed up telling yer. Being Miss Goody Two-Shoes won't get yer anywhere.'

'I don't know how yer can do that, Nellie, 'cos George is very generous with yer over money. I couldn't live with meself if I did it to Jack.'

'Ah, well, yer see, girl, me and you are as different as chalk and cheese. I don't feel bad about taking the odd tanner or shilling off George, 'cos I pay him back by being extra nice to him when we get into bed.'

'Nellie, for heaven's sake, is that all yer've ever got on yer mind? Let's change the subject, eh?'

'No, it's not all I ever have on me mind, Molly Bennett, so there! In fact, if yer put George next to a custard slice, I'd pick the cake.'

Molly shook her head. 'I give up, sunshine, so shall we just concentrate on getting to the shops before one o'clock?'

'If you say so, girl.' Nellie bent her head and muttered, 'What a miserable bleeding life she must have.'

Molly didn't answer, but she chuckled inwardly all the way to the shops.

The friends were walking up the street when Nellie said, 'Ay, girl, your Doreen's standing on the step waving to yer.'

Molly's heart jumped, and she dropped the basket. 'Oh, my God, there must be something wrong with the baby.' She began to run, saying, 'You bring the basket up, Nellie.'

Nellie picked up the heavy basket and moved as quickly as she could. 'I don't know what ye're running for, yer daft nit! Yer didn't give me a chance to tell yer that Doreen's got a big smile on her face.'

'What is it, sunshine?' Molly was out of breath and gasped, 'Has something happened to the baby?'

Doreen's face was aglow. 'Mam, he's got his first tooth!'

Molly bent down until she got her breath back, and when she lifted her head she was beaming. 'Ooh, I got the fright of me life, sunshine. I thought the worst, as usual. But isn't that wonderful news! I didn't even know he was teething.'

'Neither did we, Mam. There's never been a peep out of him, he's been as good as gold.' Doreen was so proud she wanted to tell the whole street. 'Hurry up, Auntie Nellie, I've got something to tell yer.'

Nellie let the heavy basket drop to the pavement. 'How the hell d'yer expect me to hurry when I'm carrying that thing? Yer mam went off and left me swinging, without even a please or thank you.'

Molly looked down at her. 'It's a ruddy good job there were no eggs in that basket, Nellie McDonough, 'cos they'd be smashed to smithereens.'

'Yer were glad of cracked eggs during the war, Molly

Bennett, so don't be getting on yer high horse with me.'

'Don't yer want to know me news, Auntie Nellie?' Doreen asked, while at the back of her mind she was wondering why her mam had mentioned eggs when there weren't any in the basket anyway. 'The baby's got his first tooth.'

The little woman's face was a picture. 'Go 'way! A tooth at his age? Well, I'll be blowed! If he carries on like this, he'll soon be eating yer out of house and home.'

'Or walking to work with his dad.' Molly picked up the basket. 'Let me get in to see me clever grandson.'

Victoria was nursing the baby on her lap, and she looked so pleased as she rocked her chair, anyone would think he was the first child ever to grow a tooth. 'I've never had a child meself, as yer know, Molly, but I was told by many women that they'd had to walk the floor with their babies when they were teething.'

'I had to walk the floor many nights with each one of mine,' Molly said, bending down to smile at her grandson. 'Oh, I can see the tooth! It's not quite through the skin yet. Ooh, you little love, I could eat yer. What a good boy yer've been.'

Nellie tapped her on the back. 'Would yer mind moving away and giving someone else a chance? As his adopted grandma I do have some rights, yer know.'

'I can't wait for Phil to get home from work,' Doreen said, looking so pretty and so happy. 'He'll be as proud as anything, and I pity the men he works with, 'cos he'll do nothing but brag about his son. Even though most of the men are older and have kids of their own.'

'He's entitled to brag, sunshine, and yer should be glad he loves the baby enough to brag about. Yer dad was thrilled every time one of you had a tooth come through. He never even moaned when he had to take turns walking the floor through the night. And he did it with every one of yer.'

Nellie was tickling the baby's tummy, and he was loving it.

He was smiling into her face, gurgling and kicking. 'Yer love yer Grandma Nellie, don't yer, Bobby? And I'll always be here to tickle yer tummy, lad, even though a certain person tries to keep me in the shade.'

'I know someone else who'll be very happy,' Molly said, 'and that's Frances. But when me and Nellie pick her up tomorrow, we won't say a word. Let's see if she notices it herself when she's nursing him.'

'I won't be able to keep it to meself, Mam.' Doreen laughed. 'I'll tell her before she sets her foot in the door.'

'Have yer told Jill yet?'

'I've been waiting for you, so yer'd be the first to know. But I'm going to put Bobby in his pram and walk him up there. And after I've finished boasting, I can have a nurse of Molly.'

Nellie turned round. 'We were out longer than usual today, girl, 'cos we had a bit of business to do.'

'Oh, aye, and what was that?' Doreen asked. 'Was it big business, or just shopping?'

Molly groaned inwardly. 'Take no notice of her, sunshine, she's pulling yer leg.' A glare was sent in her mate's direction. 'The nearest we get to business is buying a loaf in Hanley's, or a pound of stew in the butcher's.' She chucked Nellie under the chin. 'Isn't that right, Nellie?'

'If you say so, girl, then it's right.' The little woman was disappointed. Her view was that if yer knew something of importance, then yer should share it. Why keep it to yerself when others would be very interested if yer told them? It would put a bit of spice in their life.

'We'll leave yer to get the baby ready, sunshine. Will yer tell Jill I'll be up tonight to see them all? Just for half an hour, 'cos from there I want to go and see me ma and da. And Tommy and Rosie, of course.' Molly gave her daughter a big hug. 'We're a very lucky family, yer know that, don't yer? And we're lucky to have friends like the McDonoughs and the Corkhills. We've got a lot of blessings to be thankful for.'

Some recognition at last, Nellie thought. 'Yeah, we've been friends a long time, haven't we, girl?'

'Twenty-odd years, sunshine, and that's not bad going. But let's be on our way and get this shopping home. And if yer ask me nicely, I might make yer a cup of tea.'

'Will that make it two thousand five hundred and fifty-four, girl?'

'I can't remember offhand, Nellie, but I'll look it up when we get in.' Molly kissed the baby and Victoria. 'See yer tomorrow when we bring Frances. Ta-ra for now.'

Molly helped Frances out of the taxi the next morning, and smiled at Doreen who was waiting with the door open. 'I think yer know this woman, Doreen. She said she's come to see her grandson.'

Doreen cupped Phil's mother's elbow and helped her up the two steps. 'And her grandson is waiting for her. He's been gurgling and kicking for the last hour, as though he's expecting someone very special.'

Molly waited until she and Nellie were alone on the pavement, then said softly, 'We won't stay this morning, sunshine. We'll leave them in peace today.'

'Ah, ay, Molly Bennett, I want to stay and have a cup of tea! You can go to the shops on yer own if yer want, but I'm staying here for a cuppa.'

Molly had a good reason for what she was doing. She knew without any doubt that Nellie wouldn't be able to keep to herself what they'd been up to the day before. She wouldn't do it out of malice or spite, but because she wouldn't see any reason not to tell them. It was too good a story to keep to herself. But Molly didn't want Claire's affairs to be aired in public. 'I thought perhaps yer'd like to do a bit of business for the Bennett and McDonough Private Detective Agency. We don't need much in the way of shopping, and I believed yer'd be happier doing a bit of spying. We'd get some walking done in the fresh air, and it would do us good.'

Her friend was suspicious. 'What did yer have in mind, and why didn't yer mention it when we were in the taxi going to pick Frances up?'

'I thought yer'd be all for it, that's why! But if yer don't want to, then we'll forget it and spend an hour here.'

'Ay, hang on the bell, Molly, I didn't say I didn't want to, did I? But whatever yer have in mind had better be more appetising than a cream slice.'

'We know where the woman he was with yesterday lives, and we know his address. Why don't we go for a walk which happens to take us past both houses? We might not see anything today, but then again, we might hop in lucky. And I noticed the corner shop, which would be just the place for you to do a bit of acting. Yer might just find something out.' Molly knew her mate inside out. 'Still, if yer don't feel like it, we'll stay here and have a cup of tea and a natter.'

'Nah, let's go where the excitement is. I'm all for it, girl, so lead the way.'

'We can't just walk off. I'll have to tell Doreen we're going somewhere. So come in with me and tell them we're going on a message and will see them later.'

Nellie's face was a joy to behold. 'Oh boy, oh boy, oh boy! Yer can't beat a bit of excitement in yer life, it bucks yer up no end.'

'Come in with me, but you don't say anything. Leave the talking to me.'

Chapter Seventeen

'It's a lovely day, isn't it, sunshine?' Molly smiled down at her mate. 'Even if we don't uncover any mystery, the walk will do us good.'

'Yeah, my George is always saying I should walk more than I do, so I could lose some weight. He says I'm carrying too much fat, and it must put a strain on me heart.' Nellie chuckled. 'He's proper cheerful, is my feller, always ready with a joke to cheer me up.'

'He's only thinking of you, Nellie, 'cos he loves yer. Your trouble is that yer have a sweet tooth and eat too many cakes and chocolates. When it comes to custard creams and cream slices, yer've got no willpower whatsoever.'

'Never mind, eh, girl? When yer time is up, there's nowt yer can do about it. So enjoy life while yer can, that's my motto.'

'It's easy to talk when ye're hale and hearty, Nellie, but yer may regret it when yer get older. It wouldn't hurt yer to do without a cake every day, and go for a little walk.'

'Okay, girl, I don't need a lecture.' Nellie couldn't be serious for long, however, and mischief appeared in her eyes. 'I'll do without me cake today, and I haven't had a custard cream 'cos we had to be out early to pick Frances up. On top of that, I'm having a walk which will be well over a mile by the time we've finished. But I know a better way of taking the fat off, and that's by energetic exercise.'

Molly grinned. 'Oh, aye, I can just see you exercising.

Stretching yer arms towards the ceiling, and then bending down to touch yer toes. That's something I'd like to see, Nellie, 'cos it would only happen once.'

'That's where ye're wrong, girl. Ye're the same age as meself, but yer haven't learned as much over the years as I have. Yer see, the best place to exercise is in bed. The energy yer use, well it burns some of the fat off. And the more yer go at it, the more fat yer lose.' Before Molly could shut her up, she added, 'And what a way to lose it, eh? With a ruddy big smile on yer face.'

Molly, however, had decided not to rise to the occasion, or Nellie would carry on and go into more detail. 'From what I've heard about your bedroom antics over the years, sunshine, how come ye're not as thin as a rake?'

Nellie had the answer ready. 'Well, it's like this, yer see, girl. What I take off at night when me and George are going at it hell for leather, I put on again next day with me custard creams and a cream slice.'

'I can't win, can I, sunshine? I give in, as long as yer change the topic of conversation.'

'The reason I go on about me love-life, girl, is because it's about the only thing I'm good at. Whereas you are good at lots of things. Yer never get yer knickers in a twist, yer always know what to say to people, and yer know more long words than anyone I know.' Nellie's grin was cheeky. 'Mind you, there's something I've never thought of. Perhaps yer never get yer knickers in a twist because yer don't wear no knickers.'

'And that's given yer food for thought, has it, sunshine? Well, can yer now put yer mind to the reason for us being in this street? We're coming to the corner shop I mentioned. Shall we go in and see how the land lies? We could buy something, then if whoever serves us is friendly and talkative, we could perhaps say we know someone who lives round here, but we're not sure exactly which street. We don't know the woman's name, but we could say she's a friend of Graham Collins.'

Looking doubtful, Nellie shook her head. 'No, we'd never get away with that, girl. We'll have to come up with something more believable. And I don't think yer should mention that Graham feller's name. If his girlfriend goes in the shop and she's told someone was asking after her boyfriend, then we'd be rumbled. So why don't we walk down past her house and see if we notice anything that might give us a clue? Then we could walk to the queer feller's house. It's not far from here. It might be a waste of time, but, then again, we might learn something.'

'Good thinking, sunshine, we'll do just that.' Molly squeezed her mate's arm. 'We can't rush an undercover job, can we?'

Nellie nodded knowingly. She liked the word 'undercover', it made her sound important. 'Like William Powell and Myrna Loy. They're undercover investigators, and they always solve the crime. And no one would ever guess they were detectives, 'cos they're man and wife.'

Molly chuckled. 'And don't forget their dog, Nellie, because it solves most of the crimes for them.'

'Ay, it might be a good idea for us to get a dog, Molly. Mind you, on second thoughts, George would go mad if I walked in with a dog in tow.' After a short silence, when there was no reply from her friend, Nellie ventured to say, 'Unless you kept it in your house. I'd help yer buying the food for it.'

'Don't even think about it, Nellie. Get it right out of yer head 'cos it's not going to happen. Don't yer realise I've got enough on me plate as it is? Two new grandchildren on top of the rest of the family.'

'I didn't really think yer'd go for the idea, girl, but it was worth a try. Yer don't get nowhere if yer don't try.'

'Trying to palm me off with a dog wasn't a very good idea, Nellie. Yer've come up with some hare-brained schemes over the years, but that one is probably the worst. Not that I've anything against dogs, but they leave hairs everywhere, and it wouldn't be wise where the two babies are concerned.'

Nellie didn't think the idea was that bad. 'Not even if yer kept it tied up in yer yard, girl? It couldn't do no harm there. And we could teach it to help us catch any baddies.'

'I don't know why I'm wasting me breath asking yer this, but how would we teach it? It takes years of experience to train them to do tricks, or to catch people, and no matter how clever the dog was, it wouldn't learn much in our backyard.'

'William Powell and Myrna Loy manage,' Nellie said, not to be outdone. 'They trained their dog, and it's only a fiddling little thing.'

'They live in a mansion, Nellie, or they do in the films. And their garden is as big as a field.' Molly was asking herself why she bothered, for the whole conversation wasn't getting them anywhere. Still, she'd say what she had in mind, then forget it. 'And because a dog is small, it doesn't mean it's less intelligent than a whopping big dog.'

Nellie was biting on her bottom lip when she said, 'I can tell ye're getting a cob on, girl, so we'll forget about a dog. I don't want to see yer getting upset and thinking yerself mean because yer won't give a home to a poor little puppy.'

'That sob story isn't going to work, sunshine, so forget it. The only way I want to see a dog is on the front of a box of Cadbury's chocolates. I wouldn't harm any creature, and would feed one if it was hungry. And I would never stand by and see one being ill-treated. But owning an animal brings responsibility, and I have enough without taking on any more.'

'Never mind, girl. We've managed all these years without one, and we've done very well for ourselves.'

Molly glanced at the number on the door of the house they were passing. 'We're near that woman's house, Nellie, so you walk on and I'll follow a little way behind yer. Have a quick look to see if there's anything to give us a clue about her, and I'll do the same.'

Nellie reached the bottom of the street first, and shook her head when Molly caught up with her. 'Nothing out of the ordinary, girl, and no sign of anyone. She keeps the windows clean, and the nets are nice and white, but that's all I had time to take in.' She drew herself up to her full height. 'I didn't want to walk too slow in case one of the neighbours opposite saw me and became suspicious. I acted just like what a proper detective would, and I didn't draw attention to meself.'

'Keeps her step nice and white, too,' Molly said, 'but that doesn't tell us anything. I've got a feeling our little outing isn't going to bear any fruit, but it would be asking too much to expect success every day. And anyway, it's been a nice walk for us, and I'm enjoying the fresh air.'

'Yeah, we can't expect to be lucky every day, girl. Some detectives have to work months before they solve a case. And we'll be seeing Claire on Friday. She might have something to tell us which will help us find out more about him.'

Molly nodded. 'We'll listen to what she's got to say, sunshine, but not by word or deed will we tell her what we've seen, or what we've been up to. So yer'll have to keep yer wits about yer, Nellie, and think before yer speak.'

'Oh, I will! Yer can rely on me. I'll be the soul of . . . er, the soul of . . . what will I be the soul of, girl?'

'The soul of discretion, sunshine.'

'Yeah, that's what I'll be, the soul of discretion.'

When Friday afternoon came, Nellie was pacing Molly's living room like a caged tiger. She couldn't sit still, even though Claire wasn't due for another half an hour. 'Where the hell has she got to? She should be here by now.' With her hips swaying from side to side, the little woman made her way out to the kitchen, where Molly was putting the finishing touches to the plates of sandwiches and cakes. 'It doesn't look as though she's coming.'

'Nellie, if yer keep this up, ye're going to have us both nervous wrecks by the time Claire gets here.' Molly struck a match and set alight to the gas ring under the kettle. 'Why don't yer sit down and relax? If she sees yer like this, she'll twig there's something up. So do us both a favour and go and sit in the living room. I've got everything ready out here, so I'll come in and sit with yer. But for heaven's sake, sunshine, for once in yer life will yer think before yer open yer mouth? I like Claire, and I want her to stay friends with us. But if she knows what we've been up to, she'll wish she'd never set eyes on us.'

'We're doing it for her, girl, so she wouldn't fall out with us. But I won't say a word out of place, I promise yer.' Nellie stiffened a finger and made a cross somewhere in the region of her heart. 'Cross my heart and hope to die, if this day I tell a lie.'

Molly wanted to laugh, but managed to keep her face straight. 'Yer dice with death every time yer say that, sunshine. Aren't yer frightened?'

Nellie's brow creased. 'How d'yer make that out, girl?'

'That yer hope to die if yer tell a lie! In the course of one day, yer must tell at least ten or twelve lies. And that's only in the time I spend with yer; it doesn't include any fibs that yer tell in yer own home. Particularly those yer tell to George.'

Nellie's neck seemed to disappear between her shoulders when she spread out her hands. 'But they're only little white lies, girl, and everyone tells white lies. Even Saint Peter knows they don't do no harm.'

'Oh, Saint Peter's told yer that, has he? Yer must be very

well in with him if he's told yer that little white lies don't count as sins. It's the first I've ever heard of it.'

'Well, he doesn't need to tell you, does he? I mean, he'd only be wasting his breath 'cos yer don't tell any.' Nellie suddenly had a thought. 'Ay, Saint Peter won't like you, yer know, girl. Ye're so good, he'll think ye're after his job, and he won't let yer through the pearly gates.'

'Not even when he knows I'm your best mate?'

Her lips pursed, Nellie nodded. 'I'll have to remind him that you and me are best mates. Once he knows that, yer'll get a ticket on the front row next to me.'

Molly chuckled. 'I didn't know whether to look on that as a threat or a promise, sunshine. Don't yer think I will have had enough of yer on earth? And besides, wouldn't yer worry about me getting in the way of yer harp?'

When the knock came on the door both women moved as one. And as one wouldn't give way to the other, they both got stuck in the frame of the kitchen door. 'Get out of the way, girl, the bleeding door's not wide enough for both of us.'

'I know that, Nellie, but as it's my bleeding door, I should be the one to get through it first.' Molly managed to turn sideways and inched her way through; then, with Nellie hot on her heels, she hurried to open the front door. 'Hello, sunshine. It's nice to see yer. Come on in.'

After a greeting, Claire was able to get past Molly, but as Nellie was the width of the hall, only a ghost could have got past her. 'Hello, Nellie.'

'Hello, girl. Ye're looking well.'

'She'll look even better when she gets in, sunshine.' There were three women in the tiny hall, and two of the women were being kept there by the third, who was afraid to turn round in case she missed something. Molly would laugh about it later, with Jack, but at that moment she wasn't finding it funny. 'Nellie, for heaven's sake will yer move yerself and let me and Claire get in? Ye're taking up the whole space.'

Nellie walked backwards, with her hands on the wall so she'd know when she came to the stairs. This was one time she didn't want to fall and break a leg. 'Come in, girl. We've got the kettle on ready for yer.'

Molly stood in the doorway of the living room and let out a long sigh of relief. 'D'yer know, Nellie, I thought me and Claire were going to be held prisoner until Jack came in from work and paid a ransom for us.'

'Ooh, did yer hear that, Claire?' Nellie picked up her carver chair and carried it to the table. 'Talk about being big-headed isn't in it. Her Jack wouldn't pay no ransom for her. He'd go out and find himself a young bit of stuff.'

Claire laughed. Two minutes in the house and she was feeling at home already. 'Oh, I doubt that, Nellie. He'd go a long way to find a woman as good looking as his wife.'

'He wouldn't have to go far, girl. I only live three doors away. And Jack would have much more fun with me than he does with Molly. Every night would be Christmas Eve for him. He wouldn't know he was born.'

Molly sat down facing Claire. 'My feller wouldn't last a week with Nellie. She'd wear him out in no time.'

'I haven't worn George out.' Nellie gave a sharp sideways jerk of her head, and bragged, 'He must be made of stronger stuff, my feller.'

'For the sake of keeping the peace, Nellie, I'll agree with yer. But don't be making yerself comfortable on that chair 'cos yer can help me bring the tray in. I'm sure Claire is gasping for a drink.'

Nellie didn't waste time, but was up like a shot. The sooner they were settled, the sooner they'd hear what news Claire had.

Had she made a date with the Collins bloke, or not? 'I'll be glad of a drink meself. Me mouth is parched.'

'I'm not surprised, sunshine, 'cos yer never stop talking. And before yer start reminding me that God gave us mouths so we could speak, come out and give me a hand.'

Never had Nellie moved so quickly or so willingly. In no time at all the table was set, and they each had a drink in front of them. Her legs swinging like mad, the little woman kept her eyes on Claire, willing her to start giving out the news. When it wasn't forthcoming quickly enough, Nellie avoided Molly's eyes, and took things into her own hands. 'Any news for us, Claire? Did yer tell the bloke yer'd go out with him, or did yer tell him to sling his hook?'

Claire placed her cup carefully in the saucer, then smiled. 'I've been and gone and done it, Nellie. I went to the Royal Court with him last night.'

Molly was stunned into silence, leaving the talking to Nellie. 'Oh, come on, girl, tell us all about it. Dish the dirt with yer mates.'

'Don't be so nosy, Nellie,' Molly said. 'Claire will tell us what she wants us to know. But I'm surprised, to say the least. I thought yer'd keep him dangling a bit longer.'

'It was the kids who made the decision for me,' Claire told them. 'I thought they wouldn't like the idea, and if that was the case I would have turned him down. But the kids were all for it, and said it would do me good to get out.'

'Oh, well, that would make yer feel better, Claire, wouldn't it?' Molly tried to put some enthusiasm into her voice, but in her mind she was apprehensive. She didn't have a good feeling about this Graham Collins, and was fearful that the beautiful woman sitting across the table from her might be in for some heartbreak. 'How did yer get on with him?'

'All right.' Claire pulled a face. 'I felt so shy I hardly said a word. And every time he spoke to me, I blushed like a schoolgirl. I'm not used to talking to members of the opposite sex, 'cos it's been so long since my husband died, and I couldn't find anything to talk about.'

'Tell us all about it,' Nellie said, leaning forward and lifting her bosom on to the table. 'Did he take yer in the best seats, and buy yer some chocolates?'

'Yes, they were good seats, very near the front, and he did buy me some chocolates. It was the first time in me life I went to see a play, and once I got accustomed to him sitting next to me, I really enjoyed it.'

Nellie's chin was almost touching the table by this time. 'Did he hold yer hand?'

Claire's laugh rang out. 'Certainly not! I'm not a young girl any more, Nellie, I'm a widow with two children. But apart from that, I wouldn't have let him hold me hand anyway, 'cos I hardly know the man. He seems respectable enough, and I suppose you could say he is charming. Very good company, and considering he's a bachelor he knows how to treat a lady and make her feel special.'

'Did yer find out any more about him?' Molly asked. 'Like where he lives, and what he does for a living? He must have money to take you to the theatre, in the best seats, and with chocolates. My Jack never had enough money to treat me to those luxuries.'

'Neither did Bill, Molly, so we were in the same boat. And if I could just have one wish, it would be to have Bill back and I'd never moan again about being hard up. Graham Collins is a nice bloke, but he certainly doesn't make me heart beat faster, like Bill did every time he walked through the door.'

Molly's eyes gave out a warning to Nellie before she asked, 'He'd already told yer he lived with his mother. Did he say where?'

'He didn't say the name of the street, at least I don't think so. But apparently it's not too far away from here. It's a six-roomed house, and he has someone come in to clean 'cos his mother is getting on in years. And he deals in antiques.'

'Ooh, he must have money, girl, and he must be clever. I'd say he was a real toff.' Nellie would have loved to have said her and Molly knew where he lived because they'd passed the house. But with Molly's eyes boring into her, she was careful with her words. 'Does he speak frightfully far back, like what posh people do?'

'He's well spoken,' Claire told her, 'but he doesn't act like a toff. What I mean is, he doesn't make yer feel as though he comes from a better class. If I'd thought for one minute he was talking down to me, I'd have been off like a ruddy shot.'

'I should think so, sunshine,' Molly told her. 'I'm sure he was very proud of himself having someone so beautiful on his arm.'

'Beauty is skin deep, Molly, it's what's inside which is more important. Anyway, I had a nice night out, and he was good company. Never once did he get too familiar, or try to overstep the mark.'

Nellie was thinking it was a pity he'd acted like a gentleman. How much more exciting it would have been if he'd tried to have his wicked way with Claire. 'Did he ask yer for another date, girl?'

Claire nodded. 'I'm going out with him on Tuesday night. Ken said he'd stay in with Amy, 'cos I wouldn't leave her on her own, she's too young. I've told the kids that when I know him a bit better, I'll take him home so they can meet him. It won't be for a while, though, 'cos I don't want him to think I'm looking for a husband. It's nice to have a gentleman friend, but that's as far as it goes. At least for the foreseeable future.'

'That's wise of yer, sunshine,' Molly said. 'There's nothing to be gained by rushing into something without giving it plenty of thought. But I'm sure yer don't need me to tell yer that, Claire, 'cos I think yer've got yer head screwed on the right way.'

'If I didn't, our Ken would soon tell me,' Claire said with a smile. 'Since Bill died, my son has always been there for me. He watches over me like a hawk. He's a very sensible lad for his age, and if I was to take Graham home, and Ken didn't take to him, then he'd soon let me know. He's the man of the house since he started work, and that's the way we both like it.'

Molly nodded in agreement. She hadn't known Claire long, but she had taken a strong liking to her, and would be sorry to see her hurt. But from what she'd just heard, Claire had her two feet firmly on the ground. 'There's still a few sandwiches left, so I'll make a fresh pot of tea to wash them down with.'

Nellie sat up straight in her chair. 'D'yer want me to come and help yer, girl?'

'No, you stay and talk to Claire, sunshine. It won't take me five minutes to boil the kettle.' After putting a light to one of the gas rings, Molly popped her head round the door. 'Try and keep yer conversation away from yer bedroom, sunshine, there's a good girl.'

'I'd better bring these cups out to rinse, 'cos there's leaves on the bottom. Yer should have used the strainer, girl.'

'Oh, I forgot! I'll come and get them, sunshine. Don't you bother getting up.'

Nellie winked at Claire when Molly came in and collected the empty cups. 'She's a good mate is Molly, one in a million. I don't know what I'd do without her. I'd be lost.'

'Flattery will get yer one custard cream, sunshine. Will that do yer? Yer'd have got two if yer'd piled it on.'

Nellie grinned. 'Am I too late to say that me life would be empty without yer?'

'Don't push yer luck, Nellie: it's one custard cream each. Yer've had a cream slice – that should have been enough for yer.'

'Oh, it was, girl, it was! I'm only having a custard cream 'cos yer've talked me into it.'

When Molly came back into the living room she was carrying the empty cups, the pot of fresh tea, and a determination to keep the conversation away from Graham Collins. 'Have yer got good neighbours, Claire?'

'Yes, Molly, I've got good neighbours. They'd do yer a good turn before they'd do yer a bad one. But I haven't got one I'm particularly friendly with, not like you and Nellie. Me best mate is our Ken. He doesn't go out much once he gets home from work, but stays in and keeps me company.'

'Hasn't he got any friends? Lads of his own age?'

'There's a few he knows from his school days, but I believe the reason he doesn't go out is because he doesn't like leaving me. I know it's wrong, and I've told him, but I think he feels guilty about me being alone. Amy goes to bed about eight or half past, but I don't mind being on me own. It gives me a chance to catch up on me housework.'

'If I'd known that, I'd have told yer to ask him to come last Friday night.' Molly was remembering the lad who delivered her greens last Christmas, and how she'd taken to him. 'Our Ruthie had a few friends in for a game of cards, and Ken would have been welcome. They had a good laugh and enjoyed themselves. There was Ruthie and her friend Bella, and three local lads. Next time there's something going on, I'll tell Phil to let Ken know. He would enjoy himself, 'cos they're all nice kids.'

'It's what he needs, Molly, to mix with youngsters his own age. So if there's ever a game of cards going, let me know and I'll make sure he comes.' Claire glanced at the clock. 'I don't feel like moving, but I know I've got to. Amy doesn't like coming home to an empty house.'

'Me and Nellie will come to the door with yer, to get a bit of fresh air.' Molly grinned at her mate. 'We'll leave the dishes and do them later, eh, sunshine? Come on, let's see if any of the neighbours are having a fight so we can stand and watch.' She chuckled as she pushed her chair back under the table. 'Come to think of it, Nellie, every fight I've ever known in this street has been between you and Elsie Flanaghan.'

Molly stepped down to the pavement and looked up at the lovely blue sky. 'It's a beautiful day. Just look at those puffs of white clouds floating in the air. That means God is in his heaven and all is right with the world.'

'Don't be going all sloppy on us, or yer'll have me crying.' Nellie suddenly lifted her hand and waved. 'Look who's coming up the street, girl.'

Molly's face lit up when she saw Jill and Doreen on the opposite side of the street, pushing prams. 'Oh, it's me daughters, Claire. Don't rush off without meeting them.' And like the proud grandmother she was, she added, 'And yer must see me grandchildren.'

'Good grief, Molly, they're the spitting image of yer,' Claire said as they crossed the cobbles. 'They're lovely girls.'

Molly made the introductions. 'Claire hasn't got much time; she has to be home for her daughter. But let her have a peep at Bobby and little Molly.'

'I know all about you from Phil,' Doreen said. 'He told me your son is always singing your praises. And my husband said he's a lovely lad, and a real grafter.'

'It's thanks to your husband that Ken's got a job,' Claire said with feeling. 'We both owe a great deal to him, and to all your family, and Nellie's. And now, before I have to dash off, can I see the babies I've heard so much about?'

Bobby was gurgling as usual, his small face alight with laughter. 'Oh, he's lovely.' Claire held out a finger which Bobby gripped. 'He seems a contented baby.'

Doreen was delighted to sing her son's praises. 'He's just got his first tooth through, and there's never been a peep out of him. And no more getting up in the night to feed him; he sleeps right through till seven o'clock every day.'

'You're very lucky. Not many babies do that.' Claire laughed. 'Both of mine had a hard time when they were cutting their teeth.'

'This is my lovely daughter,' Jill said, lifting Molly from the pram. 'She's too young to be cutting teeth, so I've got that to come.'

'Oh, she's beautiful! Just like a little doll.'

Nellie felt she'd been left out long enough, so she pushed Molly aside. 'Jill is my daughter-in-law, and the baby is me granddaughter. Couldn't yer just eat her?'

'I certainly could.' Claire gently ran a finger down a cheek as soft as silk. 'With two beautiful mothers, and loving grandparents, these two babies are going to have a life of love and laughter.'

'You get going, Claire, or yer'll be a nervous wreck,' Molly said. 'If ye're coming next week yer'll see the children again, and yer might have more time than yer've got today.'

Claire smiled at Molly and Nellie. 'I'll see yer next week, same time.' Then she turned to the girls. 'It's been a pleasure meeting you, and your lovely babies. I hope to see more of you another time.' With a quick wave, she took to her heels and covered the ground with speed, watched by members of the Bennett and McDonough clan.

'Mam, she is beautiful,' Jill said. 'And so nice with it.'

'She's like a film star.' Doreen voiced her thoughts. 'In fact she's more beautiful than some film stars.'

'And d'yer know the nicest thing about her?' Molly asked. 'Well, she doesn't realise just how beautiful she is. There's no eyelash fluttering with her, no acting coy, or showing off. Just a really nice person who's had more sadness in her life than any of us will ever know, please God.'

'And it was only 'cos yer've got a soft heart, Mam, that yer met her.' Jill saw her mother-in-law standing near, and quickly added, 'And Auntie Nellie, of course, 'cos everyone got stuck in to help Ken. And I'm glad me and Doreen did too, 'cos she's a really lovely person.'

Doreen nodded. 'Phil said the boy adores his mam, and I can see why. Yer'll have to bring her over when she comes next week, Mam, so Aunt Vicky can meet her.'

'We'll see how she's off for time, sunshine.' Molly didn't want to leave her mate out. 'What do yer say, Nellie? Shall we cut ten minutes off her visits to us, and next week we can take her to meet Victoria, and the week after to meet Lizzie Corkhill? How does that suit you, sunshine?'

'Suits me fine, girl, suits me fine.'

'That's settled, then, so let's go back to our homes and get dinner ready for the hard-working men in our lives.' Molly kissed her daughters and grandchildren, then, taking Nellie's arm, she hurried her across the cobbles, 'I'll see yer in the morning, sunshine, to do our shopping.'

Nellie's face fell. 'Ah, can't I come in for a few minutes to talk about what we think of Claire and that bloke?'

'Tomorrow morning, Nellie.' Then, because she thought that sounded too blunt, Molly added, 'There's a lot I want to talk about, regarding Claire, and I don't want to hurry it. We'll have more time in the morning, over a cup of tea.'

'And a custard cream, girl?'

'And a custard cream, sunshine.'

Chapter Eighteen

Molly was ready with her coat on, and her basket over her arm, when Nellie knocked on Saturday morning. 'No time for tea today, sunshine. I want to call in and see me ma and da before going to the shops. Tommy and Rosie will be at work, so we can have a nice quiet little chat.'

Nellie looked suspicious. 'When yer say "we", girl, I hope that means you and me. Ye're not thinking of sloping off there on yer own, are yer?'

Molly closed the door behind her. 'Now would I have a snowball's chance in hell of sloping off and not taking you with me?'

'No, yer wouldn't, girl, 'cos I'd follow yer.' The round fat face beamed. 'I was going to say I would dog yer footsteps, like what we do when we're acting private detectives. That sounds good, don't yer think, girl? Real professional, like.'

Anything for a quiet life, Molly thought as she nodded. 'Very professional, sunshine, and another one for yer to remember is, when yer follow a suspect, yer say ye're shadowing them.' She moved the basket to her other arm and linked her friend. 'Come on. We'll get a cup of tea at me ma's.'

Walking up the street, Nellie said, 'Ay, what d'yer think about Claire going out with that bloke? Shouldn't we tell her he's got another woman on the go?'

'I think we should go slow and see what comes.' Molly freed her arm from Nellie's and stepped round the back of her to link her other arm. 'I'm safer here, sunshine, if yer don't mind. Another few steps and I'd have been in the ruddy gutter.'

'Ah, ye're not at that again, are yer, girl? I'm walking in a straight line, so it must be yerself what's cock-eyed.'

'All right, I'll take the blame. It's easier to agree to being cock-eyed than it is to argue the toss with yer. So let's get back to Claire. As I said, I think we should go slowly and carefully. I feel very uneasy about Graham Collins – he just doesn't ring true. And I think perhaps we should spend a bit of time finding out who, and what, he really is. The best way to do that is to follow him, and the only time we're sure of seeing him is on a Monday and Tuesday, when he calls for his laundry. So shall we start this coming Monday, and see how we get on?'

Nellie was so keen she nodded her head quickly, sending her chins in all directions. 'Ooh, that's a cracking idea, girl. We'll have to make sure we get there for eleven o'clock, so we don't miss him.'

By this time they were turning into the street where Molly's parents lived. 'In the meanwhile, Nellie, not a word to a soul. It's really important that nobody knows, 'cos I don't want to hurt Claire, or lose her friendship.'

Nellie put her thumb and forefinger together and drew them across her mouth. 'My lips are sealed, girl, and that's a promise.'

When Bridie opened her front door and saw who her visitors were, she was delighted. 'Molly, me darlin', it's yerself come to see us, so it is. And sure, you and Nellie are very welcome.' She stood back to let them pass. 'Bob will be over the moon when he sees yer. And while ye're talking to him, I'll go straight through to the kitchen and put the kettle on.' She raised her brows at Nellie. 'Is it too early in the morning for a custard cream biscuit?'

'Bridie, me darlin', if me eyes are open then it isn't too early.' Nellie's attempt at an Irish accent was passable, but she wasn't in the same league as Molly, who had been hearing it all her life. 'And as me two eyes are open, sure isn't it meself that could eat two custard creams?'

Bob Jackson was sitting on the couch looking happy, and neatly dressed as always. He loved it when Nellie called, for she never failed to make him laugh. 'Ye're doing well with the accent, Nellie. Nearly as good as me.'

'Da, seeing as yer've been married to me ma for over fifty years, yer should be perfect at it. More so, seeing as Rosie's lived with yer for a few years now.' Then Molly called to her mother, who could be heard filling the kettle. 'Ay, Ma, how long has Rosie been over here? I keep saying a few years, but it must be longer than that.'

'She was fourteen when she came, me darlin', and she'll be twenty-one in August. That makes it seven years, so it does! My, how those years have flown. Sure, it seems no time at all since you and me were going down to meet her off the Dublin boat. Time goes so quickly yer hardly notice it passing, and isn't that the truth of it?'

'It certainly is, Ma, and even just thinking about it is enough to frighten the life out of me. Me and Jack have been married twenty-three years now, but I try not to let me mind dwell on it 'cos it puts years on me.'

'Ay, girl, I should be more worried than you. My old ma, God bless her, was only in her fifties when she died, and I lost me dad two years later. Which is young to die. And as they say it runs in families, and Bridie and Bob are hale and hearty at seventy, then you should still be on yer perch in forty years' time.' Nellie's head fell back and her whole body shook with laughter. 'I've just thought on, girl, that if ye're so much later getting to heaven than I am, then I might not be able to keep a front seat for yer.'

'Now, it doesn't always run in families, me darlin',' Bridie told her. For although Nellie was making a joke of it, she wouldn't have mentioned her parents dying young if it wasn't on her mind. And as Bridie loved the little woman who brought laughter into all their lives, she didn't want her secretly worrying as the years went by. 'My dear ma, God rest her soul, was only fifty when she died, but aren't I here still?'

'Same in my family, Nellie,' Bob said. 'Me mam died at fifty-eight, and we lost me dad when he was sixty. And like me darling wife, I'm living proof that the length of anyone's life isn't determined by their parents. So yer'll still be here entertaining us for another forty years.'

Nellie's eyes were lost to sight as she tried to work out how old she'd be in forty years. 'Yer'll be eighty-three then, sunshine,' Molly said, coming to her rescue. 'Roughly the same age as meself.'

'Eighty-three! Bloody hell, girl, I'll have white hair by then, and more wrinkles than a walnut. And I won't be able to tell no dirty jokes to make yer blush, 'cos I'll be too old to remember them.' She grinned at Molly. 'At least you'll be happy, girl, 'cos I won't be able to embarrass yer. I'll be that forgetful, I won't remember where the bedroom is, never mind what goes on in it.'

Molly tutted, embarrassed in front of her parents. But then looking at her friend's chubby face, she chuckled. 'Just listen to her, Ma. Eighty-three years old and the only thing she's worried about is that she can't find her way to the bedroom.'

'I'll see to the tea.' Bridie decided she'd be better off listening to what Nellie had to say from the kitchen. No one could see her blushing then, or hear her soft laughter. And there would be laughter, for the little woman wouldn't let Molly's remark go without a quick cheeky reply. 'The kettle will be boiling by now.' But although the kettle was boiling, Bridie couldn't attend to it for she was bent over the sink, doubled up with laughter.

'I know how I could find me way to the bedroom, girl, and it's not half clever.'

Molly scratched her head. 'I know I'm a fool for falling for it, sunshine, but go on, tell me how yer could find yer way to the bedroom when ye're eighty-three?'

'I could put a bell round George's neck, and I'd know where he was 'cos every time he moved, I'd hear the bell.' Nellie nodded, and it was a nod that said she thought she'd been very clever in figuring that out. 'Isn't that a brainwave?'

'It would be, if George was able to find his way to the bedroom,' Molly said dryly. 'Don't forget, sunshine, George is a few years older than you. It's you who should wear the bell, so he can find you.'

'Oh, yeah, I forgot about that. Silly old me, eh? Still, if we both had bells, we'd always be able to find each other.' Nellie's shaking bosom was the warning of what was to come. 'Ay, girl, seeing as you and me are about the same age, that means yer'll be needing bells for you and Jack. And if the four of us were looking for each other, and the bells were ringing, all the neighbours would put their coats on, thinking it was time for church.'

As Bob wiped away the laughter tears, Bridie had to put the tray down on the draining board for the tea was spilling over on to her hand-embroidered cloth. Molly was leaning her elbows on the sideboard, and Nellie was standing in the middle of the room with a smile as wide as a mile. There was nothing in life she liked more than making people happy. Well, there was one thing she liked more, but if she said so, her mate would have her guts for garters.

When the laughter had subsided, and Bridie was able to carry the tray in, there was a plate with half a dozen custard creams on it. And when Nellie's eyes lighted on them, she rubbed her tummy. 'Things look good, there, Bridie!'

'Well, me darlin', I thought yer deserved a couple of extra biscuits for brightening up the morning for me and Bob.'

'Ma, ye're not doing her any favours, yer know. She eats far too much sweet stuff. She'll never lose any weight at the rate she goes on.'

Nellie groaned, 'Oh, here she goes again, old misery guts. What harm can two fiddling little custard creams do me?'

'Not much on their own, sunshine, I admit. But if yer add them to the two yer'll expect in our house when we've finished our shopping, plus the cream slice yer've just got to have because yer mouth is watering, then they all add up to another pound of weight yer'll put on. Yer have no willpower, Nellie McDonough, and yer should be ashamed of yerself.' Molly looked at her mother. 'Ma, I know yer think I'm making a mountain out of a molehill, but you aren't with her all the time to see the amount of sweet stuff she gets through in a day. She's like a kid with a penny in her hand, looking in the window of a sweet shop. That kid doesn't know that if she keeps on eating sweet things, then when she's older it will affect her health.'

Nellie was listening with interest, her head slightly tilted. 'Which kid is that, girl? Does she live in our street?'

'There is no kid, Nellie. I'm just trying to point out that too many sweets and cakes can be bad for yer health.'

'Then why couldn't yer have just said that, girl, instead of going all round the houses before yer make yer point?'

Bridie didn't know whether to look serious or smile. It was always difficult to know when her daughter and friend were acting daft just for the fun of it. 'Had I better take the biscuits out, then, so there's no temptation?'

Molly took a deep breath. 'If yer do that, Ma, then me mate will go back to being the little girl standing looking in the sweet shop window. She's crying now 'cos someone has taken her penny off her.'

Nellie pretended to roll up her sleeves. 'Ay, who is this flaming girl? She's beginning to get on me nerves now, and I'd like to give her a piece of me mind. If someone did steal her penny, it was her own fault for taking so long to make up her mind what sweets she wanted.'

'Yer still haven't told me whether I should take the biscuits away,' Bridie said, 'or if I should leave them and let Nellie succumb to temptation?'

Nellie solved the problem, and restored humour, when she swiped two biscuits from the plate, before saying, 'Yer better take the plate out now, Bridie, so Molly isn't tempted. Yer see, she hasn't got the same willpower as what I've got.'

For the next half hour the Jacksons' living room was filled with laughter. Molly and Nellie made a perfect double act, just bouncing off each other. Bob thought his sides would split, and Bridie's face was sore, all with laughter. And when the friends were leaving, to get their weekend shopping in, Bridie said she'd remember every word, so she could tell Tommy and Rosie what fun they'd had.

Tony saw the two mates standing on the opposite side, waiting to cross the busy main road, and he said to Ellen, 'Yer mates are on their way over.'

'Yeah, I've seen them,' Ellen told him, before smiling at the customer she'd just served. 'Here's yer threepence change, Mrs Garrett. Try not to spend it all in the one shop.'

'It's not worth much now, Ellen, but when I was younger yer could buy the makings of a dinner with a threepenny bit.'

'Yer don't need to tell me that, Mrs Garrett, 'cos I've had to do it many times meself. Blind scouse they call it. Yer needed a magnifying glass to find the meat.'

Hetty Garrett sighed as she put her purse in the wicker basket on her arm. 'They call them the bad old days, and in a way they were. But at least they taught us the value of money, and it was something yer had to work for. These days, the youngsters seem to get everything they want. And what gets me is, they believe they're entitled to it!'

'Not all youngsters are like that, Mrs Garrett. I know mine aren't. They have respect for people, and for money. They know it doesn't grow on trees.'

Nellie waddled into the shop ahead of Molly. 'What doesn't grow on trees, girl? Money, or a good man?'

'Neither, Nellie!' Hetty smiled at the woman whose back entry door faced hers. 'My feller didn't grow on a tree, and he never has any ruddy money.'

'He's no different to any other man,' Molly said, placing her basket on the counter. 'Ask any husband to lend his wife a shilling until pay day, and he'll tell her he hasn't got a penny to his name. And later, in the pub with his mates, he'll down a few pints and never give a thought to where his poor wife is going to find the money for his dinner the next day.'

Nellie pretended to play a violin. 'This is like a scene from an old silent film, where the woman is being thrown out on the streets with her children 'cos she can't pay the rent.'

Molly joined her mate in the middle of the shop, saying, 'I remember that film, even though it's many years ago. You pretend to be the wicked landlord, sunshine, and I'll be the broken-hearted heroine.'

Nellie walked to the counter with her arms outstretched. 'Here, Ellen, take this violin and supply the music while I go about my dastardly deed.'

Hetty wasn't going to miss this, so she stood back to give the actors room, as did the two customers who had just come into the shop. They all knew Nellie, and although they wouldn't like to cross swords with her, they were well aware she could put on a show worth watching. 'We're in no hurry, Tony, lad,' the woman called Vera said. 'We'll wait until Nellie and Molly have been served.'

Since he had been going non-stop since eight o'clock, this suited Tony down the ground. A little light diversion, with a laugh thrown in, was more than welcome. So he folded his arms, leaned back against the chopping table, and prayed there would be no more customers for at least ten minutes.

Throwing her shoulders back, and coughing into her hand, Nellie geared herself up to give a fine performance. 'Are yer ready, girl?'

'Ready, willing and able, sunshine.' Molly let her body go limp, her shoulders slumped in despair. She raised the back of a hand to her forehead, and cried, 'I beg you, don't throw me and the children out in the snow. We have no money and nowhere to go.'

Nellie, standing as upright as possible, pointed a stiffened finger towards the door. 'Pay me the two shillings rent you owe, or get out.'

'Oh, please, sir, I implore you.' Molly fell to her knees and pulled on the pretend villain's coat. 'I beg you to take pity on me and the children.'

'I gave you the chance to stay, woman, but you refused.' There was a sneer on Nellie's face as she stroked a pretend beard. 'Out, before I have you thrown out.'

Molly sobbed, her two arms round the villain's legs. 'I couldn't let you have your wicked way with me, not when my husband was laid to rest only yesterday.'

'Take your filthy hands off me, woman! Be off, with your children and what bits of furniture you possess.' There was a sneer as he went on. 'Throw yourself on the mercy of the poorhouse. They're the only ones who care for down and outs like you. Remove your arms from my legs before I set the bailiffs on to you.'

Unnoticed by the two actors, who were wrapped up in the roles they were playing, two regular customers had been about to enter the shop, chatting away to each other. Tony raised a hand to get their attention, then put a finger to his lips for silence. So they stood quietly just inside the door, their faces agog at what they were seeing. And a further three customers watched from the doorway. At first Tony was worried about keeping customers waiting, then he told himself it was daft to worry. These women were all regulars. They wouldn't walk off in a huff and buy their meat elsewhere. Where else could they go and be served the best meat, and be entertained into the bargain? So he relaxed and enjoyed the funniest double act he'd ever seen. Oh, he'd seen Molly and Nellie doing all sorts of things that made him laugh, but they'd never put a play on before.

Ellen pretended to be playing the invisible violin, while humming a sad dirge. She really put her heart and soul into it. And when the villain kicked Molly to free his legs, her cry of pain was so realistic it brought forth a hearty response. Amid the loud boos and hisses, there were shouts of 'Leave the woman alone, you swine', and 'Pick on someone yer own size, mate'. And the best was, 'Let's teach him a lesson and lynch him to the nearest lamp-post.'

'Yer can't do that, Vera,' Tony called. 'Yer need rope and we haven't got any. Anyhow, it's against the law and we'll all end up in jail.'

'Oh, I can't let that happen,' Hetty said. 'My feller likes his meal on the table when he gets in from work. He wouldn't be happy with me in jail and no dinner in the oven.'

Molly and Nellie did themselves proud. Nellie was fantastic as the rich landlord who had a habit of twisting the ends of an imaginary moustache, and her sneer was a masterpiece, contorting her chubby face. While Molly, surprising herself, played her part well. She did all the over-acting she remembered from the silent film her ma had taken her to see when she was a young girl. She could remember crying herself to sleep that night because the woman and her children would be out in the snow, with no roof over their heads.

When the scene came to an end, Molly and Nellie joined hands and were bowing to the applause when Tony came out of the storeroom carrying a piece of rope. 'Here, I've found this rope, ladies, if yer still want to lynch the miserable skinflint. But don't do it on the lamp-post outside me shop, 'cos it'll be bad for trade.'

'Here, give it to me,' Hetty said, holding out a hand. 'There's been a few times in the last twenty years when I've felt like hanging Nellie McDonough. I've never had the rope before, or the opportunity, but now I have, I'll make use of it.' She curled the rope into a noose. 'Come here, Nellie, and stick yer neck in this.'

'Yer can sod off, Hetty Garrett, 'cos I know yer only want to see me dangling from the lamp-post so yer can look up me clothes and see if I'm wearing my knickers.'

Hetty clicked her tongue. 'There's only one thing in life I would find more distasteful than my feller's underpants, and that's a pair of your knickers.'

Nellie didn't take offence at the insult, for she had known Hetty many years and got on well with her. 'Me heart bleeds for yer, girl, it really does. I've seen your feller's long johns on the line, wafting in the breeze, and they are not a pretty sight. At least my knickers are a nice shade of blue or pink, but I can't say anything nice about those long johns. Except, of course, that it's your line they're on, and not mine. My George doesn't wear those long kecks now, he wears short ones. And can yer guess the reason for him liking short ones better?'

Hetty shrugged her shoulders. 'I dunno. I suppose they're better in this warm weather.'

'No, ye're miles out, Hetty. He likes the short ones 'cos they're quicker to get off when he's in bed. He's hot-blooded is my George, and he doesn't waste time messing about.'

Hetty's lips twitched. That last remark of Nellie's had been a direct criticism of her husband's virility, and she wasn't going to stand for that! She might call him fit to burn, but she wasn't having anyone else make little of him. 'The people what have a big mouth and brag a lot are the ones whose life is so dull they have to make things up. It's the quiet ones that don't say much who have the best of everything in life.'

Molly stood by, listening, and wishing that Hetty wouldn't keep on digging a hole for herself. She should know by now that no one ever got the better of Helen Theresa McDonough. Still, Molly told herself, it wasn't up to her to interfere.

'What d'yer mean, Hetty?' Nellie's voice was deceptively low. 'I don't understand what yer said, so explain it to me.'

Hetty was beginning to feel uncomfortable, but she couldn't back down now, not when there were seven or eight people hanging on to every word. 'Well, it's like this, Nellie. Yer always talk about the bedroom, as though it's the only room in the house. But the living room is as important, and what is on the table.'

Nellie gave an exaggerated gasp, and put a hand across her mouth. 'Hetty Garrett, I'm surprised at yer. It's a good job there's no children in the shop.'

'I haven't said nothing that couldn't be said in front of children,' said an indignant Hetty. 'I never use bad language, not like some I could name.'

Nellie shook her head slowly. 'Yer do surprise me over your feller – I would never have thought that of him. It's a good job your Letty is married. It would be terrible if she had to witness the wild goings on.'

Hetty appealed to those watching. 'What is she on about? I think she must be going daft in the head. I haven't said nothing out of place.'

The waiting customers shrugged their shoulders. They had no intention of letting Tony or Ellen serve them before they knew what Nellie was up to. Even if the dinner was late being put on the table.

However, Molly knew Hetty had bitten off more than she could chew, and thought it was time to interfere. 'Don't worry about it, Hetty; get off home and see to the dinner. Nellie's in one of her funny moods, and yer could be here all day.'

'I'm not moving from here until she tells me what she means by the wild goings on.' Hetty put her basket down on the floor and folded her arms. 'Out with it, Nellie McDonough.'

The little woman had trouble keeping her face straight, but she was determined she wouldn't laugh. She spread out her hands. 'I don't know anything about the wild goings on in your house, 'cos I've never seen them. I wish I had, though – it sounds very interesting. But I wouldn't have even thought of it if you hadn't said it yerself. I mean, what would you think if someone said to you that the dining table was every bit as good as the bed? What crossed my mind right away was that your feller is so eager, he can't wait to get to the bedroom, and the table is the first thing to hand. I'll tell yer what, Hetty, I'll be looking at your husband in a different light in future. And yer can thank him from me, and say I'll be asking my feller if he wants his daily dose on the table or in bed.'

There was little Hetty could do but join in the laughter. 'I'll be telling my feller no such thing, or he'd never look yer in the face again. In fact, if he saw yer in the distance walking towards him, he'd run a mile.' She picked up the basket from the floor.

'It was a good laugh, though, Nellie, and we've all enjoyed ourselves. So I'll wish everyone a very good day.'

As she was passing, Nellie tapped her on the shoulder. 'I'll never have another cup of tea off that dining table of yours, girl.'

'In twenty years, Nellie, yer've never had a cup of tea off my table.'

'I know that, Hetty. I was just dropping a gentle hint to remind yer. Neighbours for twenty years, and never once invited in for a friendly chat and a cup of tea. Now anybody hearing that would think yer weren't a very generous person.'

Hetty was prepared for her this time. 'The day you invite me into your house for a cuppa, Nellie, will be the day I invite yer into mine.'

Nellie was looking very happy as she smiled up into Molly's face. 'Ay, that was good, wasn't it, girl? I really enjoyed meself, and it didn't half go down well with Tony and his customers. We'll have to do it again some time, so our crowd can see it. How about next time yer have a party?'

Molly gasped. 'The next time I have a party! Ye're a cheeky article, Nellie McDonough, yer really are. Why can't you have a party for a change? Mind you, if by some freak act of nature yer did ask me to a party in your house, I'd die of shock.'

'That's why I don't ask yer, girl 'cos I know the surprise would be too much for yer. It's you I'm thinking about, Molly. I'd hate to be the one what brought on a heart attack.'

'Listen, sunshine, I take a chance on having a heart attack every time I go out with yer. There are times when I don't know where to put me face, and I could willingly strangle yer.'

'If ye're getting a cob on 'cos I mentioned having a party in your house, girl, then forget I said it. Give me a great big smile, then I'll know yer haven't fallen out with me.' When there was no response, Nellie squeezed her friend's arm. 'What's wrong, Molly? Are yer feeling out of sorts?'

'No, I'm fine, sunshine, and I did enjoy our Lionel and Ethel Barrymore show. But yer do go too far sometimes, Nellie, and I don't know where to put meself. I felt sorry for poor Hetty. There was no need for yer to pull her leg like that. She's not as outgoing as you, and yer could see she was embarrassed.'

The little woman looked genuinely surprised. 'Why? I didn't say nothing to upset Hetty, so why would she be embarrassed?'

'It's not only Hetty, sunshine, it's everyone! This obsession of yours with the goings on in people's bedrooms, well, it's not everyone's cup of tea.'

'Oh, yeah, I know what yer mean now, girl. Hetty did mention she'd never had a cup of tea in my house.' Nellie's thoughts had her nodding her head as they approached Hanley's cake shop. 'It would be neighbourly to invite Hetty in for a cuppa some time, wouldn't it? After all, we've lived by each other for long enough.' Leaning heavily on her mate's arm to help her up the two steps, Nellie said, 'Shall I ask her to come to yours one morning, so she can have a nice cup of tea with us?'

'Sod off, Nellie McDonough. To pinch Hetty Garrett's words, "The day yer invite me to yours for a cup of tea, then that's the day I'll invite yer to mine." '

'Ah, well, it was worth a try, girl.' Nellie approached the glass display cabinet. 'Ay, Molly, see that cream slice, the third one from the end? Well, it's just waved to me, and because it's friendly, I'm going to buy it.'

'It's a nice bit of liver, this, love,' Jack said, 'it almost melts in the mouth.'

Ruthie nodded in agreement. 'Yeah, it is nice, Mam, and I'm going to eat it all up. But I don't think I can manage all the mashed potato, so can I ask me dad if he'd take some off me?'

'It's all right with me, sunshine, but hadn't yer better ask him yerself?'

'Pass yer plate over, pet, I've got room for a bit more.' Jack used his knife to transfer some of the potato from his daughter's plate to his. 'Yer grandma is always saying it's a sin to throw food away when there's people starving.'

'The six years of war, when food was hard to come by, taught us all a lesson,' Molly said. 'Most women are more careful with food now. I know by listening to them in the shops.'

'Did Nellie buy liver as well?' Jack asked. 'George would be happy because I know it's a favourite of his.'

'We always get the same, me and Nellie. Whatever I buy, she buys. The only difference in my shopping basket and hers is the bag of cream cakes. She bought six cream slices, and I'll bet that George and Paul will never see all those cakes on the same plate. She'll put three on the table, and the other three will go in the larder, to be eaten by my mate when no one is looking.'

Ruthie's brow shot up. 'Auntie Nellie wouldn't eat three cream slices on her own, would she, Mam?'

Molly nodded. 'Oh, yes, sunshine, she'll eat those cakes without any trouble, and she won't feel guilty. She loves her cakes, does Nellie.'

Jack chuckled, as in his mind's eye he could see Nellie with a cake in her hand and cream round her mouth. 'What's she been up to today, love? Anything interesting?'

'Not really, no!' Molly held out her hands for the empty plates. 'In fact she was very quiet. An uneventful morning really. Nothing to write home about.'

Chapter Nineteen

'Are yer not putting a coat or a cardi on, girl?' Nellie asked, looking surprised to see Molly in a short-sleeved cotton dress. 'Yer'll catch yer death of cold in that.'

'Nellie, it's a beautiful sunny morning. There's not a cloud in the sky, so it's going to stay fine all day. Yer can't go out in that coat, sunshine, 'cos yer'd swelter in it.' Molly grinned. 'I was going to say yer'd be reduced to a grease spot, but I won't 'cos I wouldn't hurt yer feelings for the world.'

'I've got to keep this coat on, I've nothing else to wear.' Nellie wiped a hand across her brow to brush away the beads of sweat. 'It's all right for you, going out in yer figure, but there's no chance of me doing it.'

Molly decided to try another tactic. She wasted a few minutes rooting in a drawer for the want of something to do, then, with her back to Nellie, she asked, 'Are yer hot, sunshine?'

'Hot! I'm bleeding roasting, girl, it's just pouring off me.'

Molly spun round. 'Then take that ruddy coat off yer! Let's see what yer've got on underneath it.'

Slipping her coat off, Nellie threw it over the back of a chair. Then she lifted both arms and pulled a face. 'As yer will agree, I can't walk out in this. It's got a pin keeping the hem up, and there's a few rips and split seams.'

'I wouldn't be seen dead with yer in it,' Molly said. 'Surely yer can do better than that old thing? It should have been given to the rag and bone man ages ago. But what about the navy one yer got from the market? That really looked nice on yer, and yer could walk out in it knowing it fitted yer perfectly and yer looked good.'

'D'yer really think so, girl? I'd feel really conscious walking out in just a dress. I've hardly got the figure for it.'

'Nellie, we don't have time to argue if we intend being near the laundry by eleven. So nip home, pick up the navy dress, and bring it back here to change into. And look sharpish, don't loiter. I want yer back here in the time it takes me to hang yer coat up.'

The little woman walked out with her head down, muttering, 'I wonder who her bleeding servant was before I came along?'

Molly smiled as she hung the coat up. She loved her mate like a sister, and at the moment she felt sorry for her. It must be awful carrying so much weight around in this hot weather. But Nellie would grin and bear it, for she knew if she complained she'd get a lecture on her eating habits. And really, Molly admitted to herself, Nellie wouldn't be the same if she was slim. She wouldn't suit it.

'Are you still hanging that ruddy coat up?' When Nellie pushed on the front door, Molly was thrown face forward on to the wall. 'Oh, sorry, girl, I didn't mean to hurt yer. The trouble is, I don't know me own strength.' With the navy dress over her arm, she waddled through the living room to the kitchen. 'I'll change out here if yer don't mind, girl. I won't be two shakes of a lamb's tail.'

'You better hadn't be, sunshine, 'cos it's a good walk down to the shop, and we need to be there before eleven.'

'It's no good talking while I've got me head inside a dress, girl, so save yer breath.' A few seconds later, Nellie came out wearing the dress and looking as pleased as Punch. 'It still fits me, so I haven't put any more weight on.' She did a twirl. 'How does it look, girl?'

'Oh, yer look wonderful, a real treat. Honestly, it's a lovely fit on yer. I bet yer'll feel nice and cool going out in that.' Molly was pleased because her friend was happy. 'Have yer got any money to spare, sunshine?'

Nellie looked suspicious. 'Yeah, I've always got a bit of spare money, but why d'yer want to know? Are yer skint?'

Molly raised her eyes to the ceiling. 'Nellie, it's only Monday. It would be God help me if I was skint and had to feed the family for the rest of the week. No, I was going to suggest that if yer have got a few bob to spare, we could go down to the market and see if yer can find another bargain like the dress yer've got on now. If yer had a couple more, yer'd be able to go out every day without yer coat, and without sweating cobs.'

'Ooh, yeah, that's a good idea that, girl. We haven't seen Mary Ann or Sadie since Christmas. They'll think we've fallen out with them. Can we go this afternoon, when we've finished our detective work?'

'Let's wait and see how we get on this morning. If we find ourselves at a dead end, then we can take a tram or a bus to Great Homer Street. But the whole idea of going down to stand near Claire's shop is to find out more about the bloke she's getting involved with.'

Nellie nodded. 'We'll see how it goes. But would yer do me a favour, girl, and comb me hair for me? It's no good looking good in this dress if me hair's a mess.'

Molly opened one of the sideboard drawers and took out a comb. 'Come here, sunshine, and let's titivate yer up. But don't forget, if yer click with a feller, yer've got to ask him if he's got a mate. And also if the mate is good-looking and has plenty of money.'

'Blimey, ye're not asking for much, are yer?' Nellie's eyes disappeared behind her chubby cheeks. 'Ay, if this feller I'm going to click with has got a friend what's handsome and with plenty of money, then I'd be daft if I didn't take the friend and leave you with the feller I've clicked with.'

Molly chuckled. 'Ye're not as daft as yer look, sunshine, are yer? Not where men and money are concerned, anyway.' She nodded towards the front door. 'Now let's put a move on so we get there before the queer feller.'

'Are yer taking yer basket, girl?'

'No, it's too hot to be carrying that thing around. And I don't need much shopping; we're having bacon and egg tonight. All I need is bread and milk. So I'm only taking me handbag with me.'

'Then can I put me purse in it, girl, save lugging me ruddy big handbag around? If we have time to go to the market, I'll look for a small one for meself.'

Molly opened her bag. 'Put it in, sunshine. It'll be safe in there.'

The two friends were nearing the block of shops where Claire worked when they saw Graham Collins. He was nearing the laundry from the opposite direction, and soon disappeared inside.

'Blimey, that was close,' Molly said. 'At least we know he's here, and we're not wasting our time. Another ten minutes and we'd have missed him.'

'Are we going to split up again, girl, like we did last time?'

'I think so, sunshine, it's safer that way. We won't be so noticeable. And each time we come we'll have to wear a different dress. I don't mean we'll have to buy more clothes, just that we'll have to change what we've got.'

'I haven't got one to swap with, only me mother-of-the-bride dress. D'yer think that would stand out too much?'

'Oh, I think so, sunshine. Yer'd stick out like a sore thumb. It's hardly the sort of dress yer'd go to the shops in. We need to look like two ordinary housewives, and nobody will take any notice of us. We can change our appearance by doing our hair a new way. I could comb mine back and tie it with a ribbon.'

'Well, it's God help me, then, girl, 'cos I haven't got enough hair to tie back. I could put a scarf on me head, though – that would make me look different.'

'Good idea, sunshine! Ay, yer can borrow the one Doreen bought me for Christmas. It's a pale blue voile, with pretty flowers on. It'll look nice and summery, and it won't be too hot for yer.'

Nellie was over the moon. She remembered the scarf, and though she hadn't said anything at the time, she'd wished one of her family had bought her something as pretty. 'I know the scarf you mean, girl, and it is nice. But are yer sure yer wouldn't mind me wearing it, with Doreen buying it as a present for yer?'

'Of course I don't mind, soft girl, and neither would Doreen! It's only a flaming scarf. If it was a gold necklace, that would be different. I'd have to think twice about it.' Molly put a hand on her mate's hand. 'He's just come out, sunshine. Now, no matter which way he goes, we'll follow him.'

'D'yer want me to walk on the opposite side, like last time?'

'No, let's be daring and stick together.' Molly fixed her eyes on the man as he stood at the edge of the pavement waiting for a break in the traffic so he could cross the busy road. 'He's crossing over, sunshine, so we'll do the same thing.' She bent her elbow. 'Stick yer arm in, and try to keep up with me if I run. There's a lot of cars and vans on the road today, but I suppose most of the shops will be having a delivery, seeing as it's Monday.'

Nellie didn't need the help of Molly's arm. She seemed to bounce across the road and actually reached the other side before her friend. 'Come on, slowcoach.' She grinned. 'What took yer so long?'

'I was keeping me eye on the traffic, sunshine, dodging the ruddy cars. It's a wonder yer didn't get run over, 'cos yer didn't even look to see if it was safe! One van driver had to slam his brakes on, and he was calling yer for all the silly buggers going.'

'Ooh, I'm not worried about him, girl, 'cos brakes were made for stopping quickly. That's what they're in his van for.'

'So, if he'd knocked yer down, it would have been his fault, would it?'

'Of course it would! Blimey, girl, I'm big enough for him to have seen me from a distance. He'd have plenty of time to use the brake.'

'Okay, let's forget it. While we're arguing the toss, our target is getting away. He's not going to the woman's house, like he did last week, 'cos he's going in a different direction. So we'll have to stay close enough not to lose sight of him.'

Graham Collins walked jauntily along the road. He appeared to be in good spirits, without a care in the world. After five minutes he turned into one of the many streets running off the main road.

Molly looked up at the street sign. 'This is the street he lives in. Only last time we came in from the other end. So he's going to his own house.'

'We can still follow him, girl, 'cos he's probably only going home to see his mother. I bet he won't stay long, not if he's got a job.'

'I think ye're right, sunshine, but we'll walk to the top of the street and wait there. We'll hang around for twenty minutes, and if he doesn't show himself by then we'll call it a day. He lives with his mother, and for all we know he could spend the rest of the day with her. I'd say he was about the same age as us, so his mother will be getting on in years.'

'Anything yer say, girl, I'll fall in with. We'll give him twenty minutes, and if he doesn't come out by then, we could take a tram down to the market.'

'Yer'll have to wait another day for yer dress, sunshine, 'cos here he is again.' The friends were standing on the corner of the street, and Molly linked her arm through Nellie's. 'Pretend to be talking to me, sunshine, and walk slowly until he's passed us.'

Graham was whistling when he skirted the couple without giving them a second glance. His gait told them he was in a very happy frame of mind.

'He seems in good spirits,' Molly said. 'I wonder if he's going to that woman's house?'

'We'll soon find out,' Nellie answered. 'He's only a few doors away from it now.'

Sure enough, Graham turned in to a path as they were speaking, and they could hear him knocking on a door. 'I'll run past, sunshine. Stay here and wait for me.' Molly took to her heels and was just in time to see their quarry kissing the woman they'd seen him with the week before. The door was closed then, and both were lost to view.

'Well, girl, what did yer see?' Nellie asked when Molly rejoined her. 'Or were yer too late to see anything?'

'All I saw was him taking his hat off, and bending his head to kiss her. It was the same woman, all right, I could tell by the hair. I really don't know what to make of it.'

'He's having Claire on, that's what he's doing.' Nellie was nodding to show she meant what she said. 'We should tell her what we've seen or find out definitely what he's up to.'

'I agree with yer wholeheartedly, sunshine, but what can we do about it? That woman he's just kissed is definitely one of his fancy women, and God knows how many more he's got. But how come, if he deals in antiques, he's not at work?

Or is that another lie he's told Claire? For all we know, everything he's told her might be a pack of lies. He might not even live with his mother. He could be a married man, with a string of women on the side. He probably took a fancy to Claire because of her looks. Any man would be proud to have her on his arm.'

'He's a rum one, isn't he, girl? And I think someone should burst his bubble. It would be sad if Claire fell for him, and he dropped her like a hot brick if someone else came along and took his fancy.' Nellie was quiet for a while, then said, 'There's one lie we could find him out in.'

'What's that, sunshine?'

'We could easy find out whether he does live with his mother.'

'How could we do that without him knowing?'

'He's not at home now, is he? So if I knocked on the door with some cock and bull story, he's not likely to find out.'

'What d'yer mean, some cock and bull story?'

'I could knock and ask if anyone knew where Mrs Morrison lived.'

'Who's Mrs Morrison, sunshine? His name is supposed to be Collins.'

'I don't know who Mrs bleeding Morrison is, girl, and neither will his mother if she opens the door to me. I can always act daft and pretend I must have the wrong address. I'd get away with it, girl, 'cos people do get lost. And it doesn't matter if she thinks I'm not quite right in the head. At least we'll know he's telling the truth about his mother.'

Molly grinned. 'I bet yer'd get away with it, too! Yer've got the blinking nerve for it, so if yer want to try, I'm all for it. And I won't be far behind yer if yer find yerself in a pickle.'

Nellie squared her shoulders and stood to attention. Her tummy and bosom stood to attention, too. They were feeling very happy about the freedom they were enjoying. What a relief it was not to be squashed into a tight dress and coat. 'Right, girl, about turn. We'll go back to his house and you can stand at the bottom of the path while I knock on the door.'

'I'll knock if yer like, Nellie,' Molly said, keeping her fingers crossed that her mate turned her offer down. She didn't fancy knocking on a stranger's door and telling a lie. 'But I've got to say I'd rather you did it.'

'It doesn't worry me, girl, 'cos I'm only asking if someone lives in the road. There's no harm in that.'

So the friends about-turned and walked back to the house where Graham Collins lived with his mother. Molly stood at the bottom of the small path, fearful of what was about to come. But there was no answer to Nellie's first knock, and no answer to her second. She shrugged her shoulders and pulled a face at Molly. 'I'll try once more, girl, but there doesn't seem to be anyone at home.' She had the knocker in her hand when the next door opened.

'There's no one in there, love,' said a pretty woman in her thirties. 'Would yer like to leave a message and I'll pass it on?'

Molly was quick to note that Nellie seemed stuck for words, so she smiled at the woman and said, 'We're not sure we've got the right address, love, so perhaps yer can help us. We're looking for an elderly lady, name of Mrs Morrison.'

'Oh, there's no elderly lady lives there, love. A man lives there on his own, and his name's not Morrison. Actually, he only went out about ten minutes ago, so he won't be back for a while. Not that he'd be much use to yer, 'cos his name isn't Morrison. Sorry I can't help yer, but there's no one of that name in this road.'

'Thanks for yer help, anyway.' Nellie gave her a wide smile.

'We'll have to go back and get the proper address. Sorry to have bothered yer.'

'No bother at all, love! Ta-ra.'

The friends didn't speak until they were out of the street, then they stood and looked at each other. 'Well, what d'yer make of that?' Nellie asked. 'It seems our Mr Collins is a bit of a mystery.'

'I think he's more than a mystery, sunshine, I think he's a down and out rotter.' Molly sighed as she gazed down into Nellie's face. 'It was a good idea of yours to knock at that house. At least we've learned a bit more about him. But where we go from here I don't know. He seems to have a pattern, at least on a Monday and Tuesday morning. That's the laundry, then his lady friends. If we knew how long he stayed there, we could watch out for him and follow to see where he goes. From what we've seen, he doesn't spend much time dealing in antiques. So where does he get the money from to dress like a dandy, and take women to the theatre?'

'I don't know, girl. I'm as wise as you are.'

'I won't rest until I find out what's going on,' Molly said. 'If it wasn't for Claire, he could go to hell as far as I'm concerned. But I'd hate to see her made a fool of. She's had enough heartache in her life.'

'We can hang around now if yer like, girl. I'm not in any hurry. Then we could see what he does with the rest of the day.'

Molly shook her head. 'No, we've spent enough time on him today. It was really clever of you to knock at his house, I would never have thought of it. So yer deserve a little treat. We'll forget about Mr Graham Collins for now, and when we get home we can sit and plan what our next move will be. But right now, we'll hop on the first tram that comes along to take us to Great Homer Street. As I said, that brainwave yer had was brilliant, and yer deserve a treat.'

Nellie grew upwards and outwards with pride. 'I do get some things right, don't I, girl? And I bet you and me will catch the bugger out in the end. It'll be another successful result for the McDonough and Bennett Private Detective Agency.'

Molly put a hand on Nellie's arm and smiled. 'We'll not let him hurt a friend of ours, will we, sunshine? Sort him out good and proper, that's what we'll do. He won't know what's hit him by the time we've finished. Together, Nellie, you and me could conquer the whole world.'

'Ay, it's not half quiet here today,' Molly said when they got to the market. 'The place is almost deserted.'

'It's like a ghost town, like what yer see in the cowboy pictures.' Nellie looked at the empty stalls. 'Yer don't think everyone's died off, girl, do yer?'

'Nothing so drastic, sunshine. There's not many customers, and not much stuff on the stalls, but the stallholders are here, so perhaps it'll get busy later.'

They made straight for Mary Ann's stall, which was usually a hive of activity. But that too was very quiet. Mary Ann was attending to the few customers that were there, and Sadie was straightening the goods on display. 'Where's all yer customers, Mary Ann?' Nellie called. 'Have they been and gone, or have they all fallen out with yer?'

Mary Ann welcomed them warmly. 'Me and Sadie were only talking about you two this morning. We decided that yer were either dead, or yer'd emigrated to Australia.' She let out a hearty chuckle. 'But I can see yer haven't emigrated.'

'Ay, you, watch yerself.' Nellie sounded indignant. 'We're not ruddy well dead either.'

Mary Ann's red hair shone in the bright sunlight. She wore it piled into a bun on top, and kept it in place with a tortoiseshell comb. She was a typical Liverpool Mary Ellen, in her long black shirt, buttoned-up boots and hand-knitted black woollen shawl. Like most of the other stallholders, her stall had been handed down to her by her mother. It had been in the family for generations, but Mary Ann had turned it into the largest stall in the market. And she did this by sheer hard work, plus a liking for people and a wonderful sense of humour. 'I could tell yer weren't dead, Nellie, when I saw yer lips move. It's always a good indication, queen, so if ye're ever in doubt about whether a person is dead or not, tell a joke. If it's a good joke, and they don't laugh, then it's time to send for the undertaker.'

'This isn't the sort of conversation to be having on a beautiful day like today,' Molly said. 'Can't yer find something more pleasant to talk about?'

Just then Sadie came running over, a huge grin on her pretty face. 'Where have you two been hiding yerselves? Every time we got some good quality clothes in, I've been putting them away for yer. Then, when yer didn't come, I had to put them out.'

'It's very quiet here today.' Molly looked round at the half-empty stalls. 'I've never seen it as quiet as it is now.'

'It's Monday, queen, hard-up day.' Mary Ann waved to a woman who was holding a blouse up. 'I'll be over in a minute, Ethel, just have a bit of patience.' She pulled a face. 'Honest to God, they expect yer to be at their beck and call, all for a sixpenny blouse. I've been thinking of getting meself a pair of skates, but when I mentioned it to my feller, he roared his head off.'

Nellie gawped. 'Yer weren't thinking of getting skates, were yer?'

Mary Ann bit on her bottom lip to keep the smile back. She'd done many things in her life, but skating wasn't one of them. And she could imagine the fun her customers would have seeing her falling on her bottom. 'It was only a passing thought, queen; it didn't stay very long.' Her sharp eyes were watching the customer, and she shouted, 'The bleeding blouse will be worn out if yer handle it any more. And the price will still be sixpence even if yer do pull it to pieces.'

'I'm only looking at it, Mary Ann,' Ethel shouted back. 'Yer can't expect me to buy it without seeing there's no tears in it. I haven't got money to throw away.'

'Shall I see to her, Mary Ann?' Sadie asked.

The stallholder shook her head. 'No, I'm up to Ethel's tricks, girl, so if yer'll excuse me for a minute, I'll go and sort her out.'

The three women stood watching as Mary Ann approached the customer. 'That's a nice blouse, Ethel, and well worth a tanner.'

'But it's got a button missing, so yer should knock tuppence off.'

'The button is easy enough to sew on, Ethel. It won't take two minutes.'

'How can I sew it on when it's missing?'

'It's not really missing, is it, Ethel? I saw yer pulling it off and sneaking it into yer pocket. So hand the tanner over, before I really lose me temper with yer.'

But Ethel was all for bluffing it out, until a woman standing by the next trestle table called, 'It is in her bleeding pocket, Mary Ann. I saw it with me own eyes. She's a liar, that's what she is. Fancy doing that when the blouse is a ruddy bargain at sixpence. If it was a size bigger, I'd have it meself.'

Mary Ann chuckled. 'Lizzie, it wouldn't even go over yer head, queen. Yer need one twice the size to go over those mountains what are sticking out in front of yer.'

'Ay, less of that, Mary Ann. I'm proud of me breasts. At least I've got something for my feller to get hold of, not like some, who are as flat as a pancake.'

Ethel's nostrils flared. 'Are yer referring to me, by any chance? I'll have yer know I'm very proud of me trim figure.'

'Okay, ladies, let's call it quits. Lizzie is happy with her mountains, and Ethel is happy being as flat as a pancake. So pass me a sixpence over, Ethel, and be on yer way. As soon as yer get in, sew the button back on.' It was with great reluctance that the money changed hands, and with the blouse tucked under her arm, and her head in the air, Ethel flounced away, sending daggers to the two women over her shoulder.

Mary Ann moved to stand in front of Lizzie, who was one of her oldest customers, and one of her favourites. 'That jumper yer've got in yer hands has got a small hole in, queen.'

'Yes, I know, girl, but it's under the arm and it won't be noticed after I've darned it. It'll do me a turn.' Lizzie took a well-worn purse out of her pocket. 'I've got a sixpence in here somewhere.'

'Give us threepence, queen, seeing as it's you and I'm feeling in a generous mood.'

Lizzie beamed. 'Oh, God bless yer, Mary Ann. Ye're one in a million, so yer are. I can treat meself to a pennyworth of Mint Imperials now, and five Woodbines for my feller. If it wasn't for this table, I'd kiss yer.'

'Oh no yer wouldn't, Lizzie. The last time yer kissed me, yer nearly smothered me in those breasts of yours. I was fighting for breath, and thought me number was up. So just settle for blowing me a kiss, eh? And I'll say ta-ra to yer now, queen, 'cos I've got friends waiting for me.'

Molly had watched the scene in amazement. 'That woman didn't really pull a button off on purpose, did she?'

Sadie nodded. 'You wouldn't believe some of the things they get up to. Especially on a Saturday, when the market is packed, yer need eyes in the back of yer head.' Her face glowing with laughter, she added, 'Mary Ann doesn't miss much, though, she's brilliant. And most of the customers are regulars, been coming for years and think the world her. She helps a lot of poor people, and they'd lynch anyone they thought was stealing from her.'

The stallholder was rubbing her hands when she returned. 'Can't be up to them, can yer? But while there's a few like Ethel, who would steal the eye out of yer head and come back for the socket, most of me regulars are as honest as the day is long.'

If Nellie's dress had sleeves in, she'd have been rolling them up as a sign she meant what she was about to say. 'Ooh, a job here would suit me down to the ground. That one what pulled the button off, I'd have stood her on her head until it rolled out of her pocket. She thought she was Miss High and Mighty, but I'd have been in me apple cart pulling her down a peg or two. The thieving cow.'

'Ah, well, me and Sadie have our own way of dealing with people like that. Next time she comes, we'll charge her a couple of coppers more than we would our regular customers. Take Lizzie, now. Her and her husband are as poor as church mice, trying to get by on a pittance. But both as honest as the day is long, and wouldn't do yer out of a penny. So what we make on the likes of Ethel, well, it means we can help the likes of Lizzie.'

'Nellie is looking for a couple of summer dresses,' Sadie told the stallholder, who was like a mother to her. 'I think there's some in the box yer husband brought before, so can I open it and see if there's anything suitable?'

'Of course yer can. Empty it out and let Nellie and Molly have a root through them. There's a few likely customers hovering around, queen, so I'll leave yer to it, while I try and drum up some custom.' Mary Ann was smiling as she walked towards a white-haired woman. 'Hello, Milly. Ye're looking well, queen, I must say. Is it your feller looking after yer that keeps yer so young, or is it Carter's Little Liver Pills?'

'It's a combination of both, Mary Ann. My husband looks after my heart, and the pills attend to the rest of me body.'

'It's a pity there's not more people around like Mary Ann.' Molly had a soft spot for the stallholder because she had heard the story of how she had taken Sadie under her wing when the girl was forced to leave home because of her cruel parents. 'The world would be a better place if there were.'

'I'm living proof of Mary Ann's goodness, Molly, and I say a prayer for her every night.' Sadie nodded to a trestle table at the back of them, and the trio walked over to it. 'Give us a hand with this cardboard box, will yer, Molly, and we can empty it on the table.'

As the box was turned upside down, and the assortment of clothes came tumbling out, Nellie was rubbing her hands in anticipation. She could see clothing of every description and colour. There was bound to be something to fit her in that lot. Perhaps, with a bit of luck, there'd be more than one summer dress in her size.

'Nellie, will yer give Sadie time to sort things out before yer start rooting?' Molly put a hand on her friend's arm to keep her back. 'The clothes are not going to disappear, they'll still be here in five minutes' time.'

Nellie's chubby face was creased in a smile. 'Yer know how petious I am, girl, I can't wait for anything. Ask George, he'll tell yer. I don't give him time to get into bed.'

'Oh dear, oh dear.' Molly didn't know whether to laugh, cry, or let it pass. 'Nellie, I think what yer meant to say was that ye're impetuous.'

'Yeah, I'm that as well, girl.' Nellie didn't care what she was, for in the mound of clothes she could see a blue floral cotton dress that, with a bit of luck, would be big enough for her. And shaking herself free of her mate's hand, she made a grab for it. 'Ooh, ay, girl, look at this. D'yer think there's any chance of me fitting into it?'

Molly eyed the dress being held up for her inspection. 'That's a lovely dress, sunshine, and I'd say there's a good chance it will fit yer.' She grinned at Nellie's excitement. 'With your luck, I'd say it'll fit yer like a glove.'

Sadie took the dress and held it up to Nellie's shoulders. 'Will yer hold it there for me, Molly, and I'll see if it fits round her waist and tummy.'

When Mary Ann heard a whoop of delight, she turned her head to see Nellie doing a war dance, waving a cotton dress in the air. 'Sounds like another satisfied customer, Milly. That's what I like to see, 'cos it means me family will be getting fed tonight.'

Milly smiled. 'I'm sure your family are very well looked after, Mary Ann, even if yer are always pleading poverty.'

'This pleading poverty lark has become a habit with me now, Milly, 'cos I've been doing it for so long. And ye're right, me family are well fed. There's many a poor soul would be happy with a fraction of what my family eat.'

Both women turned when there came another loud 'Whoopee!', and they roared with laughter at Nellie's antics. Sadie had come up with another cotton dress which was her size, and Nellie was performing a dance which was a cross between a war dance and a tango. 'I'd better go and see what's going on, Milly. I hate to miss out on anything. And that little woman is the funniest thing on two legs.'

'She certainly looks a happy soul,' Milly agreed, moving the handle of her bag to the crook of her arm. 'I'll see yer later on in the week.'

'Don't think I'm chasing yer, queen,' Mary Ann said, 'but if

I'm not taking any money I may as well go mad and enjoy meself. Take care now, Milly.'

By the time Mary Ann joined the friends, Sadie had not only found the two dresses for Nellie, she'd also found a really nice one for Molly. 'It's all right for some folk enjoying themselves,' the stallholder said. 'Here's me losing money hand over fist and all you lot can do is laugh and dance.'

'I'm sorry ye're having a bad day, sunshine, but me and Nellie will be adding a bit to yer coffers.' Molly was looking very pleased. She hadn't intended to buy anything for herself, but just couldn't resist the soft green cotton dress when Sadie fished it out of the pile. 'We won't be giving yer enough to splash out on pork chops and apple sauce all round, but it'll be a help towards a tasty meal.'

'Don't take any notice of me moaning, queen, it's become second nature to me to moan on a Monday. I'm only happy when the place is heaving with people, and me and Sadie are kept on the go all day. I love all the hustle and bustle, lots of people around to have a laugh with. If my customers are happy, then I'm happy too!'

'I'm more than happy, Mary Ann,' Nellie said, 'I'm over the bleeding moon! Just fancy finding two dresses what fit me. I can't believe me luck.'

'I asked Sadie how much we owe yer, Mary Ann,' Molly told her, 'but she wasn't sure, and said to wait until you came. So what do we owe yer for each of the dresses? They're all in very good condition, no tears in them and the material isn't faded. In fact they've hardly had any wear.' She opened her purse. 'So, what's the damage, sunshine?'

Mary Ann tapped a finger on her chin. 'What d'yer think, Sadie? Would they be put on yer superior quality stall, or not?'

'It's up to you, Mary Ann,' Sadie said. 'All the stuff in that box is good quality and the dresses are well worth three bob each. But, as I said, it's up to you.'

Molly waved a hand. 'I'll settle it for yer, shall I? These dresses are worth five bob each at the very least, and that's what me and Nellie are more than prepared to pay. Isn't that right, sunshine?'

Nellie was so happy, she would have agreed no matter what she was asked. 'Cheap at half the price, girl, that's what I say. Cheap at half the price.'

Molly smiled at Mary Ann and Sadie. 'My mate has a queer way of putting things at times, but she means she thinks we're getting a bargain at five bob.' She opened her purse. 'Here's my five bob, and Nellie will give yer her ten bob.'

While Nellie was sorting her money out, Molly spoke to Sadie. 'How's the boyfriend, sunshine? Are yer still crazy about each other?'

Sadie's eyes lit up at the mention of her darling Harry. 'It wouldn't be possible to love each other any more than we do. We are both so happy.'

'Are yer still getting married this year?'

'We may have to postpone it until next Easter. We both want a nice wedding with all the trimmings, but when we added up what it would cost, well, we would never have enough to marry this year. I've priced some wedding dresses, and they're really expensive. Then there's bridesmaids' dresses for me two sisters, and suits for me two brothers. Me and Harry would rather wait and do the job properly, than skimp on things. I want to look nice for him, Molly, 'cos he's been so good to me. No one will ever know how good he was when I lived next door to him. He was the only one in the street who ever spoke to me. Even defied his parents, who wanted him to have nothing to do with me because of me parents. I really love him to pieces, Molly, and I know I'm very lucky to have him.'

Having settled up with Nellie, Mary Ann joined in the conversation she'd been half listening to. 'It cuts two ways, queen, because Harry is lucky to have someone as beautiful on the inside as you are on the outside. And he has told me more times than I can remember that he's the luckiest man alive. Yer make a lovely couple, both kind, thoughtful and loving. And yer've looked after old Sarah and her husband as if they were yer own grandparents.'

'Except in name, they are my grandparents, Mary Ann. They took me in when I had nowhere to go, and for the first time in me life I was living with people who respected me and in time came to love me. I'll never be able to repay them for what they've done for me. As I will never be able to repay you, Mary Ann, for you were the one who took me under your wing and set me on the road to happiness.' Sadie wiped away a tear of emotion. 'And that is the end of today's lesson, folks, so all put a smile back on yer faces.'

'Whenever yer wedding is, sunshine, you make sure yer let me and Nellie know. It is one wedding we wouldn't miss for all the world, isn't it, Nellie?'

'I've already got me wedding dress and hat, girl, and Molly will tell yer, I look like a million dollars in them.'

'She's not pulling yer leg,' Molly told them. 'Her daughter got married at Easter and Nellie was the best-dressed woman there. Except for the bride, no one could hold a candle to her.'

Nellie's face was a joy to see. 'I was, yer know. Everyone said how nice I looked.'

Molly knew if she didn't stop it right now they'd be there for ages. 'All right, sunshine, next time we come yer can tell them about the wedding. But right now we've got to make tracks.'

'Don't leave it so long next time,' said Mary Ann, while Sadie nodded agreement.

'Oh, we won't, girl,' Nellie said. 'And I'm made up with me dresses. See yer soon.'

'That goes for me too,' Molly told them. 'It's been lovely seeing yer again. Next time we come we'll be wearing our Sadie's superior quality frocks. Ta-ra for now.'

Chapter Twenty

'That looks nice on yer, love,' Jack said as his wife did a twirl in her new dress. 'And yer said yer got it for five bob?'

Molly grinned. 'Me and Nellie went to the market and she got two smashing dresses that fit her fine. I just bought the one, 'cos I didn't have much money on me. And they were only five bob each. Mind you, we're well in with the stallholder and get the best of what's going. When we got home, I told Nellie to skedaddle so I could wash mine and get it on the line. But as usual, she got round me and I ended up putting the three in the sink and washing them. I pegged them out on the line, and with the weather being so nice they were dry in half an hour, and I ended up ironing the three of them.'

Ruthie had been listening with interest. 'Me Auntie Nellie can't half get round you, Mam, she gets away with murder.'

'Tell me something I don't know, sunshine! I keep telling meself not to be so soft with her, but it always ends up with her getting her own way.' Molly chuckled. 'If yer want to know how really daft I am, wait until I tell yer this. I was ironing the dresses, with the sweat running off me, while she sat in her posh chair watching! She was drinking a cup of tea and eating my custard creams. And she even had the nerve to tell me I'd left a crease in one of her dresses and would I run the iron over it again!'

Jack thought that was hilarious. 'Yer've got to hand it to her, love, she does have a certain way with her. I don't think yer've ever refused her once, have yer?'

'Oh, I must have done some time in the last twenty years. But when she puts on that innocent, little girl lost look, well, I can't refuse her.'

'I'm going to ask her how she does it,' Ruthie said. 'She gets away with far more than I do. I don't get all me own way with yer.'

'If yer've got any complaints, sunshine, then wait until I've got the dinner on the table and then yer can get them off yer chest. But saying that doesn't mean I'm going to agree with everything yer want, so bear that in mind.'

Ruthie looked to her dad for sympathy. 'See what I mean, Dad? I don't stand a chance against Auntie Nellie.'

Molly came in from the kitchen carrying three dinner plates. 'It's bacon, egg and tomato, and I've done a round of fried bread each.'

'Mam, if I give yer an innocent, butter-wouldn't-melt-in-me-mouth look, would yer bring the HP sauce in with yer?'

'Don't push yer luck, sunshine, and remember, yer legs are younger than mine.'

Ruthie smiled as she stood up. 'Okay, I'll get the sauce. I'd better keep yer sweet 'cos I've got a favour to ask of yer.'

'I thought there was something in the wind.' Molly winked at her husband. 'If her favour is to ask me to wash and iron three dresses for her, then I'm afraid she's in for a let-down.'

Ruthie came from the kitchen carrying a bottle of HP sauce. 'No, it's not that, Mam. If it was, I'd ask Auntie Nellie to ask yer on my behalf. She'd have more luck than me.' She put the sauce on the table and sat facing her mother. 'Are yer in a good mood, Mam, seeing as yer've got a nice dress?'

Molly picked up her knife and fork and used them to lift the egg on top of the round of fried bread. 'Yeah, I'm feeling quite chuffed with meself. So fire away, sunshine, while I spread the soft yolk over the bread. Me mouth's watering just looking at it.'

'Can I invite me friends in again for a game of cards on Friday night? Bella's mam said we could go there, but I'd rather be in me own house. So look at yer nice dress, Mam, and yer runny egg, and then find it in yer heart to say I can.'

Molly was thoughtful as she chewed on the piece of fried bread in her mouth, then she said, 'I'll agree on one condition.'

'What's that, Mam?'

'That I can invite someone to join yer.'

'Ah, ay, Mam, who is that?'

'He's the son of a friend of mine, and he's a nice young lad. He works with Phil, so yer can ask him what he's like. But I will tell yer he's a smashing-looking lad.'

Ruthie's feet stopped swinging and there was interest in her eyes. 'How do you know him, and how old is he?'

'Same age as you, sunshine. He left school the same time as you.'

Jack was showing interest now. 'Do I know him?'

Molly wasn't going to mention that the lad was the one they collected clothes for at Christmas. What Ruthie didn't know wouldn't hurt her. 'Yer've heard me mention Claire, the women me and Nellie see on a Friday? Well it's her son, and Claire was only saying last week that he didn't go out much. When he gets home from work every night he sits in to keep her company. I've told yer the story of how her husband died young, when Ken, the boy I'm talking about, was only ten. And his young sister was a baby at the time.'

'I remember yer telling me now.' Jack recalled seeing the boy when he came to pick up the clothes. 'From what yer say, he's a thoughtful lad. Not many kids would sit in every night to keep their mother company.'

'It's funny yer asking about having a game of cards here, Ruthie, 'cos on Friday Claire was saying how she wished he'd make some friends. She feels guilty 'cos he thinks she'll be lonely if he leaves her on her own. So would yer like to invite him to come on Friday?'

'How can I invite him if I don't know him?'

'Yer can pass an invitation to him through Phil, who, incidentally, thinks he's a cracking lad. And apparently a real grafter at work.'

The young girl looked down at her plate. 'Mam, yer know I'd sit in with yer every night if yer were lonely. I wouldn't leave yer on yer own.'

'I know yer would, sunshine, ye're like yer two sisters in that respect. Jill and Doreen are very thoughtful, too! And Tommy, I mustn't leave me lovely son out. Me and yer dad are well blessed with all our children.'

That brought a lump to Ruthie's throat. She was too young to know the right words to tell her parents how much she loved them. For she did love them. And if her mam wanted her to invite a boy to come to the card party, then she would. 'When I've finished me tea, shall I go over and see Phil? Or will you see him, 'cos I don't even know the boy's name.'

'His name is Kenneth Thompson, and he likes to be called Ken. I'm going over to see the baby after, so I'll ask Phil to pass the invitation on. I'm not saying he'll come, 'cos he might be too shy but there's no harm in asking. I hope he does come, for Claire would be made up if her son found some friends.'

'I'll come over with yer tonight,' Jack said. 'I haven't seen the baby for a few days.'

'Well, yer can please yerself, sunshine, but I'm going from Doreen's up to Jill's. I like to see me grandchildren every day. I'm not making fish of one and flesh of the other. And that means, my dearest heart, that the *Echo* will have to take second place tonight. Yer can read it when we get back; we won't be late.'

'Me and Bella are going for a walk in the park, Mam, with the weather being so nice. If the park-keeper isn't around, we'll sneak a go on the swings.'

'Well mind yer don't get locked in, sunshine, 'cos the keeper locks the gates when it starts going dusk. And I'd hate to think yer were locked in the park until it opens in the morning.'

'Ooh ay, Mam, we're not that daft. We could easy climb over the railings.'

While Molly's jaw dropped in horror, Jack was equally concerned. 'Don't try that, love, whatever yer do. Those railings might look easy to climb, but believe me they're not. If yer fell on one of the spikes yer could really hurt yerself.'

Molly found her voice. 'Don't you dare try to climb the railings! Yer could kill yerself! If yer did get stuck, and yer'd have to be pretty stupid to do so, then call someone walking past and tell them ye're locked in and would they get help.'

Ruthie burst out laughing. 'If you two could see yer faces, yer'd do no more good! Yer really fell for that, didn't yer? I would no more try to climb those railings than fly. They're over six feet high: me and Bella would never make it. We could perhaps manage to shin up a tree, but not those slippery railings.'

Jack scratched his head. 'I really thought yer meant it, love, and I had visions of someone knocking on the door saying yer were impaled on one of the spikes.'

'She's another Nellie McDonough,' Molly said. 'As though I'm not tormented enough with one, I've got two to cope with.'

'I wouldn't mind being like Auntie Nellie.' Ruthie had a piece of bread speared on a fork and ready to pop in her mouth. 'I don't mean I'd like to be fat like her, but I'd like to be as funny, and make people happy.' A chuckle filled the air. 'And

I'd like to be able to talk people into doing things for me . . . such as ironing three dresses.'

'Yer need to be clever to make people laugh, sunshine, and crafty. For instance, if Nellie was here now, she'd be looking at yer dad with her eyes screwed up. Then after a few seconds she'd ask, "Ay, lad, what does impaled mean?" ' Molly could see her mate in her mind. 'And when yer told her that, for instance, it could be a spike going through yer leg, she'd look down at the floor, and under her breath she'd mutter, "Why the bleeding hell couldn't he have just said that in the first place?" '

Ruthie chuckled. 'Yer sounded just like her then. I hope when I'm older and I get married, I'll have a next-door neighbour like her, and we can be friends.'

'Oh, I'm sorry to be the bearer of bad news, sunshine, but I have it on good authority that after Nellie was born, they broke the mould. If yer live to be a hundred, yer'll never come across another one like her. The woman at the market, Mary Ann, she's a very funny woman, with an answer for everything. But it's Nellie's face that gives her the final touch. She can pull that chubby face into every shape imaginable. And that's what gives her the edge over everyone else.'

'Nellie is at her funniest when she's with you, love,' Jack said. 'You are just as funny, but yours is a dry humour. The pair of yer remind me of Laurel and Hardy. Laurel acts the goat and Hardy is the straight man.'

Molly pushed her chair back and jumped to her feet. Then she folded her arms, screwed up her eyes, and impersonated her mate. 'Ay, listen here, lad, will yer just explain yerself? If ye're saying that me and my mate are a couple of clowns, then I'll bleeding clock yer one.'

Jack tried to sound contrite. 'Now, would I say that about you and my wife? No, what I meant was, ye're both good enough to be film stars. Yer should be earning a fortune.'

Molly didn't have the chubby cheeks, the mountainous breasts or the huge tummy, but her actions were those of Nellie. She stood to attention, her shoulders squared, and her hands laced in front of her. 'Ah, that's nice of yer, lad. I keep telling my George that if ever a talent scout comes down this street, or into Tony's butcher's shop, and sees me and me mate in action, he'll take us back to Hollywood with him. And he'll do it right away, no messing around, in case someone else snaps us up.'

It was hard for Jack to keep a straight face with his wife standing over him. 'And what does George say when yer tell him that?'

'Well, I've got to admit that my feller is a bit slow on the uptake.' Molly heaved the imaginary bosom. 'All he said was, I could go to Hollywood with the bloke, as long as I left his dinner ready in the oven for him.'

'Ah, well, he can't say fairer than that, can he?'

'What! Well, you would say that, wouldn't yer?' The eyes were like slits now, and her teeth were grinding. 'You bleeding men stick together like glue. Well, I'll tell yer this, Jack Bennett, my feller lived to regret those words. For he was having a roast dinner at the time, and he said afterwards he didn't remember eating it.' Her head nodded knowingly. 'Well, I told him he wouldn't remember eating it because I'd hit him over the head with it! And to this day, if we're having a roast dinner, he never opens his mouth till his plate's empty.'

'Brilliant, Mam,' Ruthie said. 'I wonder if I can get Bella to take Auntie Nellie off like that? We could do a turn when we have a party.'

'Somehow I can't see Bella being agreeable to that.' Molly smiled inwardly at the idea. She was very fond of Bella, and happy that she was Ruthie's friend. But by no stretch of the imagination could she see the shy, pretty girl standing in front of a group of people and either singing or telling jokes. 'To take Auntie Nellie off, yer have to be able to use swear words, and neither Bella or her mam would be happy about that.'

Ruthie shrugged her shoulders. 'Yeah, Auntie Mary would have a duck egg if she heard Bella swearing. Besides, it's not very ladylike, is it?'

'No, it isn't, sunshine. My mate can get away with it, but most people can't. And no decent lad would like a girlfriend who used bad language. He'd be afraid to take her home to meet his mother.'

'I better watch meself then, hadn't I?' The girl pushed her long blond hair over her shoulder. 'That's when I have a boyfriend, I mean.'

'I thought there were three or four on yer list of suitable boyfriends?' Molly sat down and smiled across the table at her youngest child. 'Haven't yer made yer mind up yet which one yer prefer?'

Jack raised his brows. 'Who are these boys? Have I met them?'

It was Molly who answered, for she wanted to spare her daughter's blushes. 'Of course yer've met them. There's Gordon Corkhill, Jeff Mowbray, Johnny Stewart, and I'm not sure whether Peter Corkhill is in the running.'

'Peter's too young!' Ruthie's face was flushed. 'He's childish.'

'He's exactly the same age as you and Bella. Do yer think you're childish?'

'Not as childish as him.'

'If I am allowed to get involved,' Jack said, 'then for what it's worth, I think he's the nicest-looking of the lot.'

'No he's not!' Ruthie shook her head quite vigorously. 'Gordon and Johnny are nicer-looking than him.'

Molly lifted her hand. 'That's quite enough now. A girl of fourteen shouldn't be seriously thinking of boyfriends.'

'I'm fourteen and eight and a half months, Mam, so I'm nearly fifteen.'

'Even so, sunshine, yer've got plenty of time to find the one who's right for you. And if ye're putting them down in the order of how handsome they are, I think yer should hedge yer bets until yer've seen Ken Thompson. And that's the end of the subject for now, so start taking the dirty dishes to the sink. By the time we get out it'll be time to come home.'

Jack made a move. 'Is Nellie coming to see the babies?'

Molly shook her head. 'No, she's seeing them tomorrow night. We decided we'd had enough of each other for one day.'

'Who decided that, love, you or Nellie?'

'It was a mutual decision, Jack. After all, yer can get too much of a good thing.'

Molly opened the door the next morning and gave a huge smile. 'Oh, that dress looks a treat on yer, sunshine! Yer couldn't have got a better fit anywhere.'

Nellie passed her with a supercilious expression on her face. Mind you, she didn't know she had a supercilious expression on her face because she didn't know there was such a word. Even if she did know, she wouldn't have been able to get her tongue round it. 'Thank you, girl, that's kind of yer. And I have to say I feel very comfortable in it. I saw myself in the mirror, and couldn't help but notice the resemblance between me and Jean Harlow.'

'Nellie, Jean Harlow is a blonde.'

'I know that, girl, but it's the only difference.'

'Which mirror where yer looking in, sunshine?'

'The one over the mantelpiece. It's the only one we've got.'

'And how much of yerself can yer see in the mirror?'

Nellie put a hand under her chin. 'From there upwards, girl.'

Molly kept her face straight until she looked into her friend's eyes and saw the devilment there. Then they collapsed, laughing, into each other's arms. 'What are you like, Nellie McDonough?'

'I'm like Jean Harlow, girl, I told yer. And if the only difference between me and her is that she's blond, well, I'll soon remedy that. I've got a bottle of bleach under the sink, what I use for the lavvy. That'll do the trick.'

'Don't even think about it, sunshine, for two reasons. First, yer wouldn't suit being a blonde. And second, it really wouldn't matter whether it suited yer or not, really, 'cos yer hair would have fallen out before yer had any choice.'

'Oh, if that's the case, girl, I'll take yer word for it and stay as I am. I like people telling me I look like Joan Bennett, anyway.'

Molly chucked her under the chin. 'Yer'll do me just as yer are, sunshine; I wouldn't want yer any different. And now we've settled on your appearance, we'll have a quick cup of tea and then start our job for the day. Which is trying to find out a bit more about the very mysterious Mr Collins.'

Nellie sat down and watched her friend walk through to the kitchen, then her chubby face creased into a mischievous grin. 'Ay, girl, we're going to get hungry if we're out a long time, so d'yer think we'd better have a few custard creams? Just to stop our tummies from rumbling, like. We could be on his trail, hoping he doesn't spot us, and suddenly my tummy lets out a noise like thunder. He'd have caught us out, girl; our cover would have been blown. And all for the sake of two custard creams.'

Molly popped her head round the door. 'Sorry, sunshine, but I haven't got one in the house. Would two arrowroot do instead?'

'Any port in a storm, girl, any port in a storm.'

* * *

The friends decided not to stand watch outside the laundry, but to go straight to the street where Graham Collins lived, and wait on the corner for him. Molly reckoned he was sure to come home: he'd have his laundry and wouldn't want to carry it around with him. So as they didn't have as far to walk, they took their time, enjoying the blue sky and the warmth of the sun.

'This is the life, eh, girl?' Nellie had never known the joy of walking in a summer dress and feeling the warmth of the sun on her arms and legs. And her pleasure could be seen in her wide smile. 'I didn't have to lie on me back on the couch and wrestle with a pair of stockings.'

'No garters to cut into yer legs, either, sunshine, that's a blessing. And summer is only just starting. We've got four months of good weather to look forward to.'

'I know something that you never noticed,' Nellie said. 'And that's not like you; yer never miss a trick as a rule.'

'It couldn't have been important,' Molly answered, 'or I wouldn't have missed it.'

'Oh, I think it was important, girl, and it's something ye're always on about.'

Molly pulled them to a halt. 'Nellie, ye're not going to ask me to guess what it is, are yer? I mean, it could be one of a million things. Like the gas meter eating money, or tomatoes not tasting like they used to before the war. I could go on for ever and not guess right.'

Nellie shook her head, and her chins. 'Yer don't half take off, girl. The least thing and ye're on yer high horse. And all over a fiddling cream slice.'

'A cream slice? What flipping cream slice?'

'The one I didn't have yesterday.'

'If yer didn't have one, how would I know about the flipping thing?'

'Because ye're always on about how I shouldn't eat them. And when I don't eat one, yer don't even notice. So, if that's all the thanks I get, I won't forget to have one in future.'

The light dawned, and Molly put a hand on each of her mate's shoulders. 'Oh, sunshine, fancy me not noticing! That's wonderful news. Why didn't yer tell me?'

'Because I didn't notice meself until I was in bed last night. And I'll tell yer what, girl, my George didn't half have a cob on when I woke him up to tell him.'

Molly dropped her hands. 'You woke George up just to tell him yer hadn't had a cream slice? I'm not surprised he had a cob on.'

'I had to tell someone, girl, and he was the only one in bed with me. Yer see, I couldn't stop thinking about the cream slice, and me mouth was watering. It was like a craving, and I used to have them when I was expecting each of me children.'

'Nellie, every woman gets cravings when they're expecting, but they don't wake their husbands up in the middle of the night. And seeing as yer haven't got the excuse of being pregnant, it's only natural George thought yer had a ruddy cheek.'

'He didn't speak to me over breakfast, just sat with a face as long as a fiddle. And he walked off to work without giving me a wave or a kiss. But I'll get me own back, girl, you just wait and see.'

'I've got no time to wait and see, Nellie, we've got a job in hand. Your ups and downs with George will have to take second place. So come on, let's get moving or we'll miss our target.'

Graham Collins didn't realise he was being followed as he strode along the road, a small case swinging from his fingers. And when he stopped at the corner of a street, opened the case and took out some papers, he didn't notice the two women who stopped just yards from him.

'I wonder what those sheets of paper were?' Nellie said, when their quarry had turned in to the street. 'Perhaps he's got clients to visit.'

'To me they looked like leaflets that come through the door now and again. You know, sunshine, like from the Salvation Army, or someone advertising soap or whatever. But I can't see him putting leaflets through letter boxes – he seems too posh.'

'My old ma used to say yer shouldn't take anything at face value, 'cos things are not always what they seem.'

'There's only one way to find out what he's up to, and that's to get after him and see for ourselves. I'll stay behind him, you cross to the other side, Nellie, and we'll take things as they come.'

There was a wide entry running behind the block of shops, and the entrance was in the street, next to the first of the terraced houses. Molly slipped into the entry at the same time as Graham Collins walked up the short path of the first house. He was blissfully unaware that he was being watched as he raised the knocker and gave three sharp raps.

'Good morning, madam.' There was a huge smile on his face as he raised his hat. 'And what a beautiful morning it is.'

'What d'yer want?' The woman eyed his case with suspicion and kept her hand on the inside door knob, ready to close it quickly if need be. 'If ye're selling anything, then ye're wasting yer time 'cos I haven't got any money.'

'Ah, but I'm not selling anything, just the opposite.' His voice was sickly sweet, and Molly, standing only yards away behind a wall, wrinkled her nose. 'In fact,' Graham went on, 'I may be in a position to put some money your way.' He handed her one of the leaflets. 'I run a very respectable business, with a shop in the city centre. I buy and sell old pictures, ornaments, and other items. If you have anything of that nature that you have no further use for, or is just cluttering up your house, then perhaps you would consider selling it and we could do a deal. Providing you have something worth selling, I would gladly buy it from you. And I would give you what it was worth. I'm sure a little extra money could come in very useful.'

'Would it be cash in hand?' the woman asked, thinking of the pictures on the wall that had belonged to her parents. After all, they were only harbouring dust. She didn't really know whether they were worth anything, but there was no harm in trying. It was all very well being sentimental, but it didn't put food on the table. 'I might have one or two things, but I can't ask yer in now 'cos it's not convenient.'

'Oh, I wouldn't expect you to! I am calling at a few houses in the street today, and will be back next Tuesday to those who are interested. Shall I put you down for a visit? I can assure you it would be worth your while. And I can also assure you that I run a legitimate business and am a well respected name in the city.'

The woman nodded, but still kept her hand on the inside knob of the door. 'This time next week will suit me fine. It'll give me time to sort out anything that might be suitable. But I'd need the money in me hand before I parted with anything.'

'You are very wise,' Graham agreed. 'One has to be very careful these days. There are some unsavoury characters about.' He raised his hat and put on what he thought was a friendly smile. 'I'll be here this time next week, and I'm sure we will be able to do business together. Until then, I wish you well.'

Molly turned her back to the street in case he happened to glance her way. Then after giving him time to move away from the house, she hurried across the cobbles to where Nellie stood on the opposite pavement. 'Are yer fed up waiting, sunshine?'

'I'm fed up pacing up and down, girl, trying to make meself invisible. I hope yer heard a bit of what he was saying so I won't feel the time has been wasted.'

'If anyone was watching, they'd think we were just two friends who happened to meet each other. And no one will suspect anything if we stand talking for a while. I've got me back to that side of the street, so you can watch what the queer feller gets up to.'

'At the present time, girl, he's knocking on the house next door. He must intend to knock on every door giving those leaflets out.' Nellie took her eyes off the man and rested them on her mate. 'I'm hoping you've got something to tell me, girl, 'cos I felt a right nit walking up and down. I imagined I was being watched.'

'I'll tell yer what I heard while you keep an eye on him. Tell me whether he gets an answer, and if whoever opens the door takes a leaflet off him and engages in conversation. Or will they send him packing?'

'The door has opened, girl, and an elderly woman is talking to him. I think she's just asking him what he wants, and she doesn't seem happy for him to be there.' Nellie felt like a real private detective now. This was the sort of undercover work they did. 'He's giving her one of the leaflets, but she's pointing to her eyes, which I think means she can't read without glasses. Oh, now he's bending down to talk to her, and he's not half ruddy smarmy. If my old ma, God rest her soul, was here now, she'd say he was too sweet to be wholesome.'

'That's just what I think, sunshine. He's up to something, and I'll lay odds it's to try and get money off these people. A genuine antique dealer wouldn't be going round knocking on doors in a poor area. He'd have a proper shop in the best part of the city.'

'Hang on, girl, I can't watch and listen to you at the same

time. He's saying something to her now, and the old lady is nodding her head.'

'He's telling her he'll call again at this time next week, and he'll buy any pictures or ornaments she has. And he'll say he'll pay good money for them and that he runs a very respectable business in the city centre.'

Nellie's jaw dropped. 'I didn't know yer could lip-read, girl! That's bleeding marvellous, that is.'

'I can't lip-read, Nellie, I'm not that clever.'

'Well how d'yer know what he said?'

'Because that's what he said to the woman in the first house. And I bet everyone who opens the door to him will get the same story, word for word. I was in a good position in that entry. I could hear every word he said.'

'And yer think he'll diddle them?'

'I wouldn't stake me life on it, sunshine, but I'd be willing to bet a tanner. He's a rotter, a scoundrel, and I hope these people can see through him.'

Nellie glared at the man who was now knocking on another door. 'Why don't we tell them they can't trust him?'

Molly shook her head. 'We can't do that without proof, sunshine, or he could see a solicitor and we'd be in trouble. Claire wouldn't have anything more to do with us, and my Jack would go mad. So would your George.'

'What shall we do then, girl?'

'I'm going to tell yer everything I heard him say, sunshine, and yer can tell me whether yer think the same as me. And if yer do, then what we'll do now is make a note of every house he calls at today.' Molly turned her head to see the man they were discussing replacing his hat before walking to the next house. 'I wouldn't trust that man as far as I could throw him.'

'Tell me what yer heard, girl, and don't miss a word out or I'll have yer guts for garters.'

Molly screwed her eyes up briefly. 'Nellie, how would yer know if I missed a word out?'

Nellie was flummoxed. How would she know? 'Well, er, well I wouldn't know, would I? But because ye're me best mate, I'll trust yer not to do it.'

So Molly repeated what she'd heard as accurately as she could. And when she'd finished, Nellie's chin was jutting out and her eyes had narrowed. 'He's a bleeding crook, that feller is. And he's not soft, either. He knows these people haven't got no money, and he'll give them buttons for pictures what have been in the family for years. Ooh, I'd like to get my hands on him. I'd ruddy throttle him.'

'Perhaps we can put a halt to his gallop, sunshine, if we put our mind to it. But it means us getting our facts right and being very careful. Right now we'll take the number of every house he knocks at where the person takes a leaflet, listens to him and nods their head. That means they've agreed he can call next week and they'll have something to sell him. But before next Tuesday comes, you and me, sunshine, have got to think of a way to stop him robbing people. Because that's what he intends doing. Otherwise, why would he say he runs a very respectable business, with a shop in the centre of the city?'

'How are we going to stop him, girl?'

'I can't tell yer off the top of me head, sunshine, but I'm determined we'll find a way. So if yer come at ten in the morning, instead of half past, we'll hatch our plan over a cup of tea and, if Ruthie hasn't been too greedy, two custard creams each.'

Nellie's face was like the rising sun. 'Sounds good, girl, it sounds good.'

Chapter Twenty-One

'What are yer standing like that for?' Molly asked, looking down on her neighbour from the top step. 'Why have yer got yer hands behind yer back?'

'It's a free country, isn't it, girl? If I want to stand with me hands behind me back there's no law what says I can't.'

Molly managed to keep a smile back, for her friend looked quite a sight. She seemed to be all bosom and tummy. 'Ye're right, Nellie, there's no law what says yer can't. But if yer intend standing there like an armless woman for any length of time, then I'll have to close the door on yer. I've put a few things on the clothes line, and I've left the back door open. So give us a knock when yer decide yer've had enough.'

'Don't close the door, girl, 'cos I'm coming in now.'

'How do yer expect to get up the steps with yer hands behind yer back? Yer need them to pull yerself up.'

'This is a nice welcome, I must say. I've got a nice surprise for yer behind me back, that's why I'm standing like this. But I don't think I'll give it to yer now, 'cos yer don't deserve it. Yer can be a miserable cow when the mood hits yer.'

'Ooh, yer've got a nice surprise for me, sunshine! Well, that's really kind of yer, and I can't wait to see what it is.'

With a look of superiority, Nellie made a great play of bringing one of her hands from behind her back. In her hand was a plate, and on the plate sat two fairy cakes, in their white ruffled cases. 'I made these meself last night, girl, so we could have them with our cup of tea. So if yer'll kindly step aside, I'll come in now.'

There was astonishment on Molly's face as she moved back while Nellie used the door frame to pull herself up with her free hand. Such was her concentration on keeping the plate with the cakes on straight, she was scarcely breathing, and her tongue was sticking out of the side of her mouth. And when she managed to reach the living room, she placed the plate on the table with a look of pride at having made it without a mishap. 'There yer are, girl, don't they look nice? Good enough to eat, eh?'

Molly nodded. 'They do indeed look very nice, sunshine, but I'll bet any money that you didn't make them. Yer've never baked a cake in yer life.' Then Molly slapped an open palm on her forehead. 'Oh, no, if my memory serves me right, yer did try yer hand at baking fairy cakes about fifteen years ago. I also remember they were so hard no one could eat them. The ones that didn't end up in the bin, your Steve and his mates used to play cricket with.'

Nellie's changing expressions had Molly turning her head away. She could just imagine the names she was being called in her mate's head. 'I bet yer telling a fib, and the truth is yer got them from the corner shop.'

'I haven't been to the corner shop, and yer can ask Maisie if yer don't believe me.' Nellie put everything she could into her look of disgust. 'They're not bought cakes, they're home-made. And if yer doubt me, then our Lily will vouch for me.'

'How the heck would your Lily know?'

'Because she made the bleeding things, that's why!'

Molly doubled up. 'Why didn't yer just bring the cakes with yer and say that? It would have been much easier and quicker than going through all that rigmarole.'

Nellie picked up the carver chair and carried it to the table. 'Yer don't have to tell me that, girl, 'cos I found out the hard way. If yer'd seen me performance, yer'd have laughed yerself sick. It took me ages to get me two hands behind me back, and I was made up when I'd managed it. That's until I realised I had no hand to knock on yer door, and I called meself all the silly buggers going. Then Mrs Seymore from the top of the street came. She was on her way to the shops, and she knocked for me.'

In her mind's eye, Molly could picture the scene. Her neighbour never did anything straightforward; she had to do things the hard way. But she always managed to turn everything into laughter. Mrs Seymore must have gone off with a smile on her face, which was a good start to her day.

'Never mind, sunshine. Everything has turned out fine, and those cakes are making me mouth water. The kettle has been boiled so in a few minutes we can sit down and relax.'

'And plan our campaign, eh, girl? Where does the McDonough and Bennett Private Detective Agency go from here with the case we're working on? The case of the mysterious Mr Graham Collins.'

'Wait until we've got a cup of tea in front of us, sunshine. My brain always works better when there's a cup at hand. It won't take a minute, and don't you dare eat my fairy cake while I'm out in the kitchen or yer won't get yer two biscuits. So think on, guzzle-guts.'

So Nellie swung her short legs back and forth, while keeping her eyes on the cakes. Her mouth was watering, but she couldn't do anything about that. George said it was something to do with her glands. She didn't know what her glands were, but she wasn't going to ask because he would say she was ignorant.

'Here yer are, sunshine.' Molly set the tray down in the middle of the table. 'I'll pour, but you can put yer own milk and sugar in. That's as long as yer remember to take it easy. I need milk for the breakfast.'

'Yer could always run to the corner shop for milk,' Nellie said in all innocence. 'Alec opens up at seven o'clock.'

'Yer can be a cheeky article at times, Nellie McDonough. Give me one good reason why I should run to the corner shop at seven o'clock in the morning, when I get enough milk off the milkman to see me through the day.'

'Well, girl, now yer ask, the only reason I can think of for yer going out at that time of a morning would be if yer had visitors what drank a lot of milk.'

'Yer hit the nail on the head, sunshine! So don't be heavy-handed when ye're putting milk in yer tea. Think of Jack and Ruthie.'

'Ah, ay, girl, how can I think of Jack and Ruthie when me mind is on business? Surely a real detective wouldn't slip up on the job just because of a lousy drop of milk?'

'In that case, Nellie, yer won't mind if I put the milk in for yer? It's not that I don't trust yer, sunshine, yer know I love the bones of yer. But as I've been married to Jack for nearly twenty-five years, I think he's entitled to be my priority.'

'Will yer put all those long words back in the dictionary where they belong, and pour the bleeding tea out before I faint with thirst.'

Molly grinned. 'Your wish is my command, sunshine.' She poured the tea and handed a cup to Nellie. 'As yer'll have seen, there's biscuits on the plate. Mind you, I don't know why I said that, 'cos the one thing yer never miss is something that goes down yer mouth and into yer tummy.'

'Blimey! There's not a mouthful in those fiddling little cakes. I could eat a dozen and still be hungry.'

Molly frowned when a thought entered her head. Knowing her mate inside out, she decided to have a bet with herself. Not for money, of course, but for satisfaction. 'It was good of Lily to think of yer, Nellie, seeing as she's out at work all day. How many did she bring down for yer?'

Nellie didn't think before she answered, which she would kick herself for later. 'She brought a dozen down, girl, straight out of the oven.'

'That was very thoughtful of her,' Molly said, while telling herself she'd half won her bet. 'And how many did George have?'

Still Nellie failed to smell a rat. 'Oh, he only had the one, girl, 'cos as yer know, George hasn't got a sweet tooth.'

'I bet Paul was pleased, though. I know for a fact that he's inherited your liking for cakes and sweets.'

'He wasn't in when Lily came down, girl, he was out with Phoebe. Yer know what they're like for dancing, and they'd gone to Blair Hall.'

'Yer saved him some, though, didn't yer?'

Only now did Nellie realise she'd walked right into a trap. Her eyes disappeared in the folds of flesh as she sought a way out. 'I did think about it, girl, and I'd actually put two on a plate in the larder for him. Then I thought he wouldn't eat them when he came home from the dance 'cos it would be very late and he'd go straight to bed. And they'd be stale by tonight, and stale cakes are not very nice.'

'So, George had one, and yer've brought those two down with yer. By my reckoning, yer'd have nine over, so what did yer do with them?'

'Well, it would have been a sin to put them in the bin, wouldn't it, girl?'

'Oh, I know yer wouldn't do that, sunshine, so what did yer do with them?'

'Well, I – erm . . .' Nellie began to get flustered. 'As I said, it was no good letting them go stale, so I couldn't do anything else but eat them.'

'You ate nine fairy cakes?' Molly's voice came out on a high note. 'Last night, after yer'd had a dinner, yer ate nine cakes?'

Nellie began to shake her head, then realised she should be nodding. 'There's not a mouthful in them, girl, so don't be looking at me as though I've committed a murder. Yer just put one in yer mouth, and then, like magic, it's gone. Yer don't even know yer've had one.'

'Perhaps not, sunshine, but yer surely would know if yer had nine. Did George know yer'd eaten them all?'

Her friend looked puzzled. 'What's it got to do with George?'

'He didn't see yer eating them, did he?'

This time Nellie had the grace to blush. 'No, I stood in the pantry and gobbled the lot down.' She went on the offensive then. With jaw jutting out, she glared at Molly. 'If our Lily went to the trouble of making us cakes, she meant us to enjoy them. If she'd known I was going to get the third degree off me mate, I bet she wouldn't have bothered.' She leaned forward, eyes narrowed to slits. 'And I did enjoy the bleeding things, too, so there!'

'Well, that's all that matters, sunshine, isn't it? In the end, we both came out happy.'

'Yer didn't sound very happy to me,' Nellie growled. 'Yer sounded like the headmistress in the school I went to. She was a right ogre, she was. The least little excuse and she'd have yer holding yer hand out for the cane.' It suddenly sank in what Molly had said. 'What did yer mean when yer said we both came out happy?'

'You had the fairy cakes that made yer happy, and I won me bet.'

'What bet was that, girl?'

'I had a little bet with meself that you had eaten all the cakes yerself. Yer see, I know yer so well, I knew yer'd never be able to go to bed and sleep while knowing there were cakes in the pantry. I don't get any money for winning, of course, but I do have the satisfaction.'

'I'm glad ye're happy with yerself, girl, but here's something for yer to dwell on. In the time yer've wasted over those fiddling ruddy cakes, we could have caught Graham Collins, got the police on his trail, and he'd now be in jail.'

'I don't think we could have done all that in twenty minutes, sunshine, but I admit I have wasted some time. So let's get down to business. We can talk while we eat and drink.'

'Have yer thought of a plan of action, girl? You know, how we are going to go about catching the rotter?'

'I've come up with a few ideas, but can't make up me mind which is the best.'

Being a private detective was a serious business, and Nellie's expression said she was treating it as such. With her elbow on the table, and her chubby face cupped in a hand, she asked, 'What have yer in mind?'

'We need to know whether he is a genuine dealer, or whether he's like those spivs we had during the war. You know, the ones who sold black market stuff. Except yer could tell them a mile off, with their long coats and greasy hair. Graham Collins is a different kettle of fish. To look at him, you'd think he's a well-to-do man of means. A lot of the people in the houses he called at yesterday would take him at face value. Well dressed, well spoken and charming. Now we can't prove he's not all those things, but our intuition tells us he's a scoundrel. So we need to find out if he is genuine, or if we are right.'

'We're right, girl, I'm sure of that. It's as plain as the nose on yer face that he's up to no good. Why would a genuine antique dealer choose to knock on doors in a poor area? Those people don't have much, but ten to one there will be quite a few who have got stuff that their parents left them.' It wasn't often that Nellie was serious, but in this case she was. 'I bet he'll offer them coppers for what they've got, when they'd get a decent price if they went to a proper, honest dealer.'

Molly's expression showed her surprise. 'My God, sunshine, yer can put yer brain to good use when yer need to. Yer've really taken this case to heart, haven't yer?'

'I might act daft most of the time, girl, but I'd never stand by and watch poor people get ripped off by a rotter. Don't yer agree that what I've just said is right?'

'I think yer've hit the nail on the head, sunshine. I was thinking exactly the same thing in bed last night. At first I wondered why he'd picked a poor area to tout for business, then it hit me that he'd deliberately chosen that area because the people are poor, and would jump at the chance of earning a few bob. Like meself, they wouldn't know the real value of an old picture or ornament. And because he looks and speaks so posh, they'd fall for anything he told them. But the question is, how do we find out if we're right about him? And if we do find out, who is going to believe us? The police would laugh their heads off and send us packing. And I wouldn't blame them, either! Two housewives walk into the station with this far-fetched story, and no proof to back it up.'

'Well, we'll just have to get it, girl! Come on, buck yer ideas up! We can't just sit on our backsides and let him get away with it. We've got Claire to think about, remember. It's better she finds out now that he's a rotter, before she gets too attached to him. We'd be doing her a favour, and all the other poor people he's planning to rob.'

'I agree with everything yer say, sunshine, but it all boils down to having no proof. Without that we haven't a leg to stand on.'

'We'll get it, girl, by hook or by crook.'

'And how do yer propose to get it, sunshine? We can hardly stop him in the street and ask him what monkey business he's up to.' Molly sighed. 'I lay awake last night thinking of a way to catch him at it, but whether it was because I was tired or not, I couldn't get the old brain cells working.'

'I was the same, girl,' Nellie said, her head and chins nodding. 'But I did come up with something. I think it would work, but you'll probably pooh pooh the idea.'

'Try me, sunshine, 'cos I haven't got a clue.'

Nellie lifted her bosom on to the table so she could lean forward. 'We've got a list of all the addresses he knocked at in that one street. And we know he's going back at the same time next Tuesday. So I thought if we knocked on one of the doors, we could make up a cock and bull story about how he's put a leaflet through our letter box but the dog had chewed it up before we had a chance to look at it. And we had heard he'd been canvassing in their street and wondered if they could let us see one of the leaflets.' She could see Molly wasn't impressed so far, and became impatient. 'Come on, girl, pull yer ruddy socks up for God's sake. At this rate we'll never get anywhere. We could tell them any tale, just to get friendly. I'm good at spinning yarns, girl, and telling lies, as yer well know. Surely out of all those houses we'd find one we could get pally with.'

Molly began to take an interest. She leaned forward and patted her friend's arms. 'That's just what I needed, sunshine, to wake me up. Ye're not just a pretty face, are yer?'

'Yer know it's not me face that men lust after, it's me voluptuous body they crave for.' Nellie was glad to see her mate back in the land of the living. 'So, yer think my idea is a good one, do yer?'

'I think it was very clever of yer to think of getting friendly with one of the women in the street. And if we move your idea around a bit, we don't really have to go knocking on doors. We could hang around the street until we see someone who looks friendly. We could still use the excuse yer made up about the dog, which I thought was brilliant. Especially as yer can't stand animals of any kind.'

'It's not that I can't stand animals, girl. I've got nothing against them, but I wouldn't want one in me house. They're too much work.'

'There's a place in the world for everything, sunshine, whether human or animal. God made it that way. The trouble is, He forgot to add that it was anywhere in the world except the home of Mrs Helen Theresa McDonough.'

'I'm not that bad, girl. I wouldn't be cruel to any animal. And you've got no room to talk, you haven't even got a ruddy mouse!'

'I did buy a trap, Nellie, and a piece of cheese. But the cheeky mouse had the nerve to leave a note saying he didn't like red cheese and would be trying elsewhere.'

Nellie's chuckle was hearty. 'Thank God yer've got yer sense of humour back, girl. I was beginning to worry about yer. And seeing as ye're beginning to come to life again, can we please get on with the business in hand?'

'Yes. I believe we should plan our next move, and when we should put it into action.'

'No time like the present,' Nellie said, eager for a bit of excitement. 'He won't be around there today, so we'd be safe.'

'It's Wednesday, sunshine, so there won't be many women out 'cos it's half-day closing.'

Looking at the clock on the mantelpiece, Nellie said, 'If we put a move on, girl, we could be there before half eleven. A lot of women like to do their housework before they go to the shops, to get it over with. There's bound to be some around.'

'Okay, now we've decided on a plan of action, let's start. I'll put these few dishes in the sink and wash them when we get back. If I do them now, it's wasting precious time. Put yer chair away, sunshine, and let's set off with determination.'

The two friends stood on the corner of the street. The main road it ran off was always busy, for there were shops selling anything and everything, and all at reasonable prices. It was an area of two-up-two-downs, where working class people struggled to make ends meet. But there wasn't a house in the street that didn't have a snow-white step and polished door knocker.

'There's a woman coming out of one of the houses halfway up, Nellie. Shall I approach her, or will you?'

'Let me have a go, girl, and if I don't have any luck, you can try the next one.'

The woman coming towards them was around the same age as themselves, with mousy hair and a slim figure. As she came abreast of them, Nellie smiled and stepped forward. 'Have yer got a minute to spare, girl? Don't worry, we're not gypsies trying to flog pegs.'

'Oh, I don't know.' The woman smiled. 'Yer don't look like a gypsy, and I can't see any pegs, but these days yer can't tell who's who.'

'I'll vouch for her,' Molly said. 'She's my best mate, and she's quite harmless.'

'In that case I can spare a few minutes of me time. What are yer after, queen?'

This is a woman after me own heart, Nellie told herself, and decided not to mess around but get straight to the point. 'Did some bloke put a leaflet through yer door yesterday?'

'Yeah. Why, did you get one?'

Nellie shook her head. 'No. We don't live round here, yer see. But we happened to be in the street yesterday visiting a friend when we saw the man handing them out, or putting them through letter boxes. We're curious about what was on the leaflet.'

The woman pursed her lips. 'I can't remember it word for word, queen, and as I was out I didn't see the bloke. But he's asking if anyone has any pictures, ornaments or glassware that they want to sell. He's coming back next Tuesday, and from what the neighbours have told me, he'll give cash in hand for anything he buys.'

Molly asked, 'Are yer thinking of selling him something?'

The woman laughed. 'My feller took one look at it and told me to put it in the bin. He said if the bloke had a good business, with a shop, then he wouldn't need to be knocking on doors. I didn't throw the leaflet away, though, I stuck it in one of the sideboard drawers.' She raised her brows. 'Why are yer so interested? I've got a feeling there's more to it than you wanting a piece of paper with writing on.'

'There is.' Molly had made up her mind she wasn't going to tell any more lies. When she was a child, she'd had it drummed into her that you always got paid back for telling untruths. 'Look, yer don't know us from Adam, but I can assure you we are just two very ordinary, but honest, housewives, who started out to help a friend of ours. She's a widow, and we're very fond of her, and we're afraid she's being taken for a ride by a man who looks, dresses and talks like a proper gentleman.'

'Ay, this is getting very interesting,' said the woman. 'Would yer stay here for about ten minutes while I run to the butcher's? Yer can come home with me then, and yer can tell me all what's going on over a cup of tea.'

'Ooh, we don't want to be a nuisance, sunshine. Yer've probably got other things to do.'

Nellie wasn't having that. She had no intention of letting this woman escape. They were lucky they hadn't stopped one who would tell them to get lost. 'I think yer'd find it very interesting, girl. And yer may be able to help us.'

The woman pointed to the pavement. 'Stay right there, and don't move until I come back.' With that, she took to her heels and made haste, darting between the other shoppers.

'Ay, we hopped in lucky there, girl.' Nellie was looking well pleased with herself. 'She seems very nice.'

Molly nodded. 'I think we should tell her the whole story, sunshine. It wouldn't be fair to ask her to help if we don't tell her the truth. So we'll tell her everything except Claire's name and where she works.' Then she had second thoughts. 'I don't think we should give our full names and addresses, either. Not until we know the woman better.'

'Yeah, yer've got a point there, Molly. My feller wouldn't be very happy if Mr Collins came knocking on our door wanting a fight. Especially if he was in the middle of his dinner.'

'Talking of husbands, hers seems to have his head screwed on, telling her to throw the leaflet away. He must have thought there was something fishy.'

'If we go about it the right way, girl, and get her on our side, she could help us nab Mr Graham bleeding Collins.'

'It would be wonderful if ye're right, sunshine, but let's not rush into anything. Best to test the waters first.'

'Yeah, okay, girl. What is it I'm going to be the soul of?'

'Discretion, sunshine.'

'That's it. One of these days I'll give yer a fright and remember it.'

The woman came running up to them. 'That wasn't long, was it? There weren't many in the shop, and I only wanted half a pound of liver. I've got the onions and potatoes in.' She grinned. 'My name's Sally. What's yours?'

Nellie banged her chest like Tarzan. 'Me Nellie, her Molly.'

'Follow me to the jungle, then, ladies, and I'll make yer a

nice pot of tea. And what yer have to tell me had better be worth it.'

'Oh, it is, girl,' Nellie said, with a hop, skip and a jump to keep up. 'Anyway, if yer don't think so, I can always make something up. My mate will tell yer, I'm very good at making stories up.'

Sally put the key in her door. 'Welcome to my humble abode, ladies. And don't bother wiping yer feet, yer'd be better off wiping them on yer way out.'

Nellie was laughing so much she fell up the two steps.

Chapter Twenty-Two

'Yer've got yer house nice, Sally,' Molly said as she gazed with approval round the well-kept room. 'As me ma would say, it's like a little palace.'

'I do me best.' Sally pulled two chairs out from the table and waved a hand, inviting them to take a seat. 'It's not perfect, but at least it's all mine. I'm not up to me eyes in debt like some people.'

'Same as us, girl,' Nellie told her. 'Me and Molly don't have anything on the never-never, either. My feller wouldn't hear of it. He says if we want anything, then we save up until we can afford it.'

Molly spoke up. 'George is right, too, 'cos once yer get yerself deep into debt, yer never get out of it.'

Sally had her back to them, rooting through one of the drawers in her sideboard. Then she gave a cry of success and held a white leaflet aloft. 'Found it! I knew I hadn't thrown it out.' She laid it on the table. 'Yer can be reading this while I make the pot of tea I promised.'

Nellie moved up closer to Molly, who had the leaflet in her hand. 'We'll read it together, eh, girl? Then if there's any big words on it, yer can tell me what they mean.'

Molly's eyes flew across the lines. 'It's what we expected, sunshine, almost word for word. In short, it's saying he'll pay good prices for pictures, ornaments and glassware, if they're in good condition.'

Sally had put a light under the kettle, and now she popped her head round the door. 'Do you two know the bloke?'

'Only by sight,' Molly told her. 'We've never spoken to him.'

'Then why are yer so interested in him? Spill the beans, or yer don't get a cup of tea. And I warn yer, I can be vicious when crossed.'

Molly grinned. 'You try that and I'll set me mate on to yer. And I warn you, Nellie doesn't fight with her hands, she uses her tummy as a battering ram.'

'How long have you two been mates?' Sally asked, then answered herself, 'Years, I bet.'

'Roughly twenty-five,' Molly told her. 'We both moved into the street after we were married, three doors away from each other. We were strangers then, of course, not pally like we are now.' She turned to look at Nellie's chubby face, which was creased in a smile. 'By my reckoning, we've been good mates for at least twenty-two years.'

When Nellie nodded, her bosom, tummy and chins did the same thing. And a wide-eyed Sally saw her table rising from the floor. 'She's right, girl, and we've never had a falling-out in all that time.'

'In twenty-two years yer've never had a row?'

'Oh, we've had rows.' Molly laughed. 'High ding-dong, calling each other for everything under the sun. Then as suddenly as it starts, it stops, and we make a pot of tea as though nothing has happened. And when we laugh about it afterwards, we can never remember what it was about.'

Nellie was bursting with pride when she said, 'My son Steve is married to Molly's daughter Jill, and they've given us a granddaughter. And her other daughter, Doreen, married a lovely bloke called Phil, and they've given us a grandson.' She couldn't get the words out fast enough, expecting Molly to interrupt at any time. 'And Molly's son, Tommy, he married an Irish girl called Rosie, but they haven't given us anything yet.'

'Nellie, sunshine, will yer stop for breath?' Molly was smiling when she shook her head. 'Yer had me breathing for yer.'

'I know, girl, but I still haven't told Sally that we're related.'

'But we're not related, sunshine, I keep telling yer that! We're only related by marriage, that's all. We're both grandma to little Molly, but you are only an adopted grandma to Bobby.'

Nellie's eyes disappeared as she sought a solution. Eventually she peeped at Molly. 'Are your Jill and Doreen sisters, or not?'

'Of course they're sisters, yer silly nit. Yer should know the answer to that after all these years.'

'So they are related? Is that right, girl?'

'Well, sisters usually are related, sunshine.' Molly was gripping her hands to stop herself from becoming impatient. 'Same as your Steve and Paul are related.'

Sally was watching this from the kitchen door. The kettle had started to boil, but she'd turned the gas low so she wouldn't miss anything. These two were like watching a short comedy at the pictures. It was no wonder they'd never fallen out in twenty-two years: they hadn't had time to.

Nellie was nodding slowly, with a smile on her face. 'Ah, well, I've got yer there, girl. Yer see, if Jill and Doreen are related, and our Steve is related because he married Jill, then there's no doubt but that his mother is related as well.' She sat back in the chair as much as to say, get out of that if you can.

Molly had no intention of getting in or out, or they'd be here all day. 'Okay, sunshine, let's agree to disagree, eh?'

It took a few seconds for Nellie to unravel that in her head. And from what she could make out, Molly had given in and admitted Nellie was in the right. 'Yeah, okay, girl. Yer know I'm not one to gloat when someone admits they were wrong.'

'Thanks, sunshine. It's very good of yer to be so magnanimous, and I do appreciate it.' Over Nellie's head, Molly's eyes told a baffled Sally that there was nothing to worry about, because most days were like this. 'Now we've sorted that out, perhaps Sally can get on making the tea.'

'Hold yer horses, girl, don't be so bleeding quick off the mark. Nothing is sorted out until I know what yer've just called me?'

Molly pretended to think. 'I can't remember now. Oh, yes I can, of course, I called yer sunshine, like I always do.'

Nellie's chins were quick off the mark: they started to shake before her head did. 'I'm not falling for that, girl. I'm not deaf or stupid. Yer said I was maggotus, and that's not a very nice thing to say about yer mate. In fact, if yer weren't me mate, yer'd be flat out on the floor by now, pleading for mercy.'

'If that's the way yer feel about it, Nellie, then I promise I'll never again say you are generous. That's as long as yer promise never to floor me.'

'Yer must think I was born yesterday, girl, to believe that. With my own ears I never heard yer saying I was generous.'

Sally was tickled pink, and wishing they were her neighbours. That was until Nellie wanted her to be a witness.

'You heard what she called me, Sally, so go on, tell her.'

'Ooh, I heard her, queen, but I couldn't get me mouth round that word. I know what it means, but I couldn't say it. I was never very good at English in school, but I do know it means good, or generous.'

Nellie's expression changed to one of sweetness and light. 'I was only pulling yer leg, girl. I knew what it meant all along. I mean, no one could say I wasn't generous, now could they? If

I saw someone in the street what was hungry, I'd share me dinner with them.'

Molly raised her brows. 'What about yer last custard slice? Would yer give that to someone who was starving?'

That needed some serious thought. And the solution came to Nellie like a flash of lightning. 'Well, perhaps not, girl, but I'd give them the money to go and buy themselves one.'

When Molly heard Sally's hearty chortle, she looked across at her. 'We could still be here when yer family come in from work, sunshine, so take my advice and make that pot of tea. We can be drinking it while we tell yer how we came to be standing on the corner of your street. If yer can help, we'll be very grateful. If yer can't, then nothing has been lost. We'll get out of the way and let yer get on with what yer would have been doing if we hadn't come on the scene and turned yer routine upside down.'

'I'll make the tea, queen, but don't worry about being in the way. I've had a good laugh, and if I can help yer, then I will. If not, yer've still been like a breath of fresh air. I'm not surprised yer haven't fallen out in twenty-odd years. Yer haven't had time.'

Nellie shook with laughter, and so did the table. 'Ay, that was good, girl. I'll have to tell George that in bed tonight.'

Molly's hand across her mouth prevented Nellie from saying any more. 'Make the tea, Sally, before Nellie gets to her bedroom. If she beats yer to it, we will definitely be here when yer family get in from work.' She began to chuckle. 'Did I hear yer say yer husband had a good sense of humour?'

'I didn't say, it, queen, but yeah, he's got a great sense of humour. He can always see the funny side of life.'

'So he'll have a good laugh when yer tell him yer went out for half a pound of liver and picked us up on the way. It's enough to put the poor man off liver for the rest of his life.'

Nellie had been looking from one to the other, and now she said, 'Ah, ay, girl, we won't be here when her husband comes home, so don't be frightening the woman. We've got to be home to see to the dinners for our family, don't forget.'

'I'm definitely going to make the tea now, ladies, and it'll be on the table in five minutes. D'yer think yer can keep mum for that length of time?'

Looking at Nellie, Molly pursed her lips. She'd never known her mate to be silent for five whole minutes. 'Ooh, that's asking something, sunshine. Could yer make it four minutes and I'll do me best?'

'Has this good friend of yours known the bloke for long?' Sally asked as they sat round the table with a cup of tea and a plate of arrowroot biscuits in front of them. 'I mean, is she courting him?'

Molly shook her head. 'She's only known him a few weeks. She's a beautiful-looking woman, and really nice. Her husband died about five years ago, leaving her to bring up two children on a meagre widow's pension. So she's had a hard time. Her eldest, a boy, left school at Christmas and got a job, but as an apprentice he only gets paid in buttons. So she managed to get herself taken on in a shop, and with the two lots of money coming in life is a little easier for her. She doesn't work full time, though, 'cos she likes to be home for her daughter coming in from school. She's a good mother, and a really smashing person. Yer can't help but like her.'

Molly took a sip of her tea before carrying on. 'This man comes in the shop where she works: that's how she met him. He began by being friendly, then each time he came in he would stay a little longer, chatting to her. He told her he was a bachelor, and lived with his aged mother. Then he asked her out. And because he dresses like a toff, talks like a toff, and acts like a toff, we think she was flattered. She'd been lonely since her husband died, and she agreed to go out with him. That was last week, and he took her to a theatre, with a box of chocolates thrown in for good measure. And she's going out with him again this week. Now that would be fine, and me and Nellie would be really made up for her because she deserves some happiness in her life. And she spoke so highly of him, we were nosy, and wanted to see this paragon of virtue for ourselves. We didn't tell her, of course, which seems underhanded, but we were curious because he sounded too good to be true. Too sweet to be wholesome, as Nellie's ma would have said. So we went and stood by the shop where she works, until he came. Not that we stood there on the off chance; she'd told us he came in the same time each Monday and Tuesday. Anyway, along he comes, walking with a swagger, as though he owned the ruddy street, and me and Nellie took an instant dislike to him. He appeared too cocky for our liking. Oh, he was well dressed and looked quite the man about town, but we both agreed that he's not what he seems. In other words, we don't think he's genuine, and we don't want to see our friend hurt.'

Nellie had been quiet long enough. 'Molly's right, girl, he's a real smarmy bugger. And we've found out he's a bleeding liar. He hasn't got a mother, he lives alone, and he's got another woman on the go as well. At least he's got one we know of, but he could have half a dozen or more. I wouldn't put it past him.'

'How d'yer know all this?' Sally asked. 'Did someone tell yer?'

Before Molly could stop her, Nellie carried on. 'We followed him, girl. That's how we found out.' She looked well pleased with herself. 'Yes, me and Molly followed him and caught him red-handed, kissing a woman outside her house. And we heard her trying to coax him in, and him saying he'd be back later.'

'But how d'yer know he hasn't got an elderly mother?' Sally was intrigued. 'Yer didn't stop him and ask him, did yer?'

Molly cut in before Nellie's imagination ran riot. 'We found out where he lived, sunshine, and spoke to one of the neighbours. We told a few white lies, but from what she told us he definitely lives alone.'

'Are yer going to tell your friend what you've found out? Better put her wise before she gets in too deep.'

'We will when we can prove we're right about him. We think he's a scoundrel, but we can't prove it yet. That's where the leaflets come into it. Yer see, we followed him on Tuesday, and saw him knocking on doors and giving the leaflets out. I was near the entry at the top of the street, and I heard everything he said to the woman who lives in the first house.'

Sally nodded. 'That's Mrs Seddon. I was talking to her at the shops yesterday. She said she's rooting a few things out, 'cos she could do with the money.'

'We think he's a con man, and on the make. He'll probably give her a fraction of what the things are worth. I'd tell the woman if I knew her, 'cos I hate to see anyone taken for a ride.'

'But yer don't really know that, do yer, Molly?'

'Not for sure, Sally – that's why me and Nellie are looking for proof. And although we started off to find out about him on account of our friend getting involved with him, we'd like to stop him from hurting other people too. I'd bet a pound to a pinch of snuff that he's up to no good. If he had a thriving business in the city centre, why would he be going round knocking on doors? And another thing I've noticed: this leaflet doesn't have his name on, or any address. So if anyone discovered they'd been swindled, there'd be no way of finding him.' Molly sat back and sighed. 'He's a rogue, Sally. That's how he can afford his fine clothes, and is able to take women to the theatre and buy them boxes of chocolates. He's a charmer, a sweet talker, who preys on people. He'll have a smile on his face while he's robbing yer.'

Sally picked the leaflet off the table. 'I never noticed there was no name and address. And I don't suppose anyone else has noticed, either! He's a crafty beggar.' She was thoughtful for a while, for the omission of name and address had added weight to the story she'd been told. Besides, she liked the two women. They weren't stupid, especially Molly, and they wouldn't be wasting their time if they didn't think they were right. 'If I can help in any way, queen, then count me in. I'll give it a bash.'

There was a crafty look on Nellie's face. 'It's no good waiting until he's been and the people have been taken in by him. That's like closing the stable door after the horse has bolted. It'll be far too late; he'll have scarpered . . . done a vanishing act. But besides all that, if the people don't know the value of what they're selling to him, how the heck will they know he's pulled a fast one on them?'

'If yer have any bright ideas, sunshine,' Molly said, 'and I'm sure yer have, then now is the time to share them with us.'

'Well, the best way would be to get a couple of things valued before he comes.' Nellie turned to Sally. 'How well d'yer know the woman what lives in the first house?'

'I'm friendly with everyone in the street, queen, 'cos we've all lived here donkey's years. Why do you ask?'

'Is she an easy-going woman, like yerself? I mean, would she listen to what we've got to say without thinking we were crazy? Or would she tell us to sod off?'

'Oh, she's a friendly woman, is Gertie. She's like yerself – enjoys a good laugh.'

Molly butted in. 'Before yer go any further, don't yer think it would be far better if she was just told that we'd heard he was a trickster? There's no need to tell anyone about our friend, or how we came to follow him. It would only make things more complicated and drawn out.'

Sally nodded. 'I agree it would be much simpler and wouldn't take so long. But what I'd like to know is, how would we go about getting an item valued before he comes next Tuesday?'

'That wouldn't be hard, girl,' Nellie said. 'I know someone who would help us.'

Molly's raised brows showed her surprise. 'Who do you know? We're together everywhere we go, and I certainly don't know anyone who could do it.'

'Yes, yer do, girl, it's just that yer've forgotten yer know him.'

'That remark is as clear as mud, sunshine, so spell it out for us. Who do we know who is clever enough to value a picture?'

'If yer cast yer mind back twenty years, girl, yer'll remember we had to go to a pawn shop on several occasions. It was either that or starve to death. Don't yer remember the shop on Scotland Road with the three brass balls hanging outside? Or don't yer want to remember?'

Molly's mouth gaped. 'I do remember, and I'm not afraid to say so 'cos I'm not a snob. But, Nellie, that was years and years ago! The bloke that we knew won't still be there. He'll have retired ages ago.'

'The shop is still there, girl. We pass it when we go to the market, or into town. It wouldn't matter whether we know the man behind the counter or not, we can always ask whoever's in charge if they'll do us a favour.'

'But a pawn shop wouldn't be able to value anything,' Sally said. 'They don't sell things, they only lend yer money on anything yer pawn, and they charge interest on the money they give yer until yer redeem the item.'

'I know all that, girl, 'cos me and Molly were glad of the pawn shop many a time. And I know they don't lend a fraction of the true value of the item. They wouldn't be in business long if they did. But I bet they know exactly what the real worth is, because if it isn't redeemed by a certain date they have to sell it. And they're not in the business of losing money.'

'I don't know how yer think that would help,' Molly said. 'There'd be no point in asking one of the women to pawn something, they still wouldn't find out its true worth.'

'Gertie wouldn't pawn anything,' Sally said, nodding her head knowingly. 'She's always saying, "Out of debt, out of danger." And like Molly, I can't see how a pawn shop would help.'

'The pawn shop wouldn't, soft girl.' Nellie was getting flustered because the other two weren't keeping up with her. 'It's the man behind the ruddy counter what could help. They know exactly how much every item under the sun is worth, and I'll put money on them being right any day.'

'Oh, yeah.' Molly huffed. 'D'yer think anyone could walk in and ask them to value something for them without being charged?'

'I would,' the little woman said, 'and I bet I'd get them to do it, as well.'

'Yer wouldn't, sunshine, 'cos we all know that pawn shops are after every ha'penny they can lay their hands on. They won't do yer any favours.'

Nellie shook her head and clicked her tongue. 'After all the tricks I've pulled over the years, and the scrapes I've got us out of, yer haven't got any faith in me. Shame on yer, Molly Bennett, when ye're supposed to be me mate.'

'This is a bit different to haggling with a stallholder at the market, sunshine. Pawnbrokers are noted for having no hearts. They don't do favours.'

'I'll show yer whether I can do it or not, even if I have to take one of the pictures off me own ruddy wall. I'll do it if it kills me, for spite.'

Sally grinned. 'I believe yer would, queen, and I bet yer'd get away with it.'

'Well I'm glad someone has faith in me. It's coming to something when yer own mate lets yer down.'

'Oh, I've every confidence in yer, sunshine. I've never doubted for a second that yer could do it. But I do doubt whether the man in the pawn shop will be so bountiful as to do it for yer as a favour. Even yer voluptuous body what every man craves after wouldn't be enough to melt the heart of a pawnbroker.'

But Nellie had an ace up her sleeve, which she now produced. Lifting the leaflet from the table, she waved it in the faces of the two women. 'This will help me pull it off. With a few little lies thrown in, like. I'll show it to the man behind the counter and tell him there's a bloke putting them through every letterbox in all the surrounding streets, flooding the area with them. Now he won't like that one little bit because it could take all his business away. They rely on local people to make a living. And to make him more interested, and worried, I'll say I know lots of the local women are searching their houses for stuff to sell to the bloke. Attics and cellars are being cleared out.'

Molly and Sally were silent as their minds digested what they'd heard. But Nellie wanted to get it all out while the plan was still fresh in her mind. 'I'll say I wasn't being taken in by this bloke, not like the other women. He came across to me as not being genuine, and I think he's out to fiddle people.'

There still wasn't a sound came from the two women listening intently, so Nellie took a deep breath and carried on. 'He'll be more than interested by then, knowing he could well lose a lot of regular customers. And that's when I'll tell him how I think the bloke could be stopped from robbing people if he will help me. I'll let him think I'm more interested in helping the poor than in putting a halt to Graham Collins's gallop.'

'D'yer know,' Sally said, looking at Molly, 'I think she might get away with it.'

However, Molly was too busy looking at her mate to answer right away. 'Have you been going to night school to brush up on your English grammar, sunshine? Have yer been keeping a secret from me? For you've been talking non stop for the last fifteen minutes, and there wasn't a word out of place, and no swearing. Full marks to yer, Nellie, yer can go to the top of the class.'

'Thanks, girl.' Nellie's face creased with happiness at the praise, and her bust also showed its pleasure by standing to attention. 'I can be serious when I put me mind to it.'

'So it seems, sunshine, but don't be serious too often or I'd miss the laughs we have.'

'Oh, yer won't be short of laughs, girl, not when we put paid to the shenanigans of the lying Mr Collins. This time next week, please God, he won't know what's hit him.'

'Well, it's fingers crossed, sunshine, while we wait to see what happens.'

'I think Nellie could pull it off, Molly,' Sally said. 'She's talked me into it, so I'm sure she'll talk the pawnbroker round.'

'Oh, she'll talk him round all right.' Molly laughed. 'He'd give in to her just to shut her up. But to do that, she needs something to take in to have valued. I don't have anything for her to take; most of my stuff would only bring coppers. Besides, having one thing valued wouldn't really help. It would take a few items to prove whether Mr Collins is genuine or not.'

'I've got an idea,' Sally told them, 'but if yer don't like the sound of it, just say so. I don't get upset easily.'

'Spit it out, girl, every little helps.'

'Well, how about if I get three women involved? All I need to say is I've heard the bloke isn't genuine, and will they help us find out. I know three women who'd jump at the chance, just for the excitement. And they all live in the right houses for what we want. There's Mrs Seddon in the first house, her next-door neighbour, and the woman next door but one. All sensible women around the same age as ourselves.'

Nellie's legs were swinging like mad under the chair. This was going to be a good case for the McDonough and Bennett Private Detective Agency. And they'd win it too, if she had anything to do with it. 'That would be marvellous, Sally! Yer've come up with a great idea.'

'Would it be possible for the two of yer to come down one day and meet the three women?' Sally raised her brows questioningly. 'It's too late to do it now – there wouldn't be enough time to go over it properly. And I don't know whether they'd be at home now. How about tomorrow? Have yer got an hour to spare?'

Molly glanced at Nellie. 'We've got nothing important on, have we, sunshine?'

'Nothing that I can think of, girl.' Nellie gave one of her creased-up-face smiles. 'I didn't notice anything in me diary when I looked this morning. Nothing so important that my secretary can't cancel.'

'Could we make it about eleven o'clock, Sally? That's the best time for me and Nellie. It would give us time to get our shopping in.'

Sally nodded. 'I'll do my best to have the three of them here.' She had an idea. 'Shall I ask if they'll bring with them any one article they've earmarked to sell to this bloke?'

Molly didn't want to steal Nellie's limelight, seeing as it was her idea. 'That's up to me mate. She's the one who thought it up, and the only one with the guts to carry it out.'

'Ooh, I can't wait,' Sally said. 'Yer've brought a bit of excitement into me life. One day is just like any other day, usually, with not very much happening. Luck was on my side when it sent me to the shops at the time you two were standing on the corner. Think what I would have missed if I'd gone out five minutes earlier or later. Today would have been as dull as any other day.'

'Ah, it's nice of yer to say that, Sally. Don't yer think so, girl?'

Molly chuckled. 'I just hope she doesn't live to regret her stroke of luck.' She winked across the table at Sally. 'There's never a dull moment with Nellie. She's always up to something, and that something is mischief. Under different circumstances, I would have some pity for the man in the pawnshop when Nellie walks through his door. But seeing her mission is of interest to us all, instead of feeling sorry for him, I'll wish them both luck. May they get on like a house on fire.' She pushed her chair back and got to her feet. 'Come on, sunshine, we've got work to do, and a dinner to get ready for the family. But thanks for having us, Sally. It was good of yer to take two strangers in like yer did.'

'It's me who should be thanking you! I've really enjoyed being in yer company, and yer've brightened me day. I'll look forward to seeing yer both tomorrow, eleven o'clock.' Sally followed them to the door and stood on the step to wave them off. 'Take care now and, Nellie, make sure no men get their hands on that voluptuous body of yours.'

Nellie was grinning when she turned round. 'Ay, Sally, I didn't have time to tell yer about my George, and what he gets up to at night.'

Molly took her by the scruff of the neck and started to push her up the street. 'One thing at a time, sunshine. Just stick to the job in hand and forget yer've got a bedroom in your house.'

Sally was on the top step shaking with laughter as she watched Nellie trying to turn her head to say, 'Ah, ay, Molly, ye're choking me! And anyway, yer wouldn't be saying that if yer had as much fun in your bedroom as me and George have in ours.'

Chapter Twenty-Three

There was a warm smile of welcome on Sally's face when she opened the door to Molly and Nellie the next day. 'Come on in, we've all been waiting patiently for yer.' And with a grand backward sweep of her hand, she invited them in.

When the friends entered the living room, it was to see three of Sally's neighbours seated on the wooden dining chairs at the table. And there was a smile on each face as they were introduced. 'This is Gertie from number two, Harriet from number four and Alice from number six.' Sally had been looking forward to this gathering for she'd never entertained so many of her neighbours before. Not at eleven o'clock in the morning, anyway. There'd been parties in the house for birthdays and Christmas, but they were celebrations, and noisy affairs with singing and dancing. Plus drinks to put the guests in the party mood.

Then Sally introduced her two new friends. 'This is Molly, and her best mate, Nellie.' After hands were shaken and greetings exchanged, she waved a hand towards the couch. 'Make yerselves comfortable, ladies, while I make a pot of tea.'

Nellie looked at the couch in dismay, and shook her head. 'If I get on that thing, girl, I'll never get off it again. Yer'd have to send to the docks for the loan of a bleeding crane to lift me off. Death traps, they are.'

Her words, and screwed-up face, brought laughter, and an

immediate offer from Gertie. 'We'll help yer up, girl, there's enough of us.'

Nellie grinned. 'In case yer hadn't noticed, Gertie, there's more of me than there is of the lot of yer put together. When God gave me this voluptuous figure what men crave for, he didn't take into consideration that me legs were too short to sit on a couch. It wasn't often he slipped up, but when I pointed it out to him it was too late. Me body had set by then.'

At first Sally's three neighbours didn't know whether they should laugh, in case the little woman was conscious of her figure, and they didn't want to upset her. But when Molly's hearty chuckle filled the room, they felt free to let their hilarity out. 'Nellie,' Harriet said, 'we'll have no trouble lifting yer off the couch.'

'Oh, I know yer won't, girl, because I'm not sitting on the ruddy thing. There's a spare chair at the table, I'll sit on that.'

Molly clicked her tongue. 'I think that chair is meant for Sally, sunshine, so don't be so flaming cheeky. 'Ye're not in yer own house now, yer know, so behave yerself.'

Nellie's face was contorted as she tried to explain. 'I will behave meself, girl, but not on that bleeding couch!'

'I'll tell yer what,' Sally said. 'We'll all sit at the table. There's a chair in the kitchen we can use, and the one under the window. It'll be a crush, but yer'll have to put up with it. Yer can't have everything.'

Nellie made a dash for the vacant chair at the table. Then, having been victorious, she bestowed her brightest smile on the occupants of the other chairs. 'This is nice, isn't it, girls? Now we can all see what we're doing.'

'Don't make yerself too comfortable, sunshine, 'cos there's another two chairs to go in there. So move up a bit and give someone else a chance.'

'Ah, don't be so miserable, girl, me backside doesn't want

to move. It's making friends with the seat of the chair, and yer wouldn't want to spoil a budding friendship, would yer?'

'There's the kettle whistling,' Sally said, turning towards the kitchen. 'Will yer sort the chairs out, Gertie? Two either side and one each end.'

'I'll have an end one,' Molly told them, 'so stay where yer are. I'll pick up the chair from under the window.'

This arrangement wasn't to Nellie's liking, for she saw it as giving Molly pride of place. She'd be like a teacher at the top of the class, where she could keep an eye on everyone. 'I'll sit at the other end then, girl, and Sally can have her chair back.'

'Make up yer mind, sunshine, before we all get settled. I thought your backside was making friends with the chair seat?'

Nellie pulled a face. 'No, girl, it was a short-lived romance. It was going great guns until the chair told me backside to sit still. I mean, like, no self-respecting backside is going to take that from a piece of wood, is it? And the cheeky bugger refused to apologise. So I'm taking me backside to another chair for spite.'

'I wouldn't bother if I were you, sunshine,' Molly said, her head shaking slowly. 'The four chairs belong to one family, and they're bound to stick up for each other. It wouldn't surprise me if yer sat on the other chair and got a splinter in yer backside.'

'Nah, my backside's tough. It wouldn't worry about a little thing like a splinter. And anyway, if the chair was bad enough to do that, I'd give it a real hard time by swinging me legs back and forth. Chairs don't like that.'

Molly nodded. 'Yeah, my chairs have complained to me about yer swinging yer legs. I promised I'd have a word with yer about it.'

Gertie, Harriet and Alice were drinking in every word. Sally had told them that the couple were a good laugh, but they weren't just a laugh, they were hilarious. Nellie's bosom was resting on the table, and her tummy fitted in nicely underneath. That was unless she moved. Then her tummy pushed the table up, and her bosom pressed it down again. This was much better than going to the pictures any day. And it didn't cost anything.

'Sally's coming in with the tea now, sunshine, so sit back and give her room on the table. And don't be swinging yer legs, ye're a big girl now.' Molly stood up to take the tray off Sally. 'My mate has changed her seat again, but as this is your house, yer have a right to tell her to move if you wish.'

'No, I don't care where I sit, queen.' Sally began to pour the tea out. 'Besides, as you are guests, we'll indulge yer.'

Nellie bent her head, her brow creased in concentration. Then, after a few seconds, she waved her hand in the air. 'It's no good, I have to ask or I won't be able to sleep tonight. What did Sally say she'd do to us, girl, because we're guests?'

'She said she'd indulge us, sunshine.'

'I heard what she said, soft girl, but what does it mean?'

'Sally meant we would get special treatment because we're guests.'

Molly's words had Nellie sitting up straight in the chair, shoulders back and bosom to attention. Proud as a peacock, she was. 'Ah, that's real nice of yer, Sally, but me and Molly won't take vantage of yer.'

Molly shook her head. 'Advantage, sunshine! We won't take advantage.'

'Yeah, that's what I said, girl.'

Molly closed her eyes. 'Don't answer that, Molly,' she said aloud. 'Life will be much easier if yer pretend yer never heard.'

'Ooh, it's a bad sign that, girl,' Nellie said, her lips pursed. 'Talking to yerself is the first sign ye're going doolally. But don't let it worry yer, girl, 'cos I'll always be here to look after yer. I'll take yer to the shops and make sure no one diddles yer.

And I'll make sure yer get plenty of fresh air every day, even though yer won't know where yer are, or how good I'm being to yer.'

'Nellie, if I ever reach that state, God forbid, then there's something yer should know. That you're the cause of it.'

Sally had placed a cup and saucer in front of each of the ladies, and now showed that she too had a sense of humour. 'Before you two come to blows, can I say that this is me best tea set, real bone china. And it'll be woe betide anyone who breaks anything. It only sees daylight on high days and holidays, so yer should all be honoured.'

'I was going to say I'd never seen it before,' Harriet said. 'Not that I object to the mugs yer normally use, Sally, 'cos that's all I use at home. I don't have any bone china ones, sad to say.'

Alice shrugged her shoulders. 'Me neither! At one time, if I had a few coppers to spare, I'd take the tram down to T.J.'s and buy meself a china cup and saucer. And over the weeks I managed to get a set of three. I thought I was Lady Muck, but soon found it didn't pay to show off. Instead of keeping them for best, I started using them every day, and within a week all the cups and one saucer were broken. My feller's got hands as big as shovels and I must have been crazy giving him a small china cup to drink out of. Anyway, it taught me a lesson I'll never forget. Never show off, 'cos it's not worth it.'

Sally took the empty tray out to the kitchen, and came back to sit at the table, next to Molly. 'Time marches on, so shall we get down to business?'

Nellie was very eager. 'Good idea, girl. Time and tide wait for no man.'

'Well, I've explained to me mates here what yer said about the bloke with the leaflets, and how yer think he's not to be trusted. And they're willing to go along with anything yer have in mind.'

'I'd got some stuff ready for him,' Gertie said, ''cos I have to say a few bob would come in handy. But I wasn't keen on the man. There was something about him I couldn't take to. He spoke proper posh and was dressed like a toff, but I got the feeling he was too good to be true. That's why I said if I sold him anything, it had to be cash in hand.'

'Me and Alice didn't see him. We were at the shops when he came, and he'd put a leaflet through our doors,' Harriet said. 'So we haven't a clue what he's like to look at, or talk to. But when Sally told us she'd met you, and what yer'd said, we took a good look at the leaflet. And as she said, it seems fishy that he hasn't put his name or address on it.'

Molly leaned forward. 'Look, we don't want to stop yer from doing something yer want to do. He'll buy whatever yer want to sell, but will he give yer what the item is really worth? We think he's a crook, and he won't be doing yer any favours. Yes, he speaks frightfully far back and dresses in only the best, but why would a wealthy man go round delivering leaflets? It doesn't make sense. But as I've said, you must do what yer want to do.'

'Have yer ever met him?' Alice asked.

'No, we haven't met him. We've seen him several times, and we've heard him speak. We know exactly the patter he uses when he's trying to talk someone into telling him unwanted pictures, glassware or ornaments. And we are quite sure that his clothes and lifestyle are paid for by the likes of yourselves.'

'Sally said you could get them valued before he comes on Tuesday,' Harriet said. 'How would yer go about that?'

Molly nodded her head to where Nellie sat. 'My mate knows a way she might be able to do it. But before she tells yer, can I say that while she acts daft, she is far from it. We both act daft, come to that, and have done for twenty years, but we know a crook when we see one. And now Nellie will tell yer the rest while I drink me tea before it goes cold.'

Once again Nellie sat up straight and squared her shoulders. Then she closed her eyes and breathed in deeply. This was a drama queen, preparing herself for the big moment. There wasn't a sound. It was like sitting in the theatre waiting for the curtain to roll back and the play to begin.

When Nellie let out her breath, five people joined her and it sounded like a light breeze rustling the leaves on a tree. Then Nellie's voice brought them down to earth. 'I bet there isn't a woman in this room who hasn't, at some time in her life, been forced to pawn something to put food on yer table. Me and Molly had to do it when the kids were little, and we're not ashamed to say so.' She saw heads nodding knowingly, and went on. 'Well, I believe the man behind the counter, in any pawn shop, would know the value of any item at first sight. They have to otherwise they'd be giving too much out. They couldn't afford to do that, 'cos if they gave too much, the person would never be able to redeem what she'd pawned, and they'd lose all the interest. They rely on people like us, and they wouldn't be too happy if they knew this bloke was knocking on doors and putting them out of business.'

Gertie nodded. 'Ye're dead right, queen. I go along with every word what yer said, 'cos it stands to sense.'

'It does make sense,' Harriet agreed. 'But I can't see how yer can get them valued without having to pay. Pawnbrokers don't do nothing for nothing.'

'They're not all skinflints,' Molly said. 'The one me and Nellie used to go to didn't have a heart of stone. He wouldn't do yer any favours, but he was fair. And he was friendly – always had a smile and a cheery word for us.'

Sally spoke for the first time. 'Well he would, wouldn't he? For his smile and cheery word, he was taking money off yer. As Harriet said, pawnbrokers don't do nothing for nothing.'

'They might if they thought their livelihood was in danger,' Molly told them. 'If leaflets are put through every door in this neighbourhood, then it could take a lot of business away from them. Anyway, we can only try! If it doesn't come off, then that's just too bad. But before parting with anything in my home, I'd want to know I wasn't being taken for a ride.'

All eyes turned to Nellie. 'Would yer really have the nerve to go in a shop and ask the man behind the counter to value, say, a picture, for nothing?' This was from Gertie. 'Yer've got some guts if yer do.'

'Of course I will! The worst that can happen is being chased out of the shop. And that wouldn't worry me.'

'Which pawn shop would yer try?' Alice asked. 'One near where you live?'

Nellie shook her head. 'The nearest one to here is in Scotland Road, and it's the one me and Molly used to go to. We don't live round here, but we used that shop 'cos no one would know us. The same man won't be there because we're talking about ten to fifteen years ago. But if there's no joy there, I could try the one near Everton Valley. It's not too far to walk to.'

This situation had brought interest into their lives, and Harriet wanted to know the ins and outs. 'How would yer go about it, Nellie? What would yer say to the man behind the counter?'

'Ooh, I don't know, girl. I'll worry about that when I'm facing him. But I'd like all the leaflets yer've got, to prove I'm not having him on.'

'There's four of them on the draining board in the kitchen, queen,' Sally told her, 'with a picture belonging to Gertie, an ornament of Alice's, and a crystal bowl of Harriet's. All the items belonged to their parents, so they are really old. They're in very good condition, and should be worth more than a few bob.'

'To be honest,' Gertie said, 'I don't think I'd sell the picture no matter how much I was offered. It belonged to me mam and she was so proud of it. I'd never be able to live with meself if I sold it for a few bob. Her memory is worth a lot more than that.'

Harriet nodded. 'Me and Alice feel the same. We were talking about it before we came here, and neither of us want to part with something that meant a lot to our parents.'

Molly's smile was understanding. 'I know how yer feel. I'm lucky to still have me ma and da, and I could never bear to part with anything of theirs 'cos I love the bones of them.'

Nellie thought of the picture on the wall in her living room. That had belonged to her ma, and even in the days when they were really skint, she had never once thought of selling it. She had pawned it, but it was never out of the house for more than a week. As soon as George handed his wage packet over, she was down to the shop to redeem it. 'Don't sell those things to anyone, then. Yer'd regret it as soon as yer'd spent the money yer got for it. And yer'd have to live with that for the rest of yer life.'

'It's not like you to be sentimental, sunshine,' Molly said. 'Yer always make out ye're so tough. But I know different, 'cos I remember yer've still got that picture on the wall.'

'All this aside,' Nellie said, 'we can still put a stop to some poor buggers being robbed. So are yer all willing to go along with it? I could take the things to the pawn shop now, and yer'd have them back in half an hour. I'll tell yer what the bloke in the shop values them at, and yer can see what the queer fellow offers when he comes next Tuesday. If he offers yer more than the figure I'll have given yer, then me and Molly are wrong. But I somehow don't think we are.'

It suddenly hit Molly that these people didn't know her and Nellie from Adam, and may worry that once their goods were taken away they might never see them again. It was asking a great deal, expecting them to trust strangers. So she sought to relieve their worries. 'I'll go in the shop with Nellie for a bit of moral support, but there's nothing to stop yer coming with us. Yer could always stand outside and wait for us. And it's a nice day for a walk.'

This brought a very favourable response. 'That's a very good idea. As yer say, it's a nice day for a walk.' This was from Gertie. 'It's better than sitting here wondering what's going on.'

Harriet and Alice nodded. 'We'll all go,' said Alice. 'We could help pick yer up if yer get thrown out.'

Nellie's bosom swelled. 'It would need a very strong man to throw me out, girl, and a very foolish one. He'd be lying flat out on the pavement before he knew what hit him.'

Sally jumped up, having made a decision. 'I'm coming with yer, even though I never had any intention of even opening the door to the man. I'd kick meself if I didn't go along and missed some excitement. I'll leave the table as it is. It won't take long to clear when I get back.'

Nellie spread out her hands. 'I need the picture and other things, girl. It's no good going empty-handed. And they'll have to be well wrapped up so they won't come to any harm.'

'There's some newspapers under the cushion on the couch, Gertie. Will yer get them out for me? I keep them here, handy for when the fire wants lighting in the cold weather.' Sally hurried out to the kitchen. 'I'll put them in me basket when they're wrapped up. Oh, and I'll put the leaflets in with them.'

'Leave the leaflets on the top, girl,' Nellie called to her. 'I want to show them to him first to get him interested.'

When Sally closed her front door, Molly took the basket from her. 'I'll carry this, sunshine.' Not for the world would she say she didn't trust Nellie with it. Her mate never walked in a straight line, and it was possible the basket would end up being banged against a wall. But there was no need for the other woman to know that. 'It's not heavy. I can manage it.'

The ladies paired off, with Molly and Nellie leading. It would normally have been a brisk ten-minute walk to the shop, but with the weather being so warm the ladies took their time. Nellie talked non-stop, and there was much laughter. No one would have thought she was about to ask a pawnbroker something no one else would have dared to. But then Nellie never was afraid of anything, or anybody.

'Right, here we are.' Molly brought them to a halt a few yards from the pawn shop. She noticed it had been recently painted, and the three brass balls hanging above the door were highly polished. 'The shop is looking a lot smarter than it used to, sunshine. Business must be good.'

'Well, let's go and get it over with, girl,' Nellie said, her face bright as she looked forward with anticipation to the challenge ahead. 'We might be fifteen or twenty minutes, ladies, it depends how easy he is to get on with.' She smiled at the four new friends. 'Not to worry, the worst he can do is show us the door.'

'She's got more guts than me,' Gertie said, when the two mates had disappeared into the shop. 'I couldn't do that to save me life.'

Harriet agreed. 'Me neither. Anything for a quiet life, that's me.'

'I wish they lived in our street,' Sally said. 'It wouldn't half liven the place up.'

Alice asked, 'D'yer think she'll get away with it?'

'I'll lay odds that she will.' Sally sounded very definite. 'Nellie's got a lot more on top than she lets on. My money's on her.'

* * *

Nellie walked straight to the counter, leaving Molly to close the door. The man behind the counter was of medium height and heavily built. He had grey hair, and looked to be in his late fifties. 'Can I help you?'

'We haven't come to pawn nothing, we've come to tell you about something that might interest yer. It'll certainly do yer business a lot of harm.' Nellie put one of the leaflets on the counter. 'Did yer know these are being put through every door in every street in the neighbourhood?'

The man looked at her under bushy eyebrows before picking up the leaflet. Then he scanned the white piece of paper. 'Where did you get this?'

Nellie picked the other three leaflets out of the basket and put them in front of him. 'There's thousands of them floating around. The bloke's been going down every street knocking on doors. If he gets an answer he tells the people he'll pay good money for anything they sell to him, and he'll be back on Tuesday. And he's promising cash in hand for anything they have, as long as it's in good condition.'

Again the man peered under his bushy eyebrows. 'Why are yer telling me this? It's got nothing to do with me.'

Nellie pulled a face as she snatched the leaflet out of his hand, and gathered the three off the counter. 'Oh, well, I thought I was doing yer a good turn, but if yer don't mind yer bleeding business going bust, it's no skin off my nose.' She turned her back on him. 'Come on, Molly. Whatever happens is his own lookout.'

'I thought there was something familiar about you both!' The man's voice rose. 'It's Mrs McDonough and Mrs Bennett, isn't it?'

Molly looked surprised. 'It's not Bob, surely?'

The man nodded. 'A much older Bob, as you can see.' He shook his head. 'I knew I'd seen you before, but I'd never have guessed if it wasn't for hearing you being called Molly. Like meself, yer've both changed. Not as much as me, though, I must say.' Now he was shaking his head. 'Nellie Mac and Molly Bennett! Who'd have thought I'd see you again?'

Nellie chuckled. 'We didn't think yer'd recognise us, seeing it's so long ago. And I'm twice the size I was then. Molly hasn't changed so much 'cos she doesn't eat as many cream cakes as me.'

'I wondered why you suddenly stopped coming in, then decided you must have left the area. Did you move house?'

'We never did live round here, Bob,' Molly told him. 'We came here because we were snobs and didn't want our neighbours to know we were pawning things. And because we always got a fair deal off yer.'

Bob pointed to the leaflets in Nellie's hand. 'If you don't live round here, why are you so interested in those?'

'It's a long story, Bob. If yer've got time to listen I could explain why we want to know about the bloke who's flooding the area with the leaflets.' When Bob nodded, Molly said, 'I'll just nip outside and tell our friends we'll be a bit longer than we thought we'd be.'

'I'll go and tell them, girl, while you start telling him what's going on. They won't mind waiting another ten minutes or so.'

Molly started at the beginning and told the surprised, but now interested, pawnbroker everything that had happened. From Claire, to how she and Nellie had been nosy enough to want to see for themselves the man who seemed too good to be true. She described his fine clothes, his posh accent, and how the elderly mother he said he lived with didn't exist. There were other things they'd found out that had given them cause to dislike and distrust the man, and they were certain he was out to rob people.

When Nellie came back into the shop, she nodded to agree with everything Molly was saying. 'He's a right rotter, Bob, and we would love to put a halt to his gallop. There are three women outside, waiting for us. They believed what he said to them, and had gathered things together to sell to him. They're nice, ordinary working-class people like ourselves, and we don't want to see them robbed.'

'And what made you come here?'

'The first reason was to let yer know what was going on, 'cos it would affect your business,' Molly told him. 'He's a fly-by-night, who I think will try to make a killing in this area, then move on elsewhere. As yer can see, he's crafty enough not to put his name and address to anything.' Molly took a deep breath. 'Now I'll let Nellie carry on to tell yer about the favour we'd like yer to do to help us stop this swindler.'

Nellie lifted her bosom on to the counter, folded her arms over it, and grinned into Bob's face. It was a grin he remembered well, and the laughter that usually came with it. 'It's a big favour, Bob, and I know yer'll think we've got a bleeding cheek. But it's the only way we could think of to stop this bloke. In that basket there's three things what belong to the three women waiting outside. Three family heirlooms what have been in the families for donkey's years. We thought if we could get some clever person to value them for us, before this bloke comes round on Tuesday, then we'd know if he was robbing people. And if it turned out he is a crook, then he wouldn't be able to show his face round here again, or anywhere from here to the Pier Head.' Bob's expression didn't change, and Nellie sighed. 'I told yer we had a bleeding cheek, but we're not asking for ourselves. Anyway, we did try, and God loves a trier.'

'Yer want me to put a price on three articles?'

Molly's hopes were raised. 'We don't expect yer to know exactly how much they're worth, just approximate. Like, should they be offered coppers, shillings or pounds. We'd be very grateful, Bob, 'cos I know we're asking a lot.' She glanced at the door at the rear of the shop. 'Is the boss in? Would we be getting yer into trouble?'

'I am the boss now, Molly. I own the shop, and have done for several years. Put the items on the counter and let's have a look.'

When Molly was carefully unwrapping the ornament, picture and crystal bowl, Nellie was leaning on the counter giving Bob the benefit of her smile. 'It's good of yer, Bob, and I could kiss yer for it.'

Bob stepped back, his hands raised and a look of mock horror on his face. 'Oh, not that, Nellie! Anything but that.'

'There's something wrong with yer then, 'cos ye're the only man what hasn't fallen in love with me voluptuous body.'

'Will yer get yer voluptuous body out of the way, Nellie,' Molly said, 'and mind yer don't knock any of these off the counter.'

'Ye're only jealous, that's what yer are.'

'Yes, I know I am, sunshine, but over the years I have resigned meself to the fact that the good Lord couldn't give everyone a voluptuous body. If He did – and He realised this – no man would ever go out to work. The world would come to a standstill.'

Bob couldn't believe his ears. These two hadn't changed a bit. Many's the laugh he had with them. The man who had owned the shop before him hadn't thought the pair a bit funny. But then again, he didn't know what a sense of humour was.

He picked up the picture first. It was a country scene, and the frame was heavy. 'You have to understand that the prices I am going to give are not dead on the nose, but they will be near enough to what they would be offered if they took the goods to a bona fide dealer. This picture is by a good artist, and the frame is original. I'd say it's worth four or five pounds.'

Molly looked at Nellie with eyes wide with surprise. 'Ooh, I didn't expect that, did you, sunshine?'

Nellie shook her head. 'Five pounds, eh? What about the ornament and bowl?'

Bob examined them, then said, 'Not quite as much as the picture. The bowl about three pound, and the ornament two pound ten shillings. If they are offered ten bob less than the amounts I've given to you, then tell the ladies not to sell. Or go elsewhere for a better deal.'

'I don't think they'd part with them no matter what they were offered,' Molly told him. 'They've done a lot of thinking since the bloke came round, and now they feel they'd be selling things their parents were proud of. And to most people, the memory of their parents is more important than money.'

'Can you remember the prices I've given you?' Bob asked. 'Or shall I write them down for you?'

Nellie, who had a lousy memory, jumped at the offer. 'Write them down for us, Bob, if yer don't mind. And when I say it's been smashing seeing yer again, I'm not saying it just 'cos yer've done us a favour. It reminds me of the old days, when we used to haggle with yer. But yer were always fair, I'll say that for yer.'

Molly took the slip of paper Bob handed over. 'Thanks, Bob, I really appreciate what yer've done. And we'll call in next week and let yer know what happens. The three ladies outside are the first ones he'll be calling to, and if he tries to fool them, well, they'll tell him to take a running jump. And within no time the news will be round every street in the neighbourhood. He'll not be able to show his face again.'

'I hope you do call in – it would be nice to see you and find out whether your work has been rewarded. But I'm going to ask a favour of you, now. Please don't tell anyone I valued the items, or I'll be snowed under with requests. Say you were very lucky that a man who deals in antiques was paying me a visit. And you can tell them I remembered you from years ago and talked the man into looking at the items you'd brought in. Will you do that?'

It was Nellie who nodded. 'I'll tell them, Bob. I'm a better liar than Molly.'

Molly picked the basket up off the counter, making sure the goods were well wrapped. 'Telling lies is nothing to be proud of, sunshine. Saint Peter will put that down in his book as a black mark against your name.' She walked towards the door with Nellie following closely on her heels, saying, 'No he won't, girl, 'cos I'll say an extra prayer tonight to make up for it.'

'I hope you ladies don't forget to call next week,' Bob said again as Molly was opening the door. He was feeling a little sad at seeing them go, for he was remembering the way they had always been able to bring a smile to his face. 'I'd like to know how things go.'

Molly turned. 'We won't forget, Bob, that's a promise. Nor will we forget what yer've done for us today. We'll be here next Tuesday, come hell or high water.'

Sally and her neighbours made to rush forward when the friends came out of the shop, but Molly put a finger to her lips. 'Let's walk to the corner of the street. We can't talk here.'

There was a crush as all the ladies moved together, all eager to hear the news, and Molly was fearful of the basket's being knocked. She caught hold of Sally's hand. 'You take this basket, sunshine. I don't want to be responsible for any breakage.'

'How did yer get on, queen?' Sally asked, as the ladies gathered round. 'Did yer talk him into putting a value on them?'

Molly was quick to answer in case Nellie, in her excitement, let the cat out of the bag. 'The pawnbroker didn't, but we were dead lucky on two counts. First, the pawnbroker, Bob, remembered us from all those years back. He only worked there then, but now he owns the shop. And ye're not going to believe our second piece of luck. There just happened to be a business acquaintance of his there, a man who deals in antiques. And with a little persuasion from Bob, he agreed to value the goods for us. We were very lucky to have been at the right place at the right time.'

'What did the man say about the leaflets?' Gertie asked. 'Did he think there's something fishy about them?'

Molly shook her head. 'He wouldn't comment on them, sunshine; it wouldn't be business-like. But he did say if yer were offered ten bob less for yer goods than the prices he's written down, then you shouldn't sell to the man. He's not going to say more than that, Gertie, 'cos he wouldn't want to get involved in what me and Nellie are trying to do.'

'What did he say me picture was worth, queen?' Gertie asked. 'Is it worth a few bob?'

'Look, we can't stand talking here,' Sally said. 'Let's go back to mine.'

'Oh, we can't come back to yours, sunshine, 'cos me and Nellie haven't got our shopping in yet, and I've got a stack of ironing to do.'

'I've finished my housework,' Nellie said. She loved being in company and would happily spend the day nattering. And she didn't give a toss if there were jobs in her house that needed doing. 'We can get what shopping we want from the corner shop.'

'Not on your life, Nellie McDonough! When my Jack gets in from work he expects a dinner put in front of him, not two ounces of corned beef. And a dinner is what he deserves and what he'll get.' She saw the crestfallen faces of Sally and her neighbours. 'I'm sorry, but I have to be making tracks home. But here's the list of what the items were valued at.' She handed the list to Gertie. 'I think that'll be a pleasant surprise to yer, sunshine?'

Gertie gasped. 'Five pounds! Oh, my God, I thought it would only be worth a couple of bob.' She passed the list to Harriet. 'I still won't sell. I'll keep it to pass on to my kids.'

Alice was peering over Harriet's shoulder. 'Ooh er. Look, Harriet. Three pound for yer bowl, and two pound ten shillings for the ornament of me mam's. I never thought they'd be worth that much. It just goes to show, doesn't it? We could have been daft enough to sell them for coppers if we hadn't decided we wouldn't sell them for any amount of money.'

'I hope ye're still prepared to help find out if that bloke what came round is a fraud?' Molly asked. 'One good turn deserves another.'

Gertie was the first to speak, while the others nodded. 'Oh, we'll do that, Molly, have no fear. We won't say nothing to him if he offers us less than what's on the paper, we'll just say we've changed our mind. And then we'll pass the word on to all the neighbours that he's a con-man, and it'll be all over the neighbourhood like wildfire. Why don't you and Nellie come on Tuesday, and find out for yerselves? Yer can sit in my house and hear what he's got to say.'

Molly grinned. 'Me and Nellie would love to. We'll be there at half ten on Tuesday. Does that suit you, sunshine?'

'Down to the ground, girl.' Nellie's smile was a joy to behold. 'Down to the ground.'

'Ay, don't think ye're leaving me out,' Sally said. 'I'll be there to supervise operations.'

Chapter Twenty-Four

Walking back from the shops on Friday morning, Nellie could hardly contain her excitement. 'Ay, aren't yer going to say anything to Claire when she comes this afternoon? Perhaps yer could just drop a hint.'

Molly stopped walking and placed her heavy basket on the pavement. 'Nellie, I'm fed up telling yer that if we tell Claire what we've been up to, the chances are she won't ever speak to us again. So one word out of you, sunshine, and so help me, I'll brain yer.'

Never one to take offence, Nellie grinned. 'Yer'd have a hard job there, girl, 'cos I've got no brains to speak of.'

'Who are yer trying to kid, Nellie?' Molly wiped the back of a hand across her brow. 'Who is sweating cobs, carrying your potatoes on top of all her own shopping, while you trip along swinging a half-empty basket? I am, of course, and I must want me ruddy bumps feeling.'

'Let's swap over then, girl, and I'll carry the heavy basket while you take this one.'

'Nellie, in case yer haven't noticed, we're in our street. It would be pointless to swap over now. Yer should have thought of that when we came out of the greengrocer's.'

'I couldn't put the spuds in my basket, girl, 'cos I've got the cakes in there. Yer wouldn't want them to get squashed, would yer?'

Molly bent and picked up the basket. 'No, sunshine, I

wouldn't want to give a squashed cake to a visitor. But I can't see you worrying, 'cos there's nothing in this world yer enjoy more than sinking yer teeth into a cream slice and squashing the life out of it.'

'Ah, now, girl, that's not true. There's two things I enjoy more in this world than cream slices. One is being in bed with my George when he's in one of his passionate moods, and the other is seeing the blush on your face when I describe it to yer.'

Molly grinned as she put the basket down to root in her pocket for the door key. She never won a battle of wits with her mate, and she should know that by now. 'Come in while I separate our shopping. Yer can take yours home with yer, and I'll put my stuff away in the larder. Then I'm going to sit down and have a nice cup of tea. I'll swill me face in cold water first, though, 'cos the sweat's been rolling off me.'

'I'll tell yer what I'll do, girl, to make up for leaving yer to carry that heavy basket. I'll come in with yer and make a pot of tea while you sit and calm down.' Nellie's eyes were like slits, as they always were when she was playing crafty. 'I'll put the shopping away for yer as well, save yer bothering, and I'll pour our cups of tea out. Yer'll feel much better after that.'

Molly closed her eyes, then raised them to the sky before looking down at her friend. 'Did I hear yer say *our* cups of tea? Listen, sunshine, if you think ye're coming in with me to sit for a couple of hours nattering, then yer've got another think coming. I'm going to have a couple of hours to meself, all nice and quiet. So I'll take the cakes off yer now, 'cos I wouldn't trust yer with them, and yer can take yerself to yer own house, where yer belong.'

'Ah, come on, girl, don't be so bleeding miserable! If yer're making a pot of tea, yer'll never drink it all yerself, and yer'll end up pouring half down the sink. And just think of the waste!

Yer'd be the first one to say it's a sin to waste good food when there's people starving.'

'Yes, I know I would, Nellie, but you aren't starving, are yer? In fact, yer look more healthy than anyone I know. And if yer're so worried about waste, then I'll make yer a solemn promise that I won't waste any tea. I'll drink it all, right to the very last drop.'

Nellie's head wagged from side to side. This was an action that pleased her chins, for they could feel a cool breeze. 'Yer'll never drink a whole pot full of tea – yer'd never get it all down. Anyway, it would be greedy.'

'Then if it is your considered option that I could never drink a full pot of tea, sunshine, I will just make myself half a pot. So hand the cakes over, and then toddle off home. I'll put your potatoes in a bag and give them to yer when yer come back at half past three. That should be just before Claire gets here.'

With ill grace, Nellie took the cake bag out of her basket and handed it over. 'For being so mean, I hope yer swollen ankles don't go down, and I hope after yer've poured yerself a cup of tea out, yer find the milk's gone sour.' She turned away, and with her head held high she waddled the few yards to her door.

Molly had a smile on her face. 'I'll see yer half three then, sunshine?'

Nellie had put her basket down and was standing on tiptoe to put her key in the lock. 'Okay, girl! Oh, and when yer're making the ham sandwiches, don't spread the butter on the bread and then scrape if off again. Leave enough so we can taste it.'

'I'll try, sunshine, but it'll be a hard battle. It's the miser in me, yer see. I can't help it.'

'Well, if I can't taste the butter, I'll make a holy show of yer in front of Claire. And don't think I won't, either.'

'Oh, I know ye're bad enough to. Well, two can play at that game, so it's tit for tat. You mention the word butter in front of Claire, and I'll tell her I saw yer sneaking yer hand in the cake bag when yer thought I wasn't looking. And as yer were turning yer head away, I saw a chubby finger, covered in white cream, making its way up to your mouth.'

'Trust me to have a mate with eyes in the back of her head and in her backside.' Nellie finally managed to fit her key in the lock and she pushed the door open. 'D'yer know, girl, while yer've been arguing the toss with me out here, we could have been comfortably seated in your house with a cup of tea in our hand. Yer'll never learn, will yer?'

'It's a bit late in the day for that, sunshine. But I can still tell the time, so I'll see yer here at half three.'

Claire was wearing a happy smile when Molly opened the door. 'Hi, Molly. Enjoying the lovely weather I hope?'

'You're looking very pleased with yerself.' Molly stood aside to let her pass, then closed the door. 'Yer look as though yer've lost sixpence and found a shilling.'

'I'm always happy when the weather's nice and I can feel the sun on me face.' Claire put her bag on the floor by the sideboard. 'Hello, Nellie. It's nice to see yer sitting on yer throne again. And you and Molly look well, getting brown with the sun.'

'Yeah, we're both browned off, girl, and we won't blame the sun for it. It's lack of interest, that's our problem. Not enough excitement in our lives.' A cheeky grin appeared. 'I get a bit more excitement than Molly, but she doesn't like me to talk about it.'

Molly wagged a finger. 'For being so cheeky, Nellie McDonough, yer can go and pour the water into the teapot. I'll fetch the plates in.'

Nellie gave a weary sigh. 'See, Claire, having a throne doesn't get yer out of doing jobs. In fact, it makes yer an easy target 'cos yer stick out like a sore thumb.'

'Go on, move yerself.' Molly gave her a gentle push towards the kitchen. 'I'll be right behind yer.' With her hand on the kitchen door, Molly turned. 'Yer always look well, Claire, but yer seem to have a sparkle in yer eyes today. Is there a reason for this?'

Nellie moved like a streak of lightning to stand inside the kitchen door beside her mate. If there was any juicy gossip on the menu, then she wanted to hear it first hand. 'Yeah, I thought yer looked very perky today, girl!'

'Well, I have got something to tell yer, but it'll wait until ye're sitting down. And then yer'll either think it's sad, mad, or yer'll laugh yer heads off.'

'Don't stand there gawping, girl, put a move on.' Nellie gave her friend a none too gentle dig in the ribs. 'It'll be time for Claire to go home if yer carry on at this rate.'

'I haven't anything to do, sunshine, but carry the sandwiches in. They're ready for eating. But, unfortunately, you are going to have to bring the kettle to the boil again. It's not me holding us back, it's you.'

Claire grinned when Molly came in carrying two plates. 'Does anyone ever win in these little spats you two have?'

'Nobody wins, sunshine, and nobody loses.' Molly put the plates down and pulled out a chair for herself. 'Me and me mate would think there was something wrong if we didn't have a few minor disagreements each day. Life would be very boring.'

Nellie came in carrying a steaming teapot in one hand, and a silver teapot stand in the other. 'You can carry the tray in, girl, and then yer'll know yer crockery is safe. I did try to pick it up, then I thought sod it! I'd never hear the last of it if I broke one of yer cups.'

Finally they were all settled down with a cup of tea in front of them and a ham sandwich in their hand. 'Well, Claire, me and Nellie are on pins to know how something can make us either sad, mad, or laugh our heads off. Come on, has this anything to do with Mr Graham Collins, or am I way off track?'

Claire felt a crumb on her bottom lip, and she pushed it into her mouth before answering. 'Mostly, yes. Yer see, I went out with him on Tuesday night, and while he wanted to go to a threatre again, I said I would prefer to go for a drink. And perhaps he'd like to come home with me after we'd had a drink, and he could meet my children.'

Molly put her sandwich down and cleared her mouth before saying, 'I hadn't realised the friendship had progressed that quickly.'

'Oh, it hasn't, Molly, but I was feeling guilty about leaving Ken to look after Amy. If we'd gone to a theatre it would have been nearly eleven when we got home, and I really don't think it's fair to leave the children alone till that time of night.'

'So ye're still going out with the bloke, then?' Nellie asked. 'Yer must think something of him to take him home with yer.'

'No, Nellie, nothing like that! It was nice to have some male company after years of being alone, I admit that. He's very attentive, holding my elbow when crossing the road, and things like that. But my heart didn't miss a beat, I'm too old for that. There was no fluttering of eyelashes, or being coy. I didn't behave like a young girl out on her first date, nor was I over familiar with him. I was just my normal self.'

Molly was eager to know. 'Did yer take him home to meet the kids?'

However, Nellie got in before Claire could answer. 'I'm dying to know, girl, if ye're seeing him again?'

'Hang on, you two, and don't be putting the cart before the

horse!' Claire was chuckling at the expectancy on the two faces watching her. 'Yes, I took him home with me and he met the children. He was very nice with them, very friendly. But I didn't encourage him to stay long, for it was past Amy's bedtime.'

'Is that all?' Nellie looked disgusted. 'No goodnight kiss or anything?'

'No, Nellie, that was never on the cards. I went to the door with him, shook his hand and thanked him for a pleasant evening. He asked when he could see me again, and I told him I'd see him when he comes to the shop on Monday with his laundry. Then I got Amy off to bed before making a pot of tea for me and Ken. And this is where the sadness, madness and hilarity comes into it. But let me finish me tea before it goes cold.'

'Yes, and have another sandwich,' Molly told her, 'for I'm sick of watching Nellie licking her lips when she looks at the cakes. I don't know whether she's more interested in yer love-life, Claire, or whether she wants yer to get on with it so we can get to the cake stage.'

'Then the best thing is for me to keep quiet until the plates are empty. Is that all right with you, Nellie?'

'Ooh, I don't know now,' said the little woman. 'Me head wants yer to finish yer story, but me tummy has different ideas.'

Molly tutted. 'You and yer tummy, sunshine, come between me and me sleep. I say let's eat up, and then when Claire carries on with her story, it won't be spoilt for me by the sound of you smacking yer lips.'

'Good idea, girl, good idea.' Nellie looked relieved. 'Yer see, that cream slice what is the nearest to me, well it's been giving me the eye since we sat down. It's just begging me to sink me teeth into it.'

'All right, sunshine, don't be making a drama out of a cream slice, me and Claire get the drift. Finish the plate of sandwiches first, though, or yer'll be eating back to front.'

'Yer've got some smashing sayings, girl.' Nellie reached for one of the ham sandwiches, and in one bite half of it had disappeared into her mouth. 'Do yer think them up yerself, or did yer get them off yer ma?'

'Nellie, don't speak with yer mouth full, sunshine, it's bad manners.'

'It's not full now, girl, it's only half full.' The other half of the sandwich disappeared, and Nellie dusted her hands. 'There yer are, girl. Me mouth's full again, but the plate is empty. I timed that nicely.'

'Hang about, sunshine!' Molly grabbed Nellie's wrist as she was reaching towards the cake plate. 'I know one of your fingers is acquainted with one of these cakes, so let me examine them, please, to see which one.' She picked up the plate and pretended to examine each of the cream slices. Then she pointed to the one which had been nearest to Nellie. 'The reason it was making eyes at yer, sunshine, was because it couldn't speak. Had it been able to, it would have asked yer to let it join the rest of the cake inside yer tummy.'

'Uh, uh!' Nellie's chins weren't going to stand for that. 'I didn't eat no cake before, girl, so don't be trying to make me look bad in front of Claire. I know yer saw a bit of cream on me finger, but that was only because it rubbed off on me.'

'To have rubbed off on yer, Nellie, yer would have had to have yer hand inside the cake bag.' Molly moved her foot to give Claire a nudge. 'I can't think of any reason for yer to have yer hand in the bag, sunshine, but, then again, yer might have a perfectly good excuse.' Molly was dying to laugh at the expression on her friend's face. She'd need divine intervention to get herself out of this pickle.

Nellie was indeed looking upwards towards the ceiling, but

it wasn't to seek help from on high. She was getting the words right for her reply, which would have Molly laughing the other side of her face.

'Oh, I don't need no excuse, girl, 'cos it had nothing to do with me really. It was Edna Hanley. And if yer hadn't been so busy yapping, as usual, yer would have seen for yerself. What happened was, Edna had put the cakes in the bag, but when she handed it to me her hand was on a slant, and the cakes all moved to the one end of the bag. She didn't see what happened, and I thought she'd think I was being petty if I told her. So I opened the bag and put the cakes straight. And that's how I come to have a bit of cream on me finger. If yer don't believe me, then it's just too bleeding bad.'

Claire burst out laughing. 'Nellie, yer deserve a medal for thinking that up.'

Nellie's face was the picture of pride and happiness. 'It was good, wasn't it, girl?'

Molly felt like cupping that face and planting a kiss on it. But she resisted, and said, 'If Nellie got a medal every time she made up a cock and bull story, Claire, she'd be weighed down with them. For she comes out with gems like that at least twice a day.' Turning to her mate, she patted her arm. 'I have to admit, though, sunshine, that was one of yer best. Considering yer had so little time, it was really clever of yer to come up with something that laid the blame at Edna Hanley's door. And I bet Edna will laugh her head off tomorrow when I tell her that she gave yer a bag of squashed cakes.'

'Ah, yer don't have to tell her, girl, she'd be really upset.' Nellie always got the pick of the cream slices off Edna, the ones with the most cream in. Now, in her mind's eye, she could see the shopkeeper getting her revenge by giving her the ones with hardly any. And that didn't bear thinking about. 'Yer wouldn't be so miserable, would yer, 'cos I think it would be a lousy trick to upset someone what's done yer no harm.'

'I wouldn't upset Edna, no, but I'd frighten the ruddy life out of you. There'd be no running to the shop at closing time, when yer know they'll be selling off any left-over cream cakes for half price.'

Nellie's jaw dropped. 'Who's been telling tales out of school? Go on, tell me who's snitched on me, and I'll strangle them.'

Molly grinned. 'I knew I was right.'

Nellie banged a fist on the table. 'I want to know who's been telling yer lies about me?'

Claire was looking from one to the other. If she didn't know them, she'd think they were going to come to blows any minute. But she knew they'd end up laughing as though there'd been no raised voices or threats. So she sat back and enjoyed the banter, while wishing she had a friend she was as close to as this pair.

'Nobody told me, Nellie, I found out for meself.' Molly had mastered the art of keeping her face deadpan while howling with laughter inside. 'And it's been going on for ages. Yer must think I'm deaf, dumb and blind, not to hear yer kitchen door close at the same time every night, then yer feet tripping down the cobbles, and the latch on the yard door going. It was so regular, I couldn't help but notice. So one night, after I'd heard yer kitchen door close, I went upstairs to the back bedroom and saw yer scurrying down the entry. Yer had yer head bent as though yer didn't want anyone to see yer. But yer have to admit, sunshine, it would be very hard to miss yer.'

Nellie's head was nodding and shaking, causing mayhem for her chins. They were forced to change direction every two seconds and were totally confused. 'If yer saw me, I must have been on me way to the corner shop. I often run out of things, and there's nothing wrong with that. Anyway, ye're a nosy bugger, aren't yer?'

Molly nodded. 'Dead nosy, sunshine. And many a time I've meant to ask yer the next day where yer'd been off to, but then forgot. Until the afternoon I saw yer close the entry door, stand there and wipe yer mouth with the back of a hand, and then screw up a white paper cake bag and put it in the bin. It was then I cottoned on to what yer were up to.'

'And yer've never mentioned it in all these years, girl? Ye're a dark horse, you are.'

'What are yer talking about, all these years?' Surprise was high in Molly's voice. 'How long have yer been doing it for?'

'For as long as you've been watching me, that's how long.'

'But I only noticed yer yesterday. And that's 'cos I was cleaning the back bedroom window.'

'Well, that's how long I've been doing it for. We were only having salad, if yer remember, because of the weather being so hot, and it was all ready to put on the table. So rather than hang around for the family to come in, I nipped out and got meself a cake. And so yer know every little detail, girl, I didn't half enjoy that bleeding cake.' Nellie's eyes, and nodding head, went to the plate. 'Same as I'm going to enjoy that cake, when yer stop bleeding talking long enough for me to pick it up. And if yer don't hurry, I'll have gone off the ruddy thing.'

'Seeing as yer've explained yerself to my satisfaction, sunshine, I'll be gracious in defeat and hand yer the plate.'

Nellie appealed to Claire. 'D'yer think a ruddy cake is worth going through all that for, girl? Honest, except I don't want to hurt her feelings, seeing as she's me best mate, I'd tell her to eat the ruddy thing herself.'

'Yer can do if yer like, queen, but I don't think Molly could eat two cream slices.'

'She wouldn't get the chance, 'cos there's only one each.'

'On the plate there is, but there's another three in my bag.

Yer know I always bring cakes with me. I was going to get them out when that plate was empty.'

Molly put the plate under Nellie's nose. 'Come on, sunshine, we both talk too much. Claire will be wanting to go home before we hear the rest of her story. I'll take me cake into the kitchen with me and eat it while I'm waiting for the kettle to boil. I'm sure we all feel like a fresh pot of tea.'

'Ken was quiet after Graham left and Amy was in bed,' Claire told Molly and Nellie after the table had been cleared and they had a fresh cup of tea in front of them. 'Usually when we're on our own he talks about his mates in work and what he's been working on that day. But on Tuesday night I couldn't get him talking at all. I asked him how the day had gone and he just said it was the same as usual. Then he suddenly blurted out, "Ye're not getting serious with that bloke, are yer, Mam?" It was the way he said it that caught my attention the most – he looked both sad and angry. I told him I'd only been out with Graham the twice, and as far as I was concerned, it wasn't serious. Then I asked him why he wanted to know, and did he object? "I don't like him, and I don't want yer to go out with him any more." ' Claire's smile was tender. 'I felt like hugging the life out of him for he looked so sad. Like he was being the man of the house and looking after me. I asked him why he didn't like Graham, and how he could say that about someone he'd only just met, and he said, "He's not like us, Ma. He's trying to make out he's posh, and better than us, but he's not. Yer don't want to fall for his fancy words, 'cos I wouldn't trust him. I know yer must get lonely, but there's better men than him around. Men like me dad – now he was a real man." '

Nellie looked on while Molly caught hold of Claire's hand. 'He's a good lad is your Ken, and no matter what he said, he was only saying what he thought was right for you. Don't get upset about it. He meant well.'

'Oh, I'm not upset, Molly. I would never get upset over anything Ken said, 'cos he's a wonderful son, and I love him to pieces. No, I wasn't upset, I was mad at meself for doing something that put that sad look in his eyes.'

'Did he put yer off the bloke, girl?' Nellie asked. 'It would make it awkward for yer going out with a feller yer children didn't like. But fancy him saying that about yer friend. Weren't yer surprised?'

'I was surprised, yes, 'cos it sounded strange coming from a boy who's not fifteen yet. But as for putting me off Graham, well, I really didn't have any feelings for him anyway. It was a change for me to get out, but if I don't see him any more it won't worry me. I know I'll see him in the shop, but I'll have second thoughts about going out with him if he asks.'

'Sometimes a young person's intuitions can surprise yer, sunshine,' Molly said, hoping her mate wouldn't think this was a good time to tell Claire her son was right. 'Your Ken struck me as being very level-headed and grown-up for his age. Perhaps he saw something in your Graham Collins that you can't see. Who knows? In any case, whatever it was, he was only thinking about your welfare, and I say good for him.'

Nellie's chins seemed to dance in slow motion as her head didn't know whether to nod or shake. 'Wait until yer see him in the shop on Monday, girl. Take a good look at him and ask yerself if yer really like him or not. If ye're not keen, then I wouldn't bother going out with him 'cos it wouldn't be worth upsetting the kids for.'

'I don't need to take a good look at him, Nellie, 'cos I've already made up my mind. I'll not be going out with Graham again, and I'll tell him so on Monday.'

'What excuse will yer give, sunshine?' While Molly asked

this, she was thinking that young Ken may have saved her and Nellie the unpleasant task of telling Claire the truth about the man in question. 'He's bound to ask why.'

'There's nothing wrong in telling him the truth, Molly, which is what I'm going to do. I'm not prepared to go out any evening and leave my children alone in the house. It's as simple as that, and nothing will persuade me to change my mind. I've got two wonderful kids, and they're all I need to make me happy.'

'Good for you, sunshine. I think ye're doing the right thing if yer've no feelings for this man Graham. Perhaps young Ken did yer a favour by causing yer to look closely at yer friendship with him. And who knows, there might be someone come along, out of the blue, and sweep yer off yer feet.'

'That only happens in films, Molly, not in real life. One thing I realise now is that I had ten marvellous years with a man in a million. There'll never be another one like him.'

'Ay, girl, don't be saying that,' Nellie scolded, ''cos never is a long time.'

'It is, Nellie, and talking about time, I think I'd better start making tracks. I don't half enjoy me Friday afternoon visits, though. I look forward to them.' With her hands flat on the table, Claire pushed herself to her feet. 'Thanks for having me, and can I come back next week, please?'

Molly suddenly put a hand to her forehead. 'Oh, my God, I nearly forgot! Our Ruthie's having some friends in at half seven tonight, and I've to ask yer if Ken would like to come? They only play cards and have a laugh, but I think he'd enjoy himself. Will yer ask him?'

'Oh, yeah, of course I'll ask him. I'd like him to come because he needs the company of kids the same age. But he is a bit shy, and I can't make him say yes.'

'You bring him, sunshine, then he won't feel so shy. Once he's met Ruthie and the gang, you could come across to Doreen's with me. And bring Amy with yer, because there's no school tomorrow and it won't hurt if she goes to bed late for once.'

'Haven't yer had enough of me for one day? I'd love to come, but I don't want to make a nuisance of meself.'

Nellie struggled to her feet. She knew Molly would be seeing Claire out, and she didn't want to miss anything. 'I'll be here, girl, and I'm not a nuisance, I'm a very welcome guest.'

'And so say all of us!' Molly winked at Claire. 'She's got no etiquette, my mate, she doesn't bother waiting to be asked. And if I was to say she couldn't come, she'd stand outside our Doreen's window and pull faces at us all night. So to stop the neighbours from talking, Doreen would have to let her in.'

Taking that as a compliment, Nellie grinned. 'She's right, yer know. I'd make a holy show of them.'

Telling herself she'd be crazy to pass over the chance of spending a couple of hours in the company of these two friends, Claire said, 'I'd love to come, Molly, and I'll be here for half seven with the two kids.' She started to make her way towards the front door. 'Come and throw me out.'

Molly was stepping down on to the pavement after Claire when she found herself being lifted off her feet. She looked down into the smiling blue eyes of her neighbour, Corker. 'Put me down, yer soft nit. Yer'll have the neighbours talking.'

But Corker wasn't the type to worry about neighbours. 'Molly, me darlin', every time I see yer, yer look prettier.' He grinned at the man at his side. 'Next to me wife, Derek, this is my favourite woman. Many is the favour she and Nellie have done for me and my family.'

As he lowered Molly to the ground, Corker smiled at Nellie and then rested his eyes on Claire. She had been watching with eyes wide. She'd seen Corker briefly on one of her visits, but seeing him up close was a different matter. Six foot five, weather-beaten face, bright blue eyes and a huge moustache and beard.

'Hello, me darlin'. Yer mustn't think I'm taking liberties, for me and Molly go back a long way, and it's all in fun.'

As she was straightening her dress, Molly said, 'Claire, this giant of a man is Corker, from next door, and this is his friend, Derek.'

When Corker shook her hand, Claire felt she was shaking hands with a giant. But a very handsome giant. His mate, Derek, was around the six foot mark, but he looked small beside his friend. 'It's nice to meet you both,' Claire said, 'but I'm going to have to run. I want to be home for my daughter coming from school.'

The group watched her walking swiftly down the street, and Corker was the first to speak. 'What a good-looking woman. Have yer known her long, Molly?'

'Not all that long, but we've become good friends. She's a widow with two children, and her nature is as lovely as her face.' Molly's eyes warned Nellie not to reveal any secrets. 'She calls every Friday afternoon for a few hours, but always leaves in time for her daughter coming in from school. Me and Nellie are very fond of her.'

Derek said, 'Her face looks as though it was sculpted out of ivory.'

Corker nodded. 'She's a rare beauty, all right.' He turned to Molly. 'I was going to give yer a knock, me darlin', 'cos I need to ask a favour of yer.'

'If it's within my power, Corker, then consider it done.'

'Would you ask in the cake shop if we can hire their reception room one evening? I'd do it meself, but you've had so many parties there I thought you'd handle it better than me.'

Nellie came to stand beside Molly. If there was a party going, she would demand the job of assistant hostess, which she always was. 'What's the celebration, Corker?' Molly asked. 'Phoebe and Paul haven't decided to get married, have they?'

Corker's loud guffaw rang the full length of the street. 'No, me darlin', that's next year, they tell me. Which I'm glad about, for neither of them are grown-up enough to get married. No, it's not a celebration for any event in particular, but for several birthdays and whatnots. Phoebe didn't have a party for her last birthday, and neither did Gordon or Dorothy. In fact, me darlin', we've never had a party for anything before. So I thought of all the parties you and Nellie have had in Hanley's, where everyone was invited and had a whale of a time. Whereas me and Ellen have never given one. So how does the idea of a real knees-up jars out sound?'

'Sounds wonderful, Corker. But I'd have to have date, time, numbers, do yer want music, and what would you want in the way of food for the buffet?'

'I was hoping you'd help me out there, me darlin'. Derek is home for good now, so any Saturday would suit. We would want music, same as you had. As for numbers, I'll make a list out when Ellen comes in from work, and she can say what she would like in the way of food.'

'If yer could let me have the list tonight, Corker, I'll see Edna Hanley tomorrow. Best to get the date sorted before she gets booked up.'

'Yer'll have it tonight. Derek is staying to eat with us, then we're going for a pint. I'll pass the list in on the way out. And if Jack, George and Phil would like to join us at the pub, we'd like their company.'

'It might be best if yer knock at Doreen's for me. Ruthie is having the gang in tonight for a game of cards, so we'll have to move camp to let them have the house to themselves. Oh, and Claire's bringing her son down to play cards, and she's coming over to Doreen's with me and Nellie.' Molly took a deep breath and then blew out. 'I hope I've got all me facts straight there. It sounded a bit mixed up to my ears.'

'Message received and understood, me darlin'. We'll be knocking about eight with the list. Oh, and don't forget to tell the men about coming to the pub.'

Molly caught his arm as he moved away. 'Corker, have yer given this party any thought? If yer intend to ask all the Bennetts and McDonoughs, plus the Higginses and Jacksons, it adds up to a fair number. Yer might well get a shock.'

Corker put his huge hands round her waist and lifted her from the ground. 'Molly, me darlin', when are yer going to stop worrying about other people? Yer've done yer fair share over the years, now let me show a little bit of appreciation. Both to you and to Nellie.' He set her down and bent down to look into Nellie's face. 'I'd lift yer up if I could, me darlin', but I'm sure yer wouldn't want the neighbours to see those blue fleecy-lined bloomers of yours.'

Nellie stuck out her tongue and pulled on his beard. 'I've got yer there, smart lad, 'cos I've got me pink ones on today.'

Chapter Twenty-Five

Ruthie and Bella were in the kitchen making sandwiches, and giggling in excited anticipation as the time drew nearer to half past seven. Molly had given the kitchen over to them and they felt really grown up because they were doing their own thing without being supervised. 'I think there'll be plenty here,' Ruthie said, counting twenty sandwiches in all. They were only small, but no one would be very hungry after their dinner, so there should be enough. And Bella's mam had given two large bottles of lemonade, while Ruthie's mam had bought the filling for the sandwiches. The girls themselves had bought a pound of assorted biscuits from the corner shop, and they were quite happy with themselves.

Bella caught Ruthie's arm. 'That was a knock on the front door.'

'Ooh, that'll be Ken. I'm dying to see what he looks like.'

'Let him get in first, Ruthie. Yer don't want to embarrass him.'

So the girls stayed quiet, listening to introductions being made. But Ruthie was nosy, and didn't have the patience to wait, so she peeped through the opening at the side of the door. When she turned back to her friend, she had a hand over her mouth and her eyes were wide. 'Oh, yer should see him, Bella, he's dead handsome. He's tall, too, like a film star.'

Bella quickly took over the speck by the door. 'Yes, ye're

right, Ruthie, he's gorgeous. He's even better-looking than Gordon, or Johnny.'

'I'll put a cloth over the plates, then we'll go in. But don't start going all shy on me, Bella, or he'll think we're childish.'

Molly poked her head round the door. 'Come and meet Mrs Thompson, and her son and daughter.'

Things got a bit hectic right then, as Gordon, Jeff and Johnny arrived, and once again there were introductions all round. But these were greeted with nods, and not handshakes, as the youngsters were shy and ill at ease.

'Have yer finished in the kitchen, sunshine?' Molly asked. 'Come and let's see where ye're up to.'

She led the way, followed by her daughter and Bella. 'They look good enough to eat, girls. Ye're getting a dab hand at it. There should be plenty there.' She put the cloth back over the plates and lowered her voice. 'I want yer to look after Ken, 'cos I think he's feeling a bit out of it. It can't be helped, the other boys have known each other all their lives, but try to make him feel at ease.'

'Ay, Mam, yer were right about him being good-looking, he's really handsome. I think me and Bella are going to have a fight over him.'

A blush came over Bella's face. 'Don't be saying that, Ruthie. I'm not going to fight over any boy. They're all nice. No one is better than the other.' Bella surprised herself by being so outspoken. 'Anyway, as me mam says, looks are not everything.'

Ruthie put a hand over her mouth to stifle a giggle. 'They help though. I mean, you wouldn't go out with a boy whose face was covered in pimples, would yer?'

'If I liked him, yes, I would! Most boys get spots or pimples, but they grow out of them.'

Molly put a finger under her daughter's chin and lifted her face until their eyes were on a level. 'Bella is right, sunshine.

Yer can never judge a book by its cover. And before yer criticise someone else, don't forget ye're often moaning yerself because yer've got a spot or pimple on yer face.'

'Yes, but I'm not going out with meself, am I?' There was mischief in the girl's eyes. 'I don't have to look at meself.'

'You, young lady, get more like yer Auntie Nellie every day. Like her, yer've got an answer to everything.'

Jack's voice floated through to them. 'What's going on out there? Yer've got visitors standing here like statues. Show some manners, will yer?'

'Coming, Dad! It's me mam who's keeping us. She's giving us a lecture on how to behave and how not to behave.'

Molly hurried through to the living room. 'Take no notice of her. Bella doesn't need a lecture on how to behave, and if I was of a mind to give our daughter one, I'd pick a time when I had a few hours to spare.' She pulled all the chairs from under the table. 'Sit yerselves down, lads, and Ruthie will fetch another two chairs. Is your Peter coming, Gordon?'

'Yeah, when he's finished doing himself up.' Corker's son sat himself down, a grin on his pleasant face. 'Honest, every hair has to be in position before he goes anywhere. And he goes through a jar of Brylcreem every week.'

'Ye're only jealous,' Ruthie said, ''cos he's got more hair than you.'

Molly winked at Ken, who had chosen a chair facing Gordon. 'If they start fighting in earnest, Ken, yer know where our Doreen lives, so nip over and tell us before the neighbours call the police in.'

Ken was feeling more relaxed now, happy there were three other lads there. 'If yer see me running hell for leather down the street, Mrs Bennett, yer'll know there's a free-for-all going on and yer'd be advised to get over quick before they start breaking up yer happy home.'

'I know it's a daft question, son,' Claire said, 'but why would yer be running hell for leather down the street, instead of over the road to where we'll be?'

'Think about it, Mam! My first time here and a fight breaks out! I'd be the one the finger of guilt would be pointed at, so it would make sense for me to disappear.'

'If a fight broke out, you and me would get stuck in the door, then.' Johnny laughed. 'I'm not very good at fisticuffs, and besides, like Peter I'm fussy about me hair getting upset.'

Jeff Mowbray wasn't going to be left out. Not when there were two pretty young girls there who would be giving them points on looks. 'Yer've got straight hair, Johnny, so no one would know whether it was upset or not.'

'Okay, that's enough. Ye're all as vain as one another,' Molly said jokingly. 'We're going to have to leave yer to it, or Doreen will think we've changed our minds.' She held out a hand to Amy. 'Come on, sunshine, so yer can see the baby before he goes to bed. And Jack, are you calling for Corker?'

Jack nodded. 'I'll come out with you. I've only got to take me jacket off the hook.'

'Yer won't forget to call for George, will yer? I wouldn't like him to be left out. And Phil will probably follow yer up.' Molly gave the youngsters one more warning. 'On yer best behaviour, kids. No throwing cups at the wall and no rowdy songs. All right?'

'We'll be as good as gold, Auntie Molly,' Gordon said. 'When yer come back, yer won't know anyone has been.'

Claire dropped a kiss on Ken's head. 'We'll be back just before ten, love. I believe that's the time the card game finishes.'

'Around that time,' Molly said, 'give or take a few minutes. But let's move, or we'll be here all night.'

* * *

Ruthie brought a chair down from her bedroom, and Bella carried in the one from the kitchen. The two packs of cards were on the table and the six youngsters settled down. Ruthie had cleverly manoeuvred herself on to the chair next to Ken, much to the disgust of Gordon and Johnny. Although they didn't know it, they were both of the same mind. When the break came for refreshments, they'd make sure positions were changed. 'Who's going to deal?' Ruthie asked. 'Shall we all pick a card from the top of the pack and the one with the highest number gets to deal?'

Before anyone could answer, the back kitchen door opened and in walked Peter Corkhill. 'I came the back way, save any of yer getting off yer bottom.'

'Oh, we're a chair short,' Ruthie said, stating the obvious, while at the same time determined not to give up the one she'd cleverly bagged. 'Gordon, would you share yer chair with Peter?'

'I'll share with him,' Bella said, having always had a soft spot for Peter, and thinking he was the nicest of the lot. 'I'm the smallest, so we'll easy manage on one chair. But that's as long as he promises not to cheat.'

That arrangement suited the boy, who had spent ages in front of the mirror making his hair neat and tidy to impress Bella. 'I promise I won't look at the cards in yer hand, unless yer stick them right in front of me face.'

'Yer won't get the chance,' Bella told him as she edged along her chair. 'I'll keep me hand over them.'

Gordon had other ideas. It was bad enough having to vie with Johnny for Ruthie's attention, but it was going too far to have another bloke to contend with. So perhaps if he paid a little attention to Bella, Ruthie would get jealous. 'Let's push both of our chairs together and Bella can sit in the middle. She'll have more room then.'

Ruthie did feel a pang of jealousy, but it only lasted a couple of seconds. She lived next door to Gordon and saw him every night, while she wouldn't get the chance of seeing Ken very often. She didn't know where he lived but it couldn't be local or she would have seen him before now. 'If we're settled at last, let's all pick a card to see who deals.'

Ken picked a queen, which turned out to be the highest, and when he began to deal it was easy to see he was no novice. 'I'd say this wasn't the first time yer've dealt cards,' Johnny said. 'Yer handle them as though yer play often.'

Ken nodded, as he tried to keep an eye on the number of cards he dealt to each one. 'Me and me mam have a couple of games most nights. Not for money, just to pass the time. Me dad died five years ago, and I don't like me mam being on her own every night, so we play cards for the sake of something to do.'

'Your mam is beautiful,' Gordon said. 'And she doesn't look old enough to be yer mam. She could pass for yer sister.'

'I know yer were paying me mam a compliment, and ye're right she is beautiful. And I'm very proud of her. But I don't know whether to clock yer one for saying she looks like me sister. That doesn't say much for me, and I feel as old as the hills now. Next thing, I'll be buying meself a walking stick.'

'Gordon didn't mean it that way,' Ruthie was quick to tell him. 'And I was going to say the same about yer mam. She is lovely. Yer should be proud of her.'

None of the friends could imagine being without their father, and their sympathy went out to Ken. And from that moment, he became one of the gang.

'Will yer be looking for a shore job now, Derek?' Jack asked, as the friends sat round the small table in the smoke-filled snug. 'Or are yer giving yerself a break first?'

'I'll take it easy for a week or two, spend a bit of time with me ma.' Derek drank from the pint glass then placed it on the table. 'Corker is going to ask his boss if there's any jobs going where he works. That would suit me fine, because he's out in the open all the time, with the smell of the sea in the air.'

'I don't think I'll have any trouble getting him a job with the company I work for.' Corker wiped the froth from his moustache. 'I get on well with me boss, and without wanting to sound as though I'm bragging, I have about ten men working under me now.'

'What is it yer actually do, Corker?' George asked. 'I know yer work for a shipping firm down at the docks, but don't know what the job entails.'

'Well, when I first got the job, it was loading and unloading the ships that come into port. Then a month or so ago, I got promoted. Now I oversee the loading and unloading. It requires a lot of paperwork, keeping a log book of goods that come in and go out, and the tonnage. It took some getting used to, but now I find it as easy as falling off a bike.' He lifted his pint glass, his blue eyes twinkling in the still weather-beaten face. 'And I have to say the rise in pay wasn't to be sneezed at.'

Derek grinned. 'In the hopeful event I manage to get a job with that firm, how long will I have to be there to get a job like yours?'

'I've got another twenty years to go before I retire,' Corker told him, 'but there's a bloke who does the same type of work as me, and he's sixty. Only a matter of five years, me old mate, and time goes by quickly.'

'Not that ruddy quick,' Derek said, laughing. 'Ye're making an old man of me, and I haven't started living yet.'

'Find yerself a good woman, like I did,' Corker said. 'It'll take yer a few months to get used to walking straight, but with a woman in yer life yer'll get over that.'

'It's going to be more difficult finding a good woman than finding a job.' Derek gazed at the faces round the table. 'It's not as though I'm in the flush of youth and can go jazzing. A nice slow waltz is about my heavy.'

Phil smiled at the memory he had of the first time he saw Doreen, and how he'd asked her for a dance. 'There's men older than you go dancing, Derek, but they go to the likes of the Grafton.' Then he shrugged his shoulders. 'Mind you, listening to the men in work, most of the women that go there are middle-aged and out for a good time.'

'He'll have no trouble finding himself a good woman,' Corker said with good faith. 'A fine-looking man like him, he'll not go short.'

Derek chortled. 'As a last resort, I can always go knocking on doors.'

'Just keep away from four houses in our street, though,' Jack said. 'We're four happily married men, all very content with what we have.'

'A fine lot of mates you are, if yer won't even share yer wife and contentment with a bloke desperate for tender loving care. I'll remember that when I'm writing out me last will and testament.'

There was much shouting and laughter in the Bennett house, with the youngsters enjoying every minute of it. Ken was really happy being with kids his own age. And he proved to have a good sense of humour when it came to forfeits. He seemed to have a never-ending stream of jokes which brought forth laughter, applause and whistles. He was definitely a hit with the boys as well as the girls, for he didn't brag or try to be big in front of Ruthie and Bella. And as the night wore on, he felt he'd known them all his life. What they didn't suspect was that he'd deliberately lost a few hands of cards because he didn't want them to think he was showing off.

Ruthie was sad when she looked at the clock and saw it was a quarter to ten. 'We haven't got time for another game, so shall we put the cards away and just talk until me mam and dad come home?'

'What about washing the dishes?' Ken asked. 'I'll give yer a hand with those, save yer mam having to do them.'

'Yeah, and I'll help,' Bella said, missing the daggers that came her way from Ruthie. 'We can have them done in no time.'

'While you're doing that, we'll tidy up in here and put the chairs back,' Gordon said. 'And if we see any crumbs on the floor we'll pick them up.'

Ruthie was smiling when she pushed her chair back. 'It's been a good night, hasn't it?' There was a chorus of approval, and Johnny said, 'Ask yer mam if we can come again next Friday. We should all club together to pay for the food and lemonade, so how about the boys giving sixpence each?'

Ruthie knew her mother would go mad if she took money off them, so she shook her head. 'No, leave it for now. I'll ask me mam about next Friday and let yer know. And if she says it's all right, yer can club together for the lemonade, and me and Bella will fork out for the sandwiches.'

The boys were well pleased with that, and already looking forward to the following Friday. 'Let's get the dishes washed and the place tidied up then, and make a good impression on Mrs Bennett.' Johnny was thinking that some time in the future she could well be his mother-in-law. 'We need to get in her good books.'

Across the road in Doreen's, there was much hilarity as Nellie was in excellent form. She was in the middle of the floor, where she liked to be, doing her impressions. She did a perfect Elsie Flanaghan, with her arms folded and her head nodding as she pretended to be standing on the corner of the street gossiping to everyone who passed. She even changed position when she took the part of the poor soul held captive by Elsie, and forced to listen as she bad-mouthed all their neighbours. She had Edna Hanley spot on, too, in mannerisms and speech. And she even took herself off, pointing to an invisible tray of cakes and pointing out to Edna which one she wanted. 'No, not that one, yer silly nit! The one next to it!' She impersonated film stars from Mae West to Laurel and Hardy. She needed the help of Molly for the latter, and they were so funny they had their audience doubled up.

There was one person, a very small one, who enjoyed herself more than anyone. And that was young Amy Thompson. For the first half hour she'd sat on the couch pressed close to her mother because she was shy. She wasn't used to being amongst so many strangers, or being up so late. But Nellie's magic worked its charm on her, and soon her giggles joined the laughter of the grown-ups. And to give Nellie her due, she never let one swear word leave her lips. Mind you, she'd been warned by Molly to watch herself or she'd be sent home in disgrace.

'Oh dear,' Claire said, wiping her eyes. 'I've never laughed so much in me life, and me ribs are sore.'

Amy spoke for the first time since she'd entered the house. 'So are mine, Mam, and me cheeks are sore, too!'

Nellie's eyes narrowed and she tapped her chin as she looked down on the girl. 'Well, let's see now. For the entertainment, it'll be threepence for yer mam, but we'll only charge you a penny 'cos ye're only little.'

Amy thought of a funny answer, but wondered whether they'd think she was cheeky if she spoke out. But looking at Nellie, so fat and cuddly, she knew she wouldn't get into trouble. 'I'm sorry, I haven't brought me purse out with me.'

They all laughed, but none so heartily as Nellie, her tummy, bosom and chins. 'Oh, aye, letting secrets out of school are yer? Is that what yer mam says when she wants a loaf on the slate?'

'Take no notice of her, sunshine,' Molly said. 'Everyone knows their own tricks best. And believe me, no one knows more tricks than my mate.'

'She's never been up this late before, have yer, sweetheart?' Claire stroked her daughter's hair. There was a strong resemblance between mother and daughter, indicating Amy would grow into a beauty. 'It's five to ten now, so I think we'd better give yer brother a knock. We've got a good fifteen-minute walk before us.'

'Yes, time marches on,' Molly said, pushing a chair back under the table. 'It's work tomorrow for most of them, so we'd better be on our way.' She gave Victoria a kiss, and said, 'It's time you were in bed, sunshine, yer need yer beauty sleep.'

'A good laugh does me more good, Molly, 'cos then when I go to sleep I have a smile on me face, and it stays there until the next morning.'

'I didn't get to see your baby again after all, Doreen.' Claire had her arm across Amy's shoulders. 'He's good for sleeping right through the noise we made.'

'She doesn't know she's born,' Molly said, hugging Doreen. 'He's one in a million is young Bobby. Eats and sleeps when it's time, and is happy and contented. Perhaps next time yer come, Claire, he'll be awake.'

Amy took a deep breath before daring to ask, 'Can I come again, please?'

'Of course yer can, sunshine! Yer can come here, or to my house, any time yer like. But right now I'd better get across the street or I'll have a few mothers after me.'

Molly was the first to step down on to the pavement, and she looked up the street in surprise when she heard her name called. 'Oh, blimey, here's a crowd of drunken men who must have been thrown out of the pub.'

'Now, Molly, me darlin',' Corker boomed, 'have yer ever seen me drunk?'

'The pub doesn't stock enough beer to make Corker drunk, love,' Jack said. He, with George and Phil, only ever had one pint to every two of Corker's. 'And before yer start on me, I'm as sober as a judge.'

'I thought yer were bringing me a list, Corker.' Molly shook a fist in his face. 'Were yer so eager to get to the pub yer didn't have time?'

'I did start it, Molly, me darlin', and Derek here can verify that. But I left it to Ellen to write out what she'd like for the buffet. She'll have it ready, so let's cross over and I'll get it off her.'

Corker put the key in the door, and turned his head. 'Come in, all of yer. Ellen will be glad to see yer.'

Nellie moved towards him. 'I'll come in, Corker. Ellen's bound to be making a pot of tea.'

'Oh, no, yer don't, my precious.' To everyone's amazement, for George was usually so placid, he grabbed hold of Nellie's arm and pulled on it so hard her feet left the ground. 'It's home for you, to make yer hard-working husband a drink.'

'What on earth has George been drinking?' Molly asked. 'Whatever it was I hope you haven't been on it, Jack.'

Claire would have loved to stay longer with these people who seemed to have made a wonderful life for themselves. But she had Amy to think of. 'I won't come in if yer don't mind, Corker. I'll get Ken, and we'll be on our way. We've got a good walk in front of us, and Ken has to go to work tomorrow.'

'You tell Ken his mam's waiting, Jack,' Molly said. 'And tell the other boys it's time they went home. Remind them it's work tomorrow, and if they're anything like our Tommy used to be, they'll be holy terrors to get out of bed.' Then she said to Claire, 'I'll just go in with Corker for the list off Ellen. I won't stay too long.'

'Which way are yer walking?' Derek asked, left alone with Claire and Amy. 'I'm walking too, and if we're going in the same direction I'll see yer safely home.'

Claire shook her head. 'I wouldn't dream of it, Derek. I'll have Ken and Amy with me, and we'll be home in no time.'

'How far have yer got to go?'

When Claire gave him the name of the street she lived in, Derek chuckled. 'Now that really is a coincidence. I live three streets away from yer.'

There was surprise in Claire's voice. 'Do yer? It's funny we've never bumped into each other before now.'

'I've been going away to sea since I was seventeen, so I haven't been at home very often. I live with me ma. Me dad died a few years ago.'

There was laughter and good-humoured chattering as five boys spilled on to the pavement. Ken came first, followed by Johnny, Jeff and the two Corkhill brothers. Ken was more animated than Claire had ever seen him, and her heart lifted. This is what his life should be about. Mixing and enjoying the things other boys his age were doing. 'Might see yer next Friday, then,' he called as the others moved away. 'I'll keep me fingers crossed.'

Claire waited until the boys were out of earshot before asking, 'Oh, aye, and am I allowed to ask what ye're hoping for next Friday?'

The boy was in very high spirits. 'We've had a smashing time, Mam. We were supposed to be playing cards, but we did more laughing. Ruthie is going to ask Mrs B. if we can come again next week.'

'I hope you weren't the one who suggested it, son, 'cos

that's asking a lot of Mrs Bennett. Don't forget, she has to move out to let yer have the place to yerselves.'

'I didn't suggest it, Mam, I wouldn't do that. It was Gordon Corkhill I think, but it might have been Ruthie herself.' His heartbeat was slowing down when he asked, 'Did you and Amy enjoy yerselves?'

'Enjoy meself! Me sides are still aching from laughing.'

'So are mine, Ken,' Amy said. 'It's been smashing. I've never seen anyone as funny as Mrs McDonough. She doesn't half make me laugh.'

Claire glanced at the Corkhills' house. There was no sign of Molly, and time was getting on. 'I feel mean not waiting to see Molly and thanking her for having us, but it's late for Amy to be up, so we'll head home and I'll call here through the week to see Molly and Nellie.'

'I'll be coming to Corker's tomorrow,' Derek said, 'so I'll explain to Molly. She won't mind. She isn't one to take offence easily.'

There was little Claire could do but introduce Derek. 'He's a friend of Mr Corkhill, and I've just found out he lives near us.'

Derek nodded. 'I'll walk home with yer. We can keep each other company. You and me can walk behind, Ken, and yer can tell me about yer job. I heard yer work with Phil?'

That was all Ken needed. Doreen's husband was Ken's hero: he really looked up to him. So he didn't find it hard talking about Phil to a man he'd only just met. Conversation between them flowed easily as the lad talked about his job, and Derek told of his love of the sea, and how he'd found it exciting visiting some of the most exotic countries in the world. 'The war was no picnic, though. Many's the time I thought me number was up.'

Walking ahead with her arm across her daughter's shoulders, Claire thought this was the night her son began to live the life of a boy who was nearly fifteen. And she prayed he would go forth and have a smooth journey into manhood.

They reached the corner of her street, and Claire said, 'This is where we part company. You don't have to come to the door with us – we'll be fine.'

Derek didn't want to push himself on them, so he nodded. 'I'll see yer around. Goodnight.'

It was when Claire was putting the key in the door that Ken said, 'I like Derek. He's what I call a man, like me dad was. Not like Mr Collins.'

Her hand still on the key in the lock, Claire looked over her shoulder. 'Ken, that's not a very nice thing to say.'

'I'm only saying what I think, Mam! Yer wouldn't want me to lie, would yer? I liked Derek, and I didn't like Mr Collins.'

Claire pushed the door open. 'Yer wouldn't be trying to matchmake, would yer, Ken? 'Cos yer'd be wasting yer time. I've already made up me mind not to see Mr Collins again, and tonight is the first time I've spoken to Derek.'

'Okay, Mam, I get yer drift. I won't mention it again.' But as he closed and bolted the door behind them, Ken was making up his mind to find out if Derek was married.

Back in the Corkhill house, Molly was staring at Corker in disbelief. 'Thirty people! Corker, it'll cost yer a fortune! And how do yer get the number to so many?'

'I want all me friends and family there, Molly, young and old. And Ellen agrees with me. We've never given a proper party before, and as we've got the money, we've decided to push the boat out. With the Bennetts, McDonoughs, Corkhills, Jacksons and Higginses, plus all the young ones at your house tonight, it comes to thirty. There was nobody I could leave out, Molly: I want everyone there. Derek and his ma are on the list, and with you saying you and Nellie are fond of Claire,

I've got her name on there as well. That makes it a nice round number.'

Gordon had been listening, and now he asked, 'Did yer say yer had all our mates down, Dad, and Ken?'

'All down, son, and if I think of anyone I've left off, I'm sure Edna Hanley would be able to squeeze them in.'

'Well, on yer own head be it, Corker,' Molly said. 'But depending on what yer want for the buffet, it's going to add up to a fair amount.'

Ellen passed another sheet of paper over. 'See what yer think, Molly. I've got pies and sausage rolls down, plus a variety of sandwiches and cakes. But if you and Edna come up with something different, then go ahead and order it. You've never been let down by the Hanleys regarding food, so we'll be guided by them.'

'Right, I'll see Edna tomorrow.' Molly was folding the two sheets of paper when she suddenly said, 'Oh, my God, I've forgotten about Claire! She'll think I'm a fine one leaving her standing outside.'

'She won't be there now, Auntie Molly,' Peter told her, ''cos I heard Derek say he'd walk them home.'

Molly breathed a sigh of relief. 'Thank goodness for that! Now I'll go and see if Ruthie's gone to bed, and if Jack has a hot cup of tea ready for his ever-loving wife.'

Corker saw her to the door. 'Tell Edna Hanley not to worry about the money side, I don't want her to spare anything. I'd like the do to be on a level with the parties you and Nellie have had there. And I'll make sure the drinks are delivered.'

'I'll let yer know tomorrow what she says. And I'll have a list of available dates for yer. Goodnight and God bless, Corker.'

He bent his huge frame to kiss her cheek. 'Goodnight and God bless, Molly, me darlin'.'

Chapter Twenty-Six

When Molly and Nellie arrived at the baker's shop on the Saturday morning, they found the shop bursting at the seams, with customers waiting outside to get in. Through the window Molly could see that Edna and her daughter Emily were rushed off their feet. 'It's no good waiting here, sunshine,' she said, 'we'd be here for ages. And I couldn't expect Edna to leave her customers long enough for me to tell her about Corker wanting to book her upstairs room. I think we'd be better doing the rest of our shopping and coming back here later, when it might not be so busy.'

'Suits me, girl, but yer'd better try and catch Edna's eye and remind her to put our bread aside, in case she's sold out by the time we get back.'

'Yeah, that's a good idea.' Molly stood in front of the window waiting to catch Edna's attention. She could see the woman was red in the face as she raced to serve impatient customers. Even over the noise, Molly could hear one irate shopper arguing that she was next to be served. And although it was only faint, she heard an equally irate Edna telling the woman, 'For heaven's sake, Rita, I've only got one pair of hands. I'll see to yer next, when I've sorted Ivy out. Just keep yer flipping hair on.'

Molly banged on the window and caught Edna's attention. Mouthing the words, she said, 'Keep our bread till we come back.' Then she could feel Nellie pulling on her dress, and knew without asking what she wanted. Once again she caught the shopkeeper's eye and lifted two fingers. 'Nellie's cakes.'

Even though she was run off her feet, Edna saw the funny side and lifted two fingers back, shouting, 'And the same to you.'

'Will she know what yer meant, girl?' Nellie asked, thinking of her Saturday morning treat of two cream slices, which she would eat before George and Paul came home from work. 'They'll be sold out by the time we come back.'

'She won't forget to put them away, sunshine, so don't be worrying.' Molly bent her arm for Nellie to link. 'Tell yer what, sunshine, I wouldn't have her job for a big clock. All those bad-tempered women wanting serving at the same time, I'd be telling them to get lost. And with it being a warm day, it must be like an oven in there.'

'I'd have her job any day.' Nellie had no doubts. 'Just think of all those cakes what yer could eat any time yer liked. That would be my idea of heaven.'

'That would be my idea of greed, Nellie McDonough. Yer'd be eating the cakes as they came out of the oven, and in no time yer'd be as big as a house. Yer wouldn't be looking for a dress to fit yer, it would be a tent.'

'I know I'd get fatter, girl, but just think of the fun I'd have on the way.'

'Can I ask yer who'd be the one baking the cakes fast enough for yer to eat them? Don't forget, if you had the shop, yer wouldn't have Edna and Emily serving, or Tom to make the cakes and bread yer love so much.'

'George could do what Tom does, easy-peasy. He'd be as happy as Larry in the bakery, and I'd be in heaven amongst the cakes.'

Molly glanced sideways. 'When we go back, why don't yer mention it to Edna? She's often told me she'd be glad to pack in. Tom has to be up about four in the morning to get the bread in the ovens, then he's got all those cakes to make. So I'm sure if yer said yer would be interested in buying the business, they'd be over the moon to sell it to yer. Mind you, they'd probably want a good price for the business 'cos they do a roaring trade.'

Nellie tilted her head sideways to look up at her friend. 'What are yer going on about, girl? I know I like cakes, but not enough to be getting out of me bed at all hours of the morning. So don't be getting carried away, and don't say nothing to Edna 'cos yer'll only end up making a fool of yerself. My George doesn't know one end of a loaf from another – he'd be hopeless in the bakery. Besides, where d'yer think we'd get the money from to buy the bleeding shop? It doesn't grow on ruddy trees, yer know.'

'And here was me thinking yer'd be made up at the idea of being a shop owner. Yer couldn't half do some swanking. And all the neighbours that yer don't like, yer could sell the stale bread to. Yer'd like that, wouldn't yer?'

Laughter rumbled in Nellie's tummy. 'Ay, I've just had a smashing thought, girl. Say I did buy the shop, and Elsie Flanaghan came in for a loaf one day. She wouldn't half get a shock if she saw me behind the counter. Ooh, I can just imagine the look on her face.'

'I don't think yer'd get a chance to see her face, sunshine, 'cos one look at you and she'd be out of that shop like a bat out of hell.'

When they were nearing the butcher's shop, Molly pulled them to a halt. 'Listen, Nellie, if I tell yer something, and then ask for yer advice, will yer promise yer won't breathe a word to a living soul?'

'Okay, girl, I won't tell a living soul. But I might go down to the cemetery and tell a few of the poor souls in there.'

'This is not funny, Nellie, so keep yer jokes to yerself till after I've got something off me chest. Now are yer going to behave yerself, or shall I ask someone else for advice?'

'I'm the best one to advise yer, girl, 'cos I'm the only one here. I'm not very clever, but I'm better than any port in a storm.'

Molly looked puzzled. Surely her mate had got that the wrong way round? Still, there was no time to worry about that now. 'Yer know I've got the list that Ellen gave me to show to Edna? Well, there's someone not on the list who you and me always invite to parties. Now, I don't know whether Ellen and Corker have decided not to ask them, or whether they've just slipped up. And I don't know whether to mention it to Ellen, or leave well alone.'

'Who've they left out, girl?'

'Maisie and Alec from the corner shop. I don't know whether to mention it or not. What d'yer think I should do, sunshine?'

Nellie's eyes disappeared and her mouth was making queer shapes. 'Ooh, that's a hard one, girl, I have to say. We always ask them because they've always been good to us and they're like best friends. But I don't know if Corker and Ellen know them as well as we do.' The little woman scratched her head. 'I wouldn't like to say, girl, so I'm afraid ye're on yer own this time. Wait until we get in the butcher's and see how yer feel then.'

'There's nothing else I can do.' Molly sighed. 'I'll take things as they come.'

When they entered the butcher's shop they were greeted with a smile from Tony and Ellen. There were a few customers waiting to be served, but it was only a matter of a few minutes before they were both standing in front of the counter. 'I'll serve them, Tony,' Ellen said. 'You go and make yerself a cup of tea. I'll give yer a shout if we have a stampede.'

'I hate to miss anything,' Tony laughed, 'so before I go and make me tea I'll ask Nellie if she's got any news for me?'

'Oh, yeah, I have, Tony.' Nellie's shoulders went back and her bosom and tummy stood to attention. 'Me and my husband, George, well, we are going to buy Hanley's cake shop.'

Nellie's face was so serious, Tony looked at Molly. 'What's this? I haven't heard anything about the Hanleys selling up.'

'No, neither have the Hanleys, Tony, so don't think ye're missing out on anything.' Molly's wink was exaggerated. 'It's all in me mate's head. She was swooning before at the very thought of owning the cake shop. George in the bakery sweating cobs to get the bread and cakes made, and Nellie eating the cakes as quick as he could bake them. I don't think the idea will take off, mind. It's wishful thinking on Nellie's part.'

'I never mentioned nothing about buying the bleeding shop!' Nellie was on her high horse. 'It was you what brought it up, and the only bit I had anything to do with was me mouth watering every time yer mentioned the cakes. But the rest was all your doing, Molly Bennett, so don't be bringing me into it.'

Tony leaned on the counter and said softly, 'Ay, Nellie, if you and your feller ever think of going into business, come and see me. It's a good little business this, and George could be eating lamb chops until they come out of his ears.'

'There's an easy solution to this, yer know,' Ellen said. 'Yer could buy both shops, Nellie, and George could have his lamb chops, and you'd have as many cream slices as yer heart desired. So yer'd have a main course and a dessert every day of yer life.'

Nellie put her basket down, then flung her arms wide. 'Oh, for a life of bliss, with a cream slice after every meal.' Her eyes went towards the ceiling. 'Are yer listening, Saint Peter? If I'm coming to you eventually, then make a note. Helen Theresa McDonough requests a seat on the front row, a halo and a harp.

And for good behaviour an unlimited supply of cakes. But the cakes must be from Hanley's, no others will do.'

'What happens if Edna Hanley goes before you, sunshine?' Molly asked. 'Or haven't yer thought of that?'

'Yer've got a point there, girl.' Nellie's chins were very much in agreement on this. 'She's very hardworking, is Edna; she could well go before me. But if she was inconsiderate enough to beat me to it, well, I'd kill her with me own bare hands.' And when her audience of three doubled up with laughter, she couldn't make out what she'd said that was so funny.

Two customers came in then, and Ellen put on a sad face. 'Ye're too late now, Tony. Yer've missed out on yer cup of tea. I'll serve Molly and Nellie, while you attend to Mrs Sloan and Mrs Ashcroft.'

'I want three chops, Ellen,' Molly said. 'And pick nice lean ones with plenty of meat on them. And I'll have six beef sausages as well.'

'Ooh, are yer having chops, girl?' Nellie opened her eyes as wide as she could to show surprise. 'That's funny, 'cos I was about to ask for the same. And sausages, as well! It just goes to show that great minds think alike.'

'I thought I heard yer say yer were having liver today, and stew for tomorrow? I must be hearing things, sunshine.' Molly tried to stare her friend out, to make her blush for telling fibs, but the face staring back at her was the picture of innocence. 'Okay, it's not you telling lies, it's me what's going hard of hearing.'

Ellen jerked her head sideways, inviting Molly to move down the counter. 'Have yer been able to see Edna Hanley yet?'

Molly shook her head. 'We couldn't get in the shop, the queue was outside. Me and Nellie are going back later when the rush is over for our bread.'

'I'm glad yer haven't talked to her yet, 'cos I've got the numbers wrong. I forgot to put Maisie and Alec on the list, and it's worried me all night. I don't know how I came to forget them, but I'm going to blame Corker for expecting me to have the lists ready so quickly. He's no patience, has my husband: when he thinks of something it has to be done right away. So will yer stick their names on for me, Molly, there's an angel?'

Molly felt a sense of relief, as though a burden had been lifted from her heart. It was daft to worry so much, but she'd never forgotten the kindness and help she and Nellie had got from Maisie and Alec during the war years. And they were still good to them, adding extra biscuits, or the odd slice of boiled ham.

'Are they lean enough for yer, Molly?' Ellen was holding out a piece of greaseproof paper to display three nice, meaty chops. 'There's plenty on them.'

'Mmm, they look very tasty, Ellen. They'll do nicely.'

As Ellen went to fold the paper over, Nellie piped up, 'Don't wrap them up yet, girl. I want to make sure my three are exactly the same size and weight. It was me what first thought of chops, so I should really have first choice.'

Molly gasped. 'You cheeky article! Yer'd never mentioned chops until I did!'

'I did too!' Nellie stepped back and stood with feet apart and eyes narrowed. 'I thought of them at half past eleven last night, when I was lying in bed.'

With her hand clamped over her mouth, Molly closed her eyes. She was telling herself not to say what she was thinking, or she'd live to regret it. But she couldn't keep the words back. 'When me and Jack went to bed last night, we thought it was quiet. Were yer so wrapped up in thinking of chops, George did the dirty on yer and went to sleep?'

Nellie tried to put a look of disgust on her face. 'Ha, ha, very funny, girl. But I work quicker than you, smarty pants. My George didn't go to sleep until I was ready for him to go to sleep. I'm not like you and Jack, yer know, I don't hang around. I'd had—' Nellie's eyes widened as a hand covered her mouth and cut off her speech.

'All right, sunshine, I know what ye're going to say, so save yer breath. And save Mrs Sloan and Mrs Ashcroft the embarrassment of having to listen to what yer do in private.'

Nellie pushed her hand away. 'How do you know what Mrs Sloan and Mrs Ashcroft would like or wouldn't like? They might not be miserable stick-in-the-muds like you, so there!'

'Oh, we are stick-in-the-muds, Nellie,' Nancy Sloan said quickly. 'Me and Tessie have got no sense of humour. Particularly over something as private as the bedroom. We're regular churchgoers, yer see.' Nancy took her change from Tony, dropped it into her pocket, then grabbed her friend's arm. 'Come on, Tessie. We've still got to get our potatoes and veg.'

Nellie had a sharp retort on her lips, but once again Molly's hand covered her mouth until the two ladies were out of the shop. 'What did yer do that for, girl? I was going to say something to Nancy and Tessie.'

'Yes, I know yer were, sunshine; that's why I stopped yer. The ladies wouldn't appreciate your sense of humour, or an account of yer antics in bed.'

'That's where ye're wrong, see!' Nellie poked her tongue out. 'I wasn't going to tell them anything about me bedroom.'

'What were yer going to say to them, then? Were yer going to say yer hoped they had a nice day?'

Nellie shook her head slowly, to give her chins a chance to get into step. 'No, I wasn't going to say anything about the day. What I had in mind, if you hadn't been so ruddy quick off the mark, was to remind them to go to confession tonight. Yer see, just 'cos someone mentions their bedroom, it doesn't automatically follow that they've been doing what comes naturally, does it? So they are two bad-minded so-and-sos. And as it's a sin to think bad about someone when it isn't true, they deserve to get a penance of six Hail Marys, and a lecture off Father Kelly.'

'Don't get carried away, Nellie, 'cos you really are not in a position to criticise anyone. If Father Kelly had heard what yer've just said, he'd have laughed his socks off.'

'No, he wouldn't, yer see, 'cos me and Father Kelly have an agreement. As long as I don't take up too much of his time in the confessional box, and I finish off by telling him a joke what he can repeat to Father Ryan, then he'll stick to giving me six Hail Marys and no lecture.'

Molly shook her head at Ellen and Tony. 'The funny thing is, Nellie firmly believes she'll end up in heaven. She's broken most of the Ten Commandments to my knowledge, but for some unknown reason she thinks Saint Peter will forgive her 'cos he's her mate. That's the funny part, but the not-so-funny part is she thinks she's going to get a seat next to mine! As though I won't have had enough of her down here!'

Nellie's grin was wide. 'She's only pulling yer leg, 'cos she loves me really and wouldn't know what to do without me.' She rubbed her chubby hands together. 'She loves me so much, if you try to palm me off with chops what are smaller than hers, she'll do a swap and give me the big ones.'

'She doesn't need to,' Tony said, walking down the counter towards them. 'I've found three just as big. They're so alike yer wouldn't be able to tell them apart. So there'll be no reason to fight over whose chops have the most meat on.'

'Put them down, and go and make a pot of tea, there's a good lad.' Ellen jerked her head towards the back room. 'There's a packet of biscuits in me basket. Yer can put a couple on a plate for me when yer bring me cup of tea through.'

'That's what I call a good boss,' Molly said when Tony walked through to the stock room. 'But then again, he's got a good worker in you.' She tilted her head. 'How long have yer worked here now, Ellen?'

'Me and Tony were only talking about it this morning. It's five years. The reason I know is because it was the end of the war, remember? Nobby was out celebrating VE Day when he got knocked over by a tram. Not that he needed an excuse to get drunk; he was seldom sober. But it was when he was in hospital and we had no money coming in that I got the job here. And it was all down to you and Nellie. Left to meself, I wouldn't have had the strength to go after a job, or the courage. God knows what my life would have been like but for you two. And I dread to think of what would have happened to the kids.' She smiled from one to the other. 'You two made me do me hair, got me a decent dress to wear, and dragged me down here. And in doing so, yer gave me me pride back.'

Nellie, who always acted tough, as though she wouldn't care if her backside was on fire, sniffed. 'Don't say any more, girl, 'cos I haven't got me hanky with me. Me and Molly were glad to help, so let's leave it at that, eh? Right, Molly?'

'Right, sunshine. And now Ellen will finish serving us and we can get the rest of our shopping in before making our way back to Hanley's. There's not a lot of panic, but I do like to have the dinner on the go when Jack and Ruthie come in from work.'

Ellen began to wrap the chops and sausages, saying, 'Will yer let me know what Edna has to say? And don't forget to add the two names on.'

'I doubt if I'll make it back here, Ellen, 'cos after I've been to Hanley's I'll have to dash home to get the dinner on. And once that's over and everything washed and cleared away, then I want to do the rounds of the family. I see Doreen and Jill every day, and the babies, but I haven't been to me ma's for a few days, and they'll think I've forgotten them. But I'll give yer a knock tonight with all the information. Say about seven o'clock, when yer've got yer dinner over and tidied up. Will that be all right?'

'That's fine, Molly. Ye're an angel for seeing to Hanley's for us.'

'I'll come with yer tonight to see yer ma,' Nellie said, a woebegone expression on her face. 'Save me sitting talking to meself while George reads the ruddy paper inside out.'

It was a look Molly couldn't refuse. 'Okay, sunshine. Yer can keep me company while I do the rounds. Now let's pay Ellen and be on our merry way.'

'Thirty-two people?' Edna Hanley pulled a face. 'That would be pushing it a bit, Molly. I don't believe we've got that many chairs up there.'

'Eight of them are youngsters, Edna – they wouldn't care if they had to share seats as long as they were there. Anyway, we could always lend yer half a dozen chairs, no problem.'

'I'll get Tom to check them tomorrow, see how many we've got. Now for dates. I've got a few weddings booked in, but if I give yer the dates I've got free, that would be the easiest way of doing it. Let's see now. There's a Saturday free three weeks tonight, another in five weeks and the next is eight weeks off. I'll jot the dates down for yer, and yer can see what Ellen and Corker say. Now, what do they want for the buffet?'

'I think they were hoping you'd help them with that, as ye're used to catering. What would you suggest?'

'I've got a menu you can take with yer to show them. It's only something I've written out, it's nothing posh. But it'll give them an idea. It's got thirty shillings a head written on it, but with there being youngsters, and 'cos ye're good customers, I'm sure Tom would agree to twenty-five bob a head. That will include pots of tea, but yer'll have to sort yer own drinks out.

We'll supply the records as usual, and with it being Sunday the next day, yer know yer'll have to be off the premises before midnight.' Edna closed the large black book. 'I think that's about it, Molly, so see what they have to say and let me know first thing Monday morning so I can fill the date in.'

'Thanks, Edna. That all sounds fine to me. What do you think, sunshine?'

'I think it's just the job, girl, just the job!' Nellie was nodding as though she'd just agreed to a very important deal. 'Can't wait for it.'

'I'm afraid yer'll have to wait, sunshine, unless yer can talk Edna into letting yer stay here until the night of the party. You could always get behind the counter and help her serve.'

Edna Hanley had her first real laugh of what had been a very busy, and very hot, day. 'Oh, Molly, can yer just picture it? Nellie in an apron that fitted where it touched, and giving daggers to anyone wanting to buy a cream slice? In fact she'd probably hide the tray under the counter and tell customers we'd none left.' There came another bout of laughter before she said, 'By the end of the first day, she'd have insulted every one of me customers, and sent them off with a flea in their ear.'

Nellie looked proper put out. 'No I wouldn't! Not all of them, anyway. Only the ones what I don't like.'

'Nellie,' Molly said, clicking her tongue, 'that would include half the people who live round here.' Then suddenly Molly seemed to come to life. 'Ay, Edna, on second thoughts Nellie could possibly bring yer more custom than yer could cope with. When the women in the neighbourhood heard Nellie was serving here, they'd be round like a shot to witness the fights. She'd be great entertainment value, 'cos they'd come from as far afield as the Pier Head to Seaforth docks. Particularly if they knew the time Elsie Flanaghan came in for her loaf. Yer'd have all the women getting their housework done very early, so they could spend the rest of the day outside this shop being entertained for nothing.'

Edna raised her brows and pursued her lips. 'I think yer might have something there, Molly. It would put a bit of excitement into me life. All I'd have to do is put a chair behind the counter and let the fun begin.' She nodded her head slowly. 'Yeah, I'll mention it to Tom tonight when we're having our meal. The only thing is, though, being in the bakery every morning, he'd miss half the fun, and that might influence his thinking.'

'Excuse me,' Nellie said, leaning on the counter, 'but do I get a say in this? Before yer say anything to yer husband, let me tell yer what me terms are. I don't put on shows for nothing, yer know. As a highly professional entertainer, I would expect a reasonable fee from yer, plus as many cream slices a day as I could eat. Now those are my terms, so yer can take it or leave it.'

'Far be it from me to interfere,' Molly said, 'but I can get yer a better deal than that, Edna. I could arrange for Nellie to trip up one of the women she doesn't like, right outside yer shop. Yer'd get the publicity and it wouldn't cost yer a penny.'

'Since when have you been my manager, girl?' Nellie was still leaning on the counter and she had to half turn her body to look up at her mate. 'I'd never get to be famous with you telling folk I'll trip people up for nothing. And I wouldn't trip anyone up, either.' After a few seconds her chubby fingers began to tap on the counter. 'Well, perhaps there's one or two who I'd like to see with a flat face. But if it ever comes to pass, Edna Hanley, I want two free cream slices.'

'Ah, that's nice of yer to think of treating Molly to a cake.'

It didn't take Nellie long to be upstanding. 'What d'yer mean, treat Molly to a cake? She might be me best mate what loves the bones of me, but not where cream slices are concerned. If she wants one, let her trip someone up for a change.'

'Ooh, look at the time,' Molly said, glancing at the clock on the wall. 'Come on, sunshine, let's put our skates on. I'll see Corker tonight, Edna, and let yer know first thing on Monday morning.'

'Ask him if there's any invites going,' Edna called after her. 'I've always promised meself to come to one of your parties, but I've never had the nerve to ask.'

Molly turned round. 'There was nothing to stop yer joining in, Edna. We would have been made up to have yer. After all, it's your room we're in. And I'm sure Corker wouldn't mind yer coming up and sharing the fun. Because we've had loads of fun in that room upstairs. Not that I need to tell yer that – yer must hear it for yerself.'

'I know, that's why I'm cadging an invite! I'm fed up hearing the laughter and cheering, and never hearing the joke! But if yer think it sounds cheeky, don't mention it to Corker.'

'I'll ask him in a nice way, sunshine, don't worry.'

Nellie nodded. 'My mate's very good at asking people in a nice way. It's the way she does it that counts, and it shows she was well brought up. She wouldn't trip anyone up, even if she hated the sight of them.'

There was a loud gasp from Molly. 'Even if I hated them? Nellie, there's no one in the whole wide world that I hate. There may be a few I wouldn't choose to be friends with, but I don't hate them.'

'Yer did hate somebody once, girl, I remember.'

'And who was that, Nellie?'

Nellie looked smug. 'Adolf Hitler. Yer hated him, and don't try saying yer didn't 'cos yer told me yer would strangle him if yer could get yer hands on him. That's when the war was on, and Steve, Phil and Tommy were in the army.'

Molly looked back at Edna and shrugged her shoulders. 'There's no answer to that, is there? And I may as well tell yer, before my mate does, that there was a time during the war when I wondered how to get in touch with Mr Churchill, so I could suggest to him that Nellie would make an ideal secret weapon.'

'Oh, yeah, I remember that, and yer—' Nellie didn't get any further, for she was literally yanked off her feet. But not to be outdone, when she was standing on the pavement with Molly, she shouted in, 'I'll tell yer the rest next time I see yer. Me mate seems to be in a hurry right now, so I won't upset her any more 'cos I hate to see a grown woman cry.'

After Edna had waved them off, she went into the bakery where her husband was busy washing the ovens and baking tins. 'Jimmy Corkhill is booking the room upstairs for a party one Saturday night. All the gang are coming, the Bennetts, the McDonoughs and the rest. And if yer remember at their last party, when Lily McDonough got married, I vowed I'd go to the next one they had. So, after I've seen to everything, I'm going to doll meself up and join them.'

Tom threw the wet cloth back into the water. 'Yer can't just walk in and join a party, love, no matter how much yer'd like to. They're customers. They'll be paying to use the room and they won't expect you to invite yerself.'

'Oh, I know that, light of my life – that's why I've asked Molly to ask for me. For the last four or five years, my one ambition in life has been to go to one of their parties. I'm fed up listening to the laughter and jollification. I want to be part of it. I don't think it's too much to ask, do you?'

'No, it isn't, love, I agree. And I hope yer get the invitations.' Tom narrowed his eyes. 'Did yer notice I said invitations, which means yer take me with yer?'

'It hadn't gone unnoticed, my love, so we'll both have to

keep our fingers crossed. Molly's coming in early Monday morning with the date and details of the buffet.' Edna turned to go back into the shop, and said over her shoulder, 'Oh, and without you and me, there'll be thirty-two to cater for.' She hurried away before the flood of questions started. What was the use of worrying about being overcrowded when the people having the party wouldn't care if they had to sit on the floor? And if there was going to be anything to worry about, it could keep until Monday. She was talking to herself as she walked into the shop, 'The only thing I'll worry about is not being invited. Even that won't stop me, 'cos I'll gatecrash.'

There was a strange look on her daughter's face. 'Mam, am I hearing things, or were you just talking to yerself?'

'Was I, love? I couldn't tell yer, 'cos I was too busy listening to what I was saying.' She grinned. 'Don't worry, Emily, I don't think it's time to send for the men in white coats. Not for a while, anyway.'

Chapter Twenty-Seven

'This basket's not half heavy, girl, me arm's dropping off.' Nellie was red in the face and the perspiration rolled down her forehead. 'We should have got the spuds in yesterday, and made life easier for ourselves.'

'I'm sorry I can't help yer, sunshine, but my basket's just as heavy, and there's no way I could carry both.' Molly gave a smile of encouragement. 'Not far now, we're nearly home.'

They turned the corner into their street, and Molly was surprised to see Corker walking ahead of them. 'Oh, I forgot it's only half day Saturday. I can give Corker the list now, save calling tonight.' She put her free hand to the side of her mouth, and shouted, 'Corker, hang on, I've got something for yer.'

Ever the gallant gentleman, Corker hurried towards them and relieved them of their baskets. 'Let me give yer a hand, ladies.'

'Ooh, thanks, Corker, ye're a godsend,' Nellie told him. 'It weighs a ton, that ruddy basket. Look, that arm is six inches longer than the other.'

The big man chortled. 'Did yer not think of swapping over now and again, to spread the weight a bit? Then each of yer arms would be three inches longer.'

'It's too bleeding hot to think, Corker. But next time I'm weighed down I'll remember what yer said.'

'I've got all the information off Edna Hanley for yer, Corker,' Molly said. 'Dates available, menu for the buffet, and the charge. So if yer want to come in for a minute I can let yer have them, and you and Ellen can see what yer think.' She took the front door key from her pocket, then said, 'Would yer be an angel and help Nellie into her house with her basket? If yer put mine down, I'll manage to take it through to the kitchen.'

'No, that's all right, Corker,' Nellie was quick to say. 'I'll come in with Molly and yer can carry it home for me when I leave.'

'Oh, no, yer don't, sunshine,' Molly said from the top step. 'I've got no time to stand talking, 'cos Jack and Ruthie will be in soon. While Corker's looking at the list, I'll be putting me sausages on.' Molly raised her eyes to the sky. 'Don't be giving me that forlorn look, either, 'cos it won't work right now. I'll be seeing yer tonight, and if there's anything to tell, I'll tell yer then. So off yer go, sunshine, and get the dinner ready for yer family.'

As she turned towards her house, her head hung low, Corker heard her muttering, 'Calls herself a friend! Some ruddy friend she is. The trouble with her is she's man mad. Can't wait to get Corker on his own. I feel sorry for him – he doesn't stand a chance. I bet she puts the sausages on as fast as she can, so when he goes back there she can have her wicked way with him before Jack comes in.'

With her basket in one of his huge hands, Corker put an arm across her shoulder. 'Nellie, me darlin', I've never been that lucky in me life.'

She twisted her neck to look up at him. 'Well, yer ship might have come in today, Corker. If I see yer coming out of her house with a smile on yer face, I'll tell Ellen on yer.'

Corker took Nellie's front door key from her. 'Let me open the door for yer, me darlin', and I'll take the basket through to yer kitchen.' He placed the heavy basket on the draining board, put a serious expression on his face and bent down so their eyes were on a level. 'Nellie, me darlin', if I come out of Molly's with a smile on me face, I'll give yer a knock.'

Nellie's body shook with laughter. 'Ooh, it won't be no good knocking here, Corker. I wouldn't have time to broaden that smile, 'cos George and Paul will be in any minute. Catch me another time, eh?'

'Ooh, I doubt that. For if Jack doesn't kill me, me wife definitely will.'

Nellie walked behind him to the door. 'I'm not a snitch, lad, so yer secret will be safe with me. I'll snitch on Molly, though, after she turned me away from her door.'

'Didn't I hear Molly telling yer to get the sausages on for yer husband's dinner? I bet when I go in her house I'll smell the sausages and hear them sizzling away.'

'Okay, Corker, I get the point. Before yer put yer foot on Molly's step, my sausages will be in the frying pan. They won't be smelling or sizzling, but they'll be in the frying pan, so at least when George comes in I'll have shown willing.'

The big man was grinning when he walked into Molly's. 'Don't ask me to tell yer why, but make sure I don't go out of here with a smile on me face.'

Molly frowned. 'I don't understand. What do yer mean?' Then she shook her head. 'It's that mate of mine, isn't it?' Then she lifted an open hand. 'No, don't answer that, Corker, 'cos I know I'll end up with a face the colour of beetroot.'

'I was pulling yer leg, Molly, for yer mate didn't say a word out of place. But she has a way with words that nobody else has. Harmless, but funny.'

'Sit yerself down, Corker, and yer can look at the menu while I see to the sausages. My husband is a very easy-going man, but when it comes to food, he has one hate. He can't stand burnt sausages.'

After a few minutes, Corker came to stand at the kitchen door. 'The menu seems fine, I couldn't fault it. And the charge is fair enough. I can't see Ellen disagreeing, either, so as far as I'm concerned we can go ahead.'

'Edna's reduced the charge to twenty-five bob, Corker, 'cos I told her there were youngsters coming, and she took into account we are good customers.'

Corker pulled on his beard. 'That's good of her, I must say. I know she'll put a good table on for us. She always has done for your weddings.'

Molly turned the sausages over before asking, 'Would yer think I was cheeky if I asked a favour of yer?'

'After all the favours yer've done for me and Ellen over the years, Molly, you can have anything yer ask for.'

'Well, it's not for me personally, Corker, it's for Edna Hanley. Yer see, she told me today that the one ambition in her life has been to come to one of our parties. She said she's had to listen to the laughter and singing, and has always been jealous. And she has been very good to my family, when the girls got married, and our Tommy, so I wondered if yer'd mind if she showed her face at your party?'

Corker's blue eyes twinkled. 'Molly, me darlin', yer can tell Edna it would be a pleasure to have her and her husband at the party. They'll both be very welcome.' Again he pulled on his beard. 'In fact perhaps it would be nice if I called in the shop one day and invited her and Tom. What do yer say?'

'That would be lovely, Corker. She'd be so pleased.'

'What would be lovely?' Jack asked, coming in from the hall. 'And who would be so pleased?'

Corker slapped Jack on the back, nearly knocking him over. 'We're all fixed up for the party, me old mate, so it's all systems go. It's either three weeks tonight or five weeks, but I'll check that with Ellen when she comes in. And to answer yer question, the person who would be so pleased is Edna Hanley. Her and Tom are now on the guest list.'

Ruthie had come in unnoticed, and heard the last part of the conversation. 'What guest list, Uncle Corker? Is someone getting married?'

'No, me darlin', no one is getting married.' His hands spanned her slim waist and she was lifted high. 'Me and yer Auntie Ellen are giving a party for all our friends and neighbours.'

She looked down into his bright blue eyes. 'Am I going to be invited? I'm both a friend and a neighbour?'

'Of course yer are, and yer friend Bella. It goes without saying that my children will be there, and yer friends Johnny and Jeff. It'll be a grand party, with all our friends, and we'll have a wonderful time.'

The girl's face was aglow as she pulled on the end of his bushy moustache. 'Thank you, Uncle Corker, and as me grandma would say, it's a fine figure of a man yer are, to be sure. I know it will be a fantastic party, and it's given me something to look forward to. Will yer put me down now, so I can go and tell Bella? She'll be thrilled to bits.'

Molly came through wiping her hands down her pinny. 'I'll agree to Corker putting you down, sunshine, but not about yer going to Bella's. Yer'll be seeing her later, so yer can tell her then. But don't get too excited 'cos we haven't got a definite date yet.'

'I'll have to get a new dress for it, Mam. I've got nothing good enough for a party.'

'There's plenty of time, sunshine. And the way yer said that, anyone would think yer didn't have a stitch to yer back.'

'Well, I'm sure yer wouldn't want a daughter of yours to look frumpy, would yer, Mam? Think what people would say.'

'She's fourteen, Corker, and acts like twenty-four.'

'Mam, I'm fourteen years, nine months and five days. So as I'm fed up telling yer, I'm nearer fifteen than fourteen.'

'She's got a point,' Corker said, while thinking this youngest daughter of Molly's was going to be as headstrong as Doreen was at her age. It was falling in love with Phil that had changed Doreen into the loving, caring wife and mother she was now. 'She is just like Doreen was at this stage.'

'Well she certainly doesn't take after Jill, that's for sure.' Molly opened a drawer in the sideboard and brought out a white tablecloth. 'And I have to say me and Jack have given in to Ruthie far more than we did with the two girls and Tommy. It's with her being the youngest, I suppose, and the only one left at home.'

'Tommy and Jill were the least trouble,' Jack said. 'Never answered us back or gave cheek. Nor did they ask for something they knew we couldn't afford.'

Ruthie was digesting every word. 'I don't give yer cheek, Mam, do I? I'm not as quiet as our Jill, I know that, or as nice and gentle as she is. I love our Jill, but we can't all be alike, can we, or it would be very dull.'

Molly was worrying about her sausages in the frying pan, and decided it was better to be thought rude than dish hard, burnt sausages to a man just come home from work. 'I'll leave yer for a minute to take the pan off the stove, but you carry on, Corker. I know yer were about to say something when I interrupted.'

'That's all right, Molly, me darlin', you see to the dinner. I was going to say to yer, Ruthie, that Doreen has changed a lot since she was your age. And that's because she met the man of her dreams. And one day, darlin', you'll meet a boy who yer'll love enough to marry, and that's when the three Bennett sisters will not only be the most beautiful girls in the street, but the most kind and caring.' He chucked her under the chin. 'And ye're fourteen years, nine months and five days towards meeting that boy.'

Molly came in from the kitchen determined the dinner wasn't going to be ruined. 'I'm sorry to interrupt again, but it's getting urgent now.' She gave the tablecloth a shake before throwing it across the table. 'When the sausages start to tell yer they'll jump out of the frying pan if I don't get a move on, then yer know it's time to move.'

Corker's guffaw ricocheted from wall to wall. 'A nod is as good as a wink to a blind man, Molly, so I'll love yer and leave yer. Sometime tomorrow I'll let yer have the date, and a deposit to secure the room.'

Standing on tiptoe, Molly put her arms round his neck and kissed his cheek. 'The size of me to be throwing a giant like you out. But it's you or the sausages, and I'm afraid the sausages have won.'

'Ay, Mam, don't you be kissing strange men,' Ruthie said, tutting like an old lady. 'What will the neighbours say? Particularly Auntie Nellie, who's peeping at yer through the window.'

Molly's hand flew to her mouth, for it was the sort of trick her mate would pull. Then she saw Ruthie winking at her dad. 'I fell for that, sunshine, hook, line and sinker. Yer really had me going there.'

'Well, I'm on me way now, me darlin', so I'll tell Nellie I got a kiss from yer, but it was with the approval of yer husband.'

Molly could tell her daughter had something on her mind by the way she was wriggling on her chair. 'What are you after, sunshine? The sooner yer come out with it, the sooner the poor chair will have a bit of peace.'

Ruthie tried to look innocent but wasn't very good at it. 'Nothing much, Mam, only I was wondering if your friend Mrs Thompson was being invited to the party?'

Well, the little minx, Molly was thinking. She couldn't care less whether Claire is invited, it's Ken she's interested in. But let's see if she blushes. 'Don't yer mean is Ken being invited? That's what yer really want to know, isn't it?'

Ruthie didn't blush, she grinned. 'It would be no good lying to yer, Mam, 'cos yer know me too well. Yeah, I was wondering if Ken would be invited.'

'Why is that, love?' Jack asked. 'Yer hardly know the lad, and I don't think Corker knows him from Adam. So why would yer think he'd be invited?'

It was Molly who answered. 'Because Ken is the new heart-throb, love, just to bring yer up to date with yer daughter's romances. Ken's a novelty because he's new on the scene, but eventually he'll join the line of Gordon, Jeff, and Johnny. You have a very fickle daughter, Jack: she can't make up her mind. Not like Bella, who's a one-man woman. It's always been Peter for her, and I believe her feelings are reciprocated.'

Jack laughed. 'Ay, love, we'll get back to our daughter's friends in a minute. But before I forget that word, which I can't get me tongue round, why don't yer try it out on Nellie tomorrow? I'd love to see her face if yer came out with that mouthful.'

'Well, first of all, love, I would have to wait for the opportunity to fit the word in. I mean it's not one of yer everyday words, is it? But I'll tell yer what would happen if I did use it on her. She would hang her head, giving herself time to think if she'd ever heard it before and what it meant. But she wouldn't give up and ask. She'd wait until the time was right, then try in a roundabout way to get it out of me. When that didn't work, she'd ask me why I didn't talk like what everybody else did? Then she'd tell me to throw the bleeding dictionary away 'cos she was fed up having a mate what talked in a foreign language.'

'Auntie Nellie's not the only stupid one, Mam,' Ruthie

admitted. 'I haven't a clue what yer meant when yer were talking about Bella and Peter.'

'Oh dear, oh dear! I've always said yer were another Nellie McDonough in the making. But you've not long left school, and yer had a good report from the headmistress, so yer should know what reciprocate means.'

The girl's eyes were dancing with mischief. 'Oh, I know what reciprocate means, Mam. It was what yer meant by Bella being a one-man woman.'

'Ay, ay,' Jack said, 'before we get away from the subject, can yer tell me about these boys yer have lined up? We've told yer, ye're far too young to be having boyfriends, even though they are all decent boys and come from good families. Except Ken, of course, who we know very little about.'

Before Jack could bat an eye, Ruthie had pushed her chair back, picked up her plate with her knife and fork, and disappeared into the kitchen. 'Mam, will yer tell me dad about Ken, and how he does come from a good family?' She raised her voice so they could hear over the sound of running water. 'And will yer also remind him that you were only my age when he first set eyes on yer? I do like Gordon, Johnny, Jeff and Ken, but it doesn't mean I'm going to marry them.'

'Seeing as ye're shouting loud enough for the neighbours to hear yer, I don't think I need to repeat it to yer dad. And, seeing as he's got a grin on his face, I think it's safe for yer to come back in here now.'

'Is the coast clear, then?'

'Yes, sunshine, I think yer can say the coast is clear. There may be a small dark cloud hovering over the Pier Head, but I'm sure you can chase it away, and satisfy your worried father, by answering just one simple question.'

'Don't ask me a question on history, Dad, 'cos that was my worst subject.'

Molly was shaking her head and mouthing, 'Tell her it's not history.'

'No, sweetheart, it's not history.'

'I'm not very good on geography, either, Dad.' There was a hint of laughter in Ruthie's voice. 'That was my second worst subject.'

Once again Molly was shaking her head, but she didn't need words this time. Jack called, 'No, it's not geography either, love.'

A beaming Ruthie came in from the kitchen. 'In that case, I'm on safe ground, 'cos I was near top of the class in all the other subjects.'

Molly waved her daughter to a chair. 'I'm going to ask yer the question, sunshine, but I'm only doing it for yer dad. Say, just for instance, Gordon or Ken asked yer to go to the pictures with them one night, what would yer do?'

'Well, I'd ask you and Auntie Mary if we could go first.'

'But Bella hasn't been asked, only you. Would yer go?'

'Yer mean leave Bella on her own, while I go out with one of the boys?'

'That's right, sunshine.'

Ruthie huffed. 'That's a daft question, isn't it? I wouldn't go, of course, 'cos I wouldn't leave Bella. She's me best friend. I wouldn't let her down for some lad.'

Molly smiled. 'I know that, sunshine, and I think yer've put yer dad's mind at rest now. Yer see, all fathers worry about their children, especially girls. And I think all these boys hanging around frighten him a bit. Like they would any loving parent. He is no different to my ma and da when I was your age.'

Ruthie went and put her arms round Jack's neck. 'Yer don't have to worry about me, Dad. I'm not daft, even though I sometimes act it. But me and Bella go everywhere together. She comes before any of the lads.' She chuckled into his ear. 'It won't always be like that, though, Dad, 'cos this time next year I'll be fifteen years, nine months and five days towards being sixteen. That's the age me mam was when yer first took her out. After being looked over by me grandma and granda, of course. Me and Bella will always be best mates, but I think we'll be old enough to go to the pictures, or a dance, on our own with a boy. What d'yer think me chances are of that happening, Dad?'

He stroked the slim firm arms of his youngest child. 'I think yer'd be in with a good chance, as long as me and yer mam can sit in the row behind yer at the pictures. Anyway, I'll have a year to think about that, love. And when you are ready to go steady with a boy, I only hope that, like yer two sisters and yer brother, it's someone we'll be happy to welcome into the family.'

She took her arms away so she could look him in the face. 'Dad, I'll make sure he's someone who will fit in. Someone who will have my family's approval, me Auntie Nellie's, and Uncle Corker's. I could go on, of course, and say he'll have to be someone who me grandma and granda approve of, as well! Blimey, if he has to walk the plank, he'll chuck me before we get any further than Auntie Nellie's. Unless he's a superman, like, who'll fight everyone who gets in his way.'

'He'll have to be all things to all men, eh, sunshine?' Molly remembered how she had to go through a grilling when she told her parents about Jack. 'But when the time comes, yer won't need a lecture from us, yer'll know right away he's the man for you. It might be a complete stranger, or it might be a lad yer've known all yer life. Only time will tell, sunshine.'

'Yeah, and time is telling me now to swill me face and then go and tell Bella the good news about the party.' Ruthie's shoulders began to shake with hidden laughter. 'If I happen to bump into a nice lad when I'm crossing the cobbles to get to

Bella's, I'll take him with me to me friend's, then bring him back here for your inspection.'

'D'yer know,' Molly said, 'we don't know the lad yet, but already I'm feeling sorry for the poor blighter. There's about thirty of us altogether, families and friends, and that's an awful lot of people to please.'

Ruthie was rinsing her face when she had a thought. 'Ay, Dad,' she called. 'D'yer know that apprentice what works with you? Well, what's he like?'

Jack's cheeks lifted as he gave his wife a broad wink. 'Well, now there's a lad I'd welcome into the family. A really nice lad, and handsome with it. Tall, broad, and hair the colour of spun gold.'

Ruthie stood in the kitchen doorway, her eyes wide. 'Go 'way! Is he really as handsome as that?'

'That would depend upon yer taste, love. He's a smashing lad, and a cracking worker. The only drawback I could see would be if yer didn't like bright red hair, and a face forever sprouting pimples. Then he wouldn't be the one for you.'

Ruthie shook her head and clicked her tongue. 'I might have known yer were pulling me leg. He sounded too good to be true.'

'How many arrows do yer want for yer bow, sunshine?' Molly asked. 'Aren't the present four enough for yer.'

'It doesn't hurt to have someone waiting in the wings, Mam. After all, what's to say Gordon, Johnny or Jeff won't suddenly sprout pimples?'

'As I said before, ye're another Nellie McDonough, got an answer for everything. Now get yerself out of the kitchen so I can wash up. I want to call to Doreen's and Jill's to see the babies, 'cos I've promised Nellie she can come with me tonight to me ma's.'

'Then yer wouldn't mind if I went for a pint with Corker, would yer, love?' Jack asked. 'It would only be the one pint. I think Derek is coming down, so if yer say yer don't mind, then I'll let George know.'

'It's your money, sunshine, yer can do what yer like with it. But I don't want yer to turn into one of these men who spend every night propping the bar up.'

'We don't prop the bar up, love, we sit at a table in the snug. Yer should come with us now and again, then yer could see for yerself.'

Not wanting to be a misery-guts, Molly said, 'I will one of these nights, love. But one night through the week, when it's quiet. Not on a Saturday. And now will yer move over to yer chair and have yer ciggy, while I clear away. Ruthie, you can skedaddle out from under me feet, and before yer go to Bella's knock on yer Auntie Nellie's door and tell her to pass a message on to Uncle George that yer dad and his mates are going for a pint.'

'You're looking very glamorous, sunshine,' Molly said when she opened the door to Nellie. 'Have yer been to the hairdresser's and had yer hair set?'

'Our Lily called in with Archie, on their way into town, and she said I looked a right mess.' Nellie pulled herself up the two steps. 'So she got the curling tongs out and curled me hair for me. It won't stay like this for long, 'cos yer know what lousy hair I've got. The first sign of any wind and it'll be dead straight again.' She smiled at Jack. 'All right there, lad?'

'I'm fine, Nellie. Did Ruthie call with the message about George coming for a pint?'

Nellie started to nod, then realised it was something she shouldn't do if she wanted the curls to stay in. 'Yeah. That's why I came a bit early, so I could tell yer he'd be ready for yer about half seven.'

'I'm glad ye're early, Nellie,' Molly told her. 'I haven't been to see the girls yet, so we'll have to call in before we go to me ma's.'

'Yer haven't been to the girls yet?' Nellie wondered if shaking her head was also bad for her curls, so she didn't take the chance. 'What the hell have yer been doing with yerself all afternoon, then?' Then came that crafty smile. 'Oh, I see. You and Jack took advantage of having the house to yerselves, did yer?'

Molly pretended she didn't hear. 'Apart from having yer hair curled, Nellie, what have yer been doing all afternoon?'

'Not having as good a time as you, girl. Before our Lily came George told me he couldn't climb the stairs 'cos he had a splitting headache. And when her and Archie left, I couldn't go to bed because of me hair.' She winked knowingly at Jack. 'Life can be a bugger sometimes, can't it, lad?'

Jack egged her on, even though he knew he'd get daggers off Molly. 'I can't moan, Nellie. I've had quite a pleasant afternoon.'

Clicking her tongue, Nellie jerked her head back. 'I knew I'd done the wrong thing. I should have said sod me hair, given George two aspirin for his headache, then dragged him up the ruddy stairs.'

Molly glared at Jack. 'See what yer've started now? She'll repeat that tale in our Doreen's, then Jill's, and worse still, in me ma's.'

'No, I won't, girl, scout's honour.' Nellie made a vague cross over her bosom. 'Cross my heart and hope to die. I wouldn't play a dirty trick on yer, not when I'll be getting tea and biscuits in three houses.'

'Yer couldn't drink three lots of tea, surely?' Jack looked surprised. 'Will it be one cup in each house, or more?'

'Don't you be getting jealous, Jack Bennett.' Nellie wagged a chubby finger. 'When you were enjoying yerself this afternoon, I had to suffer getting me scalp burnt. Yer can't win 'em all, yer know, so don't be greedy.' Then she relented. 'Still, seeing as ye're married to me best mate, I'll drink a toast to yer with the first cup of tea I have in each house. Now I can't say fairer than that, can I?'

'Agree with her, Jack, for God's sake, otherwise it'll be after midnight by the time we get to me ma's.'

'No, Nellie, yer can't say fairer than that.' Then Jack decided to add, 'Well, yer could go as far as including the first custard cream, as well.'

'It's a deal, lad! I must say it's been good doing business with yer.' Then the crafty look appeared. 'But on second thoughts, I did yer a favour by not coming this afternoon and spoiling yer fun. So we'll call it even, shall we?'

'Out yer go, sunshine,' Molly said, taking the key from the bowl on the sideboard and dropping it into her pocket. 'And remember, if yer misbehave yerself when we're out, I'll disown yer.'

That was food for thought, and Nellie's brain ticked away. Then she said, 'Seeing as yer don't own me, girl, how can yer disown me?'

'One word out of place, sunshine, and yer'll soon find out. Now, on yer way before those curls drop out.'

Nellie let Molly walk ahead of her, so she could have a quick word with Jack. 'Why didn't yer marry someone like me, lad, who would treat yer proper? How come a nice bloke like you fell for a misery-guts like yer wife?'

'Well, there were a few reasons, really, Nellie. Yer see, she was very pretty, had a wonderful figure and her kisses blew me head off.'

'I thought it must have been something like that, 'cos if yer'd known before yer married her what a sourpuss she was, yer'd never have tied the knot, would yer?'

Nellie didn't get to hear his answer, for Molly had come back in the house, and had grabbed her by the back of her neck. 'Nellie McDonough, I might be a sourpuss, but I'm a sourpuss who likes to be on time and doesn't let people down.' With that, the little woman was dragged unceremoniously through the front door, all the time threatening what she'd do to her best mate when they got to the other side of the street. Some of the words she used were not very ladylike, and definitely not fit for the ears of the faint-hearted.

Chapter Twenty-Eight

'Oh, my goodness, Auntie Nellie, just look at you!' Doreen stared down in amazement. 'Yer look a million dollars! Have yer got a heavy date?'

'I would have had, only for me mate here.' Nellie pulled herself up the step with one hand, while shoving Doreen aside with the other. 'I had Jack in the palm of me hand when droopy drawers put her foot down. Miserable cow.'

'Ay, that's my mam ye're talking about, so watch it.' Doreen was chuckling when she held her cheek up for her mother's kiss. 'Would I be right in saying she's been having a go at me poor dad?'

'Don't be feeling sorry for him, sunshine, for he enjoys encouraging her. And while the pair of them are laughing, I'm the one with the red face.'

Molly entered the living room to see Phil's mother sitting back on the couch with the baby on her lap. Never a Saturday went by that Phil didn't pick her up in a taxi on his way home from work and bring her to see her grandson. 'Hello, Frances. I see yer've got the little feller laughing. He looks really happy lying there having his tummy tickled.'

Coming to see her son and grandson twice a week were the highlights of Frances's life. But she was always afraid of being thought too possessive of baby Bobby, and said, 'You can have him now, Molly. I've nursed him nearly all afternoon. Victoria doesn't get a look in when I'm here.'

'No, you keep him, Frances. He looks so contented it would be a shame to move him. I'll give him a big hug and kiss before I go. Me and Nellie won't be staying long 'cos we're calling at Jill's on our way round to see me ma and da. And our Tommy and Rosie. I mustn't leave me lovely son and his wife out.'

Victoria was eyeing Nellie's hair. 'Yer look a treat, Nellie. I don't know why yer don't keep it like that, it makes such a difference.'

Nellie pulled a chair out and sat down. 'Well, I don't know whether yer've ever tried to use curling tongs, Victoria, but I'm blowed if I can get the hang of them. I've tried a few times, but doing it in front of a mirror, everything looks back to bleeding front and I end up burning me ruddy fingers. Besides, the curls don't last long, so it's not worth the bother. The least little puff of wind and me hair's dead straight again.'

While Nellie was talking, Molly noticed Phil standing by the kitchen door. When he caught her eye, he raised his brows and jerked his head, which Molly took as a sign he wanted a quiet word with her in the kitchen. So with Nellie in full flow, holding the attention of her audience, Molly followed her son-in-law into the kitchen. In a quiet voice, she asked, 'What is it, Phil?'

'Nothing to worry about, Mrs B., in fact I think it's quite funny. But yer know what Mrs Mac is like when she gets her teeth into something, and I'd hate it if anything which was told to me as a friend was repeated.'

'Well hurry up, son, before Nellie realises I'm missing. What is it?'

'Yer know Mr Corkhill's friend, Derek, walked Ken and his mother and sister home last night? Well young Ken took a real liking to him. He confided in me that his mam had been out with a bloke a couple of times, and she'd brought him home last week to meet the children. According to Ken, the man was a real big-headed toff, and not good enough for his mam. So he asked me if Derek was married, or if he had a girlfriend.'

'Ah, God love him,' Molly said. 'He adores his mother, and I take me hat off to him for that. I knew about the bloke, so does Nellie, and Claire said he dressed like a toff and was well spoken. And she told us yesterday that Ken didn't like the man one little bit. So much so, she said she wasn't going to go out with him again. Anyway, she wasn't so keen herself. It was the male company she enjoyed, after being on her own for so long. And having a struggle with money. Now we know that ourselves from when we first met Ken last Christmas.'

Phil narrowed his eyes. 'Is that a smile I see, Mrs B?'

'It is, sunshine, but don't think I'm laughing at the expense of Ken, 'cos far from it. I think he's a smasher. I also think he's got his head screwed on the right way. That's why I would believe him if he says the bloke is not right for his mam. The words he used, according to Claire, were, "He's not one of us, Mam, not like dad." And I'd back his word any day.'

Molly folded her arms and leaned back against the sink. 'I like Derek meself. He's a good bloke. Lives with his mam, and as far as I know he hasn't got a girlfriend. I think if he had he'd have brought her to meet Corker.' Then she had an idea. 'Jack told me to tell yer he and George are going to the pub for a pint, and he asked if yer'd like to go with them for an hour. Corker and Derek will be there, so yer could find out, in a roundabout way, of course, whether there's any love interest in Derek's life.'

'Yer want me to do some detective work for yer, is that it? And if I find out, what would yer do with the information?'

'I'll tell yer something else that Claire said, Phil, and see if it gives yer any idea. She said, "I asked Ken if he was matchmaking, and he said he liked Derek, he was a good bloke, like our dad was." '

'He didn't tell me that bit.'

'What is your honest opinion of Derek, Phil? Did yer take to him?'

'Yeah, I did! I thought he was a thoroughly decent, honest, down-to-earth bloke. That he is a friend of Uncle Corker is a good enough reference for me.'

Molly nodded. 'That's my impression, and my thoughts. So perhaps it wouldn't hurt to do a bit of matchmaking ourselves. I don't mean throw them together to suit us, but arrange for them to see each other now and then, so they could make their own minds up whether there's a mutual spark of romance between them.'

'Wouldn't that be meddling in their affairs?'

'I don't think so, son. I would see it as helping two nice people to be friends. What happens after that is in the hands of the gods.'

'What's going on out here?' Nellie waddled into the kitchen. 'He's too young for yer, girl, so put him down.'

'Yer'll have to wait until I pick him up before I can put him down. Anyway, sunshine, me and Phil have only been talking about his job. Oh, and how he gets on with Ken. I'll tell yer about it on the way to Jill's, 'cos I know how yer hate to miss anything.'

Doreen followed Nellie out. 'Ye're staying for a cuppa, aren't yer, Mam?'

'Yes, love, we'll stay for a cuppa. Nellie would have me life if we didn't. Besides, I haven't had a kiss off Bobby yet, and I wouldn't miss that for the world.'

Phil pulled his wife towards him and slipped an arm round her waist. 'Would yer mind if I went out for an hour, sweetheart? The gang are going to the corner pub for a pint, and they asked yer mam if I'd join them.'

'Of course yer can go, soft lad. I know ye're not going to get into any trouble if me dad is there. But get out of me kitchen now, the lot of yer, so I can put the kettle on.'

'I've got something to tell yer, sunshine,' Molly told her mate as they walked up the street after leaving Doreen's. 'Yer know most of it, but Phil doesn't know that, and I wasn't going to tell him because it's the Bennett and McDonough Private Detective Agency business. And it wouldn't be very private if we told everyone, would it?'

Nellie nodded to show she understood. 'Okay, girl, I know ye're going to tell me to keep what yer tell me under me hat. Well I always do, yer know that. So what were yer talking about that took yer so long?'

'We're nearly at Jill's now, so I've only got time to tell yer that Ken told Phil the same as Claire told us. And that was about him saying he didn't like Graham Collins. Well, apparently Derek walked them home last night, and Ken told Claire he liked Derek, he was a good bloke, like his dad was.'

'Ooh, I didn't know Derek walked them home! How did I come to miss that, girl?'

'Because your George dragged yer home when yer wanted to go in Corker's for a cup of tea. I don't know why he did, unless he wanted to go to the lavvy, but that's his business. And that's as much as I can tell yer now, because we're here.' Molly rapped on the knocker, then said, 'I'll have more time to tell yer the rest on our way to me ma's, sunshine, and I won't forget any of it, I promise.'

Steve's brows shot up when he opened the door. 'Hello, Mrs B. It's nice to see yer. Who's the woman with yer, the one with the curly hair?'

'Don't be so sarky, son, 'cos although yer might be old enough to be married and have a baby, ye're not too old to have yer backside slapped. So step aside and let your mother get in.

Oh, and don't breathe out when I pass yer, in case yer blow me curls out. After having had me scalp burnt in half a dozen places, I'd like the curls to stay in at least until I go to bed.'

Steve winked at his mother-in-law, whom he thought the world of. He, and the rest of the family, were well aware that it was Mrs Bennett who had kept Nellie in check over the years. She was a good influence on a woman who was inclined to use her fists rather than calming words. Oh, the family idolised her, and wouldn't let an outsider say a wrong word against her. But they knew Molly was the one who kept Nellie on an even keel. And Steve had another reason for being grateful to her, for hadn't she welcomed him as a husband for her beautiful daughter, and treated him as a son? 'Who did me mam's hair, Mrs B? It makes her look so different.'

'I can't take the credit, son, it was Lily who did it.' Molly stroked his cheek, for to her he was like a son, and had been since the day he took his first steps. 'Yer mam's pretending she doesn't care, but knowing her as I do, she's feeling as good as she looks.'

Lizzie Corkhill started at Nellie's feet, then worked her way up to her head. 'My God, Nellie, it must be a hot date yer've got tonight. Who's the lucky feller?'

The little woman was thinking how good life was. They'd walked all the way from Doreen's and there hadn't been a breath of air that could have put a stop to the compliments she was getting. 'I could have had a date, Lizzie, but for my mate here. As sure as I'm standing here, I swear it was on the tip of Jack Bennett's tongue to ask me out. I could tell by the way his eyes were devouring me voluptuous body, and me new hair style, that he desired me.'

Molly's eyes went to the ceiling. 'I'm going to get that all night now. Where's the baby, so I can nurse her and take me mind of Nellie's voluptuous body?'

'I've just taken her to bed, Mam,' Jill told her, 'but she won't be asleep yet, so I'll take yer up and yer can hold her for a minute. I shouldn't do it, really, not when she's ready for sleep, but just for this once.'

'Ay, ay, ay!' Nellie was standing with her feet parted and a fierce expression on her chubby face. 'I might look different with me curly hair, but not that ruddy different. Have yer forgotten that I'm the baby's grandma as well?'

'I hadn't forgotten yer, Mrs Mac, I'd never do that. Come on upstairs and yer can both hold the baby for five minutes.' Jill put her arm across her mother-in-law's shoulder. 'Come on, let's go.'

'Listen, girl, I love the bones of yer and I think yer make a very good mother, and a good wife for me son. But take yer ruddy arm away while I've still got a few curls left, will yer! It might be donkey's years before yer see me like this again.'

'I could take a photograph of yer if yer like, Mam,' Steve said, his dimples deepening when he smiled. 'We bought a camera the other week, so we could take snaps of Molly while she's still a baby. We're going to take one every six months so when she's older she can look back and see how she's looked at each stage of her childhood.'

'Ooh, ay, that's a good idea,' Molly said. 'Me and yer mam couldn't do that 'cos we never had the money to buy a camera. Did we, Nellie?'

'When we get them developed, we're going to get four copies of the one that comes out best, so both grandmas have one, and Auntie Lizzie.'

Nellie's actions were like a peacock preening itself, she was so proud. 'Fancy you having a camera. We're going up in the world, aren't we?' She glanced at Molly to make sure the camera was duly appreciated. 'Well, it would be nice if yer could take a photo of me and Molly holding the baby. When little Molly grows up, she'll think her grandma had nice curly hair.'

'If she's still awake, I'll bring her down for a few minutes,' Jill said. 'What d'yer think Steve? Shall I bring her down and yer can take a few snaps?'

'I think there's four left on the roll, so we could use it up and yer can put it in to be developed on Monday. But if the baby is asleep, I don't think it would be fair to waken her.'

Molly agreed. 'No, don't waken her on our account. I know ye're getting her into a routine, so don't spoil it just for us.'

'Ye're right, Mam, it wouldn't be fair. Let Steve take a snap of you and Auntie Nellie, and another one with Auntie Lizzie with yer. Then tomorrow night, if yer come down earlier, he can take yer with the baby.'

Nellie grinned up at Molly. 'Ay, I bet yer never thought when yer came out tonight that yer'd be getting yer photie took, did yer? It's fate, isn't it?'

'Fate? What d'yer mean, it's fate?'

'Me having me hair curled, that's what! Ay, I won't know meself when I see meself in a photie.'

Steve's chuckle drowned out the laughter. 'Mam, yer have a lovely way with words. No one can touch yer. Who else would say they wouldn't know themselves when they saw themselves? That's a classic, that is.'

Nellie studied his face, then turned to Molly. 'Shall I kiss him, girl, or clock him one?'

'Definitely a kiss, sunshine, and he was right, it was a classic. Good enough to repeat when we get to me ma's. And good enough for yer to repeat to George in bed tonight.'

Nellie threw her a look of disgust. 'Do yer think I've got nothing better to do in bed than tell my feller I don't know whether I'm coming or going?'

'I won't answer that, if yer don't mind, sunshine. What I will do is ask Steve to take our photographs while Jill puts the kettle on.' Then Molly was hit by a brainwave. 'Oh, yer won't be telling George in bed, anyway, 'cos yer won't be going to bed tonight.'

'How d'yer make out that, girl?'

'It was just a thought flashed through me head, sunshine, that's all. I mean, yer seem to be getting very fond of yer curls, and if yer went to bed, yer'd wake up with dead straight hair again.'

'Oh, bloody hell, I never thought of that! I'll sit up in the chair all night, and make sure I keep me head straight.'

Lizzie tried to help. 'Yer could go to bed if yer wore a hair net, queen.'

A light came into Nellie's eyes, 'Oh, yeah, that's a good idea. Lend me yours, Lizzie, 'cos I haven't got one.'

'I haven't got one, queen, I'm sorry. My hair, like Corker's, has always had a bit of curl to it, so I've never needed a net.'

Nellie looked glum again. 'Me heart lifted for a minute there, Lizzie, and now I'm back to feeling miserable. I know it's no use asking Jill, or me mate, 'cos they've both got long blond hair what they only have to run a comb through. They make me bleeding sick, and that's putting it mild.'

Jill had been standing by the stove, waiting for the kettle to boil, but now she popped her head around the door. 'Yer could put a scarf round yer head, Auntie Nellie. You know, tie it like a turban, as the women did during the war. It'll flatten yer hair, but at least it might keep some of the curl in.'

Nellie seemed to cheer up. 'Ooh, I never thought of that. Ay, Molly, you've got a nice soft voile scarf. I'll borrow it off yer for tonight.'

'You can just get lost, Nellie McDonough. Ye're not having my scarf. Yer've got one yerself, exactly the same as mine. Doreen bought yer one for yer birthday because yer moaned about not having one.'

'I know she did, girl, but I don't want to get mine all creased. Lend me yours, and don't be so ruddy tight.'

Molly shook her head. 'This is one time I'm not giving in to yer, sunshine, 'cos I'd be daft if I did. Our scarves are exactly the same, so why on earth should I lend yer mine? Especially when I'd get it back all creased and in need of a wash. Use yer own.'

Nellie ground her teeth together. 'I suppose I'll have to if you're too tight to lend me yours.'

Jill came in carrying a tray. 'I hope there's no skin and hair going to fly. Yer both know I hate any sort of arguments.'

Molly took the tray from her and put it down carefully on the table. 'Yer should know by now, sunshine, that yer Auntie Nellie and me spend our day arguing over nothing. We'd think the end of the world had come if we were nice and quiet.'

Nellie chose to sit in a chair nearest the tray. Well, if there was a plate of biscuits it wouldn't be so far for her to stretch. 'Ay, girl, yer haven't told them about Corker and Ellen having a party in Hanley's.'

'I don't need to now, sunshine, 'cos you've just done it for me.'

'What's the party in aid of?' Lizzie asked. 'Paul and Phoebe are not getting married yet, are they?'

Molly shook her head. 'No, Lizzie, it's not for anything in particular. Your son decided it would be nice to have a party to celebrate the birthdays of all his family and friends. In fact, Lizzie, Corker wanted to give a party 'cos he's never had one before. And as far as I can reckon, the number of guests will be thirty-two, or thereabouts.'

'He'll be in his applecart, Corker will.' Lizzie could never keep the look of tenderness from her face when talking of her beloved son. 'He's like a big soft kid, sometimes.'

Molly wagged a finger. 'I know he's your son, Lizzie, but

I'll not have yer talking about one of my best friends like that. Of course he wants to make people happy, that's the way he's made, and I know ye're as daft about him as I am.'

Lizzie nodded. 'I've never known my son do anyone a bad turn in his life. Nor does he speak ill of anyone. He's a big man, with a big heart, and I love every inch of him.'

'We all do, Auntie Lizzie,' Jill told her. 'I've always loved Uncle Corker.'

The old lady smiled at her with great fondness. 'And like Cinderella, sweetheart, you shall go to the ball. I'll see to the baby, yer don't have to worry about that. Once she's down, she'll sleep for three or four hours.'

Steve looked pleased. 'That's something for us to look forward to, love. Yer could buy yerself a new dress for the occasion.'

'I don't need a new dress. There's nothing wrong with the ones I've got.'

'You're getting a new dress,' Steve insisted. 'Yer seldom go anywhere these days because of the baby, so I want yer to dress up while yer've got reason to.'

'Don't argue, sunshine,' Molly told her daughter. 'If yer can afford it, then it'll do yer good to dress up. It gives yer confidence when yer know yer look good.'

'She always looks good, Mrs B.,' Steve said, his eyes telling his wife he thought she was beautiful and he adored her. 'But we don't go out much, so it'll be nice to get dressed up for a change. And it'll be nice for all the gang to be together again.'

Nellie banged a clenched fist on the table. 'I don't know whether you lot like cold tea or not, but I certainly don't. And besides that, me throat is parched.'

'Yer shouldn't talk so much, Mam, that's the trouble. And I bet yer had a cup of tea in Doreen's, did yer?'

'Don't tell him, Molly,' Nellie said. 'Cheeky bugger, he'll be asking me what I had for me breakfast next.'

'I bet I know what yer had,' Steve said. 'A cup of tea and two rounds of toast with me dad and our Paul, and another cup of tea and two rounds of toast after they'd left for work.'

Nellie hoisted her bosom. 'I'm not telling yer, so there! And if somebody doesn't pour this tea out soon, I'll do it me bleeding self.'

'I'll do it,' Molly said, 'before she starts crying. And when she's got her tea, she'll be asking for biscuits because she's starving with hunger. Yer mother never has anything in moderation, Steve. She's never just thirty, she's got to be parched. And she's never peckish, always starving.'

But five minutes later, with a cup of tea in front of her, a custard cream between two of her chubby fingers, Nellie was completely happy and kept them all highly amused until it was time for her and Molly to make their way to the Jacksons'.

'Let's walk nice and slow, girl, and yer can finish telling me about Ken and what he said about Derek. When yer've finished telling me that, and there's no need to rush it, then we'll talk about what we'll wear to the party.'

'Nellie, the party is at least three weeks off, maybe five! We don't need to think about what we'll wear until the week before.'

'That's not giving your Doreen much time to make two dresses, is it? Have a little bit of thought for her. With having the baby to see to, she'll need more than a week.'

'You cheeky article!' Molly stopped in her tracks. 'Ye're not expecting our Doreen to make dresses for us, are yer? I mean, she's not only got the baby to care for, she's got the house to keep clean, Victoria to see to, the washing and ironing, the cooking and the shopping. And you expect her to make two dresses? I wouldn't have the nerve to ask her.'

As cool as a cucumber, Nellie said, 'I'll ask her for yer, girl, if you feel too shy. If I'm asking for meself, I might as well ask for you at the same time.'

'You most certainly will not! I'll either make do with a dress I've got, or see if there's anything going on Mary Ann's stall at the market.'

'I'll do the same as you, then, girl, 'cos I don't want to upset yer. So now we've sorted that out to our mutial satisfaction, carry on with the tale about young Ken.'

'Nellie, the word is mutual, not mutial.' Molly glanced at her friend, then gave in. 'Oh, what difference does it make? It's not worth wasting me breath. Yer don't take any notice anyway. It goes in one ear and out the other with you.'

Nellie grinned up at her. 'That's because there's nothing in between, girl. At least that's what George says when he's got a cob on with me.'

'Ay, you tell yer husband he's not to talk to yer like that.' Molly chuckled. 'If anyone is going to insult yer, it should be me. I'm with yer more than anyone else.'

'Quite right, girl, you stick up for yerself. And as we're not far from yer ma's house hurry up and finish the story about young Ken.'

Molly knocked on her mother's door, then stood back to wait for it to be opened. Then she felt Nellie pulling on her arm. 'Ay, girl,' the little woman said, 'don't mention me hair and see if they notice it.'

When Tommy opened the door it was to see his mother doubled up with laughter. 'Hello, Mam. What's Auntie Nellie been saying to yer now?' He kept his face straight, for he had heard what Nellie had said. 'Oh, Rosie's calling me, so see yerselves in and close the door after yer.' He then dashed into the living room and said quickly, but urgently, 'Don't mention Auntie Nellie's hair whatever yer do.'

So the two friends entered the living room to see Bridie and Bob in their usual seat on the couch. Molly made a fuss, kissing them both, and then Tommy and Rosie. 'I've no need to ask how yer are, 'cos yer all look the picture of health.'

Nellie stood in the middle of the room, her eyes going from one to the other as she waited to be noticed. Until Bridie said, 'Sit yerself down, Nellie, me darlin', and make yerself at home.'

That was the straw that broke the camel's back. 'What's the matter with the lot of yer? Are yer all blind?'

Bob was dying to laugh, for she reminded him of Curly Top, a cartoon character from many years ago. But he managed to speak in his usual low voice. 'We're all right, Nellie. What made yer ask that?'

Grinding her teeth, Nellie turned on Molly. 'Switch the ruddy light on, girl!'

Molly guessed what had happened, and went along with it. 'What d'yer want the light on for? It's still broad daylight.'

'Me hair, yer daft nit, me hair! They can't see it!'

Rosie's bonny face was full of devilment. 'Of course we can see yer hair, Auntie Nellie, and as sure as I'm standing here, I promise yer haven't gone bald. Sure yer hair is still on yer head, right enough, and I wouldn't be telling yer no lies.'

Nellie wagged her head from side to side, tutting loudly as she did so. 'I know I haven't gone bald, soft girl, but can't yer see there's something different about me hair?'

'Of course we can, sweetheart,' Bridie said. 'Sure I noticed it as soon as yer came through the door. But the truth of it is, me darlin', I didn't like to mention it in case yer were embarrassed. There's plenty of people who get embarrassed when someone pays them a compliment. And because we all know how shy and retiring you are none of us wanted to say anything that would make yer feel uncomfortable. Isn't that the truth, Tommy?'

Shy and retiring. Even Nellie could see the funny side of that. But being Nellie, she had to have the last word. 'Ye're just jealous, the lot of yer. All me life people have been jealous of me, and it's not my fault if I've got a voluptuous body what most women would die for, is it? And it's not my fault if I woke up this morning to find me hair had grown into curls while I was asleep. A miracle it was, nothing short of a miracle.'

'Yer hair looks a treat, Auntie Nellie,' Tommy told her. 'And I've got a confession to make. As I was going to open the front door to yer, I heard what yer said to me mam about not mentioning yer hair. I made an excuse that Rosie was calling me, and ran in to tell everyone to pretend not to notice yer hair. So I'm to blame for yer not getting the compliments yer should have got, but I did it 'cos I know yer can take a joke better than anyone I know. Like I know yer'll forgive me.'

There's a few nice compliments in there, Nellie told herself, as she smiled at him. 'I'll forgive yer, son, on one condition.'

'What's that, Auntie Nellie?'

'That a pot of tea is on that table in five minutes, plus a plate of biscuits. And when yer've done that, me and Molly have got some very good news for yer. So hurry up, son.'

Tommy and Rosie made a dash for the kitchen, while Bridie asked, 'And what's the good news, me darlin'?'

'Oh, I can't tell yer, Bridie, girl, 'cos it's Molly who is helping to organise everything. And me mate is better at explaining things than I am.'

'We'll wait until Tommy and Rosie are here, Ma,' Molly said. 'I don't want to have to go over it all twice. But I think yer'll like what it is me and Nellie have to tell yer.'

'There yer are, Auntie Nellie.' Rosie put the plate of biscuits near to where Nellie was sitting. 'There's a nice variety for yer to choose from, and here's me ever-loving husband with the tea. Sure, yer wouldn't be served quicker if yer went to the finest hotel in Liverpool.'

Bridie and Bob came to sit at the table, and Rosie sat on Tommy's knees as they were a chair short. But her beloved husband's knee was better than a chair any day. And Nellie, as happy as could be with the compliments, the tea, and the plate of biscuits, asked herself what more could she wish for. 'Go on, girl, they're waiting for yer. Put them out of their misery.'

So taking a sip of tea first, Molly began the tale of Corker's party. And soon the room was full of laughter, and everyone trying to speak at once. A party with all the families and neighbours was always welcome. 'Are yer sure it won't be too much for Corker, me darlin'? Me and Bob would love to be there, but we'd understand, sure enough, if he had more than enough to invite with his own family and friends.'

'Ma, if Corker heard yer say that he'd go mad. You and me da are family as far as he's concerned. Like all of us, he'd think there was something amiss if yer weren't there.'

'When is it, Mam?' Tommy asked, a smile on his handsome face. 'I hope I can still get into me wedding suit.'

'The date isn't certain yet. It could be three weeks tonight, or five weeks. I'll find out for sure tomorrow.' Molly looked at the clock. 'It's half nine now, so if me and Nellie leave here at ten to ten, we'll probably meet the men coming out of the pub. I could get the exact date then, 'cos Corker was waiting for Ellen to come in from work to choose which Saturday.' She looked across at her mother. 'Yer'll be coming round tomorrow as usual, so I can give yer a definite date then.'

'Ay, we've got another surprise for yer.' Nellie leaned forward. 'There's someone new coming to the party, and I bet yer couldn't guess in a hundred years who it is.'

'In that case, Nellie,' Bob said, 'I think yer'd better tell us 'cos we won't be around that long. And I'm sure yer wouldn't want us to die wondering what the answer was.'

Nellie didn't keep them waiting. With pride in her voice she said, 'It's Edna and Tom Hanley, them what own the place. They asked if they could come. Edna said she'd always wanted to come to one of our parties 'cos we enjoy ourselves so much.'

So Corker's party was the topic of conversation until Molly looked at the clock and gave her mate a nudge. 'We'd better make a move, sunshine, if we want to catch the men coming out of the pub. I don't want to be knocking on Corker's door on a Sunday, for it's the only day Ellen has free.'

'Ready when you are, girl, ready when you are.'

The two women couldn't have timed it better. They were just nearing the pub door when Jack and George came out, followed by Corker and Derek. 'Where's Phil?' Molly asked. Her first thought was that the baby wasn't well and Doreen had sent for him. 'Did he go home early?'

'Only a few minutes ago, love, so don't look so worried.' Jack patted her arm. 'It's a wonder yer didn't see him.'

'Your wife's the biggest worrier on God's earth,' Nellie said. 'She always thinks the worst.'

'That's because she cares for people.' Corker put his arm across Molly's shoulders. 'Me darlin', we wouldn't have yer any different. And can we ask why you and Nellie are hanging around a pub door at this time of night?'

'Me and Nellie have done the rounds. Doreen's first, then Jill's, and lastly me ma's. We've told them all about the party, and they're all thrilled to bits. All I need from yer now is a date, Corker, if yer have one.'

'Five weeks tonight, me darlin'. Ellen said three weeks was too soon, for when the children heard, they all said they wanted new clothes. Gordon said he was old enough for a proper suit now, and when the others heard that, they all put their order in. So, it's five weeks tonight.'

Molly looked at Derek, standing next to his mate. He didn't push himself forward, and that's one of the things that Molly liked about him. 'I've told most of the gang, but I'll have to wait until I see Claire, 'cos I don't know where she lives.'

'I know where she lives,' Derek said. 'I'll call and let her know if yer like.'

'Would yer do that for us, sunshine?' Molly felt a bit guilty being so underhanded, but then brushed that aside and decided all was fair in love and war. 'Don't tell her about the party. I'd like to surprise her. Just ask her to come up to mine on Monday night, 'cos I've something to tell her. She could bring the kids with her for a walk.'

'I'll do that, Molly, it's no trouble. I'm not working yet, so I've got all the time in the world.'

'Oh, that's lovely, Derek. Thanks very much. I want to make sure of the numbers so Corker doesn't pay for someone who doesn't turn up. Ask her if she'll come about half seven, to give me time to get the dinner over and tidy up.'

'Molly, yer'd have made a good secretary,' Corker said, his arm still across her shoulders. 'Every little detail attended to and filed away.'

Jack tapped him on the back. 'Would yer mind taking yer arm away from my wife, Corker, if yer don't mind? We're getting funny looks from some of the neighbours who are passing by.'

'I'm not worried what the neighbours think,' Molly said, edging away. 'But I am worried about our daughter, Jack Bennett. I told her to be home no later than ten o'clock, and it's turned that now. Me and Nellie will run on, for I know you men will stand jangling for a while. So we'll say goodnight and God bless. Come on, Nellie, let's go.' She'd gone a few steps when she turned her head. 'Thanks for offering to go on that message for me, Derek. I appreciate it.'

Nellie did a hop skip and a jump, to keep up with her friend. 'Ay, girl, yer pulled that off very well, I must say. Don't ever call me crafty again, 'cos yer don't do so bad yerself.'

'It wasn't that obvious, was it, sunshine?'

'Nah, none of the men would have given it a thought. After they've downed a few pints they're not capable of thinking straight. Right now they'll still be standing in the same place, putting the world to rights. I just hope my George hasn't had too many pints. He's hopeless in bed when he's tipsy.'

'That's all for tonight, sunshine. My work is over for the day, and I really don't need to hear that your George's work hasn't begun yet.' Molly could see Ruthie leaning against the wall outside the house. 'Goodnight and God bless, Nellie.'

As she turned away, Molly heard her mate mutter, 'Goodnight, she says. It better had be a good night, or my George is in for it.'

Chapter Twenty-Nine

It was Ken who opened the door to Derek on Sunday afternoon, and his eyes lit up with pleasure. 'Hello! This is a surprise.'

'I've got a message for yer mother from Mrs Bennett.' Derek smiled back at the boy. 'Could yer call her for me?'

'Come in, yer don't have to stand out there.'

Derek shook his head. 'No, I don't want to interrupt her afternoon. Ask her if she'd be good enough to come to the door.'

Ken turned his head and called over his shoulder, 'Mam, Derek is here with a message for yer from Mrs Bennett.'

'Well, bring the man in, son, don't leave him standing on the step. It's bad manners.'

Ken was delighted. This was what he was hoping for. He enjoyed being in the company of men, and being treated like an adult. Opening the door wider, he said, 'Come in, Derek.'

Claire nodded and smiled a welcome before facing her son. 'You shouldn't be calling him Derek. It's very forward of you.'

'But I don't know his second name, Mam, and I couldn't just say there's some bloke here to see yer.'

'Sit down, Derek,' Claire said, plumping up a cushion on the couch. 'There yer are, we don't charge.'

He hesitated. There was nothing he would like better than to stay and get to know her, but he didn't want to appear too keen. 'I don't want to upset yer day. I know yer work through the week, so I imagine yer have plenty of jobs to catch up with on a Sunday. It was Molly who asked me to call to give yer a message.'

'I'm sure yer can give the message just as well sitting down. And Ken was making a pot of tea when yer knocked, so ye're welcome to a cup. Unless ye're on yer way somewhere, then I wouldn't want to hold you back.'

Derek lowered himself to the couch. 'No, I'm not going anywhere in particular. Me mother was having her afternoon nap, and with it being such a nice day, I thought it was a shame to waste it by staying indoors.' He leaned back, made himself comfortable and crossed his legs. 'So I thought I'd call here and pass the message on, then take a tram down to the Pier Head.' He grinned, revealing a set of strong white teeth. 'I'm missing the smell of the sea, so I'll most probably take a ferry across to Seacombe. Get my sea legs back for half an hour.'

'I'll pour the tea out,' Ken said, hoping Derek would stay for a while and talk about his adventures at sea. 'Do yer take sugar . . . er . . . mister?'

Derek laughed, and both mother and son were reminded of the time, many years ago, when the sound of a man's laughter was often heard in this room. 'The name is Mattocks, son, but I would prefer yer to call me Derek. It won't make me feel so old.'

Ken made haste to the kitchen, and they could hear the sound of crockery. 'I bet he's a good son, Claire?'

She nodded. 'They don't come any better. Since his dad died, he's been my shoulder to cry on, my man of the house. I sometimes wonder if I'm making him old beyond his years. I have never asked him to be anything but my son, a young lad, but I can't stop him from doing what he wants to do, and that is to care for me and Amy. I know he still misses his dad, misses being taken to see Liverpool playing, and most of all, having a man in the house. I've noticed a difference in him since he started work, though. He seems to have suddenly become a grown-up. And I'm trying to get him to mix with lads his own age, instead of spending his spare time with me and Amy.' She let out a sigh. 'Anyway, I don't want to bore you with my life story, so what was the message Molly asked yer to pass on?'

'I don't know why she wants to see yer, but she asked if yer could call there tomorrow night. She has some news for yer.' He chortled. 'Oh, and would you call around half seven, please, to give her time to get the dinner over and tidy up.'

'That sounds just like her. Have yer ever been in her company when Nellie is with her? If not, yer don't know what ye're missing. I haven't been friends with them for very long, but they have certainly added something to my life. And laughter and friendship come top of the list.'

'Tea's up!' Ken came through carrying a wooden tray set with cups, saucers and a brown teapot. 'Are yer sitting at the table, Mam, or will yer have it where yer are?'

'We'll have it where we are, love, it's more comfortable than the wooden chairs. Not that Derek will think the couch comfortable, 'cos he's sitting on the side where the spring has come through. I suggest we change places, Derek, and you have this fireside chair. It's as old as the hills, but it is comfortable. I'll sit on the couch. I'm quite good at dodging that ruddy spring.'

'I wouldn't dream of changing places,' Derek said, humour bubbling up inside him. 'I'm blowed if I'll let a ruddy spring get the better of me. You stay where you are, Claire, and Ken can join me on the couch.'

'We don't want to spoil the day for you,' Claire told him. 'I bet yer were looking forward to going on the ferry, having the sea under yer feet again. So when yer've finished your tea, don't feel obliged to stay. It's too nice a day to waste.'

'Aren't yer going to miss going to sea?' Ken asked. 'It must be great going to all the different countries in the world. How did yer manage to speak to people who couldn't speak English?'

'No matter where yer go in the world, Ken, yer can always make yerself understood. If yer can't speak the language, yer use sign language. Yer might look daft, but sometimes it's the only way of communicating. Me and Corker have seen some sights, believe me, and we've had some laughs.'

Claire could see the eagerness on her son's face as he asked, 'Which country in the whole world would yer like to live in?'

'There are some really beautiful countries, breathtakingly beautiful, but at the end of the day, there is no place like home. And while I've enjoyed my time at sea, and happy I've had the experience of seeing those countries and the way of life of the people who live there, I've got it out of my system now, and I'll be happy to settle in dear old England, with all me memories.'

'I'd like to see the world,' Ken said. 'But I think I'd be homesick. And I'd probably be seasick as soon as the boat started to sail.'

'Why, do yer get seasick when yer go on a boat?'

The lad shrugged his shoulders. 'I dunno, I've never been on one.'

'Not even a ferry boat?'

Again Ken shrugged his shoulders. 'I think me dad took me when I was young, but I don't really remember.'

'You were only a toddler, son,' Claire said, 'so yer won't remember.'

Derek leaned over to put his cup and saucer on the table. 'In that case, why don't yer come with me? Come on the ferry across to Seacombe, and see if yer have got sea legs.'

Ken's eyes lit up. 'Ooh, ay, yeah! Mam, did yer hear that? Would yer be all right if I went with Derek?'

'I would be perfectly all right, son. I'm more than capable of looking after meself. But I feel Derek would be better to go on his own. When he gets down to the Pier Head, he might change his mind about what he wants to do. Leave it for another day and I'll take you and Amy for a trip on the ferry.'

Derek saw the eagerness fall from the lad's face. 'I would love some company, Claire, I really would. Save me talking to meself and getting strange looks from people. And where is Amy, by the way? I could take her as well.'

'One of the neighbours was taking her family to Seaforth sands, and she kindly offered to take Amy. I'm not expecting her home until six, at the earliest.'

'I'll stay with yer, Mam, save yer being on yer own.' There was a trace of sadness on Ken's face when he said, 'Thanks, Derek. It was nice of yer to ask me, but I'll stay here and keep me mam company.'

'Both of yer stay indoors on a day like this? What a waste that would be!' Derek suddenly opened his eyes wide, then looked from one to the other with a grin on his face. 'Don't laugh, but that ruddy spring has finally got me where it hurts. I think I upset it by not inviting it to come with us.' He moved his bottom and groaned. 'Oh dear, oh dear! Have yer ever seen anyone getting on the tram with a couch under his arm?'

Claire's imagination took over, and she burst out laughing. 'It seats three people, so yer'd have to fork out for three tickets, plus yer own.'

'Not if you and me sat on it, Mam.' Ken's voice hadn't broken properly yet, and it ranged from a high squeak to a deep bass. Normally he was embarrassed when the squeak came out, but today he didn't care because his mother was laughing and looked happy and relaxed. 'I'd only be half price on the tram, and the ferry, though, so that would knock the cost down a bit.'

'Yer forget I'm not going with yer, love, so it would be you and Derek carrying that ruddy big couch between yer.'

'If you don't come, then Ken won't come.' Derek tilted his head. 'Which means me being all on me lonesome.'

'But that's what yer were planning when yer left home,' Claire reminded him. 'Yer only called here to leave a message.' She chuckled. 'I'm blowed if I remember what the message was now.'

'Tomorrow night, seven thirty, at Molly's. Oh, and she said to bring Ken and Amy with yer, for the walk.'

'Oh, right! I'll remember that.' Claire noticed Ken was looking a bit down in the mouth. It wasn't often he had the chance of going anywhere, and she began to feel guilty. 'Look, son, you go with Derek. It will do yer good, and you'd enjoy it.'

But Ken wasn't feeling down in the mouth, he only wanted to look it. And he was keeping his fingers crossed in the hope his wishes came true. 'No, I'll stay in with you, Mam. I don't mind. I can go on the ferry another time.'

Claire knew she was being blackmailed, but she couldn't say this in front of Derek and embarrass her son. She said, 'Okay, you win. But I've got to be back in time for Amy coming home.'

'It's only half past two, Claire,' Derek said, 'there's plenty of time. But I really don't want yer to come against your will, and have you cursing me under yer breath.'

'Me mam doesn't curse, Derek,' Ken said, grinning because he was happy. 'She stamps her foot and goes red in the face.'

'Ooh.' Derek lifted his arm and pretended to cower in fear. 'She doesn't get violent, does she, by any chance?'

Resigning herself to having been talked into it, Claire left her chair and took a comb from a drawer in the sideboard and ran it through her thick black hair. 'I do lose me rag sometimes, but I give out a warning first. Me eyes go red.'

'Oh, I see. Well, I'll keep watch, and if yer start ranting, I'll walk on and pretend I've never seen yer in me life before.'

Claire looked down at herself. 'Do I need to get changed? I wasn't expecting visitors, never mind going out.'

Derek would have liked to say that with such a beautiful face, few people would notice what she was wearing. But she wouldn't appreciate such a compliment from a man she hardly knew. 'I'm not exactly dressed in the height of fashion meself, Claire, so don't worry. Anyway, folk don't put their glad rags on to go on a ferry trip.'

Claire felt a little better then, for she didn't have any glad rags to change in to. She only possessed two almost decent dresses, the one she was wearing, and one in the wash. 'Before we start off, can I get one thing straight? We all pay for ourselves.'

'I couldn't go along with that, Claire. I'd feel terrible if I let you and Ken pay for yourselves. It was me who asked yer to come. I don't know much about women, having been going to sea for so long, but I was under the impression it was the man who paid. So shall we be clear about that, and my pride and dignity will be intact?'

Claire met Ken's eyes and saw the pleading there. He really had taken a liking to this man, and she didn't want to be a wet blanket. 'Okay, I'll let you keep yer pride and dignity, Derek, and thank you very much for inviting me and my son on an outing.'

'Now that's been sorted, can we get started?' Ken asked, eager for the trip across the Mersey. 'It'll be time to come home before we get there.'

On the walk to the tram, Derek kept Ken busy in conversation, asking about his job, and what ambitions he had. Now and again Claire would pass a remark, but the talking was mostly conducted by the man and the boy. And when the tram arrived, Derek waited until Claire had chosen her seat by the window, with her son next to her, before taking a seat behind.

'There's not many people on the streets, is there, Mam?' Ken was taking in the sights and sounds. 'With it being so nice, yer'd expect it to be more busy.'

'It's Sunday, love, and all the shops are closed. Besides that, a lot of people go to church on a Sunday afternoon.'

Derek leaned forward, his head between theirs. 'Yer'll find it busy when we get to the Pier Head. I bet there's queues to get on the landing stage.'

And his words proved to be right, for there were hundreds of people pushing and shoving to get in line for the ticket office. There were young courting couples, happily looking forward to an afternoon in each other's company, but in the main those in the queue were families. Mothers and fathers, their nerves frayed with trying to keep their children under control. But armed with buckets and spades, and the thought of the sandcastles they'd build at New Brighton, the children were too excited and impatient to heed their parents.

'Good heavens,' Claire said, 'there doesn't seem to be much hope of getting on a ferry, Derek, not with this crowd. You'd be better coming on a weekday, if yer want to catch the sea air and test yer sea legs.'

'It isn't really as bad as it looks,' he told her. 'There's two ferry boats sailing, one each way, and yer'd be surprised at the number of people they can carry. There's one just coming in, and once the passengers are off, yer'll see this queue move very quickly.' He caught her arm as people joining the queue behind them jostled to get the best place. 'Would yer rather skip it for today? I wouldn't mind, honestly.'

Ken groaned. 'Ah, let's wait, Mam! I mightn't get the chance again.' He bent to smile in her face. 'Not until I'm earning decent wages, anyway. And when I'm in the money, I'll bring you and Amy down and treat yer to a ride on the boats.'

'And there speaks a good son,' Derek said. 'You'll be well looked after, Claire.'

'Oh, aye, I should be so lucky. By the time he's earning good money, he'll be taking girls out, not his mother and sister.' But Claire was smiling as she spoke. 'I just hope he finds himself a nice girl.'

There was a surge forward, and Ken put his arm round his mother's waist. 'We're on the move, Mam, so Derek was right.'

It took ten minutes for Derek to get the tickets and steer them on to the ferry, which, to Ken's delight, was bobbing up and down in the water. And that was the start of an afternoon of enjoyment for Claire and her son. She felt free, with the wind whipping her hair, and the cry of the seagulls following the boat. And watching her son leaning over the rails, with Derek beside him, she was happy because he looked so happy. He was being treated like a grown-up, chatting away to a man he hardly knew, but whom he'd taken a liking to. They talked the whole time, while watching the foam the ferry left in its wake. When they reached Seacombe, they watched the passengers going down the gangplank, while they stayed aboard for the journey back to the Pier Head. Derek explained he'd bought return tickets so they would be home in time for Amy.

And when the afternoon was over, and they finally stepped off the tram at the stop nearest to their house, Derek insisted on seeing them to their front door, and brushed aside their thanks. 'I've enjoyed meself as well,' he said, 'and it's me who should be thanking you for your company.'

After saying goodbye, Claire closed the front door thinking what a difference there was between him and Graham Collins. There was no side to Derek. What you saw was what you got. There was no need to watch her words, or how she spoke.

Trying to sound casual, Ken said, 'I think that was good of him to take us. He's a smashing bloke.'

Claire nodded. 'Yes, he is.' She wasn't going to say any more, for that would be admitting her son was a far better judge of character than she was.

Jack watched his wife straightening the lace runner on the sideboard, then plumping up the cushions on the couch. 'What time is Claire coming?'

'Half seven. She should be here any minute. I think she'll bring the children with her for a bit of fresh air.'

'I'll go round to yer ma's, then, love, to get out of the way. Yer don't want me sitting here cramping yer style. Is Nellie coming?'

Molly chuckled. 'She hasn't been invited, but yes, I think I can safely say that Nellie will be here about two minutes after Claire arrives. I bet any money she's standing with her nose pressed against the window right now.'

Ruthie had been hanging around, taking her time getting washed. And Molly was well aware of the reason. 'Won't Bella be expecting yer, sunshine? Ye're late tonight.'

'I was going to ask if I could bring her over here, Mam. We'd like to see Mrs Thompson again. We didn't see much of her last time.'

'Why don't yer come right out and say it's Ken yer want to see? Not that yer need to, 'cos I know how yer brain works. But whatever the reason, the answer is no. You've got yer own friends and I've got mine.'

Ruthie knew when she was beaten, then remembered something else which would please her just as much if her mother was in favour. 'Then can I invite my friends here again on Friday night, please?'

'You're a crafty little monkey, you are.' Molly tutted but knew she'd talked herself into a corner. 'I suppose so, as long as it doesn't cost me anything, and yer behave yerselves.'

When Ruthie stretched up to give her mother a kiss, she whispered in her ear, 'One out of two isn't bad going, is it, Mam?'

'Go on, away with yer. And you, Jack 'cos there's a knock at the door.'

'We're not throwing them out, are we?' Claire asked when Jack and Ruthie said they were going out. 'Don't let us chase yer.'

'No, they were going out, Claire, so don't worry.' A smile lit up Molly's face. 'Anyway, look who's here to take their place. This is a surprise, Nellie. I wasn't expecting you.'

Jack and Ruthie both went out laughing, for the expression on Nellie's face was hilarious. 'What d'yer mean, girl, yer weren't expecting me? Who were yer expecting? King Kong, or Jack the Ripper?'

'No, sunshine, neither of them are acquaintances of mine. My invited guests have arrived, and they are Claire, Ken and Amy.'

'Well that's too bad, 'cos I'm here now and I ain't leaving.' Brushing Molly aside, and to the delight of young Amy, Nellie waddled to her chair next to the sideboard, lifted it up and carried it to the table. 'Now this is where I sit, at the head of the table. You lot of invited guests can sit where yer like.'

'It's no good me arguing, I'd only lose,' Molly said. 'So I'll put the kettle on.'

'Mrs Bennett,' Amy asked, 'could I go over and see the baby?'

'Of course yer can go over, sunshine, they'd love to see yer. Bobby may be in bed though, 'cos he goes about this time every night. But go over anyway.'

'I'll go with her, if yer think they won't mind,' Ken said. 'I can have a natter to Phil, and tell him about us going to Seacombe yesterday, with Derek. I didn't get a chance to tell him today in work, 'cos he was busy.'

The jaws of both Molly and Nellie dropped. Molly was the first to recover. 'Of course yer can go with Amy.' And after the youngsters had left, she made a pot of tea quicker than she'd ever made one in her life. 'What's all this about you going to Seacombe with Derek?' And mentally calling herself a hypocrite, she added, 'I didn't think yer knew him that well?'

'I don't know him well.' Claire was determined not to blush. 'You sent him on the message, Molly, and through Ken asking about the sea, in a very roundabout way, it ended with me going to Seacombe with the pair of them. Don't ask me how, but why I went was because Ken was eager, and he gets very little out of life.' She grinned. 'That's my story and I'm sticking to it. And now what's your news?'

Nellie had been lost for words. But now she regained her power of speech. 'It's good news, girl, very good news.'

'Listen, sunshine,' Molly said to Nellie. 'Ye're not supposed to be here, so can I tell me visitor what I asked her to come for?'

'Certainly, girl! Yer know I'm not one to interfere.' Then under her breath, Nellie said, 'Anyone would think she was used to having visitors. Two-faced, that's what she is.'

Molly began the tale of Corker's party-to-be. How Claire, Ken and Amy were on the list of guests, and what wonderful parties they'd had in the reception room over Hanley's cake shop. Claire was taken by surprise. 'Corker hasn't invited the three of us, surely? I wouldn't dream of accepting, Molly, for we're practically strangers to him.'

Nellie thought she'd been well behaved for long enough. 'Listen to me, girl,' she said. 'If ye're a friend of ours, then ye're a friend of Corker's and all our families and friends. We're one big gang, and we stick together.'

'I know that, Nellie, have done since the first day I came. And I'll admit to wishing I had friends like you. But I couldn't expect Corker to invite us. I mean, it must be going to cost him a lot of money as it is.'

'I wouldn't bother arguing if I were you, Claire,' Molly told her. 'Apart from the fact yer'd be silly for missing a really good night's entertainment, Corker would be really upset if yer refused his invitation.'

Nellie nodded her agreement. 'He would be very upset, would Corker. He loves his family and his friends. And me and Molly would be upset too, 'cos we're the ones what would have to tell him our mate didn't want to come to his party.'

'I wouldn't like to embarrass you two, but to tell the truth, I haven't got anything decent to wear to a party, and neither have the children.'

Molly and Nellie looked at each other and burst out laughing. 'Join the club, sunshine, we're in the same boat. But we're not worried 'cos we've got friends at the market and they'll fix us up. They'd fix you and Amy up, too, if yer like?'

'Oh, yes, please! I'll go with yer to the market when yer go. Oh, that's made me feel better. Will yer tell Corker I'd love to come to his party, and thank him for asking me and my children.'

Molly was telling herself she was getting more crafty than Nellie every day. 'I'm not telling him, yer can tell him yerself. He only lives next door, and Ellen will be in, too. I'll come with yer – it won't take a minute. All yer have to do is thank him, and when we come back yer can tell us how yer got on with Graham Collins the other day, and what happened on the ferry trip.'

Claire patted her hair and straightened her skirt while Molly knocked on the house next door. It was Ellen who answered, and she smiled a welcome. 'This is unexpected. Come on in, ye're very welcome.'

Molly had to pretend to be surprised. 'Derek! I didn't know you were here!'

He thought that was funny, because she'd waved to him through the window as he passed. But as Claire was with her, he guessed there was method in her madness. He hoped so, 'cos he could do with someone on his side. 'I come up most nights, to go for a pint with Corker. It'll be different when I start work, so I may as well make the most of it. How are you, Claire?'

'I'm fine, thanks, Derek. I've just come to thank Corker and Ellen for inviting us to their party. It really is very kind of them, considering they hardly know us.'

'If ye're a friend of Molly's, me darlin', then ye're a friend of ours.' Corker towered over her when he kissed her cheek. 'Welcome to our gang.'

'Where's Ken and Amy?' Derek asked. 'Did they come with yer?'

'They did, but they've gone across to Doreen's. Amy to see the baby, and Ken to see his hero, Phil.'

'I'll walk yer home then,' Derek said. 'Me and Corker are only having the one pint tonight, so I'll be ready to leave by the time you are.'

'You really don't need to walk us home, Derek. We'll be all right.'

'I'll tell yer what then. I'll walk Ken home, and you take care of Amy.'

Molly thought this was a very opportune moment to leave. Another minute would give Claire time to refuse. 'Come on, sunshine, or Nellie will be spitting fire when we get back. Yer know how she hates to miss anything.'

Claire only had time to thank the Corkhills again, before she was pulled into the street and up the steps of the house next door. 'Ay, Molly, take it easy. Yer nearly pulled me arm out.'

'If I hadn't, then Nellie would, wouldn't yer, sunshine?' Molly smiled, her eyes telling her friend to go along with her.

'I'd have marmalised the two of yer, girl, 'cos I was fed up talking to meself. So sit down and dish the dirt.'

The next hour was spent with Claire telling them Graham had been in the shop that morning, and she'd made it very clear she wouldn't be going out with him again. Apparently he got quite angry, and she could see there was another side to him. So when he tried to coax her, she refused to change her mind. Then the talk went to the forthcoming party, with Claire getting excited when she heard what was in store. 'I hope they don't all go dressed up. I'd feel like a poor relation.'

'For heaven's sake stop worrying about that! Me and Nellie need something decent to wear, so we'll take yer with us to the market. Yer don't have to worry about money, 'cos the most yer'll pay for a good second-hand dress will be five bob. And I promise yer, sunshine, by the time it's been washed and ironed it will look like a new one.'

All too soon it was nine thirty, and Claire began to worry about the length of time her children had been in Doreen's. 'I hope they haven't been a nuisance. I'm surprised our Amy has stayed so long. She's usually shy with strangers.'

'I'll nip across and fetch them. And I'm sure they haven't been a nuisance. They are both very well behaved.'

Molly was crossing the cobbles with Ken and Amy when Derek came out of Corker's. 'I see I timed it nicely.' He grinned at Ken. 'I'm walking you home, and yer mam is walking Amy. Is that all right with you?'

Ken thought it was Christmas and his birthday all rolled into one. He'd been talking to Phil about work, and how he'd enjoyed going on the ferry with Mr Corkhill's friend. And as usual Phil treated him as an equal. He would always be one of Ken's favourite people, for he'd got the lad a job when the family were at rock bottom. And now seeing Derek again, well, life was really good right now.

Molly and Nellie stood at the door and waved the foursome off, Claire in front, swinging her daughter's arm, followed by Derek and Ken. And when they were near the bottom of the street, the two mates closed the door and went inside.

Nellie narrowed her eyes. 'You knew Derek was next door, didn't yer?'

Molly nodded. 'I think they make a lovely couple, and a helping hand won't go amiss.'

'Yer haven't forgotten where we're going tomorrow, girl, have yer?'

'No, sunshine, I haven't. We'll have to be out by ten in the morning to make sure we get to Gertie's before the queer feller arrives. I don't know exactly how they're going to do it, so we'll need a bit of extra time. I'm looking forward to seeing Sally and the other ladies again. And it should be interesting to see if we're right about Mr Graham Collins. I think we are, from what Claire said about him. In any case, whether we're right or not, he's out of Claire's life now, thank goodness.'

At quarter to ten the next morning they were knocking on Sally's door. 'Don't bite our heads off,' Molly said. 'We wanted to get here early to see what's happening, but I think we're a bit too early for yer.'

Sally shook her head. 'No, I've finished me housework, except for me washing. I haven't had the fire lit, so I didn't have that to clean out, which makes a difference. The washing is in steep, and I'll rinse it and have it on the line this afternoon. I'm dying to see what happens when that bloke comes. Just to see if he offers them a good price, or if he's a fraud.' She pointed to the chairs. 'Sit down and I'll tell yer what the ladies intend to do. I'm going to stand in Gertie's kitchen and listen to what he has to say. You told her the picture was worth five pound, and she shouldn't sell it if offered ten bob less than that.

If he does, she's going to refuse to sell, and I'll use the back way to get to Harriet's to put her in the picture. If he offers Harriet a lot less than three pound, she'll refuse to sell, and I'll go on to Alice's. The whole street know what we're up to, so if he undervalues the first two by a large amount, everyone in the street will be after him. And in a few hours it'll be round the neighbourhood and he's not going to do any business in these parts. Nor does he deserve to.'

'Let's not judge him until we have proof, eh?' Molly shrugged her shoulders. 'Me and Nellie could be wrong, but I don't think so. Anyway, we should know in a couple of hours' time. But where can me and me mate go while we're waiting? I don't fancy hanging around the streets for that length of time.'

'Don't be daft! Yer can stay here, of course. Gertie said it was between eleven and half past when he came last week, so the whole thing could be over before twelve. I'm not going to Gertie's yet, so yer can keep me amused for three quarters of an hour.' She grinned at Nellie, who had been very quiet. 'I'll tell yer what, queen, why don't I make a pot of tea, and when yer've wet yer whistle, yer can tell me a few jokes.'

'That's the best news I've had since I got out of bed,' Nellie said. 'But I can't tell yer any dirty jokes, 'cos me mate won't let me.'

'I'll settle for anything that'll make me laugh, queen. If yer run out of clean ones, I've got a tub full of washing, so yer can clean up some of yer dirty jokes.'

'Don't encourage her, sunshine,' Molly said. 'Just give her a cup of tea, a biscuit if yer have one, and she'll keep yer amused for as long as yer like.'

Nellie winked at Sally as she stood up to go to the kitchen. 'See how my mate looks after me? She's me manager, yer know. All professionals like me have a manager.'

'If yer keep on working that mouth of yours, sunshine, yer'll talk us both out of a cup of tea and a biscuit.'

'It's twelve o'clock, girl. What the hell is keeping Sally?' Nellie was getting restless and had been to the window half a dozen times. 'Something should have happened by now.'

'I should hope so, sunshine, or we'll have been wasting our time.'

The words were no sooner out of Molly's mouth than the back door was flung open. Sally's face was bright red and her eyes were glistening. 'I'm sorry yer've been left on yer own so long, but it couldn't be helped. My God, yer haven't half missed something. Yer were right about that swine, he's a real rotter.' Taking a deep breath, she pulled out a chair and sat down. 'He offered Gertie thirty bob for the picture, what your friend had down for five pound. And he got a right cob on when she said she didn't want to sell. I left while he was telling her she was stupid for not taking the money while she could, for she wouldn't get that much for it off anyone else.'

Molly gasped. 'Thirty bob! That's as bad as stealing. No wonder he dresses to kill. He can afford to by stealing from poor people.'

'He wants stringing up,' Nellie said, 'the bad bugger.'

'Oh, wait until yer hear the rest.' Sally leaned her elbows on the table. 'He offered Harriet one pound for her crystal bowl, where your man said three pound. And Alice was offered fifteen shillings when on the list yer gave us, it was worth two pound ten shillings.'

'He shouldn't be allowed to get away with it,' Molly said. 'Someone should stop him.'

'Well, because of you and Nellie, he has been stopped. Round here, anyway. Yer see, when I heard about Gertie and Harriet, I didn't wait to see how Alice got on, I was too busy knocking on doors. And like yerselves, the women round here don't like people who rob from the poor. And they were waiting for him when he came out of Alice's. The last I saw of him he was legging it up the street as though the devil was on his tail. He lost his hat – one of the women knocked it off his head. And when he was out of sight we all had a good laugh. He'll not show his face in this area again. In fact, me and the other ladies are taking the leaflets to the police, and we're going to tell them what their items were worth, and how much he had offered for them. His days of living the good life are over. If he wants money, then he'll have to dirty his hands and go to work for it.'

Molly gave a sigh of relief. 'I'm glad me and Nellie were right. And I'm glad the rotter won't be stealing from anyone else.'

Nellie lifted her bosom on to the table so she could look into her mate's face. 'The McDonough and Bennett Private Detective Agency have won another case, eh, girl?'

Molly shook her head, 'No, Nellie, it was the Bennett and McDonough Agency what won the case.'

Sally looked puzzled. 'What are you two talking about now?'

'It's just our little joke, Sally, take no notice of us.' Molly pushed her chair back. 'I'm glad I know the truth now, and I'm glad none of yer friends were taken for a ride. So we'll leave yer in peace to get on with yer washing. Come on, Nellie.'

'Aren't yer going to see Gertie, Harriet and Alice?' Sally looked disappointed. 'They're waiting to see yer, to thank yer.'

'We haven't got any shopping in yet, Sally, and I hadn't finished me housework when we came out. I don't like to love yer and leave yer, but we'll have to be on our way. Will yer explain to yer friends, and tell them I appreciate that they believed me and Nellie.'

'Well, will yer come and see us again some time?' Sally didn't want to think she would never see the two friends again. 'When yer've got a couple of hours to spare?'

'We'll try, won't we, Nellie?' Molly liked Sally, and knew she'd be a good friend. But a person can only have so many friends. And with the Bennetts, McDonoughs, Corkhills, Jacksons and Higginses, plus the likes of Maisie and Alec from the corner shop, well, they were enough friends to enrich her life.

The friends were walking slowly up the street, discussing the downfall of the high and mighty Graham Collins. 'When are yer going to tell Claire, girl? She won't half get a shock.'

Molly shook her head. 'No she won't, sunshine, because we're not going to tell her. She's finished with him now, so let's leave it at that. Let her get on with her life now.'

Chapter Thirty

'What time did Claire say she'd get here for?' Nellie asked as she carried her carver chair to the table. 'And how come she can get off work on a Thursday afternoon?'

'She coaxed her boss to let her have it off, saying she'd work through her dinner hour for a few days to make the time up. She's getting worried about not having anything decent for the party. And with it being only two weeks off, it's time we got ourselves sorted out as well, sunshine. I don't want to have to go in a dress I've been wearing to go shopping in for the last couple of months.'

'Yeah, I'll be glad when I've got something nice.' Nellie's chubby face creased. 'I'm going to look for something slinky, what will show off me voluptuous body.'

'That voluptuous body will come between you and yer sleep, sunshine,' Molly told her. 'It's all yer ever think about.'

'Ye're only jealous, girl, 'cos you haven't got one. It's me what the men look at as they go past. Their eyes are drawn to me.'

Molly pushed her chair back. 'I'm going to put the kettle on, and when I come back d'yer think we could find something else to talk about, instead of that ruddy voluptuous body of yours? Like how much money we've got to spend on dresses.'

Nellie pushed herself up and followed her mate into the kitchen. 'I hate talking to anyone when I can't see their face.' She folded her arms and they disappeared beneath her bosom.

'I've got two pound, girl, so I should be able to get a lot for that much.'

'I've only got thirty bob, and it's going to have to do. Jack needs a new shirt and tie, so I'll have to go careful.'

'Yer can borrow off me if ye're short. I won't be spending the whole two pound.'

'Thanks, sunshine, that's good of yer. But remember not to brag about money when we're out with Claire, 'cos she must have a struggle to make ends meet.'

'Has she seen any more of Derek, d'yer know?'

'I couldn't tell yer, sunshine. I don't know any more than you do. Derek started work last week, with Corker, so he won't be around as much.' The kettle began to whistle and Molly reached for a cloth to cover her hand and protect it from the steam. 'I'm pleased that Corker managed to get him taken on, 'cos he was getting fed up having nothing to do all day.' As she poured the boiling water into the teapot, Molly was in two minds whether to tell her mate something she'd heard. 'Oh, I suppose I'd better tell yer, 'cos Claire is bound to mention it, and yer'd think I was mean for not telling yer.'

Nellie moved away from the sink, and her arms appeared like magic. 'Oh, aye, girl, what's that? And how come you know and I don't?'

'Because I always feel a bit guilty when I pass on something I've been told. Not that I've been told in confidence, like, 'cos if I had then I wouldn't tell yer.'

Nellie blew out her breath in exasperation. 'Would yer mind speaking in plain English, girl, instead of going round the houses? Are yer going to tell me what yer know, or do I have to drag it out of yer?'

'It's nothing to get excited about, sunshine, not like another war breaking out. It's just that I heard Derek had taken Ken to Anfield to see Liverpool play last Saturday.'

'Ooh er. That sounds promising, doesn't it, girl? It looks as though yer might be right about Derek and Claire getting together.'

'Watch what yer say in front of Claire, Nellie, or yer might put her off if she thinks people are talking. And I haven't said anything about her and Derek getting together. All I said is that they'd make a nice couple.'

'Molly Bennett, I've known yer long enough to know what's running through yer mind. And I know yer'd be delighted if they did click.' Nellie waited for Molly to pick up the tray, then followed her into the living room. 'And I'll tell yer what I think, shall I? I think that with you and Ken both moving in the same direction, it's a foregone conclusion.'

Molly put the tray down before looking at her friend, surprise written on her face. 'Nellie McDonough, that was quite a speech for you. And very well spoken, too! Yer can go to the top of the class, sunshine – yer did well.'

'Ah, but was I right, girl, that's the burning question?'

'Yes, Nellie, you are right. I think Claire has had a hard time since her husband died. In fact, through Ken, we know she has. And she's a thoroughly nice woman. I like her very much, and her two children. I also believe Derek is a thoroughly nice bloke, who will one day make a very lucky woman a fantastic husband. If we put all those points together, it comes out that Claire and Derek are made for each other. And that would make me, and her children, very happy. However, yer can't force someone to love another person, can yer? With the best will in the world, I can't make them love each other.'

'Ye're having a bloody good try, girl, I'll say that for yer. And 'cos ye're me best mate, I'm going to try and get a bit of help for yer. I'll have a word with Saint Peter tonight, when I'm in bed, and with him on our side we'll be home and dry.'

Molly was pouring the tea out when the knocker sounded, and Nellie said, 'Okay, girl, I'll go.' It was so unusual for Nellie to offer to take her backside off the chair, Molly's face wore a look of utter astonishment as she watched the little woman head for the door. 'Are yer feeling all right, sunshine?'

'Top of the world, girl, top of the world,' Nellie answered before opening the door to Claire. 'You must be able to smell the tea, girl, 'cos me mate's just pouring it out.'

'I've timed it nicely, then.' Claire was looking very happy when she entered the living room. 'I've been looking forward to this trip to the market. After all yer've told me about Sadie and Mary Ann, I'm dying to meet them.'

'Yer'll love them, Claire,' Molly said. 'Apart from being nice, they're really very funny. Me and Nellie have known them a couple of years, and they've been good to us. They always manage to find something to suit us no matter what we're after. Anyway, yer'll find out for yerself. But get this cup of tea down yer first, and I've made yer a butty so yer won't be hungry. I don't suppose yer've had anything since breakfast, have yer?'

Claire shook her head. 'No, but I could have lasted out. Yer shouldn't have gone to any trouble for me.'

'I wouldn't call making a cheese sandwich going to any trouble, sunshine. It took me all of five minutes.'

'One of these days I'll pay you and Nellie back for what yer've both done for me. Not that any amount of money can repay kindness. But when Ken's earning a bit more, I'll treat yer to afternoon tea at Reece's. They bring a cake stand to the table with a variety of fresh cream cakes, so yer could have as many cream slices as yer liked, Nellie.'

'Now ye're talking my language, girl. When were yer thinking of taking us?'

'Ooh, let's see now.' Claire tapped a finger on her chin while looking thoughtful. 'Ken will be fifteen soon, so it'll be six years before he's earning a man's wage. D'yer think yer could hold out that long, Nellie?'

'With great difficulty, girl, with great difficulty.' Then she thought of something. 'Ay, your Ken in the same age as Ruthie, isn't he?'

Molly sighed inwardly. What in the name of goodness was her friend going to come out with now? Best to head her off. 'Come on, girls, drink yer tea and let's be on our way. If we leave it too late, most of the best stuff will have been snapped up.'

'Gosh, it's busy here,' Claire said, looking around in amazement. 'It must be about seven years since I was here last, and I don't remember it being so busy.'

'It's the nice weather, sunshine,' Molly said. 'A lot of people are probably just walking around. Anything to get them out of the house and in the fresh air.'

'Me and Molly come here for our Christmas shopping, don't we, girl? We know most of the stallholders, and we always manage to knock them down in price.'

'Yer mean you always manage to knock them down, Nellie – I wouldn't have the nerve. But I'm always grateful to yer for saving me a few bob.'

'I'll come with yer when yer do yer Christmas shopping, if yer'll let me. I always think it's more fun when ye're with someone.'

'Yer'll be welcome, sunshine.' Molly was wondering how she could bring up the subject of Derek, Ken and the football match. But she couldn't think of any way except to ask straight out. 'Ay, I believe Derek took Ken to see Liverpool play on Saturday.'

'Yes, and our Ken was over the moon. He came back looking

as though he'd won the pools, but with no voice. Derek said he'd lost it with shouting encouragement to the Liverpool players. And I believe that when Liverpool scored, Ken got so excited he slapped Derek on the back and nearly sent him flying.'

'It was thoughtful of Derek to take him,' Molly said, 'and I bet Ken appreciated it.'

'He did, Molly, and so did I. Honestly, I've never known my son to be as happy and outgoing since his dad died. He hasn't had much of a life in the last, what, five years. It's not been so bad for Amy, 'cos she doesn't remember her dad. But Ken does; he's never forgotten him. And because he looks so much like his dad, I am reminded of him every day.'

'Well I'm glad for Ken, 'cos I think he's a smashing lad. And I like Derek, too; he's a man I would trust with me life. And ay, he brought his mam down to Corker's a few days ago, and she's lovely. She's like Victoria, and Mrs Corkhill. I always want to hug them to pieces, and I felt the same about Derek's mam. Her name's Hannah, and she's bright and bubbly.'

Nellie pulled on her mate's arm. 'We're there now, girl. I can see Sadie's blond hair.'

At that moment, Sadie saw the women and waved. Above the hustle and bustle, she shouted, 'Go to yer usual speck and I'll be with yer as soon as I can.'

'What a lovely-looking girl,' Claire said, hanging on to Molly in case they got separated in the crowd. 'She stands out, doesn't she? I bet she has all the boys running after her.'

'Half the lads in the market have tried to date her,' Molly said. 'But she's engaged to a lad called Harry, and she's crazy about him.'

'They're getting married next year,' Nellie said, her head and chins nodding. 'Me and Molly are going to the church to see the wedding.'

Molly stopped at the last trestle table. 'This is our speck, and that's Mary Ann, the woman who owns the stall, over there. She's a character if ever there was one. Just watch the way she handles the crowd.'

Mary Ann, with her bright red hair, long black skirt and white blouse, was standing with her hands on her hips in front of one of the trestle tables. 'Aggie, I thought you and Elsie were supposed to be best mates?'

'We are, Mary Ann,' said Aggie, her huge bosom resting on top of a pile of clothes. 'But that doesn't mean I have to give her everything she wants. I saw this blouse first, and she tried to grab it off me.'

'Why, you lying cow!' Elsie was red in the face and very agitated. 'Don't yer take no notice of her, Mary Ann, she's a bleeding liar. I saw the blouse first. It was me what said it was a nice colour, and before I had a chance to pick it up, this one had it in her hand.'

Mary Ann's head wagged from side to side. 'Oh, dear, me heart bleeds for yer. It's the end of a perfect friendship, and all over a blouse what won't fit either of yer.'

'It'll fit me, Mary Ann.' Aggie wasn't going to let go of that blouse for love or money. It was a dark brown, just the colour she liked. 'I know it will fit me, and I got me hands on it first.'

'Over my dead body do yer walk off with the blouse what I was the first to see.' An equally irate Elsie made another unsuccessful attempt to grab the article which Aggie was hanging on to like grim death. 'And if I saw yer in the street with it on, so help me I'd tear the ruddy thing off yer back.'

'If ye're going to fight about it, why don't yer come round the table and fight it out inside the square? If yer want to make a spectacle of yerselves, then the least yer can do is perform in front of a crowd.' Mary Ann held out a hand. 'While ye're knocking the stuffing out of each other, I'll keep the blouse safe. Hand it over, Aggie, or d'yer want me to come round there and take it off yer?'

Knowing Mary Ann's reputation for never losing a fight, Aggie passed the blouse over. 'I want it back, though, Mary Ann, don't yer forget that. Once I've sorted Elsie out, I'll be taking that home with me.'

'This blouse is a shilling, Aggie. Will yer pay that for it?'

'I'll give yer a shilling for it, Mary Ann.' Elsie wasn't finished yet, not by a long chalk. 'Yer can have it now if yer like.'

Aggie's nostrils flared at that. 'You flaming cow!' She pushed the unsuspecting Elsie hard, and the woman would have ended up on the ground if it hadn't been for the women crowded round waiting for the fun to start. They didn't get much excitement in their lives, and they weren't going to miss a punch-up.

Elsie was rolling her sleeves up, ready for the fray, when Mary Ann said, 'Hang on a minute, ladies, before yer tear each other limb from limb. I don't care whether yer kill each other or not, but I'll not let it happen at my stall. I've got me reputation to think of.' She saw Aggie's hand curl into a fist, and Elsie's sleeves rolled up further. Then she looked round at the faces of those hoping for a free-for-all. 'Before yer get too excited, let me show yer what these two silly buggers are fighting for.' She held the blouse up, and there was a gasp from those looking on. For the blouse had been part of a school uniform, and looked about the right size for a ten-year-old girl. 'Two grown-up women didn't have the sense to see if the blouse would fit them before they let their greed get the better of them. But yer all heard Elsie offer me a shilling for it, so give me a shilling, queen, and yer can have the ruddy blouse.'

'I'm not paying a shilling for a blouse what won't fit me!

Well, the bleeding cheek of yer, Mary Ann. I've never heard nothing like it in all me life. Did yer hear that, Aggie?'

Yes, Aggie had heard, but she was in a quandary. Elsie was her mate, and lived a few doors away from her. Their husbands were mates, too, and went for a pint together every Saturday night. But Mary Ann had been good to her over the years, and she wasn't prepared to fall out with her. 'We asked for it, Elsie, and we've made a laughing stock of ourselves. I bet if we ask Mary Ann, she'll find us each a nice blouse what will fit. Eh, Mary Ann?'

But the stallholder's eyes weren't on them at the moment. She was looking at a woman standing at the next table. 'That'll be one and six, Tessie.'

The woman stared back. 'What are yer on about, Mary Ann? I haven't bought nothing yet.'

'Yer mean yer hadn't paid for anything yet, don't yer, Tessie? The blouse yer've put in yer bag is a shilling, and the underskirt a tanner.'

There were murmurs from most of the women around, for Mary Ann was the most popular stallholder in the market. You always got a square deal off her, and she was always good for a laugh. 'Oh, me mind must have been miles away, Mary Ann,' said Tessie, now sporting a very red face. 'I wasn't going to go away without paying. It's just that I was looking to see if there was anything for our Annie.'

'I'll believe yer where thousands wouldn't,' the stallholder told her. 'Give the money to Sadie, she's nearer to yer.' Then Mary Ann turned back to Aggie and Elsie. 'You two want yer heads banging together, and I'd do it meself if I wasn't frightened of the few brains yer've got falling out. Now act yer age and have a root through the stalls. Give us a shout if yer find anything that yer like. I've got to see to some friends now.'

Claire was enjoying the scene. 'I could stand here all day, just watching. Let me know next time ye're coming and I'll ask for time off again.'

Mary Ann was smiling when she approached them. 'It's good to see yer, Molly, and you, Nellie.' She rubbed her hands and laughed. 'Me takings will be healthy today, 'cos yer always spend a few bob. And I see yer've brought a mate with yer.'

Molly made the introductions. 'Each of us wants a dress, and they have to be in good nick and stylish, 'cos we've got a party coming up.'

'Yer mean stylish as in Buckingham Palace, or stylish as in a knees-up next door?'

Molly chuckled. 'Somewhere in between, Mary Ann. Have yer got anything in mind?'

'If I served you, Sadie would have me life. As far as she's concerned, you are, and always will be, her customers.' Mary Ann felt an arm go round her waist and turned her head to look into the bright blue eyes of the girl she looked on as a daughter. 'Speak of the devil and he's bound to appear. Yer mates are here, Sadie, and they're looking for ten guinea dresses for ten bob. I'll leave yer to see what yer can do for them, while I keep me eye on this lot.'

'Some good clothes came in last week, and I thought of you two right away. So I put them on one side, on the rack,' Sadie smiled at Claire. 'Is the twosome now a threesome?'

Nellie thought it was time she joined in. 'Yes, this is Claire, and she's a new friend of ours. We've all been invited to a party and want to look like film stars.'

'Come over to the rack, then, and I'll show yer what I put away. There'll be something for yer friend, too, 'cos I can think of a couple of nice dresses in her size.'

On the way over to the rack of clothes, Molly said, 'Is the

wedding still on for Easter, Sadie? Me and Nellie don't want to miss it.'

'Yes, it's still on. I wish it was tomorrow – I can't wait. But I'll see yer loads of times before that, and I can give yer a definite time and everything.' Sadie went straight to a lilac dress in soft cotton, and took the hanger off the rack. 'I thought of this for you, Molly. It would go well with yer blond colouring.'

Molly was delighted as she held the dress up for inspection. 'Oh, it's lovely, Sadie. Thank you. Ye're a pal.'

'Ay, we'll have no favouritism,' Nellie said, pretending to take the huff. 'Whatever yer've got for me will have to be as nice as that one.'

Sadie grinned and stretched to take another hanger from the rack. 'I thought royal blue for you, Nellie, with a nice white collar. It will fit yer, and there's a belt in the same material.'

'Oh, brother, will yer look at that!' To say Nellie was chuffed would be putting it mildly. 'If I don't get a feller in that, I'll never get one.'

While Nellie held the dress up to her shoulders and paraded up and down, Sadie gazed at Claire's face. What a beauty she was. There was no dress on the rack to do her justice. But then beauty wasn't reserved just for the rich. 'Ye're about my size, and there's two nice dresses on the rack that would fit. I'll show yer them both.'

With Molly and Nellie watching, Claire looked from the pale blue dress to the one in a soft green colour. Without hesitation, her hand went to the green one. 'That's my favourite colour. I like the style, too. It's lovely.' There was doubt in her eyes as she worried about the price, and this wasn't missed by Molly.

'Sadie, there's a dress at the end there. Could I have a look at it?' Molly took the girl by the arm and led her away from Claire. 'I did this on purpose, sunshine, so I could ask yer how much the dresses are. Particularly the green one, that Claire likes?'

'All the same price, seeing as it's you, Molly. Ten bob each. Is that all right?'

'Wonderful, sunshine, wonderful. Yer look like an angel, and yer are an angel. We'll be the best dressed at the party.'

All the way home on the tram, Claire couldn't stop talking about how she'd had her eyes opened. 'I never thought I'd get such a nice dress for ten bob. I can't believe it. At least I don't have to worry about the party any more.'

'The only worry you and me have, sunshine, is that Nellie will outshine the two of us.'

Sitting on the end of the seat, with half her backside hanging over and defying the law of gravity, Nellie was grinning like a Cheshire cat. Just wait. She'd show 'em. On the night of the party she'd knock 'em dead.

'No, yer can't have the gang in on Friday night, sunshine, and it's no good yer sitting there pulling faces at me.' Molly was determined to hold out this time. 'It's the party on Saturday, and I'll want to wash me hair tomorrow night. I'm not doing that with half a dozen youngsters watching.'

'Don't argue with yer mam, Ruthie,' Jack said. 'Be satisfied that yer've got the party to look forward to.'

'I know I'm lucky, Dad, but me and Bella are skint after buying new frocks for the party, so we can't go to the pictures. And it's boring sitting in the house twiddling our thumbs.'

'Then why don't the pair of yer go for a walk and get some fresh air?' Molly asked. 'Or go round to yer grandma's? Yer'd have a laugh with them, and Tommy and Rosie. It would certainly be better than twiddling yer thumbs.'

There was a spark of interest in the young girl's eyes as she sat up straight in the chair, and her legs stopped swinging.

'Could we go round there tonight, Mam? It would pass the time away, and as yer say we'd have a laugh. Then tomorrow night I'll wash me hair, same as you. I'm going to try and do something different with mine, a new style.'

Jack raised his brows. 'Yer hair is lovely the way it is. Why would yer want to change it?'

'I thought of parting it in the middle, or combing it straight back and tying it with a ribbon.'

Molly's mind took her back to when she was Ruthie's age, and how she'd tied her long hair back with a ribbon. 'If yer like, sunshine, I'll have a go at yer hair tomorrow night. I could comb it back and tie it, or perhaps a side parting would look nice. We could keep on trying until we came up with something yer liked.'

'Oh, that would be great, Mam! When yer go to the shops tomorrow, would yer get me some ribbon?'

'Yer'll have to tell me what colour yer want, how much, the width, and whether yer want it plain or in satin?'

'Well, yer've seen me dress, and it's blue and beige, so I think blue would be nice.'

'The colour of yer eyes, love,' Jack said, as proud of his youngest child as he was of the other three. He never ceased to tell himself how lucky he was to have such a wonderful wife and children. 'I'll give yer mam the money to pay for it.'

Ruthie was round the table in a flash. 'Oh, thanks, Dad. Ye're the best dad in the world, and I don't half love yer.' She took her arms from round his neck. 'I'll go over to Bella's now, and we'll walk to me grandma's. I won't be late – half nine at thc latest.'

When she'd gone, Molly looked at Jack and shook her head. 'I suppose yer know we are both too soft with her, don't yer?'

'Perhaps we are a bit soft, but she's not a spoiled brat, like some kids.'

'I know, sunshine.' Molly gave him the look that still had the power to send his heart pounding. 'I think, all in all, we've done a good job with our children. And we've made a pretty good job of our marriage.'

'We're still making a good job of it, love.' He raised his brows. 'What time did Ruthie say she'd be in?' He waited for her answer, then said, 'That gives us two hours with the house to ourselves. And I can think of better things to do than twiddle me thumbs.'

'Ooh, yer know I can't resist those brown eyes. But stay off the creaking stairs, 'cos yer know Nellie's got ears like a hawk. She can hear yer from three doors away.'

Jack reached for her hand. 'I've got more on me mind right now than your mate Nellie.'

On Friday night, while Molly and Ruthie were busy doing their hair, Claire was sitting in her fireside chair sewing a hem on the green dress she'd bought at the market. When she'd been ironing it, she'd caught the hem with the iron and broken the cotton, causing a few stitches to come loose. Now she was making it good while Ken and Amy listened to a play on the wireless. They seldom had visitors, so when the knocker sounded all three were startled. 'Who the heck can this be?'

'I'll go, Mam. You stay where yer are.'

Claire's hand was still as she listened. She heard her son saying, 'Come in, Derek. I'm just listening to a play, and it's not half exciting.'

'Are yer sure yer mam's not too busy?'

'Oh, come on in, don't be daft,' Ken said. 'Me mam is only doing a bit of sewing.'

Derek walked through to see Claire with a sewing needle between her fingers. 'Have I caught yer at a bad time?'

Claire didn't want him to see the dress, not until tomorrow night. She folded it over quickly and dropped it at the side of her chair. 'No, it's not a bad time – I do a bit of sewing most nights. I need to with two children. When the play on the wireless is over, it'll be time for Amy to go to bed.'

Although he said, 'I won't stay long,' Derek sat himself down on the couch. 'I came to say I'll come for yer tomorrow night, and take yer to the hall. Everyone's making their own way there, but Molly said she wasn't sure whether you know where it is or not. Anyway, to put her mind at rest, I said I'd pick yer up.'

'There's really no need to, Derek. I'm sure we'd find it.' Little did Claire know that her son knew exactly where it was. But he wasn't saying. 'Anyway, what about yer mother? Yer can't expect her to walk here, then all the way to the hall.'

'She's going early,' Derek explained. 'She wants to see the babies Corker's told her about: Doreen's son Bobby, and little Molly, Jill's daughter. Molly said she'd take her to see them 'cos me ma dotes on children.' He grinned. 'I think it's a dig at me because I haven't given her any grandchildren.'

'Molly really took a shine to her; she said she was a love.'

He nodded. 'She is. Me ma is one of the best, and I'm dead proud of her.'

Amy had been awkward with Derek at first, but after meeting him a few times she'd lost her shyness. Now she asked, 'Will we be seeing your mother tomorrow night?'

'You certainly will, pet, and she knows all about yer 'cos I've told her. She's looking forward to meeting the three of yer.'

'I'm not half looking forward to it,' Ken said. 'I've never been to a party in a hall before. Ruthie Bennett said there'll be food and music. And she said Mrs McDonough will keep us all entertained. It'll be smashing.'

'When it's your birthday, son, we'll throw a party, eh? Not a big one in a hall, but a party nevertheless. You can choose where yer want it.'

'Can I have a party on my birthday?' Amy asked. 'I've never had one before.'

Derek ruffled her hair. 'Of course yer can, sweetheart. Like Ken, yer can have it where yer like and invite who yer want.'

'Don't tell her any more, Derek, or she'll be too excited to sleep. And it's her bedtime now, so wash yer face and hands, love, and I'll take you upstairs.'

'I'll leave yer to get on with it,' Derek said, standing up and rubbing his bottom. 'One of these days I'll fix that for yer, Claire.'

She grinned. 'I'll hold yer to that. It definitely needs fixing.'

Ken got to his feet. 'I'll see Derek out, Mam.'

'No, son, you stay and listen to the play. I'll see him out.'

Derek stood on the pavement looking up at her. 'I'll pick yer up about half seven, is that all right?' When she nodded, he asked, with a shy but cheeky grin, 'Are yer going to have a dance with me tomorrow night?'

'It's so long since I danced, Derek, I'd be standing all over yer feet.'

'I'll take me chances. Sleep well and I'll see yer tomorrow.'

Claire watched him walk away. When he turned to wave, she waved back before closing the door with a smile on her face and a feeling of well-being in her heart.

Ruthie and Bella were the first to arrive at the reception hall, followed by Gordon and Peter Corkhill, Jeff Mowbray and Johnny Stewart. The two girls looked very pretty in their new dresses, and wearing their hair in a new style. And the boys looked very smart, all neatly dressed and not a hair out of place.

The youngsters were wide-eyed when they saw the long trestle tables laden with a wide variety of food. The vases of flowers set at intervals added a nice finishing touch. The Hanleys had certainly spared no expense on the buffet: it was fit for a king.

Corker's booming voice was heard coming up the stairs, and he entered the room with Ellen, Derek's mother Hannah, and Molly and Jack. While they were expressing their appreciation at the spread, the hall was filling up. Jill and Steve, happy to be having a rare night out while Lizzie Corkhill minded baby Molly, arrived with Doreen and Phil. Baby Bobby had been put to bed and was asleep, with Frances and Victoria listening out for him.

The corner pub had delivered the drinks ordered by Corker: crates of beer and two bottles of whisky for the men; crates of milk stout and bottles of sherry for the women; and lemonade and cream soda for the youngsters.

Nellie's grand entrance brought the first burst of laughter. She swanned in with one hand on a hip and the other touching the back of her head. Her hair in curls, and her new dress doing her proud, she swayed over to Corker and drawled, 'Why don't yer come up and see me some time, big boy, and you can peel me a grape.'

George, Paul and Lily, with Archie and his mam, laughed even more heartily than the rest, for they'd witnessed the shenanigans of Nellie while Lily was trying to curl her hair.

Bridie and Bob, with Tommy and Rosie, were just in time to see Nellie's first performance of the night, and as Bridie was to say later to Corker, 'Sure, we were laughing from the time we came into the room, so we were.'

The room was noisy with conversation and laughter, but Corker's voice brought instant silence. 'Ye're all welcome, and the food is there to be eaten, and the drinks to be drunk. The men can see to the ladies' drinks, and I'll trust Gordon to look after his young friends. And me and Ellen want yer to have the time of yer lives.'

Molly's eyes kept going to the door, and this didn't go unnoticed by Corker. 'They'll be here soon, me darlin', yer can count on that. I know yer have a healthy interest in Claire and Derek, same as meself, Molly. I know he's smitten with her, but I don't know how she feels about him. I'm optimistic, though, and hoping for a happy union.'

Molly grinned. 'I'm doing me best, Corker, whether they'll appreciate it or not. I think they are a nice couple who would be good for each other. And young Ken feels the same, although he hasn't gone as far as to tell his mam yet.'

'Well, worry no more me darlin', for they've just come through the door.'

Knowing Claire would feel shy, Molly hurried towards the troup. 'Yer know some of the people here, Claire, and the others yer'll get to know as the night wears on.'

'Don't leave me on me own, Molly. I'll feel like a wallflower.'

'In this crowd?' Molly waved her hand. 'Start off by going with Derek to meet his mam. Then take a deep breath and walk up to our Jill and her husband Steve. They're over there.'

'I can see Jill. She stands out 'cos she's very pretty. It seems to run in your family.'

'I'm going to join the gang, Mam,' Ken said, 'so don't worry about me.'

Amy pulled on Molly's skirt. 'Can I come with you, Mrs Bennett? 'Cos you're with Mrs McDonough, and she's funny. I like her.'

Derek was left with Claire, a situation he was happy with. He cupped her elbow. 'Come and meet me mam.'

'I don't like to, Derek. I'd just as soon stand here for a while, if yer don't mind.'

'Oh, but I do mind, Claire! If Corker sees me standing here like a statue, instead of mucking in, he'll have me life. And yer've seen the size of him. I'm sure yer wouldn't want me to tackle someone so much bigger than me, would yer?'

'Okay, I give in,' Claire said, 'but don't yer dare leave me on me own.'

'I have no intention of leaving yer on yer own. Yer have my promise.'

Hannah Mattocks saw her son walking towards her, his hand on a woman's arm. Her heart leapt, for Derek had told her he had met a woman he'd taken a real fancy to. If this was the woman, it wasn't surprising, for she was really beautiful. And from the way she was pulling back, she was also very shy.

'Mam, this is Claire, and Claire, this is my mother, the woman in my life.'

Hannah's handshake was firm, her smile friendly, and Claire felt the tension leaving her body. 'I'm pleased to meet yer, Mrs Mattocks. Derek has told me about you.'

'He has mentioned you, queen, and yer children, but let's chase him to get us something to drink while we get to know each other.'

Ken was standing with the young ones, a plate piled with food in one hand and a glass of lemonade in the other. But his eyes had followed Derek and his mam over to a woman who Ken knew right away, from her features, must be Derek's mother. So he put his plate and glass down, and asked Ruthie, 'Will yer keep yer eye on those for me, please? I won't be long – I just want to see if me mam's all right.' Without waiting for an answer he hurried away. Although he didn't know others were also interested, he knew that this meeting between his mam and Mrs Mattocks was important.

'Oh, here comes my son, Mrs Mattocks. This is Ken.'

When Derek came back carrying three glasses, it did his

heart good to see Claire and Ken talking happily to the mother he adored. He had just handed the glasses over when a loud roar had everyone turning to where Corker stood with his wife, the Bennetts and the McDonoughs. Nellie was trying to get her husband to do the charleston with her, but George wasn't having any. 'Do it on yer own. I'm not making a fool of meself.' He scratched his head, then said, 'Mind you, I made a fool of meself the day I married you, so I'll have a go.'

'Oh, I've gone off yer now, George McDonough. Ye're too ruddy slow to catch cold. I'll do it with Archie. I bet he's good at it.'

Lily's husband loved his mother-in-law, and he was always game for a laugh. 'I need some music, Mrs Mac. I can't dance without.'

'Hang on, son,' Corker said, pleased that the party was now starting to liven up. 'I'll put a record on.'

Archie was a good dancer, and even though the charleston had been out of fashion for years, he was putting on a good performance. But it was Nellie who had people doubled up. Her face was set as she went through the motions, every part of her body shaking. And for the size of her, she was doing a brilliant job. But every time she kicked her leg out, a roar of laughter filled the room, for she was showing quite an expanse of her pink fleecy-lined bloomers. But did she care? Did she hell, for she was enjoying every minute of it. And when Archie tried to leave the floor because he was puffed out, she dragged him back.

'Mam,' Lily called, 'yer curls are dropping out.'

'Sod the curls, girl, I'm enjoying meself.'

Paul McDonough was standing with Phoebe Corkhill, and he was red in the face with laughing. 'Mam,' he called, 'ye're showing yer bloomers.'

'Sod them as well, son, 'cos yer've all seen them before. I

hope yer have all noticed me new dress? Well, I bought this to come to a party, and a ruddy party we're going to have, whether yer like it or not. Put another record on, Corker.'

'I'll put a slow one on, Nellie, so we can all dance to it. Not everyone has your stamina, me darlin', so we'll have a nice waltz. And there's nothing to stop the youngsters from joining in. It's their party as well.'

Steve held his arms out and Jill walked into them. They danced cheek to cheek, as much in love as ever. Doreen was next on the floor with Phil, and as they held each other close Phil whispered, 'I'm thinking of the first time I saw yer at Barlows Lane. I fell in love with yer at first sight.'

Lily and Archie were next, and they really were good dancers. They covered the floor gracefully, their bodies in tune with the music. Just then, Edna and Tom Hanley, and Maisie and Alec from the corner shop, slipped into the room. The two couples made straight for the dance floor, showing they hadn't lost their touch for waltzing. For Edna it was a wish come true. She had finally made it to one of the gang's parties.

Derek looked at the dancers, then at Claire. Holding out a hand, he asked, 'May I have this dance?'

'You'll be sorry. I'll be hopeless.'

'Oh, I doubt that. Come on, let's show me mam how good her son is.'

As Derek put his arm round Claire's waist, he felt a tingle run down his spine. It took a few seconds for him to get his feet moving in time with the music. Little did he know Claire too experienced the tingle, and dropped her eyes so he wouldn't see the surprise she felt. 'See, we're not doing so bad,' Derek said, his heart thumping like mad. 'We're as good as anyone on the floor.'

Claire grinned. 'I think ye're being optimistic, Derek, but why worry?'

There was a break then for eating and drinking, and conversation with old and new friends. Derek and Claire had been introduced to those they didn't know, and soon felt they'd all been friends for ages. Corker decided that as it was his party, he should entertain. 'I'm going to sing yer a little song, and I won't be upset if yer put yer hands over yer ears. It's dedicated to the folk from dear old Ireland!

'Does your mother come from Ireland, for there's something in you Irish,
Can yer tell me where you got those Irish eyes?'

Bridie couldn't resist a song from her old country, and she ran to stand by Corker, followed by Rosie and Tommy. They sang with feeling, and Rosie's clear sweet voice filled the air.

'And before she left Killarney, did your mother kiss the blarney,
For there's something in those eyes you can't disguise.'

They got a rousing round of applause, and Tommy lifted his beloved Rosie in the air and spun her round. With Bridie, Rosie had taught him all the songs from their native land, and he could speak the lilting Irish brogue to perfection.

'Oh dear,' Claire groaned. 'They're not expecting everyone to do a turn, are they?'

'I hope not,' Derek told her. 'I can't sing for nuts. No, they'll be putting another record on for dancing.'

Corker had picked a record at random, and it happened to be a tango. It was to bring the house down. For Nellie grabbed hold of Archie and pulled him on to the dance floor. She made him hold his arm out straight as they strode down the floor, twisting their heads the way she'd seen George Raft doing in a picture. And when they reached the bottom of the room, she decided to be daring and do what George Raft's partner had done. She threw herself back, thinking Archie's arm would hold her. But Archie had never danced the tango in quite that way before, and he was laughing his head off at the spectacle they must be making of themselves. So he wasn't prepared when his mother-in-law fell backwards, and although he tried to grab her before she fell, big as he was, he couldn't cope with her weight and down he went with her. At least he landed with his dignity intact. Not like Nellie, who ended up on her back with her legs in the air.

The laughter was so loud they must have heard it miles away. And when Archie bent to cover Nellie's modesty, she slapped his hand away, saying, 'Yer silly bugger, why didn't yer catch me?' Well, the screams of laughter had Edna Hanley thinking the roof would come off her premises. Not that it would have worried her at that particular moment, for she was enjoying herself too much.

Wiping the tears from his eyes, Corker went to pick Nellie up. When she was on her feet, she pointed to Lily, and asked, 'Where did yer get this bloody husband of yours? Useless, that's what he is.'

Archie was holding the pain in his side. 'Mrs Mac, yer don't get many like you in a pound. Ye're a cracker.'

She patted his cheek. 'Ye're not bad yerself, son.' Then she looked at Corker. 'Put another record on, slow coach. Let's get the show on the road.'

Corker made sure the next record was another waltz. And when Derek held his hand out, Claire followed him on to the floor. 'D'yer know, Derek, I've never laughed so much in me life as I have since I made friends with Molly and Nellie. They are really so funny.'

'You like them, don't yer?'

'Of course I do! It would be a rare one who didn't like Molly and Nellie and the gang.'

Derek nodded. 'Yes, I agree. I like them too.' He was dithering inside, then told himself to stop acting daft: he wasn't a kid any more. He was almost thirty-six years of age, and he was holding in his arms a woman he would like to spend the rest of his life with. 'I also like you.'

Claire lowered her eyes. 'Thank you.'

He put a finger under her chin and raised her face. 'Well, can't yer return the compliment?'

'Yes, of course I can return the compliment.'

'Then say it! It's only three little words, Claire. Unless, of course, yer don't like me.'

'I like you.'

'Those are the nicest three words I've ever heard in me life. Do yer like me as a brother, as a neighbour, or as a man yer'd like to come to the pictures with on Monday night?'

'As long as it's a Doris Day film, or Cary Grant. I don't like horror films.'

He pulled her closer, his face one big smile. 'Doris Day is on at the Astoria. The children would enjoy that.'

She drew away from him so she could look him in the face. 'You are a good man, Derek. And you're right. The children will be thrilled.'

Nellie and Molly were standing either side of Corker, linking his arms. And like Hannah Mattocks and young Ken, they were closely watching the couple on the dance floor.

'I'd say ye're getting yer wish, girl,' Nellie said. 'They seem to be hitting it off.'

'I hope so, sunshine, I really do. They were made for each other.'

Secretly delighted, Corker said, 'Why doesn't he kiss the woman?'

The words were just out of his mouth when, to their amazement, Claire stood on tiptoe and kissed Derek on the cheek. And five people let out a sigh of pleasure.